# Eudora Welty

---

# *Losing Battles*

*Virago*

Published by VIRAGO PRESS Limited 1986
41 William IV Street, London WC2N 4DB

First published in the United States by
Random House, Inc., New York 1970

First published in Great Britain
by Virago Press Limited 1982

*British Library Cataloguing in Publication Data*
Welty, Eudora
 Losing battles.
 I. Title
 813'.52[F]      PS3545.E6
 ISBN 0-86068-761-9

Printed and bound in Great Britain by
Cox & Wyman Ltd, Reading

# EUDORA WELTY

was born in 1909 in Jackson, Mississippi, which is still her home. She was educated at the Mississippi State College for Women, the University of Wisconsin and the Columbia University School of Advertising in New York. After leaving College she took a job as a publicity agent with the Works Progress Administration in Mississippi which entailed travelling through the state. During this time she took numerous photographs which were published as *One Time, One Place: Mississippi in the Depression: A Snapshot Album,* in 1971.

Eudora Welty has written five novels (all published by Virago): *The Robber Bridegroom* (1942), *Delta Wedding* (1946), *The Ponder Heart* (1954), *Losing Battles* (1970) and *The Optimist's Daughter* (1972). She has also published seven books of short stories and *The Collected Stories of Eudora Welty* was published to great acclaim in 1980. Her autobiography *One Writer's Beginnings*, became a bestseller in America on publication in 1984. Eudora Welty has lectured at various colleges in the United States and has been awarded numerous honorary degrees and fellowships, including Guggenheim Fellowships in 1942 and 1968. She received the Howells Medal for Fiction for *The Ponder Heart* in 1955, the Brandeis University Creative Arts Award in 1965 and the Pulitzer Prize in 1973. Eudora Welty became a member of the American Academy of Arts and Letters in 1971 and in 1985 was the recipient of the fifth annual Commonwealth Award for distinguished service in literature. More recently she was selected by Malcolm Bradbury, Hermione Lee, and Melvyn Bragg as one of the Book Marketing Council's "Authors-USA" for her novel *Losing Battles*.

VIRAGO
MODERN
CLASSIC

NUMBER
208

*To the memory of my brothers,*
*Edward Jefferson Welty*
*Walter Andrews Welty*

## Characters in the Novel

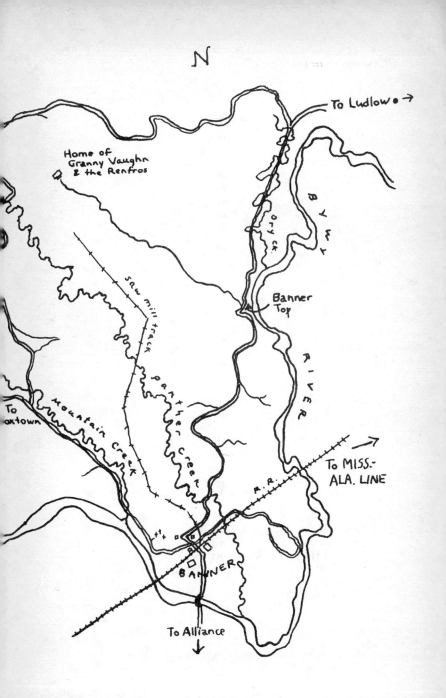

# Part 1

When the rooster crowed, the moon had still not left the world but was going down on flushed cheek, one day short of the full. A long thin cloud crossed it slowly, drawing itself out like a name being called. The air changed, as if a mile or so away a wooden door had swung open, and a smell, more of warmth than wet, from a river at low stage, moved upward into the clay hills that stood in darkness.

Then a house appeared on its ridge, like an old man's silver watch pulled once more out of its pocket. A dog leaped up from where he'd lain like a stone and began barking for today as if he meant never to stop.

Then a baby bolted naked out of the house. She monkey-climbed down the steps and ran open-armed into the yard, knocking at the walls of flowers still colorless as faces, tagging in turn the four big trees that marked off the corners of the yard, tagging the gatepost, the well-piece, the birdhouse, the bell post, a log seat, a rope swing, and then, rounding the house, she used all her strength to push over a crate that let a stream of white Plymouth Rocks loose on the world. The chickens rushed ahead of the baby, running frantic, and behind the baby came a girl in a petticoat. A wide circle of curl-papers, paler than the streak of dawn, bounced around her head, but she ran on confident tiptoe as though she believed no eye could see her. She caught the baby and carried her back inside, the baby with her little legs still running like a windmill.

The distant point of the ridge, like the tongue of a calf, put its red lick on the sky. Mists, voids, patches of woods and naked clay, flickered like live ashes, pink and blue. A mirror that hung within the porch on the house wall began to flicker as at the striking of kitchen matches. Suddenly two chinaberry trees at the foot of the yard lit up, like roosters astrut with golden tails. Caterpillar nets shone in the pecan tree. A swollen shadow bulked underneath it, familiar in shape as Noah's Ark—a school bus.

Then as if something came sliding out of the sky, the whole tin roof of the house ran with new blue. The posts along the porch softly bloomed downward, as if chalk marks were being drawn, one more time, down a still misty slate. The house was revealed as if standing there from pure memory against a now moonless sky. For the length of a breath, everything stayed shadowless, as under a lifting hand, and then a passage showed, running through the house, right through the middle of it, and at the head of the passage, in the center of the front gallery, a figure was revealed, a very old lady seated in a rocking chair with head cocked, as though wild to be seen.

Then Sunday light raced over the farm as fast as the chickens were flying. Immediately the first straight shaft of heat, solid as a hickory stick, was laid on the ridge.

Miss Beulah Renfro came out of the passage at a trot and cried in the voice of alarm which was her voice of praise, "Granny! Up, dressed, and waiting for 'em! All by yourself! Why didn't you holler?"

This old lady's one granddaughter was in her late forties, tall, bony, impatient in movement, with brilliantly scrubbed skin that stretched to the thinnest and pinkest it could over the long, talking countenance. Above the sharp cheekbones her eyes were blue as jewels. She folded the old lady very gently in her arms, kissed her on the mouth, and cried, "And the birthday cake's out of the oven!"

"Yes, I can still smell," said Granny.

Miss Beulah gave her call that clanged like a dinner bell: "Come, *children!*"

Her three daughters answered. The Renfro girls ran out of the still shadowy passageway: Ella Fay, sixteen, the only plump one; Etoyle, nine, fragrant of the cows and the morning milk; and Elvie, seven, this summer's water hauler, with her bucket and ready to go. They lined up and put a kiss apiece, quick as a bite, on Granny's hot cheek.

"Happy birthday, Granny!" all three of them said at the same time.

"I'm expecting to see all my living grandchildren, all my great-grandchildren, and all the great-great-grandchildren they care to show me, and see 'em early," said Granny. "I'm a hundred today."

"Don't contradict her," Miss Beulah commanded as Etoyle opened her mouth. "And Granny, you'll get the best present of all—the joy of your life's coming home!"

Granny nodded.

"Won't that be worth the waiting for?" cried Miss Beulah. Then she patted the old lady's trembling hand.

From the waterless earth some flowers bloomed in despite of it. Cannas came around the house on either side in a double row, like the Walls of Jericho, with their blooms unfurled—Miss Beulah's favorite colors, the kind that would brook no shadow. Rockets of morning-glory vines had been trained across the upper corners of the porch, and along the front, hanging in baskets from wires over-head, were the green stars of ferns. The sections of concrete pipe at the foot of the steps were overflowing with lacy-leaf verbena. Down the pasture-side of the yard ran a long row of montbretias blazing orange, with hummingbirds sipping without seeming to touch a flower. Red salvia, lemon lilies, and prince's-feathers were crammed together in a tub-sized bed, and an althea bush had opened its flowers from top to bottom, pink as children's faces. The big china trees at the gateposts looked bigger still for the silver antlers of last year's dead branches that radiated outside the green. The farm track entered between them, where spreading and coming to an end it became the front yard. It lay before them in morning light the color of a human palm and still more groined and horny and bare.

"He can come right now," said Granny.

"Then suppose you eat fast enough to be ready for him," said Miss Beulah.

Granny rocked herself to her feet and, fighting help, found the passage. Miss Beulah kept behind her, not touching her, as though the little pair of shoulders going low and trembling ahead of her might be fragile as butterfly wings, but framing her with both arms. The little girls followed, making up for going slowly by jumping all the way.

Then Vaughn Renfro, the younger brother, who had finished

doing what there was still nobody but him to do, catching and killing the escaped rooster and his whole escaped flock, put down his hatchet. He stepped up onto the porch and washed at the basin on the table. Taking the rag again, he swabbed the new dust off the mirror, so that it ran with a color delicate as watermelon juice on a clean plate, and looked at his face in there. This year he had turned twelve.

Then he clomped in after the girls and women.

Distance had already vanished in the haze of heat, but the passageway down which they had just gone was bright as the eye of a needle. The other end was sky. The house was just what it seemed, two in one. The second house had been built side by side with the original—all a long time ago—and the space between the two had been floored over and roofed but not to this day closed in. The passage, in which Granny's old loom could stand respected and not be in the way, was wider than the rooms on either side. The logs had been chinked tight with clay and limestone, in places faced with cedar board, now weathered almost pink. Chimneys rose from the side at either end. The galleries ran the full width of the house back and front, and under the roof's low swing, the six slender posts along the front stood hewn four-square and even-spaced by rule of a true eye. Pegs in the wood showed square as thumbnails along the seams; in the posts, the heart-grain rose to the touch. The makings of the house had never been hidden to the Mississippi air, which was now, this first Sunday in August, and at this hour, still soft as milk.

When Granny, Miss Beulah, and the children took their places at the kitchen table, Mr. Renfro came in and joined them. He was smaller than Miss Beulah his wife, and walked with a kind of hobble that made him seem to give a little bow with every step. He came to the table bowing to Granny, to his wife, to his children, bowing to the day. He took his place at the foot of the table.

"Now where's *she?*" asked Miss Beulah.

The three young sisters raising their voices together called through their noses, "Glo-ri-a! Sister Gloria!"

From the company room up front a sweet cool voice called back, "We're busy right now. Go on without us."

"Well, ask the blessing like a streak o' lightning, Mr. Renfro," Miss Beulah told her husband. "The rest of us has got a world to do!"

All heads were bowed. Mr. Renfro's was bald, darkened by the sun and marked with little humped veins in the same pattern on both sides, like the shell of a terrapin. Vaughn's was silver-pink, shaved against the heat, with ears sticking out like tabs he might be picked up and shaken by. Miss Beulah and her three daughters all raked their hair straight back, cleaved it down the middle, pulled it skin-tight into plaits. Miss Beulah ran hers straight as a railroad track around her head; they were tar-black and bradded down with the pins she'd been married in, now bright as nickel. The girls skewered their braids into wreaths tight enough to last till bedtime. Elvie's hair was still pale as wax-beans, Etoyle's was darkening in stripes, Ella Fay's was already raven. Granny's braids were no longer able to reach full circle themselves; they were wound up behind in two knots tight as a baby's pair of fists.

After the Amen, Mr. Renfro bent over and gave Granny her birthday kiss.

She said, "Young man, your nose is cold."

Miss Beulah flew to wait on them. "Now eat like a flash! Don't let 'em catch you at the table!"

"Who'll be the first to get here?" Ella Fay began.

"I say Uncle Homer will be the *last,* because we're counting on him and Auntie Fay to bring the ice," said Etoyle.

"I say Brother Bethune will be the last, because he's got to fill Grandpa's shoes today," said Elvie, an owlish look on her thin little face.

They all looked quickly at Granny, but she was busy licking up syrup in her spoon.

"I say Uncle Nathan will be the last," said Ella Fay. "He's coming afoot."

"And doing the Lord's work along his way," Miss Beulah said from the stove. "He'll never fail us, though. He's Granny's oldest."

"Jack will be the last."

"Who said that? Who said my oldest boy will be the last?" Miss Beulah whirled from the stove and began stepping fast around the table, raising high the graniteware coffee pot, with its profile like her own and George Washington's at the same time, and darting looks at each member of the family under it before she quickly poured.

"It was Vaughn," said Etoyle, smiling.

"Vaughn Renfro, have you taken it in your head to behave contrary today of all days?" cried Miss Beulah, giving him a big splash in his cup.

"Jack's got him the farthest to come. Providing he can get him started," said Vaughn, his stubborn voice still soft as a girl's.

Etoyle laughed. "How do *you* know how far it is? *You* never been out of Banner!"

Vaughn's blue eyes swam suddenly. "I've been to school! I seen a map of the whole world!"

"Fiddle. My boy'd get here today from anywhere he had to," said Miss Beulah loudly. "He knows exactly who's waiting on him."

Granny, with her spoon to her lips, paused long enough to nod.

"And as for you, Mr. Renfro!" Miss Beulah cried. "If you don't stop bringing a face like that to the table and looking like the world might come to an end today, people will turn around and start going home before they even get here!"

At that moment the barking of the little dog Sid was increased twenty-fold by the thunder of shepherd dogs and the ringing clamor of hounds. Ella Fay, Etoyle, and Elvie ran pounding up the passageway, ahead of everybody.

The three girls lined up on the gallery's edge and even before they could see a soul coming they began their waving. Their dresses, made alike from the same print of flour sack, covered with Robin Hood and his Merry Men shooting with bow and arrow, were in three orders of brightness—the oldest girl wore the newest dress. They were rattling clean, marbleized with starch, the edging on the sleeves pricking at their busy arms as sharp as little feist teeth.

A wall of copper-colored dust came moving up the hill. It was being brought by a ten-year-old Chevrolet sedan that had been made into a hauler by tearing out the back seat and the window glass. It rocked into the yard with a rider on the running board waving in a pitcher's glove, and packed inside with excited faces, some dogs' faces among them, it carried a cargo of tomato baskets spaced out on its roof, hood, and front fenders, every basket holding a red and yellow pyramid of peaches. With the dogs in the yard and the dogs in the car all barking together, the car bumped across the yard to the pecan tree, and halted behind the school bus, and then the dust caught up with it.

Uncle Curtis Beecham, next-to-oldest of Miss Beulah's brothers, climbed down from the wheel. He walked low to the ground and stepped tall, and bore shoulder-high on each slewed-out palm a basket of his peaches. Behind him a crowd of his sons and their jumping children and their wives hurrying after them poured out of the car, the dogs streaking to the four corners of the farm.

The Renfro sisters ran to take Uncle Curtis's baskets and put the little points of their tongues out sweetly to thank him.

"A new roof! You got a new roof!" Uncle Curtis shouted to his sister Miss Beulah, as though her ears wouldn't believe it.

"Jack's coming home!" she shrieked. "My oldest boy will be here!"

"That roof's sound as a drum," said Mr. Renfro, lining up on the porch with Miss Beulah and Granny. "Or better be."

"Oh, I don't blame you a bit for it," Aunt Beck protested. She climbed the steps in the wake of Uncle Curtis. Her pink, plain face was like a badge of safety. Over her pink scalp, tiny curls of a creamy color were scattered in crowds, like the stars of a clematis vine.

"You brought your chicken pie," Miss Beulah said, relieving her of the apron-covered dishpan.

"And Jack's exactly who I made it for," said Aunt Beck. "If I made my good chicken pie, he'll come eat it, I thought, every dusty mile of the way."

She and Uncle Curtis were from the Morning Star community. She kissed Granny, and kissed Mr. Renfro along with Miss Beulah and the girls, calling him Cousin Ralph. Then she went back to Granny and kissed her again, saying, "Granny stays so good and brave! What's her secret!"

The old lady took her seat in the rocking chair. She precisely adjusted her hat, a black plush of unknowable age. Her purplish-black cambric dress was by now many sizes too large and she was furled in by it. She had little black pompons on the toes of her sliding-slippers.

"Here's more!" screamed Etoyle.

Coming out of the dust that still obliterated the track appeared an old pickup riding on a flat tire, packed in behind with people too crowded in to wave, and with babies hanging over the sides on their folded arms, like the cherubs out of Heaven in pictures in the family Bible. This belonged to Uncle Dolphus and Aunt Birdie Beecham, of Harmony. In another minute the truck emptied. Little Aunt Birdie and the daughters came speeding ahead of the others, under every sort of hat and bonnet, as if dust and heat and light were one raging storm directed at women and girls. All were laden.

"If there's anything I do abhor, it's coming through the broad outdoors!" cried Aunt Birdie with elation. "New tin! Why, Beulah Renfro! What'd you give for it?"

"Ask Mr. Renfro!"

"And what's the excuse?" Aunt Birdie cried, hugging her.

"My boy's coming! My boy's coming!" cried Miss Beulah. "He's coming to surprise Granny—we just somehow know it."

Aunt Birdie with a squeal of joy opened her arms and ran to Granny. She was faded but still all animation, as if long ago she'd been teased into perpetual suspense.

"Happy birthday, Granny! Jack's coming! Won't that make up for everything?" she cried into the old lady's ear.

"My ears are perfectly good," Granny said.

Then the little Beechams came up and tried to present Granny with a double armload of dahlias, each stalk as big as a rag-doll, a bushel of plushy cockscomb, and cooking pears tied in an apron. Miss Beulah rushed to her rescue.

Uncle Dolphus, the middle Beecham brother, walked heavily across the porch and put his black-browed face down close to Granny's and kissed her. "All right, we'll help you wait on him," he told her.

As his own grandchildren swarmed around, Granny put kisses on top of their heads like a quick way to count them. From the little girls' crowns, the hair fell in sun-whitened strands as separate and straight as fork tines over the dark yellow underneath. The little boys' heads, being shaved, were albino white or even a silver gray, like the heads of little old men. Every little mouth said, "Happy birthday, Granny Vaughn!"

"Jack's coming! Jack's coming!" Miss Beulah was shrieking anew. With a sharp smell of leaking gasoline, another car had drawn up in the yard behind Uncle Dolphus's old Ford. It was another old Ford, sagging with weight, but carrying only two people.

"It's Uncle Percy and Aunt Nanny, Granny!" yelled Etoyle.

"I can still see," said Granny.

Aunt Nanny Beecham hauled herself up the steps as though she had been harnessed into her print dress along with six or seven watermelons, and only then did she try to speak. "Jack's coming? For keeps?" She looked around, already winking. "Well, where's Gloria?"

**10**

"She's over the ironing board, I reckon," Miss Beulah said.

"Wouldn't you know it?" Aunt Nanny gave over to Miss Beulah a dishpan full of honey-in-the-comb robbed that morning, tossed in peaks and giving off a clover smell as strong as hot pepper. "Got a baby here for me?" she hollered.

"Granny's being so brave behind you," Aunt Beck gently reminded her, and Aunt Nanny nearly fell over herself to hug the old lady, the cheeks in her big face splashed over red with blushes.

Uncle Curtis's sons and Uncle Dolphus's grandsons helped carry in the new load. They brought in tomatoes and bell peppers, some fall pears, and a syrup bucket full of muscadines—all that set of children were now at large with purple hands. They brought dahlias with scalded leaves hanging down their stems like petticoats, darker and heavier prince's-feathers that looked like a stormy sun-set, and a cigar box full of late figs, laid closely, almost bruising each other, in the leaves and purple and heavy as turned-over sacks, with pink bubbles rising to the top and a drunk wasp that had come with them from Peerless. They brought watermelons. They brought one watermelon that was estimated to weigh seventy-five pounds.

Uncle Percy followed it all silently. Because his voice was weak and ragged, he was considered a delicate man. He lifted up for Granny's eyes a string of little fish, twitching like a kite-tail. "Happy birthday," he said, his Adam's apple trembling like one of the fishes.

"You could fry all those in one skillet," said Granny. "I'm planning a little bigger dinner than most of you seem to think."

◆§

"And won't you be glad to see that big brother of yours come home?" Aunt Birdie cried to Vaughn.

"I don't care if he don't get here till tomorrow," said Vaughn.

"That boy's grown two feet higher since Jack's been away," said Uncle Curtis, as though that explained him.

"But if he don't get a little wider somewhere, we won't be able to see him much longer or find him when we want him," said Aunt Nanny, giving Vaughn a pinch at the waist.

"I don't care if he don't get here till the *next* reunion," Vaughn said.

"All right, Contrary!" called Miss Beulah, coming in with a pitcher and a Mason jar packed tight with flowers. "Right now you can go to the cemetery in the wagon for me. There's a foot-tub already loaded in it, and go get that churn of salvia for Mama and Papa Beecham. These dahlias go to Grandpa Vaughn. Sam Dale Beecham gets the milk-and-wine lilies in this fruit jar—I advise you to hold it steady as you can between your feet."

"Yes ma'am."

"And you know what to bring back with you! Don't leave a solitary one."

"Yes ma'am."

"Go flying. And if you meet that blessed mortal in the road, turn right around and come back with him!" yelled Miss Beulah after Vaughn. "Give him the reins! Let him drive!"

As Vaughn rattled off in the hickory wagon, Miss Beulah threw up her hands. "He'll never be Jack," she said. "Says the wrong thing, does the wrong thing, doesn't do what I tell him. And perfectly satisfied to have you say so!"

"Beulah, this may be Jack coming this minute," warned Aunt Birdie.

Vaughn had waited to let it by. An old Ford coupe, that looked for the moment like a black teakettle boiling over and being carried quick off the stove, crossed the yard. It bounced to a stop in the last bit of shade under the pecan tree, and Etoyle screamed prophetically, "It's Uncle Noah Webster back in Banner! Bringing his new wife to show us!"

The next minute, a big, mustached man with plugged watermelons under both arms and both his hands full took the force of Etoyle's running against his knees. He laughed and kept coming, carrying her with him at a run. Etoyle grabbed the banjo from one fist, Mr. Renfro took the watermelons and laid them on the porch.

"Now be careful, Sissy! That's a pretty—it'll break!" Uncle Noah Webster cried as he let Miss Beulah take the wrapped-up present out of his other hand. Then he kissed her with such a bang that she nearly dropped it. He flung his free arms around Granny, chair and all. "If you ain't the blessedest!"

"What are you doing here?" said Granny in a defensive voice. "Thought they told me you was dead."

He hugged her till she tried a smile on him, and then went all but galloping over the porch, the yard, hugging his brothers, kissing their wives, throwing their children up in the air and catching them. Clapping Mr. Renfro on the back, he roared, "Who you trying to fool with that new lid on the old house?"

"Play 'I Had a Little Donkey,' Uncle Noah Webster!" cried Etoyle.

"I'm looking for Jack!" Uncle Noah Webster hollered, with a swing of his banjo. "Ain't he here yet?"

"No, but he's coming!" cried Miss Beulah. "He's coming, to make Granny's heart glad!"

"Why, Sissy, I'm as sure of that as you are," cried Uncle Noah Webster. "And I thought if Jack can make it, I can! Where's that sweetheart of his?"

"She's putting the baby to sleep now," said Elvie, looking solemn. "So that when she opens her eyes, Jack will be here."

"Uncle Noah Webster, look behind you!" said Ella Fay.

Walking toward them came the new member of the family, Aunt Cleo, from South Mississippi, Uncle Noah Webster's new wife. She wore a dress of shirting in purple and white stripes, with sleeves so short and tight that her vaccination scar shone at them like a tricky little mirror high in her powerful upper arm.

"We try to be ready here for all comers," Miss Beulah said, facing her. "Make yourself at home. I reckon you know who I am."

"Is that your husband? He take a nail in his foot already this morning?" Aunt Cleo asked as Mr. Renfro hobbled forward.

"No'm, a little piece of dynamite accounts for that," said Miss Beulah.

"A wonder it didn't carry off more of him than it did," said Aunt Cleo.

"Well, don't think he did it just for you," said Miss Beulah. "He got on crutches just in time for our wedding day, twenty-four years ago. Here's my grandmother and she's ninety today!"

"Oh, I've nursed 'em like *you!*" said Aunt Cleo, bending down to see Granny closer. "Pat pat pat pat pat."

"Well, you needn't come patting after me," said Granny. "I'd just have to stop what I was doing and run you off, like I do some others."

"Here's my daughters," said Miss Beulah. "They've reached seven, nine, and sixteen."

"Three generations and all fixing their hair in the same pigtails. You-all must be a mighty long ways from civilization away up here," Aunt Cleo said.

The girls ran.

"It's a bigger reunion than I ever dreamed, congratulations," said Aunt Cleo.

"Listen!" Aunt Nanny cried. "But it ain't started yet, Cleo." And as Aunt Cleo began again looking around her, Aunt Nanny cried, "You'll know when it starts, all right, you'll hear the bang! That's when our boy makes it on back home. Jack Renfro!"

"Where's he?" asked Aunt Cleo.

"In the pen," came a voice that was all but a whisper—Uncle Percy's.

"The pen! The state pen? Parchman?"

"What's Noah Webster been doing all this time if he hasn't told you all the sad story?" asked Aunt Birdie.

"What did Jack do?" Aunt Cleo cried.

"Not a thing," came a chorus right on top of her.

"That's enough," said Miss Beulah.

"Then show me—who'd he marry before he went? Bet you he made sure of somebody, didn't he, to come home to?"

"Yonder she comes!" cried Ella Fay. "She likes you to wait as long as you can, then she comes out looking cooler and cleaner than you do."

"Who's this streaking up behind me?" asked the old lady. "Declare yourself."

The young girl just stepping out of the company room came forward. Dressed up in white organdy, smelling like hot bread from the near-scorch of her perfect ironing, she said, "It's Gloria."

All but Granny took a deep breath.

"A redhead. Oh-oh," said Aunt Cleo.

"You're standing on your tiptoes looking just about good enough to eat! Right this minute!" Uncle Noah Webster shouted. He ran up onto the gallery and gave her a big hug and kiss.

"Don't she look like somebody stepped out of a storybook?" exclaimed Aunt Beck in her compassionate voice.

"You look good and cool as a fresh cake of ice, sure enough," Aunt Birdie told her.

"Don't even all that hair tend to make you hot?" asked Aunt Nanny. "It'd roast me, just being the color it is."

"Well, in spite of even that hot dress, and curly hair, you con-

**14**

trive to look cooler right now than we do," said Aunt Birdie. "We're good and jealous, Gloria."

"When she wants to use it, Gloria's still got the prettiest thank-you in the family," said Aunt Beck in her gentle voice.

"Well, and I'd just like to know why she *wouldn't* have!" Miss Beulah said.

Gloria sat down in front of them all on the top step, a long board limber as leather and warmer than the skin, her starch-whitened high-heeled shoes on the mountain stone that was the bottom step. In four yards of organdy that with scratching sounds, like frolicking mice, covered all three steps, she sat with her chin in her hand, her head ablaze. The red-gold hair, a cloud almost as big around as the top of an organ stool, nearly hid what they could peep at and see of her big hazel eyes. For a space about the size of a biscuit around the small, bony points of her elbows, there were no freckles; the inner sides of her arms, too, were snowy. But every-where else, every other visible inch of her skin, even to her ears, was freckled, as if she'd been sprinkled with nutmeg while she was still dewy and it would never brush off.

Ella Fay chanted, "Sit still, Sister Gloria, keep your hands folded, don't let your dress get dirty. You just keep yourself looking pretty and be ready for your husband." The two younger sisters chanted it after her, smiling, "Keep your hands folded!"

"Yes sir, you're still here!" Uncle Noah Webster jumped heavily to the ground, ran around in front of Gloria and looked up the steps at her, slapping his hands down on his knees. "Cleo. two years ago this little bride was just as green as you are." The fading mustaches hung like crossed pistols above his radiant smile, and he cried to Gloria, "Did any of 'em ever succeed in making you tell how you ever decided to marry into this ugly family in the first place?"

"Here comes somebody new, just in time to stop her," an-nounced Aunt Cleo.

Vaughn was driving up into the yard with the tables from the church dinner grounds thumping in the back of the wagon and a passenger sitting up on the seat beside him; for a minute all they could see of her was a stylish hat with a quill slanting up from the crown. Then she put her leg over with the high white man's sock and the winter shoe.

**15**

"That's Mr. Renfro's old maid sister Lexie. Oh, ever at the wrong time!" cried Miss Beulah, running out.

The lady got down from the wagon in her Sunday dress, and reached up for a big oilcloth portmanteau and pulled it down herself.

"I stood for an hour! I'd already walked as far as across the bridge, and I stood there at the store waiting on an offer of a ride. Some of you went right by me," said Miss Lexie Renfro.

"It's that gripsack you've got along with you. They might wonder if they'd have you to carry from now on," said Miss Beulah. "I'm not sure you can find any room left to set it down here."

"Everything I've got will fit right in there together," said Miss Lexie. "Then I can tell myself I don't have to go back if I don't want to."

"Don't take a bite out of Lexie, that's a nice dog," Miss Beulah told one of the shepherds and faced Miss Lexie as she came walking up the steps.

"I borrowed a little bit of this and a little bit of that from her pantry, and made my donation to the reunion," Miss Lexie said, poking around in her portmanteau and then handing out a flattish parcel.

"What is it?" asked Miss Beulah before she'd take it.

"A pound cake. It won't kill anybody," said Miss Lexie.

Miss Beulah unwrapped it from the sheet of *The Boone County Vindicator,* and it was tied again in an old jelly-bag darkened with berry stains. She held it up by the drawstring.

"Don't everybody look at me like I'm the last thing of all," Miss Lexie said. "My sister Fay hasn't come, or her husband Homer Champion, I beat Nathan Beecham, and Brother Bethune's not yet in sight. None of which surprises me."

"No, and *Jack's* still got to come!" cried Miss Beulah.

"Now that *would* surprise me," said Miss Lexie.

"He's coming! And you needn't ask me how I know it," cried Miss Beulah.

"What kind of a postcard did he manage to send you?" asked Miss Lexie.

"My oldest boy never did unduly care for pencil and paper," Miss Beulah retorted. "But you couldn't make him forget Granny's birthday Sunday to save your life. He knows who's here and waiting on him—that's enough!"

Miss Lexie Renfro dipped her knees and tipped herself back, one tip. She didn't make a sound, but this was her laugh.

"Take your hat off, then, Lexie," said Miss Beulah.

"When I saw that hat coming, I thought—I thought you were going to be somebody else," Gloria told Miss Lexie.

"I'm wearing her Sunday hat. I make no secret of it. She'll never need a hat again," Miss Lexie said. "Miss Julia Mortimer's out of the public eye for good now."

Mr. Renfro came forward to carry in her portmanteau. "You just come off and leave your lady, Lexie?" he asked his sister.

"I may be more needed here than there, before the day gets over with," she answered.

Granny poked her shoe.

"You a nurse?" Aunt Cleo called, as Miss Lexie exchanged short greetings with the Beechams all around her and refused a seat on a nail keg.

"Well, let's say I know what to do just about as well as the next fella," said Miss Lexie.

"You've run up on the real thing now, sister," Aunt Cleo said. "And I could tell you tales—!"

Vaughn, having led the mule out of the yard, lifted out of the wagon bed the cedar buckets and milk buckets full of water drawn from Grandpa Vaughn's old well, the only one that hadn't run dry. He lugged them to the house, replenished the drinking bucket on the porch, lugged the rest to the kitchen. Then he let Mr. Renfro take an end of each of the tables he had brought up from the dinner grounds at Damascus Church in Banner, along with one or two of their better benches, and help him get them down out of the wagon.

"Vaughn! Hurry up, and get your other clothes on! Don't entertain the reunion looking like that!" called Miss Beulah.

❧

Now there was family everywhere, front gallery and back, tracking in and out of the company room, filling the bedrooms and kitchen, breasting the passage. The passageway itself was creaking; sometimes it swayed under the step and sometimes it seemed to tremble of itself, as the suspension bridge over the river at Banner had the reputation of doing. With chairs, beds, windowsills, steps, boxes, kegs, and buckets all taken up and little room left on the floor, they overflowed into the yard, and the men squatted down in the shade. Over in the pasture a baseball game had started up. The girls had the swing.

"Been coming too thick and fast for you?" Aunt Birdie asked Aunt Cleo.

"Everywheres I look is Beecham Beecham Beecham," she said.

"Beulah's brothers. Except for one, that circle is still unbroken," said Miss Lexie Renfro. "Renfros come a bit more scarce."

"Where they all get here from?" cried Aunt Cleo, looking full circle around her.

"Everywhere. Everywhere you ever heard of in Boone County—I can see faces from Banner, Peerless, Wisdom, Upright, Morning Star, Harmony, and Deepstep with no trouble at all."

"And this is Banner. The very heart," said Miss Beulah, calling from the kitchen.

"Never heard of any of it," said Aunt Cleo. "Except Banner. Banner is all Noah Webster knows how to talk about. I hail from Piney."

"I at present call Alliance my home," said Miss Lexie. "That puts me across the river from everybody I see." She went to put her hat away and came struggling backwards up the passage to them dragging something.

Miss Beulah shrieked, "Vaughn! Come get that away from your Aunt Lexie!" She was running behind it—a cactus growing in a wooden tub. "Little bantie you, pulling a forty-pound load of century plant, just to show us!"

"I've pulled a heavier load than this. And the company can just have that to march around," Miss Lexie said. "Give 'em one thing more to do today besides eat and hear 'emselves talk."

The cactus was tied up onto a broomstick but grew down in long reaches as if trying to clamber out of the tub. It was wan in color as sage or mistletoe.

"It's threatening to bloom, Mother," Mr. Renfro warned Miss Beulah.

"I see those buds as well as you do. And it's high time, say I. Bloom! Bloom!" she cried at it gaily. "Yes, it's making up its mind to bloom tonight—about time for 'em all to go home, if it knows what's good for it."

"Can't tell a century plant what to do," said Granny.

**18**

"Now, let that be enough out of you, Lexie. Set," said Miss Beulah. "And help us look for Jack."

"Jack Renfro? He won't come. He hasn't been in there long enough yet, by my reckoning," said Miss Lexie. She had a gray, tired-looking face, gray-speckled hair cut Buster Brown with her own sewing scissors that were swinging wide on the ribbon tied around her neck as she walked around looking for something to do. "Better start thinking what *you'll* look like if he *don't* get here," she said to Gloria. Her foot in its black leather, ragged-heeled shoe, feathered with dust, and wearing a skinny white sock, stepped on the end of Gloria's sash.

"What's she want to walk off and leave good company for?" asked Aunt Cleo the next minute. "She too good for us?"

For Gloria walked down the yard away from the house, through the circles of squatters, until she was all by herself. Her high heels tilted her nearly to tiptoe, like a bird ready to fly.

"Hair that flaming, it looks like it would hurt her," murmured Aunt Beck. "More especially when she carries it right out in the broil."

All the aunts, here on the gallery, were sheltering from sun as if from torrents of rain. Ferns in hanging wire baskets spread out just above their heads, dark as nests, one for each aunt but Aunt Lexie, who wouldn't sit down.

Aunt Nanny shaded her eyes and asked, "How far is Gloria going, anyway?"

Down near the gate, a trimmed section of cedar trunk lay on the ground, silver in chinaberry shade. Clean-polished by the seasons, with its knobs bright and its convolutions smooth-polished, it looked like some pistony musical instrument.

"That's her perch," said Miss Beulah as Gloria sat down on it with her back to them, her sash-ends hanging down behind her like an organist's in church.

"She's got to be ready for her husband whether he gets here or not," Aunt Beck said softly. "But she's young, she can stand the disappointment."

"She's too young to know any better. That's the poorest way in the wide world to bring him," Aunt Birdie said. "Getting ready so far ahead of time, then keeping your eyes on his road."

"Set still, Sister Gloria, keep your hands folded!" Jack's little sisters chanted together. "Don't let your dress get dirty! You got plenty-enough to do, just waiting, waiting, waiting on your husband!"

"When I can't see her determined little face any longer, but just her back, she looks mighty tender to my eyes," Aunt Beck said in a warning voice to the other women. "Around her shoulder blades, she looks a mighty tender little bride."

A big spotted cat, moulting and foolish-looking, came out onto the porch, ramming its head against their feet, standing on its hind legs and making a raucous noise.

"He's kept that up faithful. He's looking for Jack," said Etoyle. "That cat's almost got to be a dog since Jack's away."

"Think he'd better whip up his horse now and come on," said Granny.

"He's coming, Granny, just as fast as he can," Aunt Birdie promised her.

Aunt Nanny teased, "Listen, suppose they was all ready to let those boys out, then caught 'em in a fresh piece of mischief."

"They'd just hold right tight onto their ears, then," said Miss Lexie. She had a broom now and was sweeping underneath the school chair, the only one where nobody was sitting.

"You wouldn't punish a boy on his last day, would you?" Uncle Noah Webster asked. "Would you now, Lexie?"

"Yes, I would. By George, I took my turn as a teacher!" Miss Lexie cried.

Vaughn ran the little girls out of the swing, and while the uncles climbed to their feet to watch he started setting out the long plank tables. There were five, gray and weatherbeaten as old rowboats, giving off smells of wet mustard, forgotten rain, and mulberry leaves. None of them were easily persuaded to stand true on their sawhorse legs. Vaughn looked down an imaginary line from the big bois d'arc to the chinaberry. Unless Gloria were to move from where she sat, there would have to be a jog in the middle of it.

❧

Close to the house, the company dogs had fallen into long slack ranks, a congregation of leathery backs jolted like one long engine by the force of their breathing. Over the brown rocks of their foreheads flickered the yellow butterflies of August like dreams, some at their very noses. Sid, tied in the barn behind, did the barking all by himself now. His appeals, appeals, appeals rang out without stopping.

"I guess," said the new Aunt Cleo, "I guess I'm waiting for somebody to tell me what the welcome for Jack Renfro is all about! What's he done that's so much more than all these big grown uncles and boy cousins or even his cripple daddy ever done? When did he leave home, and if he ain't let you have a card from him, what makes you so sure he's coming back today? And what's his wife got her wedding dress on for?"

Aunt Cleo had been left the school chair to sit on. She leaned her elbow on the writing-arm and crossed her feet.

Then the uncles stretched and came strolling back to the house. Uncle Noah Webster skidded across the porch floor, riding his splint chair turned backwards, so as to sit at her elbow.

"If you don't know nothing to start with, I don't reckon we could tell you all that in a hundred years, Sister Cleo," said Aunt Birdie. "I'm scared Jack'd get here before we was through."

"Take a chance," she said.

There was not a breath of air. But all the heart-shaped leaves on the big bois d'arc tree by the house were as continually on the spin as if they were hung on threads. And whirly-winds of dust marched, like scatterbrained people, up and down the farm track, or pegged across the fields, popped off into nowhere.

"Can't she wait till Brother Bethune gets here for dinner and tells it to us all at the table? Surely he'll weave it into the family history," pleaded Aunt Beck.

"This'll be his first go at us," Uncle Percy reminded her.

"If he shows up as poor in comparison to Grandpa Vaughn at the reunion as he shows up in the pulpit on Second Sundays, I'll feel like he won't even earn his dinner," said Uncle Curtis.

"Brother Bethune is going to do the best he can, and we all enjoy the sound of his voice," said Aunt Birdie. "Still, his own part in this story's been fairly stingy. I wouldn't put it past a preacher like him to just leave out what he wasn't in on."

"What I mainly want to hear is what they sent Jack to the pen for," said Aunt Cleo.

Miss Beulah marched right away from them and in a moment her set of bangs and clatters came out of the kitchen.

Then a mockingbird pinwheeled, singing, to the peak of the barn roof. After moping and moulting all summer, he'd mounted to

**21**

his old perch. He began letting loose for all he was worth, singing the two sides of a fight.

Their voices went on with his—some like pans clanking on the stove, some like chains dropping into buckets, some like the pigeons in the barn, some like roosters in the morning, some like the evening song of katydids, making a chorus. The mourning dove's voice was Aunt Beck, the five-year-old child's was Aunt Birdie. But finally Aunt Nanny's fat-lady's voice prevailed: "Let Percy tell! His voice is so frail, getting frailer. Let him show how long can he last."

Only at the last minute did Aunt Cleo cry out, "Is it long?"

ᥩ

"Well, crops was laid by one more year. Time for the children to all be swallowed up in school," Uncle Percy's thready voice had already begun. "We can be sure that Grandpa Vaughn had started 'em off good, praying over 'em good and long here at the table, and they all left good and merry, fresh, clean and bright. Jack's on his best behavior. Drove 'em off in the school bus, got 'em all there a-shrieking, ran and shot two or three dozen basketball goals without a miss, hung on the oak bough while Vaughn counted to a hundred out loud, and when it's time to pledge allegiance he run up the flag and led the salute, and then come in and killed all the summer flies while the teacher was still getting started. That's from Etoyle."

"But it don't take Ella Fay long!" prompted Aunt Nanny.

"Crammed in at her desk, she took a strong notion for candy," Uncle Percy quavered. "So when the new teacher looked the other way, she's across the road and into the store after it."

"And shame once more on a big girl like that," said Miss Lexie.

"Well, wouldn't you have liked the same?" Uncle Noah Webster teased. "A little something sweet to hold in your cheek, Lexie?"

"Not I."

Aunt Nanny winked at the porchful. "The first day *I* had to go back to Banner School, I'd get a gnawing and a craving for the same thing!"

"And been switched for it!" they cheered. "By a good strong right arm!"

"It didn't take Ella Fay but one good jump across a dry mud-hole to the store. And old Curly Stovall's just waiting."

"Stovall? Wait a minute, slow down, halt," interrupted Aunt Cleo.

"You're a Stovall," several guessed.

"Wrong. I was married to one, the first time round," she said. "My first husband's folks comes from Sandy. It's a big roaring horde of 'em still there."

"The first Stovalls around here walked into Banner barefooted —three of 'em, and one of 'em's wife. I don't know what description of hog-wallow they come from," said Mr. Renfro, passing by in the yard, "but the storekeeper then alive put the one in long pants to work for him. Stovalls is with us and bury with us."

"Visit their graves," Aunt Beck invited Aunt Cleo. "They need attention."

"Don't you-all care for the Stovalls?" she asked, and Uncle Noah Webster slapped a hand on her leg and gave a shout, as though watching her find this out was one of the things he'd married her for.

"If I was any kind of a Stovall at all, I'd keep a little bit quiet for the rest of this story," came the bell-like voice of Miss Beulah up the passage out of the kitchen.

"Well, Ella Fay didn't much more than get herself inside the store than she had to start running for it," said Uncle Percy.

"What had she done?" Aunt Cleo challenged them.

"Not a thing in the world that we know of but grow a little during the summer," Uncle Percy went on mildly. " 'Well,' says Curly, 'look who they're sending to pay the store.' 'I didn't bring you anything, I come after a wineball,' she says, as polite as you are. 'Oh, you did?' " To speak the words of rascals, Uncle Percy pitched his poor voice as high as it would go into the confidential-falsetto. " 'And it'll be another wineball tomorrow,' he says, 'and another one the tomorrow after that, every school morning till planting time next spring—I can't afford it. Not another year o' you!' Jumps up. 'When am I ever going to get something back on all that candy-eating?' says he to her. And she starts to running."

"Tell what he's like, quick," said Aunt Birdie.

"He's great big and has little bitty eyes!" came the voice of Ella Fay from where she was pulling honeysuckle off the cow shed. "Baseball cap and sideburns!"

"She's got it! Feel like I can see him coming right this minute," said Aunt Nanny, hitching forward in her rocker.

" 'Don't you come a-near me,' Ella Fay says. She trots in front of Curly around the store fast as she can, threading her way—you know how Banner Store ain't *quite* as bright as day."

"Pretty as she can be!" exclaimed the aunts.

"If only she didn't have the tread of an elephant," said Miss Beulah in the kitchen.

"Girls of his own church will run from him on occasion, so I'm told. Better Friendship Methodist is where he worships, and at protracted meetings, or so I'm told, every girl younger'n forty-five runs from him," said Uncle Percy primly.

"Every bit of that is pure Baptist thinking," said Aunt Beck. "I'd like you to remember there's plenty of other reasons, just as good, to keep out of that storekeeper's way, and my sympathies go out to his sister. She can't even *bring* him to church."

"Well, he's coming behind Ella Fay and says, 'Your folks been owing me for seed and feed since time was—and when's your dad going to give me the next penny on it! You-all never did have anything and never will!' And he's just about to catch her. She turns around, reaches in, slides out in his face the most precious treasure there is, a gold ring! And that's just the way her mind works," said Aunt Nanny proudly.

"She's borrowed it out of Granny's Bible for the first day of school," said Aunt Birdie. "Yes sir, and had it tucked in where Granny tucks her silver snuffbox."

"Little devil," said Aunt Nanny.

"And he put out his great paw and taken it! Of course she right away asks him to please kindly give that back."

"And he wouldn't give it back?" a chorus of cries came, as hilarious as if none of them here had ever heard. "And what excuse did he offer for such behavior?" said Aunt Birdie in sassy tones.

"Oho, she didn't give him time to resurrect one. Out of that store she flies! Not even his wineball would she take—spit it right out in the road. And put out her tongue at him, to remind him just who she was," cried Aunt Nanny, hitching herself forward a little farther.

"Pure gold?" Aunt Cleo asked.

Uncle Noah Webster rumbled at her: "Our dead mother's. Granny's keeping it in her Bible. That's your answer."

"What was a half-grown girl like that doing with it?" she asked.

"Carrying it to school. She'd already shown it to the other girls," Aunt Beck said with a sigh. "I don't know yet how she escaped having the teacher take it up, first thing."

"Teacher's too young and green," voices teased.

Gloria sat on, before their eyes, with her back to them. Out beyond the gate, the heat flickered and danced, and devil's whirl-winds skittered across the road.

"Ella Fay Renfro'd go parading off in your *hat* if you didn't stop her," Miss Lexie Renfro said.

"She's over-hungry to be gauding herself up, living in the land o' dreams," said Aunt Nanny, winking. "Something like me, back when I was a schoolgirl."

"All right, then what does she do?" cried Aunt Cleo.

"Planted herself right there in the road and bawls: 'Big booger's got Granny's gold ring!' Etoyle says that's the swiftest she ever saw her brother Jack brought out of his desk."

"Oh, Jack is *so* dependable!" sighed Aunt Beck.

"Is it always Jack?" asked Aunt Cleo.

"Try hollering help yourself one time and see," cried Miss Beulah from the kitchen.

"Sprung over his desk like a blessed deer and tore out of the schoolhouse and in that store he prances. And in two shakes Jack Renfro and Curly Stovall's yoked up in another fight."

"A schoolboy fighting an old man?" cried Aunt Cleo.

"Listen, Curly Stovall ain't old. He's just mean!" Uncle Noah Webster told her.

"And Jack wasn't due to be a schoolboy much longer!" grinned Aunt Nanny. "He didn't know it but his days were already num-bered."

"Listen, Sister Cleo, here's what Curly Stovall is: big and broad as the kitchen stove, red in the face as Tom Turkey, and ugly as sin all over. Old Curly Stovall ain't old and I don't think he'll *get* old," said Uncle Dolphus.

"The Mr. Stovall I buried was old," she said. "Creepin'!"

"You can forget him." Uncle Dolphus brought the front legs of his chair down hard. "Had they but saved it for Saturday!" he cried to his brothers. "It wasn't only that we had to miss a good one. But fifteen or twenty more fellows at least would've been on hand, and ready and able to tell it afterwards, in Court or out, and help us give the world a little better picture of the way we do it in Banner."

"But like it was, everybody's busy getting in the last of their peas," said Uncle Percy. "Well, Curly skinned Jack's ear, and Jack had to skin Curly's ear, and so on, and old Curly's getting pretty fractious, and calling now for his pup to come and take a piece out of Jack's britches. He comes, and Jack's little dog Sid that's there waiting for the end of school, he frolics in too, with a kiss for that ugly hound! 'Sic 'em, Frosty!' Curly hollers, and if you'd been there, you'd had to stand well out of the way, or hid behind the pickle barrel. Curly even calls for his sister! Calls for Miss Ora to come out of the dwelling house back of the store and swat Jack with her broom."

"She's a pretty good artist with that broom, but she don't always make an appearance when she's called," giggled Aunt Birdie. "That's her reputation."

"A good thing for 'em both they didn't call for Lexie," said Miss Lexie. "I'd killed both of 'em right on the spot, before they went an inch further."

"If you'd got close enough to the store, you might've caught a flying rattrap, sure enough." Uncle Curtis told her. "But you couldn't expect to put a stop to Jack and Curly. Your broom ain't any longer than Miss Ora's."

" 'Hand over the ring! Where you got it hid?' Jack keeps hollering. 'What'd you do, swallow it?' he says.

" 'Let go my windpipe,' says Curly. 'And quit turning my store upside down—I put it in my safe.'

" 'Bust it open!' says Jack.

" 'I ain't a-gonna!'

" 'Don't make so much racket,' says Jack. 'The new teacher's over there trying to get a good start. Speak more quiet.'

" 'Make me!' says Curly.

"So Jack he brought down on Curly's crown with a sack of cottonseed meal—"

"Without warning?" Aunt Cleo cried.

"—of cottonseed meal that Curly had standing right there. Busted the sack wide open and covered that booger from head to foot with enough fertilize to last him the rest of his life. Then didn't old Curly whirl!

"Jack says, 'Hold it, Curly! Vaughn, go back to your desk!' Yes, that little feller's slipped out and followed his big brother into battle."

"Couldn't the new teacher hold onto her pupils any better'n

that?" teased Uncle Noah Webster. "In my day, the teacher wielded a switch as long as my arm!"

"You can't keep children of *mine* shut up in school, if they can figure there's something going on somewhere!" Miss Beulah called above the sudden spitting of the skillets in her kitchen. "They're not exactly idiots!"

" 'Vaughn, get out of men's range,' says Jack. And Vaughn's still little enough to back off like his brother tells him, but big enough not to back no further than the best place to see. He squats him on the roof of the pump box and could see and hear."

"Here it comes!" sang the aunts.

"Jack dives right over the counter into Curly and butts him out of reach of that old piece-of-mischief that Curly was whirling for, and it was loaded, you bet, and steers him out from behind that counter to the one clear spot in the middle of the floor—and the whole store busts wide open. All in a golden cloud of pure cotton-seed meal."

"That's when I wish I could've waded in on top of 'em!" hollered Aunt Nanny. "Wielding the battle-stick I stir my clothes-pot with!"

"The whole schoolhouse must've been equally ready to pop!" cried Aunt Birdie. "And the teacher, of course, she couldn't do any good."

"Maybe not a *teacher*. But what was Gloria doing all this time? Where was *she?*" asked Aunt Cleo. "She must come into this somewheres."

"If you teach, you're expected to go on teaching whatever happens," said the voice of Gloria. She spoke from her seat on the log.

"Until you die or get married, one," Aunt Birdie agreed.

"You mean *Gloria* was the teacher?" shrieked Aunt Cleo.

"That was only my first day." Gloria turned her head only the least bit to tell them. "I wasn't blind to what went on. I was taking full stock of that commotion from my windowsill, abreast the pencil sharpener. All the while careful to keep the brunt of the children behind me instead of where they were struggling for, so they couldn't learn the example that was being set. And teaching them a poem to hold them down, the one about Columbus and behind him lay the gray Azores."

"And when Curly stretched his arm for the gun?" cried Aunt Birdie.

"I rang that dinner bell," said Gloria.

"If Ella Fay could've just lasted till then! She had jelly in all her biscuits in her dinner pail, besides the rest of her dinner!" Miss Beulah cried from the kitchen.

" 'Curly, hear that bell? It's dinner time already,' says Jack. 'Give me the ring and be quick about it—you wouldn't want me to keep the new teacher waiting on me.'

" 'I ain't going to bust open that safe,' says Curly.

" 'Stay put, then,' says Jack. 'And I'll come back after dinner and bust it open for you.'

" 'What's gonna hold me?' says Curly.

" 'Well, what's that coffin been doing here in our way so long?' says Jack, and packs him in so quick!"

"Where'd it come from in such a hurry?" Aunt Cleo asked.

"Made for him. Made just to hold Curly, thanks to Miss Ora his sister," said Uncle Curtis. "It wasn't nothing new. All his trade was pretty well used to falling over it. She had Willy Trimble to get busy on that coffin when Banner in general and her in particular had it settled Curly's about to go in it—back when the Spanish Influenza was making its rounds. Then of course old Curly jumped up and fooled her. Well, that mistake is still taking up room in Curly's store to this day."

"Cleo, that's some coffin," said Uncle Noah Webster. "Made out of two kinds of wood, cedar and pine. It would hold two of you. If it wasn't Sunday, you could step in the store and take a look at the size of it."

"If it wasn't Sunday she could step in and take a look at the size of Curly," said Uncle Percy primly.

"Vaughn says, 'You can't do that to our storekeeper!'

" 'Just because nobody ever has?' says Jack."

"Didn't Curly Stovall object to being treated like that in his own store?" asked Aunt Cleo.

"He let it shortly be known he wasn't too happy about it," whispered Uncle Percy. "Stuffed in backwards the way he was, yellow as sin from cottonseed meal, and boxed in as pretty as you please—all that was lacking was the lid on."

"Squeezed in tight on his old tee-hiney!" cried Aunt Birdie.

"Right smack on his old humpty-dumpty!" shouted Aunt Nanny.

"To a tighter fit than any galvanized tub ever give him. And chalked up the side of it's running the words 'Cash Sale Only, Make Me an Offer!' I reckon up till that very day, old Curly'd been basking in the notion somebody'd come along from somewheres and cart that thing off his hands." Uncle Noah Webster groaned with laughter. "Curly says, 'Jack, wait! You go off to eat and leave me like this for my trade to find?' 'I better make sure,' says Jack, and runs a little clothesline around. Laces him tight and ties the ends behind, so fat arms can't reach. Like Nanny here—can't untie her own apron strings."

" 'Twas a mighty poor trick to play, then!" Aunt Nanny cried, delighted.

Uncle Percy went on. "Vaughn says, 'Now can I pop him?' And Jack says, 'You trot yourself back to the teacher and hand in your slingshot before she can ask you for it,' he says. 'That's a teacher I want us to hang onto. Help me keep her rejoicing in Banner, so she'll stay.' Vaughn told it on him.

"And without a word Jack skips to the safe, rakes off a forest of coal oil lamps and chimneys that's crowding the top of it, squats him under it, and ups with the whole thing on his back. Packs it right on top of him! You can bet Curly loved seeing that safe get up and walk away from him—about as well as he'd love a dose of Paris green!" sang out Uncle Noah Webster, and Uncle Percy went wavering on:

"Out Jack goes, staggers down the steps of the store, and starts across the road. The children's got their lunch pails open, they's already gobbling, but the teacher's still on the doorstep pumping that bell. I reckon now's when she drops it."

"And I reckon he was fixing to drop that safe, there at her feet," said Aunt Beck gently. "But when he gets there, she's ready for him."

They paused to look at Gloria. Small girl cousins had been drawn to her now, and marched in a circle around her, every little skirt a different length from the others.

> "*Down on this carpet you must kneel*
> *Sure as the grass grows in this field,*"

the little girls were singing, loud through their noses.

" 'You can't bring that to school,' says Miss Gloria. 'School is not the place for it. Just keep your antics to the store.' And she says,

'If all this was to make me sit under the oak tree with you and open our lunch side by side, you've gone the wrong way about it, Jack Renfro,' she says."

"My lands," said Aunt Cleo, leaning back in her chair.

"Little Elvie told it on her—she can copy Gloria just like Poll Parrot," Aunt Nanny grinned.

" 'If you took up a ton on your back to let me know how good and strong you are, I'm not going to give you the satisfaction of laying it down,' she says. 'You can just keep on going. Carry it on home and see what your grandpa will say. I've already sent your sister crying home ahead of you. And here!' She prisses to meet him, and hangs his own lunch pail on his other hand. Then she's strapping up his history and arithmetic and geography and speller, and saddling 'em around his neck. 'Go on,' she says. 'See how far this performance will carry you. If I'm going to hold down Banner School, I need to see right now what my future's going to be like.' "

"No wonder she had her pupils running out the door! I'm surprised they didn't go climbing out the windows as well," said Aunt Nanny, slapping her lap.

" 'And come right straight back! And bring me a written excuse from your mother for coming home before school is out. Or take your punishment!'

"Off he staggers."

"Say, wasn't Jack showing off a good bit for the first day of school, when you start to adding it all up?" asked Aunt Cleo.

"Oh, no more than the teacher," said Miss Beulah coolly, standing there to look at her.

A couple of butterflies flew over Gloria where she sat on her log, particles whirling around each other as though lifted through the air by an invisible eggbeater. But she sat perfectly still and stared straight ahead.

"Well, I'm ready to hear the rest!" said Aunt Cleo. "How big a safe is it?"

"It's as big as a month-old calf!" cried Aunt Nanny.

"Well, how big is Jack?"

"He's Renfro-size!" said Miss Beulah. "But he's all Beecham, every inch of him!"

"How come he didn't just crack open that safe and try carrying home nothing but the ring?" asked Aunt Cleo.

"Do you think he had all day?" cried Aunt Birdie.

**30**

"Pore Jack! How he made it up that first hill is over and beyond my comprehension," said Aunt Nanny.

"Pore Jack! It's just a wonder he didn't fall flat on his face, once and for all," said Aunt Beck.

"Carrying the safe on his back, and books and lunch pail and the rest of the burdens he's had piled on him, one on top the other! He ate the lunch, got rid of that much load—we don't need to be told that," cried Aunt Nanny.

"Didn't the safe alone pretty soon start weighing a ton?" asked Aunt Cleo.

"It's only a wonder he didn't go through a single bridge with it," Uncle Percy conceded. "It had to weigh as much as a cake of ice the same size, but a safe don't melt as you go, more is the pity."

"I could see him coming when he started up through the field," said Miss Beulah. "Oh, I wish I'd turned him around right there!"

Ella Fay in the front yard giggled. "And Mama yells, 'What're you bringing now, to get in my way?' I was crying so hard I couldn't tell her!"

"The day before, he'd brought up them old pieces of concrete pipe he'd unearthed from some bridge that's gone, and upended them there by the foot of the steps for his mother to plant—so the new teacher'd see 'em when she went up the steps or down!" cried Miss Beulah. "And now this!"

"Jack struggles through the gate and the yard and drops his load to the ground at the front steps. 'Here's Papa something to open,' says Jack."

"What ways and means has Mr. Renfro got?" asked Aunt Cleo, as Mr. Renfro came around the house carrying a watermelon. "He don't look like he's got too many left."

"Never mind, he didn't get the chance," said Miss Beulah.

"You knew something would gô awry, you was just waiting for the first hint!" Aunt Birdie said, tugging on Aunt Cleo's hefty arm. "Well, by the time that safe hits home soil, it's already open! The door's hanging wide—"

"And the cupboard was bare," whispered Uncle Percy. He turned to Granny. "There's no more ring than I can show you right now in the palm of my hand."

Granny looked back at him through the long slits of her eyes.

"*Now* what does Jack say?" Aunt Cleo asked.

" 'Bring me a swallow,' he says. So Ella Fay holds the dipper and when he can talk he says, 'If Curly wants that safe now, after the behavior it's give me, he's going to have to come with his oxen and haul it down himself.' Then he gives his mother the gist, and says, 'Don't worry about the ring, Mama. Tell Granny not to worry— somebody with bright eyes can help me find it.' And he says, 'The new teacher told me not to come back without a written excuse.' 'I wouldn't write you an excuse this minute to please Anne the Queen,' says Beulah. 'I'm too provoked to guide a pencil, and what do you suppose Grandpa's going to be?' 'Then I got to make haste,' says Jack. 'If I ain't back by the last bell to take my punishment, she's liable to kill me!' Whistles for Dan. Onto his back and shoots off like a bolt."

"And why ain't he back?" asked Granny. "I've heard this tale before."

"Never mind, Granny, he's on his way right now," boomed Uncle Noah Webster. "That's what we're doing—bringing him."

"Who'd opened the safe?" asked Aunt Cleo.

"Nobody." Uncle Noah Webster beamed at her. "It'd opened itself. Jack'd already hit the ground with it a time or two, coming."

"Wouldn't *you* have?" Miss Beulah cried. "It was as big as a house and twice as heavy!"

"Well, now, I wouldn't say it's all that sizeable," said Mr. Renfro, coming around the house with another melon to put on exhibition. "Or all that heavy. I reckon the sides of the thing may have a certain amount of tin in 'em, Mother. Or you'd expect it to go through the store floor."

"How do you know, Mr. Renfro?" asked Aunt Cleo.

"Used to be my safe," he said. "Used to be my store."

"My!" she said. "How did you come so far down in the world, then?"

"And my daddy's before me," he said. "And away back yonder, his granddaddy made the first start—trading post for the Indians. Come down to me and I lost it."

"The year we married," said Miss Beulah. "Never mind going any further."

"I *see* all the rest," Aunt Cleo told her.

"Just you be assured that that safe weighs a ton," said Miss Beulah. "I heard the noise the *ground* made when the safe came down and shook it. Just exactly like thunder."

"Let's be fair, and say it wasn't any more the fault of the safe than the fault of this here soil," said Uncle Curtis. "Banner clay is enough to break even a man's back, when rain is withholden. Ain't that the case, Mr. Renfro?" he asked. "Growing watermelons is about the best it can do now, ain't it?"

Mr. Renfro thumped his melon and left again for more.

"And just to think of an ignorant boy walking along this hilly old part of the world, dropping out pennies and nickels and dimes and quarters behind him! Wheresoever that boy walked there was good money laying in his tracks, and he didn't know it!" Aunt Cleo cried.

They all laughed but Miss Beulah.

"It was the *ring* he lost!" she shrieked. "What he went to all the trouble for!"

"How's Curly Stovall getting along?" Aunt Cleo cried.

"In his coffin? He ain't any better," said Uncle Noah Webster, giving her a clap on the shoulder.

"Curly in his own coffin is a picture I'd give anything in this world to see to this day, and just listening to his choice remarks," said Uncle Curtis. "It happened on the wrong day of the week and that's the only thing that's the matter with it."

"I reckon those precious children's the only ones got a decent look at him," said Aunt Cleo.

"That teacher, the minute they's through gobbling, she lines 'em up and marches 'em right back inside the schoolhouse," said Aunt Nanny. "They never knew what they missed. And she didn't know no more about any coffin than they did!"

"Thought she could see so good with those bright eyes," said Aunt Birdie.

"What good's her eyes? In the first place, the store scales is standing right in front of the door, trying to block you. And in the second place, it's dark inside," Aunt Beck gently reminded them.

"You don't know what's there till you get in the store, and even when you can see it, sometimes it'll bump you," said Uncle Curtis. "That coffin."

"And now there's Curly stuck in it, as tight as Dick's hatband, going sight unseen," said Uncle Percy.

"Stuck and still wearing his baseball cap," said Aunt Nanny, grinning. "Sideburns thick with meal. Like bunches of goldenrod hanging to his ears, Etoyle says."

"How'd Etoyle get a look?" asked Aunt Cleo.

**33**

"She ate the fastest and run the quickest, then told her story and didn't find any believers," said Ella Fay in the yard. "She's not but in the fourth grade and everybody knows she embroiders."

"Well, what does Curly Stovall do?" asked Aunt Cleo.

"Hollers," whispered Uncle Percy. "And not a soul can he summons. Calls again for Sister Ora. But she don't come till she's ready."

"She can't hear Curly half the time for the reason she's talking to *him*," said Aunt Birdie. "When he's in the store she's talking to him from the house. When he's in the yard she's talking to him from the store. I bet you she was there in the house talking to Curly the whole time. And he had to hear all she had to say, stuck in his own coffin."

"I'm glad he did," said Uncle Dolphus. "And for the good it done him."

"So nothing he could do but go on raising as much racket as he was able. But who was he going to bring? It wasn't Saturday. You could holler your own head off, but that don't guarantee you'll draw a soul if it ain't no further along than Monday," Uncle Percy went on.

"If I couldn't get anybody by hollering, I believe I'd use the telephone," Aunt Cleo said. "If I found myself in as friendless a spot as he's in."

"Sister Cleo, you must have walked in that store in some dream and seen where that coffin was put. It's put facing the post where the only phone in seven earthly miles is hooked up," said Aunt Birdie.

"That's right, and after while, old Curly got his head poked out, in between them hanging boots and trailing shirt-tails, and butted the receiver off," said Uncle Percy, and went into falsetto: "Hello? Find me the law! I'm tied up! Been robbed!"

"Miss Pet Hanks is Central in Medley. That means she's got a Banner phone in her dining room," said Aunt Birdie. "Sometimes when you're trying to tell somebody your woes, you hear her cuckoo clock."

"Well, you know her laugh. Miss Pet Hanks comes right back out of the receiver at him and says, '*You're* the law, you old booger!' "

"Ha, ha," said Ella Fay, coming out into the yard. She carried the preacher's stand out in front of her and placed it in the shade, ready to twine it in honeysuckle vines.

"Sure, by that time hadn't we started Curly on his way up? He was the marshal. So Miss Pet just lets him stew in his own juice awhile. She's got that job for life," Uncle Curtis said.

"Didn't one earthly soul come in?" cried Aunt Cleo.

"Do you count Brother Bethune? When he comes in it's with the one idea of helping himself to some shells out of the box. He calls to Curly how many he's taking, and goes his way. Curly don't let even a Baptist preacher have anything free. And it takes more than a Methodist storekeeper getting stuck in his own coffin to take Brother Bethune's mind off his own business," whispered Uncle Percy.

"Oh, I'm beginning to feel sorry for Curly, I can't help it," Aunt Beck warned them. "It's a human deserted from far and near."

"Are you telling me Gloria wouldn't cross a dirt road herself to help a human fight free of his coffin?" asked Aunt Cleo. "What was she doing?"

"Teaching," spoke up Gloria. "Teaching 'Sail on! Sail on!' "

"She was in her schoolroom where she belonged, trying her little best to hold down a flock of children she was just beginning to learn the first and last names of," said Aunt Beck gently.

"I was getting through my first day about as well as I expected," said Gloria from the yard. "Then when the storekeeper started making more noise than all seven grades put together, it was time to step out on the doorstep and speak to him."

"Oh-oh!" cried Aunt Nanny.

"I called for his attention. I said this was the teacher! I told him he was interrupting the recitation of a hard-learned piece of memory work and not doing the cause of education any good. And I told him all that work to attract attention had better stop right quick, because my opinion of Banner was fast going down."

"Oh-oh!" several exclaimed.

"He gave very little more contest till he heard my last bell," said Gloria. "People will learn to measure up if you just let them know what you expect of them."

"Where'd she get all that?" giggled Aunt Birdie, and Miss Lexie dipped her knees and rocked back to laugh.

"Green or not, if she'd been doomed to teach on, little Gloria might have needed to be reckoned with," said Aunt Birdie. "Some day."

"Don't forget. She knew who to copy," said Miss Lexie.

35

"Then I reckon Curly Stovall just had to wait for Jack to come on back to have enough mercy to pull him loose and finish the fight," said Aunt Cleo. "Who won?"

"Know what? Jack never did get back to the store to so much as even untie him," Uncle Percy put his head on one side and told her. "You can try naming your own reason."

"Curly Stovall belongs to be tied. That's one," Aunt Birdie offered.

"It's a plenty. But there was some reason why somebody did untie him," Uncle Percy went on.

"It was Aycock Comfort and he don't need no reason," said Uncle Curtis.

"Who's Aycock Comfort and what's wrong with *him?*" asked Aunt Cleo.

"He's a Banner boy and a friend of Jack's. What's wrong with him is he ain't Jack," said Uncle Noah Webster, with an expansive smile for his brothers.

"Had Aycock followed Jack over from school, like he follows him everywhere else? And straggling?" asked Aunt Birdie.

"Aycock ain't even reported to school. Ain't even heard there's a new teacher. He's just ready for a sour pickle. It's just as Miss Ora Stovall finds it's time to slice off some meats for her greens," said Uncle Percy. "She walks in on the vision of Curly in the coffin and she lets forth one cackle. 'I'm going to put that in the paper!' she says. She writes Banner news for *The Boone County Vindicator*. 'What happened to you?' 'School threw open this morning!' he says. 'Get me out of this harness!' 'Jack Renfro must have made up his mind mighty sudden to go on with his education,' she says, seeing what kind of knots it was. "If you-all just wouldn't bring it in the store!' 'If you could just get me loose!' says Curly. So Aycock borries the knife out of the store cheese and saws through the clothesline with it. And Curly hollers, 'Now who's going to buy that, Aycock, after you been slicing on it?' Pore Aycock, it looks like anywhere he goes he has a hard time finding him any gratitude."

"One more way he's a different breed from Jack," said Aunt Beck.

"So Miss Ora says, 'Take your pickle and go, Aycock, and stand out of busy folks' way. Me and Brother don't want to see this high varnish get scratched.' Plants her feet. Takes a good hold of that brother of hers and she pulls. And she pulls. Till out he comes like a old jaw tooth, hollering. She had to give the pull of her life to do it, and declares to the passing public she ain't over it yet," Uncle Percy said.

"And as soon as she's out of the way, Curly whirls and cuts off Aycock's shirt-tail. And if Aycock don't pick up a little two-ounce popcorn-popper and come running at him while he's nailing it up!"

Uncle Noah Webster said, "Percy, you don't give Aycock no credit at all. I feel like it was at least a churn dasher!"

"Well, he's running full-tilt with it. And right in time for the crack, in comes Homer Champion!"

"That's my sister Fay's husband," Miss Lexie told Aunt Cleo. "I'm going to get you one person told before you ask."

"And look out for him today," said Uncle Noah Webster. "He's a certified part of this reunion."

"Well, Homer comes rattling up and bringing in his bucket of eggs—he's on his egg route. 'Homer Champion,' says Curly, 'you're justice of the peace—why won't you come to the phone? I been smothered, tied and robbed, pulled on by a hundred and seventy-five pound woman, and hit a good lick with a churn dasher! Made a monkey out of by who ought to be in school, talked back to by a eight-ounce schoolteacher! Everything but have my phone used free! Well, here's Aycock by the ear—I caught you one of 'em. And you can catch you the other one. You grab hold of Jack, put 'em under arrest, and haul 'em off to jail, both of 'em.' "

" 'Did I understand you to say *Jack?*' says Homer Champion.

" 'Now he's a safe robber!' says Curly. 'You can catch him easy when he gets back to drive the school bus.'

"But Homer Champion says, 'Curly Stovall, did you suppose you could trick me that easy into riding my own wife's brother's oldest boy through the country clear across Boone County all the way to Ludlow to put him in jail—the whole Banner School basketball team in one?' 'That's what I want,' says Curly. 'I got a good mind to throw something at you,' Homer says. Or so he tells it.

" 'Now will all three of you get out from under my feet so I can clean up the store?' says Miss Ora, coming in to take the eggs away from 'em. 'Before that tide of children floods in here when the last bell rings? I wish you didn't have to act so countrified.' She sends Curly to the pump to wash some of it out of him."

"If I'd been Curly, I'd been mad at all of 'em, her included," said Aunt Cleo.

"He wasn't overly pleased," said Uncle Curtis. "Now, it's the last bell, and without a minute wasted in pours the whole horde of children for their penny stick of fresh gum to chew in the bus going home. Then they all pour out into the bus, and Jack ain't quite back yet."

"Didn't the new teacher know enough to wait on him?" teased Aunt Birdie.

"She says, 'Long skinny red-headed boy without any books, come here to me.' That's Aycock, standing there gawking at her. 'What is your name and grade?'

" 'Aycock Comfort, and I thought I'd quit.'

" 'I'm putting you to further use,' says she.

" 'Well, I'm not the one they generally calls on,' says Aycock.

" 'You're more than tall enough to see over the steering wheel,' she says. 'I'll let you carry this load of children as far as they live.'

" 'If I can get it to crank, all right,' says Aycock. 'I rather drive a pleasure car, but slide in.' The Comforts never says 'Thank you' for a favor. They say that's because they're fully as good as you are. But the teacher don't slide in with *him*. 'Just carry the children,' she says. 'I need to wait for the elected driver to get back here so I can give him his punishment. You are just the substitute.'

"Put Aycock right back in the seventh grade. He'd been out of school four years, but Jack had had to give it up for five, so as to give the little ones a chance to start. And now, for the new teacher's sake, he's determined to do everybody's work and let her teach him too. The whole five months of it out of the year." Uncle Percy's voice failed him for a minute.

"Little did Jack know, when he started back to school that morning to try out the new teacher!" Aunt Nanny said with a wide smile.

"Little did Gloria know!" Aunt Beck said. "With the tumult over, I reckon she just sat down in the school swing to wait for him."

"He had to ride her home on his horse, holding on behind him!" said Aunt Nanny.

"Why, Nanny, he sat her up in the saddle, and come home leading him," said Miss Beulah. "And the cows had been calling to him since sundown."

Gloria raised and let fall her shoulders in what looked like a

**38**

sigh. Out there with her flew the yellow butterflies of August—as wild and bright as people's notions and dreams, but filled with a dream of their own; in one bright body, as though against a head-wind, they were flying toward the east.

◄§

"All right, did the ring ever turn up?" asked Aunt Cleo.

"Cleo, what in the name of goodness did you think we ever started this in order to tell? No'm!"

"Sure enough? How hard you look for it?" she asked.

"Listen! We *all* looked till the sun went down and we was putting our eyes out trying to see," said Miss Beulah, coming to the head of the passage. "Combing the woods and pasture and that creek bank and the weeds and the briars! Here on this farm it was every hill of corn, every stick of beans—and Jack had those rows as clean as I keep this house, didn't he? And this family knows *how* to look! If something's trying to hide from us, we'll find it! But the blessed ring fooled us."

"Ha ha," Ella Fay spoke from the yard.

"And I've got a good eye on you!" Miss Beulah called to her. "I want to see you twine Grandpa's stand so thick with honeysuckle that Brother Bethune'll have a hard time finding *it*."

"Well, if you didn't see the ring anywhere, I hope you got all the money picked up," said Aunt Cleo.

"*What* money? Curly's money?" Uncle Noah Webster was asking through their shouts of laughter. "Have you heard of anybody yet that pays that billy goat cash?"

"Will you tell me where on earth they elect to keep what they run the store on?" Aunt Cleo demanded to know. "They have to keep change."

"In Ora's purse I think you'll find the majority of it today the same as then. Though I'm not trying to tell you she ain't got a sugar bin too, if you want to go knocking down the door and tromping in the house to make sure," said Miss Beulah. "I don't. I don't go *in* their house."

"Sister Cleo," Uncle Curtis said, "before Curly slapped in that gold ring, he'd put very little else in that safe worth taking out."

Aunt Birdie said, "Miss Ora kept a thing or two of hers in

there that she don't consider it nobody's business to go through."

"Her pincushion, her needles and thread, and her scissors are all things I've seen her reach out of there," Aunt Beck said. "Her specs. Bah."

"And there's that big pot o' rouge she piles on her cheeks on Saturday," said Aunt Nanny.

"The only thing anybody ever found was the mortgages," whispered Uncle Percy. "They was all together in one pile in the bed of Panther Creek. Hadn't been a single drop of rain to fall."

"Who found those? The mortgages?" Aunt Beck asked with a sigh.

"Vaughn Renfro, the little brother, and run to carry 'em straight back to the store—all Curly had to do was snap on a new rubber band. Ants had eat up the old one, but left the signatures alone. Sure is a pity the weather had been so dry."

"Just pull me out of this chair. Lead me in your woods. If all you want's that ring, I bet I could turn it up," Aunt Cleo said with spirit.

Miss Beulah was back out here, holding an egg in her hand as if ready to crack it. "Sister Cleo, if you're the one knows and can tell where that ring rolled to, you'll get a more wholehearted welcome out of this family than you'll ever know what to do with," she said. "But the truth is you don't know, nor I don't, nor anybody else within the reach of my voice, because that ring—it's our own dead mother's, Granny's one child's wedding ring, that was keeping safe in her Bible—it's gone, the same as if we never had it." She returned to the kitchen, and hard, measured strokes began in a bowl of batter.

Granny spoke. "Time's a-wasting."

"There, Granny, never mind," said Aunt Birdie. "We're all remembering it's your birthday."

"Bring him here to me, will you?" said Granny. "Don't keep Granny waiting a good deal longer."

"That's what we're doing, Granny—we're bringing him," said Uncle Noah Webster, going over to pat her shoulder, fragile as a little bit of glass. "Just as fast as we can."

"And next morning at the earliest," Uncle Percy continued, "weaving up the road to the house comes Homer Champion's chicken van from Foxtown. And when it bucks to a stop, it's two of 'em hops out—Homer and Curly Stovall! Just like they's buddies.

" 'Here's your proof, Homer Champion! Here's my safe, and Jack's turned it over to babies to play with!' says Curly. 'If they won't give it back, you can arrest him!' And it's Etoyle and Elvie and Vaughn, Beulah's three youngest, playing store to their hearts' content under a chinaberry tree. And they don't do a thing but quick sit down on that safe in a pile. Precious children, they don't get many play-pretties up this way.

" 'Climb off my safe!' says Curly. 'If you don't, old Homer'll carry you to jail, all in one load!'

"And Elvie don't do a thing but open the safe and tuck her little self inside and slam the door on him.

" 'Quit, you little mischiefs. Give it back to him like he says,' says Homer. 'The safe ain't hurt none, Curly, just the door needs a little lining up and oiling so it don't hurt your ears. Let's don't have hard feelings. Let's all just be friends.'

"Old Curly scrapes the other two children off the safe and yanks that door open and shakes Elvie by the foot. 'Hand me the money out!' he hollers.

" 'We never had any money but chinaberries, we're too little,' pipes Elvie out of the safe.

"And Curly, the big bully! Has to haul out Elvie kicking and fighting, and he pulls that safe right out through their little arms that's twined around it! Elvie cried for her safe till dark.

"Etoyle knows enough to holler Jack from the barn. Here he comes, straight from the cow, carrying two full buckets, calling to say it's never too early for company, and asking if they won't come sit on the steps and enjoy a glass of foaming milk and the sunrise.

" 'Jack, you're under arrest!' says Homer.

"Jack threw the first bucket so fast! All that new milk right in Curly's face."

"Why not Homer Champion's?" objected Aunt Cleo.

"Sister Cleo, it's Homer that's arresting him, but he's married into our family—Mr. Renfro's and Miss Lexie's sister is his wife. And you know how Jack holds the family. And all ladies especially he holds in terrible respect."

"Drummed it into him as a child!" cried Miss Beulah.

"Jack, though, had to set one bucket down before he could throw the other one—he's like anybody else—and before you know it, old Homer's give it back to him, the whole thing plumb in the face. Blinds him! Curly and Homer acting in harness lifts him blind-struggling right into Homer's van with the chickens. Somewheres they find room in there for the safe too, and Curly climbs in after it and sits on it—Etoyle was quick enough to see he was holding his nose. Homer slams 'em all in together and drives off, without ever giving this house the benefit of a good morning. Little Elvie has to go to the kitchen and cry, to break the news."

"Hasn't Homer Champion changed his tune?" asked Aunt Cleo.

"He's a little bit primed this morning. And a good thing he didn't catch any of that milk, because it ain't the drink he's most overly fond of," said Uncle Curtis.

"I still don't see why Curly Stovall couldn't do his own arresting," said Aunt Cleo. "A marshal's got every right in the world and a justice of the peace is very little better than he is."

"Curly knew better, that's why! So off Jack's carted to Foxtown and shooed in jail. And Etoyle said Homer warned him before they started that if he give any more trouble resisting arrest he'd get a bullet ploughed through his leg."

"Etoyle embroiders. What are you doing sitting down with company now, Etoyle Renfro?" asked Miss Lexie.

"I love to hear-tell."

"You slip in here for what's coming next? In time to hear how your poor mother cried?" Aunt Beck reproached her.

"Now, I'm not going to try to tell the way Beulah performed that night," Uncle Percy whispered. "I ain't got the strength to do it justice."

"And you wasn't here to see it!" called Miss Beulah.

"Well, how did Gloria here perform?" asked Aunt Cleo.

"Cleo! Gloria hadn't got to be a member of the family *that* quick!" The other aunts laughed, and Aunt Nanny called, "Had you, Gloria!"

Gloria sat without turning around or speaking a word.

"Has she got good sense?" Aunt Cleo wanted to know.

"No indeed, she's addled," Miss Beulah came out to tell her. "And there's not a thing I or you or another soul here can do about it. It'll take Jack."

"I'm wondering by now why even Homer Champion don't get here," said Aunt Cleo. "Unless he's waiting for Jack to get here first."

"Oh, I can tell you exactly what Homer's doing. He's sitting

**42**

jammed in a hot pew somewhere, waiting on the final Amen so he can shake hands with the whole congregation when they're let out the door," said Miss Beulah.

"The biggest, fullest, tightest-packed Baptist church he can find holding preaching today," said Aunt Beck.

"Then he'll hurry to shake hands again in front of the Foxtown ice house," said Uncle Percy. "He'll catch the Methodists going home to dinner."

"He'll figure a way to jar loose a few Presbyterians before the day of worship is over, if he can find some," said Miss Lexie.

"How's Curly Stovall putting in *his* last Sunday?" asked Aunt Cleo.

"He'll think of some such thing as a fish-fry to sew up all the infidels," said Miss Beulah, going.

"He figures he's got the Christians hooked like it is, blooming storekeeper!" recited Elvie, in her mother's voice.

"What're you doing here, child?" cried Aunt Beck.

"Keeping the flies killed."

"Well, sweetheart, your Uncle Homer Champion and Curly Stovall is in eternal tug-of-war for the same office now," Uncle Noah Webster told her. "You ain't likely to understand all you hear till you get up old enough to vote yourself."

"Both in the run-off?" asked Aunt Cleo.

"Why, of course. And I don't know how in the nation ol Homer's going to cheat him out of it," said Uncle Noah Webster. "Homer's my age. He can't keep a jump ahead of Curly much longer."

"Now to me," Uncle Percy was quavering, "what they ought to had sense enough to do was throw this case out that selfsame day in Foxtown."

"Think of the trouble it would have saved!" Aunt Beck sighed.

"To me and the majority," Uncle Curtis said, "Jack had acted the only way a brother and son could act, and done what any other good Mississippi boy would have done in his place. I fully expected 'em to throw the case right out the window."

"With nothing but a good word for Jack," said Aunt Birdie.

"Well, if Jack's that lucky, then Curly's just wasting his time trying to arrest him," said Aunt Cleo.

"Well, Jack *wasn't,* and Curly *wasn't.* So don't go home," Aunt Nanny teased her.

**43**

"Well, they was mighty hard up for a spring docket in Ludlow if Jack's the worst fellow they could get Foxtown to furnish," said Uncle Curtis.

"All right, Sister Cleo, would *you* call that a case?" asked Aunt Birdie in sassy tones.

They cried, "We're testing you."

"Now wait, now wait," said Aunt Cleo. "I might could."

"Why, you could no more call that a case for court than I could call my wife flying!" said Uncle Percy. He put his hand on Aunt Nanny's shoulder.

"I *might* could," said Aunt Cleo. "Even if all Jack got home with was the empty safe, I reckon you could call that safe-cracking. I don't know what else you could call it."

The beating in the kitchen stopped again. Miss Beulah came out onto the porch. "If Jack had wanted to steal something, Sister Cleo, he could have run off with Curly's fat pig and butchered it and done us all a little good at the same time! My son is not a thief."

"If a boy's brought up in Grandpa Vaughn's house, and knows drinking, dancing, and spot-card playing is a sin, you don't need to rub it into his hide to make him know there's something a little bit the matter with stealing," Uncle Noah Webster cried.

"Throwing his case out of court," said Uncle Curtis, "was the only thing for Homer Champion to do, so he didn't. He bound Jack over to the grand jury. Homer swore he couldn't afford to do anything else. They'd call him playing favorites. And said Jack hadn't done himself a world more good the way he treated the Foxtown jail," said Uncle Dolphus.

"Started nicking his way in a corner, prizing his way out as soon as he'd cleaned up his first dinner plate," said Uncle Percy. "He worked faithful. But Jack is a Banner boy, and how was he to know that if you dug your way through the brick wall of the Foxtown jail with your pie knife, you'd come out in the fire station? Chief looks up from the checkerboard and says to him: 'Son, I don't believe I ever seen you before. You better turn around and scoot back in till they make up their minds what to do with you.' And helped him scoot."

"Well, when they got Jack told they'd have to lock him up a little better now and keep him till spring, Jack just told *them* he's a farmer," said Uncle Curtis. "Jack told *them* just exactly who he was and just exactly where he lived. 'I got my daddy's hay to get in the barn, his syrup to grind, his hog to kill, his cotton to pick and the rest of it,' he says. 'His seed in the ground for next year. And I got my schooling to finish. I can't be here to sit and swing my foot while you scare up somebody to try me,' he says.

"So they told Jack, 'Go on, then.' And one of the other prisoners says, 'We don't keep room in the Foxtown jail for the likes of you country boys.' "

"And they let him go?" cried Aunt Cleo.

"Look out, don't start to saying something good about the courts, Foxtown or anywhere else!" yelled Miss Beulah. "Not when Homer had the further crust to tell Jack if he didn't show his face in Ludlow Courthouse on the very stroke of the clock when they called his name, he could look forward to being arrested the same way all over again. Don't thank Homer! And don't let me hear anybody start thanking Curly Stovall for putting up that bail!" She went.

"Now that was right outstanding of a Stovall," said Aunt Cleo. "Say as much."

"How else did he think Renfros was going to live? How else did he figure he stood a chance of getting a penny out of 'em?" laughed Uncle Noah Webster. "Oh, Jack he did sweat, early and late. And just when we didn't need it, rain. And court creeping closer and closer. So the time come when we couldn't stand sight of his face any longer and we had to tell him, 'Jack! Before you get drug off to be tried in Ludlow, what would you most rather have out of all the world? Quick!' And quick he says, 'To get married!' Didn't surprise nobody but his mother."

"You couldn't say Jack hadn't been showing signs. Now the year before, our guess would have been the little Broadwee girl," said Aunt Birdie.

"Imogene? The one that's timid?" grinned Aunt Nanny.

"Yes and she's sitting there still."

"He's chased 'em all some. But when he singles out who he wants to carry *home,* he singles out the schoolteacher!"

"Was that a pretty good shock?" asked Aunt Cleo.

"Being as she's already living here in the house and eating at the table, no'm," said Aunt Nanny.

"Gloria had a choice too, even if you leave Aycock out. Curly Stovall was right across the road from that schoolhouse, with nobody but Miss Ora to look out for, enjoying a job on the public. And in

**45**

his store carried all she wanted. But she turned up her little nose at him."

"He didn't make a good impression on me, from the first time I saw him," Gloria called in.

"But that year it's our turn to board the teacher, no hope of rescue," said Miss Beulah, coming to the head of the passage. "We'd spent the summer highly curious to see what they'd send, after the last old maid give up the battle. Well, here she came. The old fella that got it for superintendent of schools carried her up here in a car that's never been seen in my yard before or since—purse in both hands, book satchel over her shoulder, valise between her feet, and her lap cradling a basket of baby chicks for her present to whoever was to board her. I had a feeling the minute she pulled off her hat—'Here's another teacher Banner won't so easily get rid of.' "

All at once Lady May Renfro, aged fourteen months, came bolting out into their midst naked, her voice one steady holler, her little new-calloused feet pounding up through it like a drumbeat. She had sat up right out of her sleep and rolled off the bed and come. Her locomotion, the newest-learned and by no means the gentlest, shook the mirror on the wall and made its frame knock against the house front like more company coming.

"Who you hunting?" Aunt Nanny screeched at the baby.

Lady May ran through their catching hands, climbed down the steps in a good imitation of Mr. Renfro, and ran wild in the yard, with Gloria up and running after her.

"Where's your daddy, little pomegranate?" they hollered after her flying heels. "Call him! Call him!"

Elvie came third, following solemnly with the diaper.

Lady May ran around the quilt on the line and Gloria got her hands on her. There behind the quilt she knelt to her, curtained off from the house; the quilt hung motionless, just clear of the ground. It was a bed-sized square that looked rubbed over every inch with soft-colored chalks that repeated themselves, more softly than the voices sounding off on the porch. From the shadow of an iron pot nearby, rising continuously like sparks from a hearth, a pair of thrushes were courting again.

The sugar sack Gloria pinned about her baby's haunches blushed in the light and sparkled over with its tiny crystals that were never going to wash out of it. Around their shoulders the air shook with birdsong, never so loud since spring. On all the farm, the only thing bright as the new tin of the roof was the color of Gloria's hair as she bent her head over her baby. It was wedding-ring gold.

"Act like you know what you're here for, Lady May," she told the smooth, uplifted face.

The child looked back at her mother with her father's eyes—open nearly to squares, almost shadowless, the blue so clear that bright points like cloverheads could be seen in them deep down. Her hair was red as a cat's ear against the sun. It stood straight up on her head, straight as a patch of oats, high as a little tiara.

"Just you remember who to copy," Gloria told her child.

She came leading Lady May to the house and through their ranks and inside the company room and out again, and this time the little girl was tiptoeing in a petticoat.

"Have a seat with us," said Aunt Nanny. "That's better."

Gloria sat down on a keg and Lady May climbed onto her lap. She turned her little palms up in a V. Her eyebrows lifted in pink crescents upturned like the dogwood's first leaves in spring. Her unswerving eyes looked straight into her mother's.

"Learn to wait," said Gloria, pulling both baby hands down.

So the baby sat still, her lashes stiff as bird-tails; she might have been listening for her name.

"Honey, where did Banner School ever get you from?" asked Aunt Beck, leaning forward. "Has this reunion ever asked you and ever got a full reply?"

"Miss Julia Mortimer was training me to step into her shoes," said Gloria.

"Whose shoes?" asked Aunt Cleo, and everybody groaned.

"The oldest teacher that's living. She was giving me my start," said Gloria.

"You meant to teach more than the single year?" exclaimed Aunt Birdie. "Never dreamed!"

"When I came, I could see my life unwinding ahead of me smooth as a ribbon," said Gloria.

"Uh-oh!" said Aunt Cleo.

"All I had left to do was teach myself through enough more summer normals to add up to three years, and I could step right into Miss Julia's shoes. And hold down Banner School forever-more."

"But then she just happened to run into Jack," said Aunt Nanny, with a strong pinch for Gloria's arm.

"So I wonder what was everybody's first words to Jack when he says he wants to marry his teacher?" asked Aunt Cleo.

Miss Beulah called, "I told him, 'Jack, there's just one thing you need for that that you're lacking. And that's the ring. Remember the gold ring Granny was keeping in the Bible? She might have spared it to a favorite like you, at a time like this, and where did it go?' "

"I reckon his mother had him there," said Aunt Birdie.

"No she didn't. Jack said, 'Mama, I'm going to afford my bride her own ring, like she wants, and all I need is a little time.' Time! He thought he had all the time he was going to need. You had to feel sorry for the child. Sorry for both of 'em."

"Well, I see you got you one anyway," Aunt Cleo said to Gloria. "What'd you have to do? Steal it?" She laughed, showing her tongue.

"Mind out, Sister Cleo, Gloria don't like to tell her business," Miss Beulah called, while Gloria laid her cheek to the baby's. Lady May's fast hands pulled the mother's hairpins out, and the curls rolled forward over them both.

"Gloria taught Banner School a whole year long for that little ring, that's what I think," said Aunt Birdie, giggling.

"A teacher always gets a warrant she can trade with," said Miss Lexie. "It means the same as a salary. And it just depends on the teacher—what she decides to use it for, if and when and how soon. If she don't starve in the meantime."

"If you used up your warrant for your ring, what'd you have left over for that wedding dress?" asked Aunt Cleo. "I only ask because I'm curious."

"It's homemade."

"You just can't see how much sewing there is to it, because of all that baby in her lap," Aunt Nanny said.

"Just a minute! If it tore!" Gloria cautioned two little girls who had come up from either side to stare and were now holding her sleeves and the hem of her skirt between their fingers. "I rather you stood back a distance." Her short puff sleeves were ironed flat into peaks stuck flat together and canvas-stiff, almost as if they were intended to be little wings.

"Full, full skirt and deep, deep hem," said Ella Fay, bumping through them on her way into the house now. "Organdy and insertion, flower-petal sleeves, and a ribbon-rose over the stomach above the sash. That's the kind of wedding dress *I* want."

"You could almost wear hers. I can see now there's a lots of material going to waste in that," said Aunt Cleo. "Despite that baby taking up the most of her lap." She laughed. "So you was here, ready, and waiting all this time?" she asked Gloria. "Well, where'd you hold the wedding? Your church right on the road? Or do you all worship off in the woods somewhere?"

"I'm surprised you didn't see Banner flying by on your way here, Sister Cleo," said Uncle Curtis. "Didn't Noah Webster show you which church was ours?"

"I keep my eyes on the driver," she said.

"Listen, Grandpa Vaughn downed enough trees himself to raise Damascus Church. Hewed them pews out of solid cedar, and the pulpit is all one tree. And in case you're about to tell us you still don't remember it, you might remember the cemetery on beyond—it's bigger than Foxtown's got to this day."

"How many came to the wedding? Church fill up to the back?"

"Stand up now and count!" Miss Beulah cried, clattering some pans together. "And you can add on the ones still to come today—Nathan, bless his heart, Fay and Homer Champion, Brother Bethune—"

"And Jack!" they cried.

"I'd call it a fair crowd," said Uncle Curtis. "I seen Aycock Comfort propped in a window—that's what room we had left for a Methodist."

"Blessed Grandpa joined those two blushing children for life in Damascus Church on a Sunday evening in spring," said Aunt Birdie. "If I forget everything else alive, I'll remember that wedding, for the way I cried."

"Oh, Grandpa Vaughn out-delivered himself! Already the strictest marrier that ever lived—and the prayer he made *alone* was the fullest you ever heard. The advice he handed down *by itself* was a mile long!" cried Uncle Noah Webster. "It would have wilted down any bride and groom but the most sturdy."

"And Curly Stovall come down the aisle and clapped his hand on Jack's shoulder in the middle of it, I've already guessed," said Aunt Cleo.

"Sister Cleo! Curly Stovall would not dare, would not dare to walk in Damascus Church with Grandpa Vaughn standing up in his long beard and looking at him over the Bible!" Aunt Birdie cried. "And Curly ain't even a Baptist."

"Not even for the scene it'd make?" she asked them.

Miss Beulah marched in on her. "I just came to be told the name of the church *you* go to," she said.

"Defeated Creek Church of the Assembly of God. One mile south of Piney."

"Never heard of a single piece of it." She about-faced and marched out again.

"It's after we're back at the house here, Sister Cleo, cooling off with Beulah's lemonade, and seeing the sun go down, that old Curly sneaks up the road on Jack for the second time. Says Curly, 'Eight o'clock in the morning by the strike of the courthouse clock, they'll be calling your name in Ludlow!' And just to be sure Jack will answer, he gets him thrown in the Ludlow jail on his wedding night!" said Uncle Noah Webster. "And don't you know Curly enjoyed doing it?"

"Suppose *you'd* put up the bail!" Aunt Cleo said. "But what about Grandpa Vaughn—wasn't he still awake, to scare off all comers?"

"Grandpa wasn't going to stand in the way of justice, Sister Cleo. Only unless Curly had tried that in church, before Grandpa had married 'em. *Then* Curly'd seen what he got out of Grandpa."

"Or even what he got out of Jack," said gentle Aunt Beck.

"I still hold Jack Renfro wasn't *born* that easy to take by surprise," said Aunt Birdie in loyal tones.

"His wedding night may have been the prime occasion they could risk it," Uncle Curtis said.

"Who'd Curly bring along to partner him this time?" Aunt Cleo asked. "He still playing with Homer Champion?"

"Oh no, he's already declared for office against Homer!" cried Uncle Noah Webster. "Old Curly's brought Charlie Roy Hugg, the one that's got the Ludlow jail."

"What's *his* style?"

"Drunk and two pistols. Makes his wife answer the phone."

"We got his twin in Piney."

"Sister Cleo, this entire family had to sit where we're all sitting now and see Jack Jordan Renfro carried limp as a sack of meal right off this porch and down those steps on his wedding night. He's open-mouthed."

"Just the caps of his toes dragging," said Etoyle, smiling.

"Curly had to hold up his other arm. And partly hold up Charlie Roy Hugg before they all got on and fired off. And at Banner Store there sits Aycock on the bench like he's waiting for a ride. Charlie Roy stops and Curly hops out of the sidecar and they fold Aycock in. Charlie Roy carried those boys away to Ludlow in a weaving motorcycle—too drunk to drive anything better."

"If Charlie Roy Hugg hadn't been kin to Aycock's mother, and hadn't had an old daddy living in Banner, I believe Jack might have come to and tended to him before they got to Ludlow, right from where he's holding on behind him," said Uncle Curtis.

"He may have had the most he could do just keeping Charlie Roy awake. I believe Aycock went to sleep on both of 'em in the sidecar. Twenty-one miles is a heap of distance after the sun goes down," said Uncle Percy, whispering. "And with all the creeks up. And Mrs. Hugg give 'em a room in the jail and no pie at all with their supper."

"That wasn't any kind of a way to treat one of mine," Granny said. "No, it wasn't. Tell 'em I said so. I'm in a hurry for him back."

"We told 'em. Maybe they've already sent him. Maybe he's here in this crowd now, and you just can't see him," teased Aunt Cleo.

"Hush up, Sister Cleo! None of that! Take your nursing tricks away from here!" cried Miss Beulah.

❧

Uncle Noah Webster leaned away out from his chair and caught a baseball flying in from the pasture. Prancing down the steps, he wound up and threw it back into the game. "So the next thing we knew," he cried, coming back, straddling the chair as he sat down again, "there we all was at the trial. Cleo, I wish it had been your privilege to be with us our day in court."

"Even if I'd known it was going on and got a free ride to

Ludlow, my first husband wouldn't have let me sit with you all: he was still living," said Aunt Cleo.

"Excuse me," said Uncle Noah Webster.

"Though I love a good trial as well as the next fellow," she said.

"We'd had to squeeze to make room for one more, down front where we was all sitting. Grandpa was holding down one end of our pew, just a little bit more bent over on his cane than before, and Beulah held down the other end, with the rest of us in between. It's a wonder everybody could get there! It wasn't like it was any other time of year. It was spring! The whole world was popping, needing man. Oh, it needed Jack bad! And the wedding and the trial, that made two days in a row. But everybody was there, all but Nathan— he was out of reach. The majority of Banner community was there, right behind us. Harmony had another record attendance, to make Dolphus and Birdie feel real good, and Morning Star to a man was packed in behind Curtis and Beck, and I think Percy and Nanny drew at least their side of Panther Creek. Even a few Ludlow folks was there, with nothing better to do, I reckon, than come to get a peep at a bunch of country monkeys." Uncle Noah Webster smiled at them tenderly.

Uncle Percy downed a gourdful of water and shook his head. "From the opening tune he give on the gavel," he said, "I commenced praying that Judge Moody might drop dead before the trial was over and the whole thing be called off out of respect. Can happen! I never witnessed it myself, but there's such a thing in the memory of Brother Bethune—he's there telling it while Judge Moody's bringing us to order.

" 'You're pleading innocent, I suppose,' says he to Jack.

" 'Yes sir, I'm needed,' says Jack.

"Judge Moody calls, 'Hush that crying! Or I'll send the whole crowd out and order the doors shut. This is a courtroom.' That'll give you some idea. 'Call Marshal E. P. Stovall,' he says."

"Who in the world was that?" asked Aunt Cleo.

"That's Curly. His mama named him Excell Prentiss. In he comes, parading that coffin behind him. Mr. Willy Trimble's holding up the foot," said Uncle Curtis.

"Wearing his Sunday harness, sporting a tie," said Aunt Nanny. "Red tie. You could have packed Curly back in that coffin and sent him straight to meet his Maker without a thing more needed."

52

"And Mr. Willy was saying down the aisle, 'If anybody in Ludlow wants one just like it, you're looking at the artist right now.'

" 'Stand that thing in the corner until it's called for and show some respect for this court!' Judge Moody says to Curly. I don't know why I took heart," said Uncle Percy in a wavering voice. "Then they carried in the safe and the Judge wants a good look at that."

"Just as empty as before?" asked Aunt Cleo.

"Not only that, a bird had built a nest in it."

"Oh, we know how to make things dangerous around here!" cried Uncle Noah Webster. "And she was setting!"

" 'Am I going to have to forgo examining that safe in the face of a nesting robin?' That's the Judge," said Uncle Percy.

"Well, it was spring!" Aunt Nanny interrupted. "That's what Curly got for leaving the safe out front with the door wide open to show the passing public what had happened. I'd been surprised if there *wasn't* a nest in that safe, by the time it comes to the trial.

"Jack says, 'Judge Moody, I hate to come in the courthouse and act like I know more than you do, but that's a purple martin.'

" 'What kind of a *safe* is that?" says Judge Moody. 'And I want the best answer I can get from the owner.'

"Curly tells him it's a Montgomery Ward safe with a Sears Roebuck door.

" 'You kept it locked?' says Judge Moody, and Curly says he didn't have to just exactly lock it if he leaned on it good. 'Can you tell me why you don't keep it locked?' says Moody, and Curly says it's because every time he locks it it costs him another sack of coal to get Mr. Willy Trimble to stop his horses and open it again. And he says when that door is leaned on good, it's stuck so tight nothing will open it but a good rain of blows from his own fist in just the right tender spot on top, and that's where he keeps his lamps setting."

"To me, that safe looked as poor an excuse for something to make a big fuss over as anything you could hope to see at a trial," Uncle Curtis said.

"Oh, the safe was on show, the coffin was on show, everything was on show but the ring! The only thing in the world that would have told the true story and spoken for itself!" screamed Miss Beulah. "That's missing!"

"That safe was the evidence, Beulah," said Uncle Noah Webster. "And was that little rooster martin loud!"

"Hen never budged, either," Uncle Percy whispered. "Not for something as unparticular as a wagon-ride to Ludlow and a court-house trial and the same ride home again. She set right through it all."

"Don't you know she got hungry?" cried Aunt Nanny.

"She hatched 'em, too, later on," said Aunt Birdie. "It was Ora's cat that finally made a meal of 'em."

"Well, they couldn't blame Jack for that!" Aunt Beck said. "He was too far from us all to save baby birds by that time!"

"It's money they worry about in town," said Uncle Curtis.

"Curly had 'em sized up! He give a song and dance about how poor he stayed, never getting paid like he ought by the poor farmers, then to lose his safe, only to get it back full of chinaberries. I'm surprised he didn't show 'em the chinaberries," Uncle Percy said. "But finally he's through and it's Jack's turn." Uncle Percy lifted his hand for quiet and went into falsetto. " 'I'm going to question this boy myself,' Judge Moody says, and bangs till the family's all in their seats and the dogs from Banner gives up on their barking. Then says to Jack, 'All right, you heard the charge. Now did you do all that to Marshal Stovall?'

" 'Yes sir, and a little bit more.'

" 'Well, what did you do it for?'

"Jack says, 'Well, it's because he's aggravating.'

"Judge Moody cracks down with the gavel. 'No clapping and stamping in the courtroom while I'm on the bench!' he calls to the congregation. 'Try and remember you all are in Ludlow, and in this room on sufferance,' he says, and asks Jack, 'What's "aggravating" mean in your book? Give me one example,' he says.

" 'He'd just have to show you himself,' says Jack."

"Well, Jack's a bashful boy," said Aunt Birdie loyally.

"Sure-enough?"

"You'd been bashful too, Sister Cleo," said Aunt Beck, "if you'd been a boy no more than eighteen years old and just got married the night before by Grandpa Vaughn to your schoolteacher, and woke up in jail in Ludlow to be tried by a hard-to-please stranger sitting over you and in front of all your aching family and a pretty good helping of the public. And if you was the only one of 'em standing up."

"What's the trouble, couldn't Jack put up a good story?" Aunt Cleo asked. "That's what he's up there for."

"He's twenty-one country-miles from home!" Uncle Noah Webster cried.

Miss Beulah came out drying her hands on her apron. "And we knew full well he wasn't going to stand up in front of the public and tell 'em any of our business. Wasn't going to call his sister's name, even! Though she did keep standing up and setting down and standing up again, waving at him, like she's trying to tell him go ahead."

"Felt cheated, didn't she?" grinned Aunt Nanny.

"Just hungering to get up there herself and cry for a crowd of strangers!" Miss Beulah marched off again.

"Vaughn felt mighty put-upon too. Jack had told us the best place for Vaughn Renfro was setting on the steps outside and holding the dogs. Vaughn was there, boo-hooing," Aunt Nanny said with a grin.

"Judge Moody says, 'Hush that crying! Why aren't these children in school?' Then he asks Jack how many times along the way did he drop that safe, and Jack says he hadn't kept count. 'I just dropped it to mop my neck, like you're mopping yours now, sir,' he says. 'I reckon it's even hotter in Ludlow than it is in Banner.' "

"Of course it was! I could see it rolling off of both of 'em," said Aunt Birdie.

"And I was sweating right along with 'em! Pouring! Oh, I wouldn't live in a paved town for all you'd give me!" cried Aunt Nanny.

"And the flies!" Aunt Birdie said.

"Judge Moody says to Jack, 'The storekeeper aggravated you, so you carried off his safe. Was it your idea to rob him?' 'No sir,' Jack says, 'just to aggravate him.' 'Yet all that was in the safe managed to get out, vanish, disappear, melt away, never to be found,' says the Judge."

"Ain't Percy grand? He gets 'em all down pat," said Aunt Birdie. "I wish I was married to him," she told Uncle Dolphus. "He'd keep me entertained."

"Oh, I wish you could have been there, Cleo!" Uncle Noah Webster cried again into her face.

"I'd been sitting with Mr. Stovall and pulling for the other side," she reminded him.

" 'The picture I get's a familiar one,' the Judge says. Sounds not far from mournful about it, though. 'You folks around Banner trade at Stovall's store, vote him into office, and raise the roof when you feel like it.' " Uncle Noah Webster smiled.

"And keep coming back some few miles to do it," aded Uncle Percy. "Though the Saturdays now is few and far between."

"And if you *don't* give Curly your vote, what happens to your store credit? I don't know what could be easier to understand," said Uncle Dolphus.

" 'Baiting the storekeeper and thumbing your nose at the peace officer,' Moody says. 'Blessed with Excell Stovall, Banner is able to accomplish both at the same time.' "

"Moody didn't know any of that for sure—how could he?" said Uncle Dolphus. "He just makes a living off of guessing. Gets paid for it. Bound to be lucky some time."

"And then it all comes out—what Moody's up to," quavered Uncle Percy.

Miss Beulah in her kitchen yelled, "I'll tell you! He made a monkey out of Jack."

"That's right, Beulah. I can hear his voice right now." Uncle Percy prettily piped: " 'How long will it take people to start showing some respect for those they have raised to office?' "

"Whoa, I don't know as I go along with that," cried little Aunt Birdie.

"Look first!" cried Aunt Nanny. "And see if it's Curly Stovall!"

"*Or* Judge Moody!" they joined in.

"Judge was bound to miss the gist, and he's missed it now," said Uncle Curtis.

"That Judge Moody's whole battle cry was *respect*. I don't believe any of that courtroom was too well pleased. They wasn't prepared for anything they hadn't come to hear," whispered Uncle Percy.

"Why, I saw *Curly* baffled!" Uncle Noah Webster cried, and let out a laugh that sounded like reckless admiration.

" 'You-all go right ahead taking things in your own hands. Well,' says Moody, 'I'm here today to tell you it's got to stop.' He says, 'You can't *go* knocking the law down if it gets in your way, you can't keep *on* packing up the law in the nearest crate big enough to hold it'—nods at the coffin—'and go skipping out the store with a safe, so-called'—nods at the mother-bird—'and all without offering this court any better reason than "He's aggravating." Aggravating!'

" 'Judge, I reckon to do justice to Curly, you got to see him in Banner,' says Jack. 'The best place is his own store, and the best time is Saturday.'

" 'I'm doing the justice around here,' says Moody. 'When I need outside help, I'll ask for it. What if he is aggravating!'

" 'I'd like you to see him try cutting off your shirt-tail and nailing it to the beam before you make up your mind, sir,' says Jack, still polite about it. He just gets the gavel."

"But didn't you-all have a lawyer furnished to pull a better story out of Jack?" asked Aunt Cleo. "You can get those free."

"If that's what you want to call the fellow," said Uncle Curtis. "He was not there on my invitation, and I think I speak for the family. He got as much in the way as he knew how, I imagine. A good deal of what he said was drowned out. Never caught even his first name, doubt if I'd know him again if I was to see him coming."

"Well, when Moody finally pounds 'em quiet, he leans out over Jack," said Uncle Percy, "and says, 'Tell me one last thing: would you do it again?' "

"Why, Jack's as dependable as the day is long!" Aunt Birdie cried out.

"And Jack gives a great big smile to Gloria and says, 'Well, sir, I'm a married man from now on. And I reckon my wife would have to pass a law about that.'

"Bang bang and thump thump thump, says the gavel. Judge Moody tells Jack, 'Come on back here. Don't you realize the jury hasn't been charged and brought in a verdict and I haven't passed sentence yet?' Jack had been about to sit down with his family. 'I'm about to make a living example out of you, young man!' And there's a groán you could hear from one end of the State of Mississippi to the other, I bet—it's this family. 'You're going to be a lesson to the rest,' says Judge Moody, and gives the jury a strict piece of his mind too, like they's no better than the rest of us poor humans, and sent 'em out. They turned right around and came back, while Jack's still puzzling over it."

"How'd you-all like the verdict?" asked Aunt Cleo.

"Of guilty?" everybody cried, while Uncle Noah Webster sank back in the seat of his chair and opened both arms to them all, as if to bring in the word once more.

"And what of?" he begged them.

"Aggravated battery!"

"—whatever that is!" called Miss Beulah in the suddenly gay, sharp voice of the cook whose pan is ready to come out of the oven no matter what happens, and she ran feverishly onto the porch with a pan of hot gingerbread clutched in the folds of her apron.

"And robbery," said Elvie solemnly, coming behind her mother to serve the buttermilk.

At Granny's chair first, they found her with head bowed in sleep, and tiptoed past her.

"Aggravated battery and robbery, I bet you fainted," said Aunt Cleo in congratulatory tones, biting into a hot square.

"Jack all but did!" cried Aunt Birdie.

"Pole-axed is a little more like it," Aunt Nanny said, cradling a thick brown square in both hands before the big bite.

"What surprised us was the courthouse didn't fall down." Uncle Curtis reached for his portion. "When the judge says, 'Two years in the state pen, time off for good behavior.'"

"Then Grandpa Vaughn put his head right down on his cane in front of him," said Uncle Percy, his wary eye on Granny.

"We did our share of helping out his groans!" cried Aunt Nanny. "Homer Champion didn't do so bad himself. He was ever'where at once, begging 'em all for their sympathy."

"Vaughn come in with the dogs in time to hear Moody say the pen. And I saw Vaughn—he bit himself. Just turned away from Jack and took a big plug out of his arm," said Aunt Birdie.

"Bet Curly kicked up his heels," Aunt Cleo said. "Wasn't he well pleased?"

"In hog heaven. Invited everybody there but us to a fish-fry the next Sunday, told Judge Moody to come too and bring his wife if he had one. He didn't come and didn't send any wife either," said Uncle Noah Webster.

"Good. I'd hate the rankest stranger to get their notion of Banner hospitality from Curly's fish-fry. Stovalls fry their fish with the hides on," grinned Aunt Nanny.

Miss Beulah cried, "The rest was all in Damascus that Sunday listening to Grandpa heal our hearts by telling us of Heaven to come. We could smell Curly's smoke the whole sermon long. He'd dance on your grave." She whirled fiercely with the hot pan. "If I'd known what that Judge was fixing to do to Jack, I'd stood up in the courtroom right quick and told him a thing or two to his face he'd still remember! After all, I'm the boy's mother!"

"Beulah, I bet you could have!" They helped themselves in quick turn as she passed them the pan.

"For two cents I'd a-done it, too!"

"The way you know how to let fly, Beulah, if I'd been Judge Moody you'd have silenced *me*," said Aunt Birdie.

"Oh, I'd silenced him," said Miss Beulah, and she ran out and ran back with her second panful. "I'd silenced him, all right. Let 'im try it again, he'll never ruin my boy but once."

"My eyes see a sunbonnet coming this way," said Etoyle, chewing.

"Little Mis' Comfort, coming all this way up?" asked Aunt Nanny.

"It'll just be to peep at us," said Miss Beulah. "She'll just come far enough up our road to count us. She'll turn around in a minute and trail home." She laughed. "She said she's having a hen and cooking a mess of collards for Aycock, and I bet not a bit of that's so."

"You think Aycock's coming home too?" Miss Lexie asked.

"Jack's coat-tails is where he lives. He couldn't stay anywhere by himself," she said.

"Why isn't she home, then, and preparing?" cried Aunt Birdie.

"I doubt you she's even set bread," said Miss Beulah.

"Hasn't she called on kin to come be with her when he walks in?" asked Aunt Beck. "Help hold her up?"

"Besides Mr. Earl Comfort, and nobody wants Earl, there's just Mr. Comfort *to* call, and he's been gone."

"Mr. Comfort and little Mis' Comfort, they didn't gee," said Miss Lexie comfortably.

"Does this mean Aycock went to the pen with Jack?" Aunt Cleo asked.

"How'd you get so behind! Yes'm, at least Jack had Aycock with him, to keep him from being so altogether homesick. We slept better at night for that," said Aunt Beck.

"How come Aycock had to pay the penalty like Jack?" Aunt Cleo asked. "What had *he* lost?"

"Because when Aycock had his turn in court, he stood up and said he's going too! 'And how are you going to qualify yourself for the pen?' says Moody. Aycock says he'd been in the store from the beginning, propped up behind the pickle barrel. He'd set still and let goods go flying over his head if they wanted to, let Jack have

**59**

the gun pulled on him and Curly be boxed and tied, must have seen the safe get carted off, heard out all Curly's racket. And hadn't done a thing but enjoy himself and put away pickles." Uncle Noah Webster slapped Aunt Cleo's leg. "But the Judge comes down on his gavel and says, 'Well, I see no reason why I can't make a lesson of you too.' Verdict was guilty as charged."

"Goodness, that was over in a hurry," Aunt Cleo said.

"Aycock goes to the pen as big as Jack. Whether he'll come home as big is another question. The Comforts don't know what the word reunion means," said Uncle Curtis.

"Never did I have any use for those Comforts at all, they're the nearest to nothing that ever did come around here. I'm sorry we have 'em. Even the mother is a failure," said Miss Beulah.

"She's gone now," said Etoyle.

"She hadn't the least idea how to put a face on it!" said Miss Beulah.

"And there *you* was, high and dry! Wouldn't we all have hated to be in your shoes!" Aunt Birdie cried to Gloria.

"Had you finished your good-byes?" asked Aunt Beck sadly.

"No ma'am," Gloria said. "But we got our promises made. We're going to live for the future."

"Bet that made you cry!" said Aunt Nanny.

"She hasn't cried yet!" said Miss Beulah. "Not a single time when I was looking at her!"

Gloria closed her eyes. Everybody watched her cheeks. They were as speckled as sweet warm pears, but just as tearless.

"You was crying inside," Aunt Beck told her.

"Didn't you have anybody with good shoulders to cry on? Where's *your* family?" asked Aunt Cleo.

"Sister Cleo, you're asking that to the only orphan for a mile around," said Aunt Birdie. "We'll have to forgive you for your question this time."

"Who was your mama and papa?" asked Aunt Cleo.

"Nobody knows," said Gloria.

"Did they burn up, fall in, or what?"

"Nobody knows," said Gloria.

"Gloria's a little nobody from out of nowhere," said Aunt Beck fondly.

"She's from the Ludlow Presbyterian Orphan Asylum, if you want to hear it exactly," said Miss Beulah. "And how she turns all that around into something to be conceited about is a little bit more than I can tell you."

"Found on a doorstep?" cried Aunt Cleo.

"A little better than that. You may hear about it one day," said Aunt Beck soothingly. "For right now, her new husband's just been dragged away from her. And she still hasn't cried."

"What about the one that was trying to make a teacher out of you before it happened?" Aunt Cleo asked Gloria. "You could have cried on her. She'd have been the very one to offer."

"I never went back to see Miss Julia Mortimer and give her the chance."

"Well, excuse me! No wonder you're sitting up on that powder keg in your wedding dress today!" cried Aunt Cleo.

⋅⋅⋅

"I don't know today who I relish blaming the most—Judge Moody or old Curly Stovall," said Aunt Birdie.

"Moody!" Miss Beulah cried. "Moody! For the name he laid on my son. I just hope Jack's feelings get over it before mine do."

"I'll be glad to say Moody," said Aunt Beck.

"And there Jack went, trusting him!" yelled Miss Beulah. "The poor fool, I reckon he thought he was safe because he's needed. I learned my lesson then!"

Aunt Nanny said, "But it was Curly that took that ring like it was even change. I more than blame him, I look down on him. And more than that, I'm not going to vote for him Tuesday."

"Curly'd do the same thing over again, it's the only way he knows to behave at all," said Aunt Birdie. "Blame him and he don't care! Your votes is all he cares about. I swear he's too mean to live."

"And it's not like Curly would have left a wife, had somebody hauled in the store and *killed* him. He's too mean to marry! That's what I told his own preacher, Brother Dollarhide, that was taking up half my seat at the trial," said Aunt Nanny.

"Old Curly was baptized a Methodist to boot, if you can picture him being just a month old," said Uncle Percy. "A big bawler."

"While I put Judge Moody down as a Presbyterian. For one good reason. The whole way through that trial, his mouth was one straight line. He didn't look out on that crowded courtroom and smile once. Not one time." Uncle Noah Webster laid a crumb-stuck hand on his wife's leg.

"And if he never lets me see his Moody face again for the rest of his life," Miss Beulah shouted, as if she were still the length of the passage away from them, "that'd be the first kind thing I could find to thank him for."

"He's through with us now, Mother," said Mr. Renfro.

"Of course that judge never got it through his head what it was all about!" yelled Miss Beulah. "Born and bred in Ludlow, most likely in the very shadow of the courthouse! A man never spent a day of his life in Banner, never heard of a one of us!"

"I don't think there's a heap you can say on behalf of that *jury,*" said Uncle Curtis. "I wonder where they ever resurrected a bunch like that."

"All right, if I had that jury back together before me, I wouldn't mind taking a minute to skin 'em alive right now for my own satisfaction," said Miss Beulah, passing her pan again fast. "All twelve of 'em quick just for doing what Moody told 'em."

"Now and then I have to feel provoked with even Ella Fay for letting people suppose she'd trade treasure for a little bit of store candy—a precious gold band, the only one like it in Christendom!" Aunt Beck said, tears rising to her eyes.

"How long had she had it?" Aunt Cleo asked.

"A day."

"Granny kept it in the Bible knotted to a good stout string," said Miss Beulah, addressing her words to the chair where the sleeping old lady was cradled. "I thought all we had to guard it against was children swallowing it."

"All of 'em striving as one, they succeeded. That's how I look at it," said Aunt Birdie. "They locked up the sweetest and hardest-working boy in Banner and Boone County and maybe in all Creation."

"But he never got a whipping at home, I reckon, for all the trouble he caused you?" asked Aunt Cleo.

"We whipped Ella Fay," said Miss Beulah.

"Hey, Ella Fay, did you cry, darlin'?" Aunt Birdie called.

"You could've heard me clear down to the store," Ella Fay called from inside the house.

"Good."

"But I'd stick that ring in his face again if I had it back right now," she called sweetly.

"How many more chances do you suppose you've got coming to you?" called her mother sharply.

"Well, a lot grew out of one little ring, didn't it?" remarked Aunt Cleo.

"Even Sister Cleo sees that! And I'll tell you once more that's exactly what old Judge Moody lost sight of!" cried Miss Beulah. "The ring itself!"

"Not having it there in front of his eyes to remind him," said Aunt Beck sympathetically.

"Yes'm, it would've been a little mite different for Jack and us all today if he'd contented himself with spilling open that safe there in the store, and fishing out the ring, and carrying the ring home in his shirt pocket, and delivering it back to Granny. But he's a man! Done it the man's way," said Aunt Nanny.

"He did his best," Miss Beulah cried. "And it was a heap more trouble! For everybody!"

Mr. Renfro ran his eye over the parade of melons he had lined up there on the porch, then passing along them spanked each one. They resounded like horses ready to go.

"Oh, I've brought mine up on praise!" cried Miss Beulah, glaring after him.

"You get the credit, Beulah!" Aunt Birdie cried. "You get the credit for the wonderful children they are!"

"And I'll keep it up to my dying day!" she shrieked in their faces. "Praise! With now and then a little switching to even it up."

"It's the girls that gets the switchings," Elvie said, and bolted.

Aunt Nanny grinned and said, "And all this time, that ring may be laying down yonder in the Banner road in front of Stovall's store, looking no more'n a little bit of tin, a piece of grit! Bet it is right now! But you've all walked on it a hundred times! And if it had teeth it'd bite you."

"I tell you lost's lost," said Miss Beulah, and passed the pan with the last piece of gingerbread in it, which Miss Lexie didn't mind taking. "And my son in the pen for the trouble he took to save it."

⋅§

"So here's all these little sisters and a little brother, with a cripple daddy and with uncles that's had to scatter, and Grandpa and Granny Vaughn and their broken hearts, and Beulah that's beside herself for a spell, all doing without Jack. And after Jack had stayed out of school himself to give the little ones their chance, they had to pass up their own schooling half the time, smart as they was—" Uncle Percy was trying to get the story back from them.

"Well, Vaughn did Jack's work and some of mine, and I did his, and the girls they scrubbed and hauled and fetched and carried, and did every bit of their own part, and that was the system we used," said Miss Beulah.

"And Vaughn trying to trot even for little Mis' Comfort when his mother told him," said Aunt Birdie.

"I couldn't let her accept charity!" cried Miss Beulah.

"She did it anyway, behind your back," said Aunt Beck. "Our preacher carried her with him to the courthouse and they came back with a big box of commodities."

"Pity *her!*" came cries.

"Our preacher says further there wasn't anything worse served him in the United States Army than what he got at Boone County Courthouse last December."

"And here was the baby put in *her* appearance. Lady May Renfro, bless her little heart, she come as soon as she could," Aunt Beck said.

Lady May's neck, like the stem of a new tulip, held poised its perfect little globe. She had heard her name. Throwing her arms wide, she jumped from her mother's knee to the floor.

"Look how that baby can already fly!" said Miss Lexie in a voice of present warning, as Lady May ran about the porch sounding off louder than before.

"I'm going to catch you and run off with you, Britches!" Aunt Nanny called after her flying heels. "Who you hunting?"

"Pore little Lady May's running in her petticoat and it reaches to the calf of her leg," said Aunt Cleo. "Who made that!"

It had been made like a doll dress from a folded sugar sack, round holes cut for neck and arms, then stitched down the sides. A little flounce edged the bottom, a mother's touch.

"It allowed for her to grow like she's been growing—fast as a beanstalk," said Miss Beulah. "Do you raise any objection to that?"

"No'm," she said. "That's nature, you got to accept it."

"Well, *we've* been feeling mighty sorry for her!" Miss Beulah retorted.

The baby scrambled down the steps and out into the yard. In

her shoes coated white with cornstarch, their high heels tipping her a little forward, Gloria went after her. She walked fast but didn't quite run, the way a thrush skims over the ground without needing to use wings.

"Don't fall down! Don't rake your dress on the rosebush! You've got to both be ready for Jack, got to look pretty for him!" came Etoyle's cry.

The baby ran behind the quilt again and Gloria caught her on the other side. But she was already sliding, slick as a fish, from her arms and running ahead of her mother again.

Aunt Nanny headed off Lady May, and breathing hard she crouched and scooped up the baby in her arms. "I've come to steal you!" But Lady May squirmed free and charged up and down a little path that kept opening between their knees, over their patting feet.

"Well, in case anybody forgets how long Jack Renfro's been gone, feel the weight of *that*," said Miss Lexie, and stopping the baby with a broom, she caught her and loaded her onto Granny Vaughn's lap.

Even before her eyes opened, Granny had put both arms out. Lady May, the soles of her feet wrinkling like the old lady's forehead, went to the weakest and most tenacious embrace she knew. They hugged long enough to remind each other that perhaps they were rivals.

"And what's Jack know about his baby?" asked Aunt Cleo.

"Not a thing in this world. She's his surprise!" cried Aunt Birdie. "What else would she be?"

"Yes sir! I've already started to wondering when she's going to talk and what she's fixing to say," Miss Lexie said.

Lady May made a dart from Granny to Gloria, and Gloria took her up on her lap and began to make her a hat from the nearest plant stand within reach. She pinched off geranium leaves, lapping them over the child's head, fastening them with the thornless stems from the pepper plant and the potted fairy rose that she bit to the right length. Some little girls drew near in a ring to watch, their hair falling beside their cheeks in pale stems, paler across the scissors' slice, like fresh-cut lily stalks. Now Lady May had a hat.

"But where's she going, where's she going so soon?" Uncle Noah Webster teased Gloria.

"That's for the future to say," she replied.

Aunt Birdie said staunchly, "Well, a son can do something that's a whole heap harder to bear than what Jack did."

"That's right, he could've kilt somebody," said Aunt Cleo. "And been sentenced to die in the portable electric chair—they'd bring it right to your courthouse. And you-all *could* be having his funeral today, with a sealed coffin."

They cried out at her.

Aunt Beck said in shocked tones, "Now I'm not *blaming* the boy!"

"Find fault with Jack? I'd hate to see the first one try it," said Aunt Nanny.

"I'd hate to see anybody in the wide world try it!" Aunt Birdie cried.

"It'd be the easiest way to kill him," said Miss Beulah.

"If ever a man was sure of anything at all, I was sure I had to give this house a new tin top to shine in Jack's face the day he gets home," said Mr. Renfro. "That roof speaks just a world, speaks volumes."

"Mr. Renfro give up just about all we had left for that tin top over our heads," said Miss Beulah. "He had to show the reunion single-handed the world don't have to go flying to pieces when the oldest son gives trouble."

"You hammer that tin on by yourself?" protested Aunt Beck. "Since he wasn't even here to help you? Cousin Ralph, I'm more than half surprised you didn't crack at least your collarbone for today."

"He had so-called help. And I'll tell you what I got tired of was Mr. Willy Trimble scurrying and frisking around like a self-appointed squirrel up over my head," said Miss Beulah. "He was neighborly to offer, but he's taken liberties ever since. It's still our roof!"

"Paid for with what?" the new Aunt Cleo asked in complimentary tones.

"Take comfort. Our farm ain't holding together a great deal better than yours, Mr. Renfro," said Uncle Curtis. "Maybe me and Beck did raise a house full of sons, and maybe not a one of 'em had to go to Parchman, but they left home just the same. Married, and moved over to look after their wives' folks. Scattered."

"Why, of course they did," said Aunt Beck softly.

**66**

"But all nine!" said Uncle Curtis. "All nine! And they're never coming home."

"I'm thankful they can still get back all together at the old reunion," said Uncle Percy, looking over at the ball game in the pasture. "Who are they playing—their wives?" But as he stood looking, he exclaimed in his faint voice, "Look where the turkey's walking."

The Thanksgiving turkey, resembling something made on the farm out of stovepipe and wound up to go, walking anywhere he pleased with three months yet to stay alive, paraded into a grease-darkened, grassless patch of yard with a trench worn down in the clay, an oblong space staked out by the stumps of four pine trees.

"I *thought* there's something about the place that's unnatural!" said Uncle Noah Webster. "Beulah!" he hollered. "Where's Jack's truck, Jack's precious truck? It ain't picked up and gone to meet him, has it?"

"One guess."

"Oh, the skunk!" the uncles shouted, all rising.

"Now you Beechams might as well sit down. It was nothing but a dirty piece of machinery," Miss Beulah said.

"Curly didn't even let Jack get home first to make it go," said Uncle Noah Webster.

"Jack was so purely besotted *with* it, I'd been more greatly surprised to learn something hadn't happened *to* it," Uncle Dolphus said.

"But a truck? How did Jack ever get hold of such a scarcity to start with?" asked Aunt Cleo. "You-all don't look like you was ever that well-fixed."

"It fell in his lap, pretty near. Jack's just that kind of a boy, Sister Cleo," said Aunt Beck.

"The last time I seen it enthroned in your yard, Beulah, it was still asking for some little attention," said Uncle Curtis. "I don't guess it improved a great deal with the boy away."

"I hadn't let the children touch it!" she declared. She put up her hand. "And listen, everybody, don't let on to Jack about his filthy truck—not today. Don't prattle! Owing to the crowd, he might not see it's gone any quicker'n you did. Don't tell him, children!" she called widely. "Spare him that till tomorrow."

"Just lay the four stumps with some planks, like it's one more table. And Ella Fay can have it covered up with a cloth. That wouldn't be a hard trick at all," said Aunt Nanny. "I'll eat at it!"

"And there's another thing that's gone he'll come to find out." said Uncle Curtis. "That's the Boone County Courthouse. It burned to the ground, they don't like to think how."

"How many here got to see it?" asked Aunt Cleo.

Aunt Nanny said, "Me and Percy got invited to ride over with our neighbors and wait for the roof to fall in. And guess who come in sight with the fellows bringing things out, the water cooler and such as that. My own daddy! I hadn't seen him in five years, and then he was too busy to wave back. He was rescuing the postcard rack with all those postcards of the courthouse."

"It burned right at commodity time," said Uncle Percy.

"And whenever I think of it going up in smoke, I think of all that sugar!" said Aunt Nanny.

"Never mind. With the welcome he's got waiting, he won't ever start to count what's gone," said Aunt Beck.

"If he tries, then that roof ought to be enough to blind him," said Aunt Birdie, "the sweet trusting boy. It blinded *me*."

"And then when he sits, Brother Bethune will forgive him here at the table for his sins," said Aunt Beck. "I just hope *he* won't disappoint everybody. I know he's got your church now, all you Baptists—"

"Beck, if you can't forget you're the only Methodist for a mile around, how do you expect the rest of us to forget it?" said Miss Beulah. "It don't take a Methodist to see Brother Bethune as a comedown after Grandpa. Who wouldn't be?"

"There must be a dozen other Baptist preachers running loose around the Bywy Hills with their tongues hanging out for pulpits," argued Aunt Beck.

"There's a right good many who'd be tickled to steal Damascus away from him this very day," Miss Beulah granted her. "Brother Yielding of Foxtown would dearly love to add it to his string. But Brother Bethune is the one who grew up in Banner, and you've got to put up with him or explain to him that there's something the matter with him, one. So he can't be touched."

"I just feel at a time like this he won't be a match for us," Aunt Beck said with a sigh.

"Yes, it's Grandpa we need, and Grandpa's in the cemetery. It was a year ago tonight we lost him," said Uncle Curtis.

"Well, but if you had one to die, Jack could have got a pass home," said Aunt Cleo. "Ain't that good old Mississippi law?

They'd let him come to the funeral between two guards, then be led back. Handcuffed."

They cried out again. Only Granny was peaceful, head low.

"Sister Cleo, we didn't tell him about Grandpa. Jack's got that to learn today, it's part of his coming home," said Miss Beulah. "It's what's going to hurt him the most, but I can only hope it'll help him grow up a little."

"He's already a father," said Uncle Dolphus.

"He don't know that either," said Aunt Nanny.

"That's right. We'll bring out that little surprise just when he needs it most, won't we?" Aunt Birdie cried.

"She's my surprise to bring," Gloria said.

"Well, ain't *you* about ready to cry a little bit about everything, while you still got time?" Aunt Cleo asked, pointing to Gloria.

Gloria shook her head and set her teeth.

"What we say here at home is," said Miss Beulah, "Gloria's got a sweet voice when she deigns to use it, she's so spotless the sight of her hurts your eyes, she's so neat that once you've hidden her Bible, stolen her baby, put away her curl papers, and wished her writing tablet out of sight, you wouldn't find a trace of her in the company room, and she *can* be pretty. But you can't read her."

"She can roll up her hair in the dark," said Elvie devotedly.

"*There's* a sweet juicy mouthful singing!" Aunt Nanny told Lady May, when just then the mourning dove called. "It won't be long before the boy gets home who'll treat you to a morsel of that."

"I wouldn't let her have it," said Gloria. "She's a long way off from eating tough old bird."

"Listen! But I've seen 'em when their mothers' backs was turned, and they'd be sitting up eating corn on the cob!" cried Aunt Cleo.

"Stop, Sister Cleo. Gloria don't want to tell her business," Aunt Beck gently warned.

"Well, ain't you a little monkey!" Aunt Cleo laughed at Gloria, but nobody laughed with her.

Mr. Renfro counted them and then one by one he took the torpedo-shaped watermelons and loaded them carefully back into the cool cave underneath the porch.

Aunt Birdie suddenly asked, "Where *is* Parchman?"

"A fine time to be asking," said Uncle Dolphus.

Uncle Curtis said, "Well, only our brother Nathan's ever seen for himself where it is, I believe I've heard him say."

Vaughn, at the water bucket, pointed straight through them. "Go clean across Mississippi from here, go till you get ready to fall in the Mississippi River."

"Is he in *Arkansas?*" cried a boy cousin, raising a baseball bat. "If he is I'm going over there and git him out."

"Arkansas would be the crowning blow!" Miss Beulah cried. "No, my boy may be in Parchman, but he still hasn't been dragged across the state line."

"Jack's in the Delta," said Uncle Curtis. "Clear out of the hills and into the good land."

They smiled. "That Jack!"

"Where it's running with riches and swarming with niggers everywhere you look," said Uncle Curtis. "Yes, Nathan in his travels has spied out the top of its water tower. It's there, all right."

"The spring after Jack went, General Green about took over your corn, remember?" Uncle Dolphus said to Mr. Renfro, who at last came hobbling up the steps and bowing into their company. "And today, your whole farm wouldn't hardly give a weed comfort and sustenance."

Uncle Noah Webster clapped Mr. Renfro on the back and cried in the tones of a compliment, "Looks like ever' time we had a rain, you didn't!"

"And the next thing, everything's going to dry up or burn up or blow up, one, without that boy. Is that your verdict, Mr. Renfro?"

"While Jack's been sitting over there right spang in the heart of the Delta. And whatever he sticks in the ground, the Delta just grows it for him," whispered Uncle Percy.

"I'm sorry I even asked where it was," said Aunt Birdie. "I wonder now how early a start he made, if he's got all that distance to cover."

"He better start hurrying," Uncle Dolphus said. "Busted out of jail in Foxtown in less than twenty-four hours—I see little reason why he can't make it back from Parchman in a year and a half."

"Hush!" cried Miss Beulah.

"You can't get out of Parchman with a pie knife," cried Uncle Noah Webster.

"Men, hush!" ordered Miss Beulah. "He's coming just as fast as he can. He ain't going to let it be the end of the world today—he'll be right here to the table."

70

"And a good thing Jack knows it. Because the truth of the matter is," Aunt Beck murmured, gazing at the old lady in her rocker, "if we had to wait another year, who knows if Granny would've made it?"

There came a sound like a pistol shot from out in the yard. All heads turned front. Ella Fay had cracked the first starched tablecloth out of its folds—it waved like a flag. Then she dropped it on the ground and came running toward them, screaming. Dogs little and big set up a tenor barking. Dogs ran from all corners of the yard and from around the house and through the passage, streaking for the front gate.

Aunt Nanny grabbed the baby from Gloria's knees and ran to hide her in the company room, screaming as if she herself had nearly been caught in her nightgown. Miss Beulah raced to Granny's side. The barking reached frantic pitch as a whirlwind of dust filled the space between the chinaberry trees. As even those chatterers on the back porch and those filling the house started up through the passage, the floor drummed and swayed, a pan dropped from its nail in the kitchen wall, and overhead even the tin of the roof seemed to quiver with a sound like all the family spoons set to jingling in their glass.

Riding a wave of dogs, a nineteen-year-old boy leaped the steps to a halt on the front gallery. He crashed his hands together, then swung his arms wide.

"Jack Jordan Renfro," announced Miss Lexie to the company. "Well: you brought him."

⌘

He might never have been under a roof from the day he left home until this minute. His open, blunt-featured face in its morning beard had burned to a red even deeper than the home clay. He was breathing hard, his chest going up and down fast, his mouth was open, and he was pouring sweat. With his eyes flared wide, his face smileless as a child's, he stood and waited, with his arms open like gates.

Then it seemed that the whole reunion at once was trying to run in.

"Why ain't you nearly perished?" Miss Beulah shrieked as she shouldered her way through the rest and smacked his face with kisses.

"What did you bring me?" yelled Etoyle.

"What did you bring me?" yelled Elvie. They both beat their fists against him. Elvie beat on his legs, crying with joy, then found a cockleburr to pull off his pants, and Etoyle with a scream of triumph pinched a live June bug that was riding his sleeve—the torn sleeve that flowed free from his shoulder like some old flag carried home from far-off battle.

"Where's mine?" teased the boy cousins. "Where's mine, Jack?"

Ella Fay ended her shrieks at last and ran to get her hug. Then Vaughn came across the floor in long strides, his heavily starched pants weighted down by the deep folds at the bottom. He had put on his print-sack school shirt, new and readable front and back, from which the points of his collar were damply rising. Jack lunged forward looking ready to kiss him, but Vaughn said, "I've got on your pants." He had with him a pair of dried cornstalks, and offered them. Jack took one and for a moment the brothers jousted with them, shaking them like giant rattles, banging them about like papery clubs.

"Was you a trusty?" Vaughn asked, then fled.

"And oh but he's home tired, limping and sore after all his long hot way!" screamed Aunt Birdie, pulling down Jack's head to kiss his cheeks and chin, while Aunt Nanny bear-hugged him from behind.

"Honey, you don't know yet how hard we've been waiting on you," said Aunt Beck, with great care ripping a briar away from his pants leg. "I wish you did."

"Never wrote your family once—I got that out of your daddy," Miss Lexie was sweeping up the cakes of clay and strings of briars his shoes had tracked in. "Might as well be coming back from the dead."

"Don't he get here fat and fine, though?" Aunt Nanny still squeezed him around the ribs. "Believe you put a little meat on your bones while you was away!"

"But I venture to say they never did succeed in feeding you like we're fixing to feed you today," said Aunt Birdie, pulling him loose.

72

"Well, did you bring us a rain?" Uncle Noah Webster was shouting at him as though from a rooftop.

The uncles plunged forward to pull on him and pound him, while Etoyle and Elvie sat on the floor and each anchored one of his feet.

"Where's Gloria? Gloria, Glo-ri-a! Here's him! You forgotten how to act glad? Girl, can't you find him, can't you fight your way through us?" It was the aunts screaming at her, while the uncles said to the aunts, "Hold back, then."

They divided and there stood Gloria. Her hair came down in a big puff as far as her shoulders, where it broke into curls all of which would move when she did, smelling of Fairy soap. Across her forehead it hung in fine hooks, cinnamon-colored, like the stamens in a Dainty Bess rose. As though small bells had been hung, without her permission, on her shoulders, hips, breasts, even elbows, tinkling only just out of ears' range, she stepped the length of the porch to meet him.

"Look at that walk. *Now* I'd know her for a teacher anywhere," said Aunt Cleo.

Jack cocked his hands in front of his narrow-set hips as she came. Their young necks stretched, their lips tilted up, like a pair of rabbits yearning toward the same head of grass, and Jack snapped his vise around her waist with thumbs met.

"First kiss of their lives in public, I bet a hundred dollars," Aunt Cleo observed.

"Speak, Jack, speak!" shrieked his mother.

"Speak, Jack!" they were crying at him. "You ain't gone deaf and dumb, have you?"

"A new roof! I could see it a mile coming!" His lilting voice came at last. "What's happened?"

"Bless his heart!" Miss Beulah thankfully cried.

"Well, I believe it's one thing that may be on tight, son," said Mr. Renfro. He still stood back, with his arms hugged together in front and the prong of his chin in his hand. But as Jack started parting his way toward him, Granny made a little noise of her own.

"Look who's been waiting, just a speck!" Uncle Noah Webster shouted, as Jack, spinning and sweeping her from her feet, brought Granny up to meet him, chin to chin.

"Ain't you got me a little sugar?" she inquired.

"I didn't quite hear Grandpa's thunder as I came through the

**73**

lot," Jack told her after she'd got her kiss, still holding her up where he could see her. "Where have you got him hid, Granny?"

"Jack, we've lost Grandpa," Miss Beulah called up, hands frantic at her lips.

"We lost Grandpa Vaughn, one year ago today," Uncle Curtis said, and as all went quiet, like the rattle of tiny drums came the sound of one more kettle coming to a boil in the kitchen.

"You never stopped coming for long enough to see if there's a new grave in the cemetery with fresh flowers on it?" Miss Beulah asked, reading his face. "It would have been staring right at you."

"It was the last place I thought to look," gasped Jack.

"Yes, son. And oh but you know how an old lady grieves! We was all worried for fear we couldn't keep her for you, either," Miss Beulah cried.

Granny, up in the air, only looked him back cockily in the eye. Carefully he lowered her down to the floor, and when she got her footing he brushed some of his dust off her sleeves.

"Oh, Jack's cheek is ready to wipe," said Aunt Birdie.

"We've got a mighty good little surprise ready for now," Aunt Nanny said.

"When people need it most! That's the time to bring it out," said Aunt Birdie.

"Gloria! What have you got for Jack? Ain't it just about time to show him?" The crowd caught up with her in the kitchen, clamoring to her.

"I'll be the judge," said Gloria from the stove.

Jack came plunging into the smoke and steam, turned her around, circled the table at a hop, counting his mother's cakes out loud, stealing a wing from the mountain of fried chicken heaped on the bread board, and kissed the icing off the blade of a knife. Then, sinking into the kitchen rocker, he took off his shoes and held them out to the nearest sister.

Under the red dust that coated them the uppers were worn nearly through. Their soles were split. The strings hung heavy with dust and weeds and their own extra knots. They were the shoes he had left home in. Elvie bore them off to the company room, while Jack lifted a crock from the table and drank off the top of the milk.

"And here's who's been doing the most of that barking," cried Aunt Nanny.

Sid ran in panting, a festive-looking little dog with a long coat,

74

black and white with a marking down his breast like a flowing polka-dot tie. He was like a tiny shepherd. Jack gathered him onto his knee, raised the moulting cat to his shoulder, and rocked the two together.

"What would we have done if you *hadn't* got here and *wasn't* sitting right now in that chair?" Miss Beulah screamed at him.

"Well, Mama, I believe I'm right on time," he said with milky mouth.

"Jack Renfro, you're home early, by my reckoning," Miss Lexie Renfro now marched up and said with the bang of her own kiss. "Now how'd you get rewarded like that?"

"Aunt Lexie, what they told me it was for was my behavior."

"Surprised *they'd* know good behavior when they saw it!" snorted his mother, and forced a saved-up square of gingerbread whole into his mouth.

Chewing softly, he kept his eyes on Gloria, and now in a wreath of steam she came toward him. She bent to his ear and whispered her first private word.

"Jack, there's precious little water in this house, but I saved you back some and I've got it to boiling."

"Whose is it?" he whispered back.

"Lady May's."

The whole round circle of blue showed in his eyes.

"There's a foot tub waiting in you and Vaughn's old room. Scrub. Then you can shave those whiskers so they won't scare somebody else." She put into his groping hand the lump of sweet-soap, gave him a towel she had ready, stiff as pasteboard from the clothesline and hot too, and walked ahead of him carrying from the stove the boiler of slightly milky, steam-breathing water.

"I've been in the river already," he said humbly there at her heels.

"Like I couldn't help but know!"

The front porch that he had emptied of all company by going back to the kitchen was for the moment still deserted. It was only draped with their coats, set about with their packed buckets and bundles, and its floor was bulging as if pressed up from below by Mr. Renfro's melons underneath.

Jack came leaping over a banjo laid on a folded coat, and straddling a bucket of zinnias he planted himself before the mirror. She pointed out to him where all this time they'd kept his shaving brush in the dish. Then she put into his hand the razor she'd stropped.

"Don't just look at me," she said.

The mirror was mottled like a bird egg. He filled it with his urgent face.

"She's being a real little wife, she's making him earn his surprise," said Aunt Birdie. A circle had re-formed on the porch.

"Now that cheek looks more like you. It would take more'n the whole wide world to change you, Jack," said Aunt Beck.

"Don't let those fingers slip! I bet he's already lost a gallon of sweat just proving how glad he is to see us," said Aunt Birdie.

Aunt Cleo pushed in front of the others, leaned over Jack's shoulders, and got into the mirror with him.

"Who you think this is?" she asked.

He almost cut his cheek. Everybody laughed but Gloria, Granny Vaughn, Miss Beulah, and Aunt Cleo.

"Her story is," said Aunt Nanny, "your Uncle Noah Webster gave the Market Bulletin a free ad for a settled white Christian lady with no home ties and drawing a pension to come keep house for him."

"Wasn't that just the same as handing Aunt Lexie an invitation?" he asked, shaving his perplexed jaw.

"You know I'd be turned down," Miss Lexie said.

"The bus halted at Foxtown store," said Aunt Nanny. "And when she climbed off it was Cleo. 'Well, now that I've seen your house,' she says to Noah Webster when she's ready to go, 'suppose you ride back with me and I'll show you mine.' Well, he climbed on."

"I ended up my ad, 'Don't care if you drink, dip, cuss, flirt or philander, just so you can wield a broom and enjoy the banjo,' " said Uncle Noah Webster.

"I started not to even come," Aunt Cleo said.

"I got a pretty fair little set of answers altogether," said Uncle Noah Webster.

"You're still gettin' 'em. Bulletin never did know how to *quit* running an ad," said Uncle Dolphus. "Mailman says if you don't want 'em, he does."

"But Jack," said Uncle Noah Webster, "it was when I spotted the name Stovall peeping out of Cleo's answer that I saw the first familiar thing. I'd found my pick!"

"And guess what she is," they cried. "A Stovall's widow."

**76**

Gloria had to take the razor or it would have fallen out of his hand.

"Not Curly!" the circle, all except smiling Aunt Cleo, cried into his boiled, well-alarmed face.

"For a minute you had me thinking somebody had fell for Curly, married him, and the shock had killed him," Jack told Aunt Cleo. He beat his hands and face with Gloria's towel, and put his welcome on Cleo's cheek.

"And she keeps house for him fine except they're married and living in hers, and it's clear down away from us all in South Mississippi," Aunt Birdie said.

"He thinks we've forgiven him for it," called Miss Beulah.

Gloria took hold of Jack's still undried wrist, and led him straight from the porch to the door of the company room, then stopped him.

"You can't come any farther till the reunion's over—the company room is chock-full," she told him. She pushed open the door upon thick hot air as palpable as a wedge of watermelon. "Take your nose back," she warned him, and pressed the door against his naked toes, leaving only a crack.

Inside a ring of ladies' hats and tied-up presents, the width of the bed was filled with babies, as many as a dozen, all of them asleep, tumbled on top of or burrowed into one another. Gloria hovered for a minute over the baby whose eyelids were not quite sealed, and whose girl-hair streamed soft as a breath against a mother's palm. As if to show she remembered the way she'd looked when she first came, Lady May buried her face away from the light, and down the nape of her neck lay the same little trigger of hair, nasturtium pink.

Then Gloria pulled her valise from under the bed and took something out. When she slipped into the passage again, she was holding it up—a store shirt, never worn.

"Somebody that's never seen you before wants to see you a little better adorned," she whispered. "Curly Stovall traded me this for black walnuts, Jack. I picked 'em all up between here and the store, just keeping to my way. A barrel full."

"The hog," he said hoarsely.

Without ever taking his eyes from her, and without moving to get the old shirt off till she peeled it from his back, he punched one arm down the stiffened sleeve. She helped him. He drove in the other fist. It seemed to require their double strength to crack the starch she'd ironed into it, to get his wet body inside. She began to button him down, as his arms cranked down to a resting place and cocked themselves there. The smell of the cloth flooded over them, like a bottle of school ink spilled—the color was blue, a shade that after a few boilings in the pot would match her sky-blue sash.

By the time she stood with her back against the door to get the last button through the buttonhole, he was leaning like the side of a house against her. His cheek came down against hers like a hoarse voice speaking too loud.

Then the voices of others, that tread which was only just a little lighter than feet, ran over them. Somebody else was arriving.

"Uncle Homer and Auntie Fay and the ice has made it in. And Uncle Homer says for Jack to come hopping, Sister Gloria." There was Elvie's little announcing face. She was holding a present tied up in the shape of an owl and another hat for the bed.

Jack still had his weight against Gloria. She straightened him up and led him back into the midst of them.

༺

With only two newcomers, the porch now looked crammed so full that the standing room seemed to reach even beyond the floor's edge. The only thing that held the reunion from falling off appeared to be the double row of cannas that ran around it.

Aunt Nanny gave a boy's whistle as Jack walked in again, Gloria at his shoulder. "Whoo-ee! Who you dressed up for?" "Now he looks ready!" came welcoming cries. "Where'd you get that shirt? Who had that waiting for you, how'd she get that paid for?" "Ask her whereabouts is your *big* surprise!"

Auntie Fay, a little woman twice as frail as Miss Lexie and Mr. Renfro, but wearing pink in her cheeks, grabbed Jack with a shriek and with a second shriek let him go as though she'd grabbed the hot stove by mistake.

Uncle Homer Champion clicked across the floor in western boots. He carried his black alpaca coat hanging from his thumb down over the back of his shoulder. He hung it up on the antlers and then took his hat off too and hung it on top. When he turned around, a necktie with green bluejays on it was blazing down his front.

**78**

"Jack Renfro! What do you mean by showing up the Sunday before election day?"

"You've still got till Tuesday, Uncle Homer," Jack said, shaking hands. "I just had till today." His voice still croaked. "Please bring me a swallow," he told Gloria, and with his starched arm reached for the gourd she carried to him, drank, and handed it back.

"Sit down!" Uncle Homer said.

The whole company, as far as could, sat. Only the school chair was left vacant; Jack sat down in that. Gloria perched just above him on the writing-arm, where she could look down on his face.

"In all this great and sovereign State of Mississippi, how far out of your way did you have to travel today to find you trouble?" Uncle Homer began.

"I thought I was coming in a pretty straight line, sir," said Jack. When he listened to Uncle Homer it was the same as when he listened to all his family—he leaned forward with his clear eyes fixed on the speaker as though what was now being said would never be said again or repeated by anybody else.

"But you found you a car in the ditch, didn't you—while you was still a good mile from Banner?"

"Put shoulder to wheel and upped him out," said Jack. "Is that Buick back in again?"

Auntie Fay drew breath and shrieked, "Willy Trimble, trust him, saw you do it! And declared it to Homer!"

"Just tell, Jack. Who was it at the throttle of that Buick?" asked Uncle Homer. "They might all like to hear it."

"A stranger for sure. He'd never tumbled in a Boone County ditch before, to judge by the slang it drove him into using," said Jack. "An old fellow, that couldn't climb out very fast."

"Homer, won't you set and butter you a biscuit?" cried Miss Beulah. She faced him with a plate full.

"Beulah, you'd stop the very preacher about to deliver your own funeral oration to see if you couldn't make him feel more at home," said Uncle Homer. He took a biscuit but remained on his feet. "Jack, I'd be more careful before I called that man old. You could call that man more in the prime of life, about like you'd call me. Jack! Did you just get out of the pen today so's to shoulder the very man that *sent* you there up out of the ditch?" he cried, and slapped butter on his biscuit.

Jack leaped up. He nearly fell backwards, recoiling, over a

basket of dishes and a pillowcase stuffed with knives and spoons. Children ran up and grabbed him.

"It was the Judge?" yelled Etoyle. "O glory."

"Jack Jordan Renfro," came a chorus of aunts, as he slowly sat down again under Gloria's eyes.

"Judge Oscar Moody in the flesh," said Uncle Homer, and bit in. "That's exactly who you stopped and acted the Good Samaritan to before you'd so much as got home."

"Now you better think up a good one," said Aunt Cleo.

"All my children is too quick," Miss Beulah said. "Just too quick."

"Gloria, I think he needs another surprise fast," said Aunt Beck. But Gloria stayed where she was, peering into Jack's face.

"Speak, Jack!" cried Uncle Homer.

"All I need to tell is a Buick pleasure car only about five years old was spinning nice and pretty towards Banner crossroads, and Mr. Willy Trimble entered the story," said Jack.

"So Mr. Willy turned right across its path," said Uncle Curtis.

"Who *is* Willy Trimble?" asked Aunt Cleo.

"He's such an old bachelor that the way he cleans out his fireplace is to carry the ashes through the house, shovel-load at a time, and dump 'em out through the front door," said Miss Lexie Renfro. "That answer your question?"

"His ditch is pretty well all cinders," said Jack. "And that's the one that Buick went in."

"And when the fella saw where he was put—" Uncle Percy prompted.

"The same as any mortal that fell in the ditch, he hollers get-me-out, and the same as any Good Samaritan alive, Jack done it," cried Miss Beulah. "He can't help it. We make no secret of it."

"How did a man of Judge Moody's reputation find help so quick? To be right particular, how did he find Jack?" asked Uncle Curtis.

"You was riding on his tire," Vaughn said.

"I don't know how a little schoolboy like you would know that," cried Jack. "We was, though. Me and Aycock had caught on behind that Buick between Peerless and Harmony. It was heading right for Banner."

"But son, was that becoming?" cried Miss Beulah.

Jack told her, "Mama, we'd already covered ground with

three preachers, and we'd sat up front and heard 'em out for miles, and been invited to three sermons and three Sunday dinners and one river baptizing, and then I reasoned we'd get home faster if we caught on with somebody with more of their mind on the road. And when we did, that's the very fellow that before you could turn around twice was in the ditch."

"But then what?" cried Aunt Birdie.

"He was glad to have help offered!" Jack cried.

"If Willy Trimble's ditch is the ditch I'm thinking about, that Judge might've been glad to have help offered from Lucifer himself," said Aunt Nanny.

"It didn't take me but a minute to up him," said Jack.

"And wasn't you sorry then?" Aunt Birdie reproached him.

"I didn't know who it was!" cried Jack.

"Willy Trimble must have spread it like only he knows how. Everybody knew it at the ice house. Laughed!" Uncle Homer said.

"And Homer didn't dream, till he heard about that, that Jack would even get turned loose today!" Auntie Fay told them.

"Jack, you ought to be examined," said Uncle Homer. Elvie, making a sorrowful face, brought him a glass of buttermilk with a piece of his own ice in it.

"Why didn't that miserable Aycock warn you what you was doing? What was you carrying *him* along for?" Aunt Nanny cried.

"I believe when we hit the bottom of the ditch is right exactly when Aycock said 'Good evening,' Aunt Nanny, and struck off home to his mama," said Jack. "He was just about as close home as he could get."

"If we'd just been there, coming in the road behind you!" cried Uncle Dolphus.

"We'd hollered quick. *'Watch out who you're saving, Jack!'* " cried Aunt Birdie.

"Beulah, that boy's led a sheltered life," said Uncle Homer in a heavy voice. "And it don't seem to me now that he's remedied that a *great* deal where he's been."

"Some day it'll happen," Aunt Nanny cried. "He'll have a jolt and an awakening."

"Why can't Jack ever look and see where he's headed?" Uncle Homer pointed a buttery finger at Jack. "Couldn't you even spare a glance through the window into that car to see who might be driving?"

"We was riding back there with most of the dust for company, Uncle Homer," said Jack. "I did see as far as a cake I'm pretty sure was a chocolate, riding under a napkin in the back seat. I don't know where it went when we hit. Mr. Willy's team broke aloose and split up and they went on to Banner. The white one climbed to Better Friendship Church and the black one got all the way down under the bridge. I shouldered the Buick up onto the road. And on it went without me. Caught and brought both mules back and got Mr. Willy hitched up again. Then I come running on home and never thought about a one of 'em again."

"Judge Moody might even have made you his passenger and rode you home for your trouble, put you out right here at your door, and let you thank him in front of the whole reunion, and you *still* wouldn't have caught on!" Uncle Homer said. "That's what I believe of you."

"Yes, you'd have just thanked him for the ride," said Aunt Beck sadly. "You're the densest thing sometimes. Oh, I take that back!"

"Just let Moody dare to come up in my yard!" shrieked Miss Beulah. "Just let him show his Moody face at this reunion. He'll hear *me* tell him who he is!"

"Mama, I saw his face when he climbed out of his car, to get a look at the damage. I don't believe there was a *whiff* of the courthouse clinging to him," said Jack.

"Well, who did he look like?"

"He looked more like a bank robber than any judge. He had a white handkerchief tied across his nose and hanging down over his chin," said Jack.

"I guess he don't care for your dust," said Aunt Cleo.

"It was Judge Oscar Moody in the flesh, and you saved him," Uncle Homer said. "Wait till the rest of the voters hears about it."

"And they will," said Auntie Fay. "I've learned that much just putting up with Homer."

"Jack, you did Judge Moody a favor in return for him sending you to the pen. That's what it adds up to," Uncle Homer said.

"And it wasn't even hard!" Jack said. "Ditch was powder dry! Looks to me like Banner ain't had rain in a hundred years!"

"Now all it lacks is for *Curly* to tell me about it. How much notice do you think that gives me, Jack, to think up an answer and get it back to the population?" asked Uncle Homer.

"Sir Pizen Ivy is what me and Aycock called that Judge every day alive at Parchman!" said Jack in a hoarse voice.

"Then didn't know him when you met him in the road," said Aunt Cleo. "Sounds to me like a joke on *you*."

"Leave him alone!" every one of them hollered at her, all except Uncle Homer and Gloria.

"I think it's a joke on the whole reunion," said Aunt Cleo.

"Who's that?" asked Uncle Homer. He told Aunt Cleo, "Lady, you don't vote around here."

"She's a Stovall's widow. That's a shock, ain't it?" Aunt Nanny said to Uncle Homer.

"No, Nanny Broadwee. Even a Stovall in with this reunion today don't surprise me a whit." Uncle Homer told Aunt Cleo, "And you're about what I'd expect at this stage of the game."

Jack crouched forward in the chair, hands on his knees. Miss Lexie studied him. "Brother," she said to Mr. Renfro, who stood with his chin in his hand, contemplating Jack too, "these children of yours are the least prepared to be *corrected* of any I ever ran up against. How they'll conduct themselves on the Day of Judgment I find it hard to imagine."

"All I can say is, Jack, I'm glad you ain't old enough to vote," said Uncle Homer. "Or I believe you'd vote against me."

"Homer! That's a terrible thing to say!" cried Auntie Fay. "Vote against his own family?"

"And *for Curly?*" Uncle Dolphus cried.

"Homer Champion, my boy would do anything for his family, anything in the world!" cried Miss Beulah. "*Look* at him! He'd vote for you if that's what's asked of him, and not even stop there!"

"If it hadn't been for this family," Uncle Homer said, glaring around at the reunion, "I'd been no telling how high up now. Maybe even sheriff."

"Perish the day!" cried Miss Beulah. "Mr. Renfro, if you don't find something to say to this boy, you're going to have him feeling ashamed of himself in a mighty few minutes! Look at him biting his lip!"

"Judge Moody didn't make a single mistake to give himself away?" asked Aunt Beck, as if it might even then not be too late.

"He just showed himself for a stranger," said Jack. "Offered to pay me for my help. I told him I *lived* around here and it would vex me pretty hard to have to take his money."

"Oh, my boy sounds pitiful," said Miss Beulah. "Pitiful!" She stamped her foot.

"Mama!" cried Jack. "Listen: if that was the Judge and he's so smart, how come *he* didn't know *me?*"

"That's my boy!" shouted Uncle Noah Webster, and his brothers said, "He's right!"

"What good did it do him to make a living example out of me if he wasn't going to know me the next time he saw me?" Jack cried.

"And what business did he have in our part of the world anyway?" cried Miss Beulah. "Homer Champion, tell me that! What you need is a little more buttermilk to wash those crumbs down with!"

"He's politicking. That's what everybody's doing today and that's what Moody's doing. Politicking!" cried Auntie Fay. "He's got to run for office the same as other people! The sands is running out for him as fast as they is for Homer!"

"Judges ain't elected, Sister Fay, it wouldn't be safe," said Uncle Curtis.

"Where do we get so many, then?"

"For aught I know or ever give thought to it, they's self-appointed," he said.

"And that's exactly what they act like!" cried Miss Beulah. "One in particular!"

"If his memory's gotten that poor since I been gone, then I ain't much past letting him know *yet,*" said Jack.

"You mean you'd go hunt him?" Uncle Percy whispered. "Now?"

"I'd know that Buick if I saw it a mile away," said Jack.

"Then what?" Uncle Noah Webster hollered.

"I'd tell him who that Samaritan was, and no two ways about it!"

"You got to do more than announce yourself in this world, Jack," said Uncle Curtis. "We proved that in court. You're going to just about need to run headlong into the man and butt him with it like a billy goat, to make him pay you heed. But we'll be right behind you to a man. Won't we, sons?" he asked.

"Yes sir!" they cried, a chorus of uncles and boy cousins.

"If you've already rescued somebody, he's rescued," said Miss Lexie Renfro. "So give up right now."

"Now Lexie, what we all want is a second chance!" Uncle Noah Webster cried. "That's all we're asking for, ain't it, boys?"

"You saved the wrong man, but you can always go back and make him feel bad about it. That's still your privilege, I should hope," said Aunt Birdie to Jack.

"Jack, I just wish you could steal back and ruin his day," said Aunt Nanny. "That would sure help my feelings more than a little."

"Jack, honey, you don't know and never will dream what we've been through, just knowing where they had you," said Aunt Beck, the gentlest of the aunts always. "Grieving for you! Then at last to see you come—and you've saved your Judge's life before you even reached your door."

"Where you reckon he's got to by now?" Aunt Cleo asked. "Timbuktu?"

Jack shot to his feet.

"Hold yourself in one piece, son," said Uncle Noah Webster fondly. "And remember one blessed thing: he's a man that ain't at home around here. He won't know one road from another when he gets to a forks, and it's ten to one he's already lost. Lost upon the face of the wilderness! That make you feel any rosier?"

"Noah Webster, you act like you know where the man's headed," said Mr. Renfro, rocking on his feet.

"And what's him heading anywheres got to do with it?" cried Aunt Birdie loyally. "He's on our roads!"

"At least we've got bad roads!" Aunt Beck cried.

"He'll double on his tracks. These roads alone will see to that," Uncle Curtis predicted.

"And then I know what," Etoyle said, turning herself in circles to make herself dizzy. Aunt Birdie beat her to saying it: "You-all could wait for him at a real good place and when he comes past, hop on him!"

Jack made a sudden plunge for the water bucket.

"Judge Moody could end up pop in the Bywy River!" said Auntie Fay. "That's what I've been trying to get at ever since I walked in this house!"

"Well, it ain't going to be allowed!" cried Miss Beulah.

"Or just start him out across our bridge, that may be all it needs!" Aunt Nanny cried.

"The good old Banner bridge!" said Aunt Birdie. "That'd make an everlasting good drop. If it's ever going to fall in now's the day."

"No decent floor to it hardly at all," Miss Beulah said to Mr. Renfro fiercely. "Speak, Mr. Renfro, tell him what he's waiting to hear you say!"

"The old Bywy ain't deep enough in August to go over his head, Beulah. It's just deep enough to give 'im a splash," said Uncle Noah Webster with his face already beaming. "I feel like I'm getting younger by the minute!"

"When do you suppose the supervisor we all voted for is going to fix our bridge?" Aunt Beck asked, pulling him back by the arm.

"Not today!" Uncle Noah Webster cried gaily, jumping to his feet.

"I've got that supervisor in my pocket, if you all get me elected. But take care of that bridge while you got it, boys," Uncle Homer cried, pounding his fist on a barrel top. "Why does everybody think because it's falling to pieces it's a good place to have a big time on? You're misinterpreting my remarks."

"Jack ain't going to see a flea hurt, you know that!" Miss Beulah said frantically to her brothers.

Jack looked over the rim of the dipper and said, "I'm feeling harder and harder at Judge Moody. I don't think nothing much could stop me from announcing myself to him and telling him who it is that's back."

"That's right, Jack. He made a monkey out of you. Now you can make a monkey out of him," said Aunt Birdie. "That's all the reunion is asking of you."

"I tell you not so fast!" Uncle Homer shouted, with biscuit crumbs flying from his tie.

"Homer is so fickle," Miss Beulah cried. "Sometimes I wonder if he knows whose side he's on himself. He started this!"

"Jack, you *nearly* messed me up last time—getting yourself sent to the pen," said Uncle Homer. "Now you're trying to mess me up again by coming home and reminding the voters we got one like you in the family."

"Oh, go to grass!" said Miss Beulah, and ran to the kitchen.

"Homer," said Mr. Renfro, coming forward, and leveling his forefinger at Uncle Homer, "if you're speaking now of votes, my boy leaving home for the pen is just about what give you your margin in the first place. I can recall the day when you come in ninth for coroner. You wouldn't have an office to be holding *onto* if it wasn't for Jack."

"Liked on all sides as that sweet starving boy is!" cried Miss Beulah, running back in with a platter set around with hot biscuits opened and filled with melted butter in one half and pools of blackberry jelly in the other. "Yes, Homer arrested Jack, his own nephew-in-law, then electioneered for a fresh term as justice of the peace on how bad he hated to do it. Asked the voters to show they found it in their hearts to feel sorry for him. And voters is such fools! And I was one right along with 'em."

"Come on, boys!" cried Uncle Noah Webster.

"Has he even had a decent breakfast?" Miss Beulah reproached them all, while Jack was shaking his head and opening his mouth at the same time.

But before she could pop a biscuit in, the boy cousins cried:

"Hey! Jack! Are we supposed to spend the whole day waiting on you to catch up at the table?"

The men were all on their feet. At the same time the porch seemed full of liver- and lemon-spotted dogs. The barking had started over.

"Nathan ain't going to go exactly into raptures over this!" Miss Beulah cried despairingly at them. "Remember I've still got one more brother to come!"

"Beulah, by the time Nathan makes it in, things is going to be all over," Uncle Noah Webster said, "and skies clear."

"Now, then," said Uncle Curtis, "how are we all going? I ain't inclined to walk it."

At this moment Gloria rose, turned on her little white heel, and went inside the house.

"Well, you can't all load on one mule, can you?" Mr. Renfro said.

"Well, want to trust that rattletrap of ours?" asked Uncle Curtis.

"I got a slow leak in my gas tank," said Uncle Percy. "It may not last me and Nanny back to Peerless like it is, but we can always *start* in our jitney."

"There's a good old-timey Ford in my little family now that'll go anywhere and do anything. It's true the radiator's boiled over twice since it started climbing hills on the way up," said Uncle Noah Webster. "I ain't yet tried it going down."

"Well, everybody can see the nigh front tire on my son's contraption is down again flat," said Uncle Dolphus. "What do you think of all going in it?"

"You'll have to go back to driving the school bus!" cried Elvie. Under the tree it stood headed downhill and first in line, with a chunk under the wheel. It was wrapped in dust as in a pink baby blanket.

Vaughn said, "You can't. You ain't the driver, Jack, not any longer."

"I'm telling you all one thing! If I had my good truck finished now, there wouldn't be any question! I wouldn't *hear* no other offer!" Jack cried. "That is, if you-all wouldn't mind riding like we do at Parchman, standing up! It'd block any man's road—"

Jack had turned himself around to look. Ready on the moment, Ella Fay raised her lovely goose-white arms and flung wide the last tablecloth and spread it over the vacancy there.

"Jack," Miss Beulah said, "ready for some more bad news?"

"I think I'm about to guess it already, Mama," he told her.

"What's this?" Uncle Homer demanded to know. "I don't *see* that truck."

"Won't you sit back down, Homer?" Miss Beulah cried. "You need a little more biscuit to come out even on your buttermilk." She laid her hands on Jack's arms. "There's a little story about Stovall and that truck, Jack," she said. "We had to mortgage it."

Jack looked without words from one face to another.

"Curly hauled it right back to where you got it," Etoyle told Jack. "Drug it with oxen."

"He's looking almost pale," Aunt Birdie said, and Aunt Beck tremulously called for him, "Gloria!"

"I'm right in here, tending to some of my business," she called out the window of the company room. "While I can hear every word being said."

"Hauled the whole thing away?" cried Jack. "The *whole thing?*"

"Nothing left but that miserable spot of grease," said Miss Beulah.

"The skunk!" Jack cried.

"*Now* choose between us!" said Uncle Homer Champion to the world.

"Well, he'll never get that engine to hitting without me, that's one thing left to live for!" Jack shouted.

"Saturday's still coming!" Uncle Dolphus cried, to some cheers.

"All right, Vaughn, pull Dan out of the pasture and shoot the bridle on him. I'll ride ahead and the rest can follow. I'll give Dan a treat he's been going without for a long time," said Jack.

"Tell me something more easy," said Vaughn.

"Has he missed me too bad to thrive?"

"We had to part with Dan too, Jack," said Miss Beulah.

"Whoa, Elvie!" he cried, as she burst into tears for him. He broke from them, hurled himself over the steps and started racing toward the pasture, the barn, turning everywhere at once.

"Would you completely spoil his welcome?" Miss Beulah shrieked at Elvie and all the little girls. "You crybabies'll do it yet!"

"My! Who's Dan?" asked Aunt Cleo.

"It's Jack's stud, Jack's stud," they told her.

"That Dan was a horse in a million," said Uncle Noah Webster.

"That horse was as good and spoiled as anybody in this family," said Miss Lexie Renfro.

"Fib to him a little bit!" pleaded Aunt Birdie.

The cousins were chasing Jack and one of them called, "Come on back, Jack, Curly didn't get your stud." Jack stopped in his tracks.

"We had to shoot him," Aunt Beck compassionately called. "He's still taking it hard," she turned and said. "Look where he's biting down on that lip."

"And you know, it seemed like he wasn't hardly worth the powder it took," Curtis Junior kept talking persuasively as the cousins crept up on him.

"Lead me to his grave."

They grabbed him.

"Jack! Watch out! *Please* don't get your family to feeling so sorry for you before you go!" Aunt Beck begged him from the porch.

"You can't find his grave! He was drug off to the renderers," said Etoyle, hands joined at her breastbone. "Clear to Foxtown! I watched him go."

"Gloria!" he hollered.

"Be patient," her sweet voice called back. "I'll be with you when everything's all ready."

"I always said my horse was going to be buried under trees," Jack gasped out.

"We had to have coal and matches and starch," Miss Beulah listed for him. "And flour and sugar and vinegar and salt and sweet-soap. And seed and feed. And we had to keep us alive. Son, we parted first with a nanny goat, then a fat little trotter. Then the cow calved—"

"Mama, I ain't going to make you tell me any more of the tale," said Jack. "Not in front of all of 'em."

"And how is old muley?" asked Aunt Nanny.

"Bet's been doing it all, if you'd like to see her stagger," Miss Beulah replied.

"I was reading the signal from that roof pretty well," said Jack at last. "Judge Moody's got a lot on his head. I got a lot more to tell him now besides my name. Bring me my shoes."

Then Gloria came out onto the porch with his shoes in her hand. At the same minute she released Lady May from her skirts into their midst.

Jack came hurling himself up the steps. When he saw the baby aiming straight as a cannonball for him, he opened his mouth and gave a great shout. Then she veered and ran back to her mother. Jack threw himself over and stood on his head. As Lady May gazed at him, her eyes open all the way like vinca flowers at midday, he slowly pedalled his feet in the air.

"Jack!" They all began talking at once, moving their circle closer around the three of them.

"Jack! You're home after nearly two long years away—and here's your baby."

"Here's your surprise!"

"Here's your reward."

"Hold it, Jack!" Uncle Noah Webster cried when he wobbled.

"Don't he appear a little small, though, for all he's done and still got to do?" asked Aunt Cleo, her head on the horizontal.

"He's sparing—I never knew there to be a sin in that," said Miss Beulah. "All Renfros is sparing, and they just about never wear out. Now us Beechams, when we go, we go more in a flash, call it a blaze of glory."

The new shirt turned over on its tails all in one piece, like a board on its hinges, uncovering the full stretch of Jack's roasted back and the pair of pants he'd come home in—so worn and faded that they had no more color than skimmed milk. The frayed holes gaped like fish-mouths up both legs.

Lady May drew closer to him, dressed in her first colored dress, her leaf hat, and sliding-new baby shoes buttoned tight with a frill of blue sock falling over the tops. She looked at the holes in Jack's pants, all the way up, like a little buttoner, till her gaze was elevated to his feet. She moved closer, under those feet that were walking upside down on the air, dusty and with leaves sticking to the raw and bleeding toes.

"Look. He already worships her," said Aunt Beck.

Then he tumbled over, as if toppled by the baby.

"Now look at the smile he's brought to that little face! Jack's a real artist!"

Now he squatted before her, face to face. "Come here, baby, come here, baby," his lilting voice said. "Bring me what you've got."

The baby passed and re-passed him.

"He's winning her."

She kept returning him looks of her own, steady and solemn, like a woman trying on a hat. When she stood still, he laid his arms out on the air, and she walked in. He gave her a hug that looked strong enough to break her bones.

"Look at her go right to him. Look at her give him her own play-pretty!" It was her mother's comb.

"Where's mine?" one of the cousins teased the baby, but Aunt Beck said, "Hush, there's been enough of that."

Jack flicked the comb through his own sopping hair and sawed it down through the starch of his shirt pocket and put it out of sight. Lady May's mouth opened round as a plum.

"That fourteen-month-old thinks Jack is *her* surprise," said Aunt Birdie.

"Hi, Lady May," said Jack. "Lady May Renfro, how do you do?" He gave her a kiss, which she returned.

"Listen. Listen at that—he called that baby by her name," Aunt Nanny said.

"Gloria told!" cried Aunt Birdie.

"Gloria told him what she had."

"That baby's no more surprise than I am!" cried Aunt Nanny.

"*I'm* not afraid of pencil and paper," said Gloria.

"I caught her going to the road and giving letters to Uncle

Sam!" cried Etoyle. "Plus the fresh egg for the stamp!"

"Lady May all along was supposed to be his surprise. *Now* what is she?" cried Aunt Birdie.

"She was my surprise to tell," Gloria said.

"You've been just the least little bit sneaky, it seems to me," Aunt Nanny said, starting to grin.

"And where do you suppose Gloria ever got her such a dress?" cried Aunt Birdie.

Lady May's first real dress was not made of Robin Hood flour sacks, it was not handed down from Elvie. It was solid blue and had pockets—starched till the pocket flaps stood out like little handles to lift her by.

"I cut it out from mine," Gloria said. "That's the dress I wore the day I came here."

"At least I'm glad you didn't let Curly Stovall cheat you with it at his store," said Aunt Beck sympathetically.

"Look, now it's made that baby cry. She's caught on! She's no surprise at all! She heard you, poor little old thing!" said Aunt Birdie.

Jack picked her up. "Whitest little biddy!" he said softly.

"She's without blemish," said Gloria, reaching for her. "Her skin's like mine, tender tender. Till now, I've kept her pretty well shielded in the house."

He lifted the leaf hat to see what was under it, and the baby's red cockscomb sprang up like a Jack-in-the-box. Then here came his smile. It was as big as a house.

"Welcome home from the pen!" roared Uncle Noah Webster.

Lady May in her mother's arms put out a little crow.

"Laugh, baby! Ladybird, laugh, that's right!" cried Uncle Noah Webster.

"And now let's us get going!" cried some boy cousins.

While his big arched smile, gratitude and gratification in equal parts, still held on his face, Jack dropped to the floor and laced on his shoes that Gloria had scrubbed ready for him.

"Oh, ever'thing happens at once!" Uncle Noah Webster cried and almost kissed Aunt Cleo. "I wouldn't take a pretty for still being alive and able to come today!"

"All right, Homer Champion, see what you accomplished, bringing in that story!" raged Miss Beulah.

**9 2**

"Ain't you coming with us, Homer?" teased Uncle Noah Webster.

"Now listen here, bunch of idiots!" cried Miss Beulah.

"Good-bye, Granny," Jack whispered to her nodding head. "Good-bye, Mama, all my sisters and aunts and girl cousins! Good bye, Gloria—you can play with our baby girl till I get back. Keep dinner waiting!"

"Your mother is going right ahead and spread dinner when the shade gets to those tables in the front yard!" cried Miss Beulah. "And if you're all still alive, you'd better be right back here and ready to eat it! Jack, watch these idiots and don't let 'em do anything more foolish than they can help in honor of you coming home, and you lead 'em right back here, do you heed me?"

There was a general surge of men and boys departing from the house. Bird dogs, coon dogs, and squirrel dogs were jumping and pawing the air and racing for the gate, every one giving his bark.

"Let every one of you come back to your seats," came the uplifted voice of Gloria. "I don't want man or boy to leave this house, or budge an inch till Jack gets back. This is Jack Renfro's own business. And nobody's coming with him but me and the baby."

They all stopped where they were. A long shout travelled all the way down the scale. Gloria lifted her old teacher's satchel from among the plunder on the floor and hung the strap over her shoulder.

Jack's blue eyes had opened nearly to squares. He was the one to move first—he ran and brought her a dipper of water.

"No thank you," she said. "I never have got used to Banner water, and try to do without it."

"Are you really braving it?" asked Aunt Birdie in a faint voice. "Tagging along through the broil behind Jack?"

"Now I know she's addled," said Aunt Cleo.

"Waiting is the hardship," Aunt Beck said gently. "That was her part."

"But it's over! Now it's all over! Don't she know her hardship is ended?" asked Aunt Birdie.

The uncles had fallen back onto chairs as though Gloria had blown them all down with a puff of her breath.

"Just sit tight and hold my dogs, boys," Jack ordered his cousins.

"She ain't even going to let the dogs go?" they cried.

"Just one," said Gloria.

"Sid, I reckon your day has about come," said Jack.

"That dog ain't good for a thing but friendship. And you ought to learned that by now, Jack," said Uncle Dolphus as Sid rose on his hind legs.

"Oh, please wait, son!" shrieked Miss Beulah. "You haven't even had a word from your father yet!"

"Well, the roof wasn't exactly lost on him," said Mr. Renfro.

Granny opened her eyes and said, "Who now? Who's trying to sneak away from Granny?"

Jack ran to her. "I still got a little bit to do to finish getting myself home, Granny," he told her. "But it can't take long, not with the help I got." He hugged her and whispered, "You'll see us all back together again at the table." Then he swung the baby up against his hip.

"Jack's going to make a wonderful little mother himself," predicted Aunt Beck.

"Tell 'em good-bye, Lady May!" said Jack. "Wave at 'em!" Lady May, from under his arm, waved like Elvie, quick-time. He laid the palm of his other hand between Gloria's shoulder blades, pivoted her around, and they skimmed together down the steps.

Ella Fay, in the yard with all her tables spread, watched them go. "Bring me something!" she called after them.

"Even if the reunion was to stop this minute, it would have been worth coming through the dust for," Aunt Birdie said.

"You just can't read her!" Miss Beulah exploded. "It's Gloria I'm talking about. Why, I reckon this minute is all in the world she's been waiting on."

# Part 2

*T*he dust Uncle Homer had made still rolled the length of the home road, like a full red cotton shirtsleeve. Jack led off through the fields. Lady May was riding his shoulder, Gloria with her satchel marched right beside him on the narrow path.

"I hated to go off and leave the rest of 'em if it hurt their feelings," Jack said. "But they've all growed old, that's the shock! If they'd come, we'd had to find a place for 'em all to sit down."

The farm was as parched now as an old clay bell of wasp nest packed up against barn rafters. As the roar of the reunion grew faint behind them and even the barking toned itself down, heat, like the oldest hand, seized Jack and Gloria by the scruff of the neck and kept hold. They marched through the cornfield, all husks, robbed of color by drought as if by moonlight, through the cotton that had struggled no higher than halfway to Jack's knees. Jack dropped on one knee and thumped a melon his father had overlooked.

"Don't crack Lady May one," said Gloria. "I'm not anxious for her to start on common ordinary food."

"What're you trying to tell me, Possum?" he asked, turning his head to look at her.

The mule stood waiting by the pasture gate, as if thunderstruck at some idea that was floating around in the air.

"Want to see if Bet can carry us all three without any nonsense?" Jack cried as if inspired.

**97**

"I never had the wildest dream of going on a mule," said Gloria.

"She's still better than nothing and she knows it herself, bless her old black heart!" He went and hung his free arm around her neck. "She's getting a little scrawny, I'll have to feed her."

Under the shade tree shaped like a rising bird, two cows stood nose to nose in the cow-brown pond, motionless; the water in the middle was deep enough to cool their bags, but just barely. The rest of the pond baked its bottom like a mudpie made by Elvie last summer. They walked through waist-high spires of cypress weed, green as strong poison, where the smell of weed and the heat of sun made equal forces, like foes well matched or sweethearts come together. Jack unbuttoned his new shirt. He wore it like a preacher's frock-tailed coat, flying loose. They passed the cane mill and came to the top of the rise where a crop of spears, old iron spikes man-made and man-high, made a hollow squarish circle like a crown, and an old oak tree standing within it poured black shade over it. Inside lay buried old Captain Jordan under a flat tablet black as a slate, like a table that he had all to himself. A bushel of Granny's red salvia gushed from a churn on top of it. Bees were crawling like babies into the florets. Beyond this was the last fence, and there the bantam flock pecked, like one patch quilt moving with somebody under it.

Jack helped Gloria through the fence after him. Then side by side, with the baby rolled next to Jack's naked chest, they ran and slid down the claybank, which had washed away until it felt like all elbows, knees, and shoulders, cinder-hot. Bare Banner clay was the color of red-hot iron. The bank pitched them into the bed of a rusty sawmill track, overgrown like the bed of an untended grave. A stinging veil of long-dead grass flowed to meet their steps and hid cow-pats dry as gunpowder. Keeping time with each other they stepped fast without missing a tie—domino-black, flat-sunk, spongy as bread, sun-cooked, all of them. Sumac hung over the way ahead, studded with long heads like red-hot pokers. On the curve they mounted their rails and walked balancing, each with an arm arched overhead. Gloria slipped first. Jack reached for her and led her over the trestle, bleached like a ghost-trestle, then he soared into the creek bed, caught the baby from her arms, hopped Gloria down, and beat their way along a strip of path slick as leather. It was like walking through a basket.

"Lady May," Jack said, "you have to remember that when the old Bywy backs up in Panther Creek, it's an ocean where we're stepping."

"And right now it's extra-mosquitery," said Gloria.

Jack tucked the baby inside his shirt.

The high shoulders of the Bywy Hills rose ahead, near but of faint substance against the August sky. They looked no more than the smudges Lady May might have made on the pages of the Renfro Bible, turning through them with her fast little hands.

They climbed up past the old chimney that stood alone.

"But I know this is snakey," said Gloria, pulling back a little as Jack led her over the old hummocks, deep in vines too thick to see the ground through, where Grandpa Vaughn's own early home used to be, like breastworks for some battle once upon a time. Then, on the well path, piney shadows, falling soft about them, slid down their arms and sides into the early-fallen pine needles. The path was a carpet that threw off light like running water. They began to run, Gloria in front—Jack had the baby. A pack of courting squirrels electrified a pine tree in front of them, poured down it, ripped on through bushes, trees, anything, tossing the branches, sobbing and gulping like breasted doves, and veered the other way. Gloria slid on the straw, tripped on a root, and was thrown to her knees. Jack sank to his right there on the spot, and released the crowing baby. The final glare dropped from them like a set of clothes. The big old pine over them had shed years of needles into one deep bed.

Around the circle of needles, slick and hot and sweet as skin under them, and dead quiet, they chased each other on the hobble, fast as children on their knees, around and around the tree. A family of locust shells with wide-open backs went praying up the trunk. Each time she turned to go the other way, Gloria re-gathered an armload of skirt to her breast. With flushed eyes and faces straight ahead, they kept from running into each other or into the baby, who now made efforts to join in. His face rushed like an engine toward hers.

They hugged as they collided, gasping and wet. Their hearts shook them, like two people pounding at the same time on both sides of a very thin door. Then Gloria threw back her head, with all the weight of her curls, and said, "Jack! This isn't what we came out for!" She pulled herself to her feet. Lady May came, still running hard, into her legs, and she gathered up both baby and satchel before Jack climbed upright again.

Even after they started again on the path, the well at the end of it seemed to go on turning. In its canopy of trumpet-vines it only slowed down gradually, like a merry-go-round after a ride.

Jack stepped to the well for them, and after the wait it took to get the splash and haul the bucket up, its long, long shriek came up with it. By the time he came bringing the jelly glass full, Gloria and Lady May were waiting all fresh, seated straight up on a fallen tree, and Gloria was daintily strapping up her satchel.

They passed the jelly glass back and forth, Lady May sitting between them, and then Gloria emptied what was left onto the ground. It was swallowed up at once there, leaving only a little deposit of what looked like red filings.

They stood up together. In another step they were back on the farm track. Jack threw out both arms and went first, to bar Gloria and the baby from coming too fast down the perpendicular, and they were here, in a cloud of dust. Banner Road ran in front of them, standing table-high out of the ditch.

Here the road had all but reached its highest point. It came winding and climbing toward them between claybanks that reared up grooved and red as peach pits standing on end. Little pink and yellow gravelstones, set like the seeds in long cuts of watermelon, banded all the banks alike, running above the road—more gravel than the road had ever received in its life. Growing along the foot of the banks the branchy cosmos stood man-tall, lining the way. Their leaves and stalks looked dust-laden as the old carpentered chairs that take their places by more travelled roadsides in summer, but the morning's own flowers were as yellow as embroidery floss.

"Not a soul's been raising new dust. We beat Judge Moody altogether! And we're travelling with a baby and he ain't," said Jack. With Lady May astride his neck he jumped the ditch, and held out his hand. Gloria jumped to him.

Directly in front of them across the road, Banner Top rose up. In shape it was like a wedge of cake being offered to them. icing side toward them, point facing away. With Jack going in front, carrying both baby and satchel, they proceeded up to the peak of the road and came back onto Banner Top by the gentler slope where the path crawled. There was a barbed-wire fence that ran with the banks on this side of the road, climbing and dipping at sharp angles and pendant with small "Keep Off" signs ruby-red with rust, like the lavalier chains draped across the pages of a mail-order catalogue.

Jack walked a high step over the wire, holding the baby, then helped Gloria under it.

"Getting up on a rise! That's what I was homesick for," said Jack.

Up here, limestone cropped out of the clay and streaked it white. The real top of Banner Top was like part of a giant buried cup lying on its side. Taking Gloria's hand in his free one Jack made straight across it. The way underfoot was ridged with little waves the size of children's palms. There were places clean and white as if a cat's tongue had licked them. The clay that there was was set with shallow trenches, and all around the edge it was scallopy with seats and saddles. The jumping-off place itself was grooved like the lip of a pitcher, sandy, peach-colored, grainy, and warm until long after dark in summer—it faced the summer moonrise. A tall old cedar tree was stubbornly growing out of the end and standing over it. A scattering of plum bushes, delicate and quivering, already hung with orange-colored fall plums of the kind whose sucked skins tasted like pennies, furnished the only screen to keep passers in the road from seeing exactly who was up here and what their business might be.

"Now, Lady May. The first thing you do is look out and see what you got around you," Jack told the baby. "This right here is Banner Top, little girl, and around us is all its brothers and sisters." He had set the baby up to ride his shoulders. As far as eye could see, the world was billowing in its reds and pinks that the heat had pearled over and the dust had coated until it seemed that everything swam as one bubble. The sky itself looked patched here and there with the thin pink plaster of earth.

"Mind you don't step too close," said Gloria, getting behind them. "Lady May doesn't care for steep places."

"You might even call this a mountain," Jack invited Lady May. "If you do, I ain't going to argue with you."

Now the baby obscured Jack's head. Her little draped behind, white as a tureen, rested on his neck, and she looked with all the hair of her own head standing up.

"And winding along the edge of everywhere is the old Bywy.

Right now it's low as sin and you can't see it. If this was bare winter, you could look right through yonder and see Grandpa's church pointing up its finger at you."

Both the baby's hands pulled gently at the tufts of Jack's hair as he turned with her, a little at a time, showing her the world.

"You can't see dear old Banner from here. By the road it's five miles away, at the bottom of the ridge. But it's right—where— I'm pointing," Jack told her. "Like a biddie under a wing. You just follow the road."

He reached for Gloria's arm and steered her, taking them back across the Top to where it hung over Banner Road. It ran deep between its banks that were bright as a melon at that instant split open. It came over its hill, rushed to the bottom, and disappeared around a claybank.

"Right here in the world is where I call it plain beautiful," said Jack. "That way is Banner." He pointed. "And that's the other way. Your guess is as good as your daddy's which end of the road that old booger's on now."

Lady May pointed her finger straight forward.

"Why, that's Grandpa's chimney again," Jack told her.

Back on the other side, it stood drinking up the light, red like the claybanks, the same clay.

"Oh, Grandpa Vaughn! I come listening for his voice all the way up to the house this morning. And believed when he kissed me good-bye he'd live to be a hundred," said Jack.

"Showing how much more you count on everybody than I do," said Gloria. "Get back from this edge."

Jack squeezed Lady May's thin leg a little. "And listen to me: that was the strictest mortal that ever breathed. He's asleep in the ground now, and don't have us to pray over any longer. And I miss him! I miss his frowning presence just as I get myself ready to perform something."

"If you're wishing for somebody who's hard to please and wouldn't too well like what you're planning on now, there's one standing over your shoulder and alive this minute," said Gloria. "Now, haven't we had enough of Lover's Leap?" she cried.

"That's what they call Banner Top if they weren't born here," Jack told Lady May, smiling. "Gloria, there's just one word I want to tell you about where they had me for a year and a half: it was flat."

The baby complained, and Jack whispered to her, "Getting homesick? Then I can show you right back where we started. That new tin giving us the signal from away across yonder"—he pointed far—"is the roof of our house." He pointed to the farm track, red as a strand of mitten-yarn, where it showed along the curving ridge, draping it, to fall in easy stages till the last minute, when it cut through the claybank and dropped twelve feet into Banner Road, with the ditch across its foot. "And that's our road. It comes out right under our feet. Who's that holding up the mailbox?" And he told her, "Uncle Sam."

The wooden figure stood at the foot of the farm track like a paper doll made out of a plank, weatherbeaten but recognizable by its pink-tinted stripes and the shape of its overlarge hat. It held out the mailbox on a single plank arm.

"I brought you here by the short-cut," said Jack.

"Now explain to your baby what we're all here for," Gloria challenged him.

"Family duty," Jack told Lady May. "And it won't take longer than a snap of your own little finger to get Judge Moody tucked away in a ditch like he was in, long enough to learn his lesson. To save precious time, I'm going to see to it that the ditch he goes in now is one he can get *himself* out of, for a change."

"And what easy ditch do you know of?" asked Gloria.

"Ours. You just jumped it."

He trotted with the baby along the edge to where the bank stood steepest over the road. In the thin fold of the clay wall at the top, a round peephole had in some past time been leisurely carved. It gave a view of the road around the turn, toward Banner.

"Now look through that and tell me if you see anybody coming." Jack let Lady May peep, she smiled, and then he peeped and cried, "You do! You see Brother Bethune! He's coming up the road on foot and the least bit weaving!"

"That's who has to take Grandpa Vaughn's place," said Gloria. "He's in Damascus pulpit on Second Sundays. And today he's taking Grandpa's place at the reunion."

"Giving us the family history?" cried Jack. "He's licked to start with!"

"He's heard our voices. Now look who you're bringing right up here," said Gloria.

The old man came right on up Banner Top, climbing the

**103**

path like a rickety ladder of his dreams. It was when he got to the top that he stumbled and fell. He kept hold of his gun, but everything else on him pitched to the ground. Jack and Gloria raised him to his feet and straightened him up between them.

"Don't tell me where I am," the old man warned them, as Gloria beat his hat for him and put it on his head and Jack beat the dust out of his black serge pants, dropped the tuning fork back into his shirt pocket, and scooped up his Bible, and the baby stood and watched and put her finger into her mouth. "Or where you think I'm headed. I want to tell *you*. It'll all come back to me in good time."

Brother Bethune's Bible, bound in thin black leather skinned to the red of a school eraser, looked as if it had come to his door every Sunday by being thrown at it, rolled up like the Ludlow Sunday newspaper. Its pages, with rain-stained pink edges, looked as loose and fragilely layered as the feathers of a shot bird as Jack picked it out of a plum bush and blew on it to fly the dust.

"That looks like mine," said Brother Bethune, reaching for his Bible and rolling it up to go back in his pocket. "Just stand still. I want you folks to keep me company right here till I can tell you who you are."

"Jack, I wonder if this means everybody in Banner has forgotten you?" whispered Gloria.

"I hope not. And I'd be pretty quick to remind 'em!" he exclaimed. Then he cautioned her in a low voice, "But don't tell him. You got to let him do it his own way, he's old and a preacher."

"He may be with us all day."

"Suppose Judge Moody come spinning in sight before Brother Bethune knows it's me?" Jack whispered. "And I'd just have to hold my mouth shut?"

"You should have thought of that before you started."

"Vaughn!" Jack shouted, and made the sound of the name like a tree falling.

"Now you can't catch me. Vaughns is all gone, I know that much—played out and gone to mouldering," said Brother Bethune, his face beginning to light up.

Jack shouted, "If you want to start learning to be a Good Samaritan, we need a buggy ride from the mailbox!" Then he bent to Brother Bethune. "I'm just going to whisper you one thing, sir: your gun is loaded."

Brother Bethune looked back at him in a fixed way. The skin on his bony, motionless face looked like the skin on chicken gravy when it has been allowed to cool, even to the little flecks and spots of brown trapped in it. "I know good and well I'm supposed to be carrying comfort and solace to somebody," he said.

"Not today!" Jack warned him. "You can take my word for it, you're headed where you can just lend your presence in the absence of somebody mightier, eat your share, and offer a few kind words in return for hospitality."

"No death in the family, sudden or otherwise?" Brother Bethune argued. He looked from Jack to Gloria to the baby. "Now who in the world is that!" He tried to poke his finger into the baby's mouth, his own mouth stretching in delight.

The trotting of hooves and the creaking of an axle sounded, as if approaching from down under, and stopped in the road just below them. They ran to peer down over. The dust climbed to their level in clouds like boxcars. As the red faded, then turned transparent, the first thing they could see was mule ears scissoring. Then they saw a bonnety hat, stationary, at the low point of the settling dust.

"Met your mule! She's headed for the cemetery. Want to ride home with me?" called the driver.

"You don't want to go with him, sir," said Jack to Brother Bethune. "I'll just tell you one thing more—it's Mr. Willy Trimble."

"The biggest old joker in Christendom!" said Brother Bethune, looking pleased as at a favorite game. "No sir, can't catch me! No, I ain't ready yet to ride in your old wagon, not till I'm ready for King dom Come! Ha! Ha! Ha!" Brother Bethune shouted laughter into the dust rising again as the team started on its way. Then he asked a bit quaveringly, "Am I all that far from some cold water?"

Jack went, and the well-pulley gave its squeal. He came back bringing the jelly glass full, all its faces stained tea-color from the beady Banner water.

"It's warm as pee," pondered Brother Bethune, then gave a cry. "The water give it away! It's Banner! Today is First Sunday! And I'm good old Brother Bethune!"

"So far, he's remembering everything in one grand rush," said Jack.

Brother Bethune pivoted on his gun and fixed him with his loving, gimlet eye. "It's the Prodigal Son."

"Yes sir, looks like I'm just about to make it," said Jack. He blushed. On his skin shone the crystal tracks, like snail tracks at sunup, of Lady May's confidences and kisses up to now.

"Hi, Ladybug," the old man said gaily, coming to try Lady May again. "There now. Churning my finger to pieces with your little tongue? Can't talk yet? When they going to carry you to church?" He gazed at Gloria; he didn't look as sure about her. "Mother still living?" he asked in the tones of a compliment.

"I'm an orphan, sir," she said.

He made a shaming sound back at her.

"And Banner is not my home."

Brother Bethune struck a sudden attitude and fixed his eye on the jumping-off place. A small head protruded over it with the motion of a hen's. Like a long black stocking being rolled out through the wringer, all of it came up over the edge and moved on into the open over the flag-red ground and the milk-white limestone in the direction of Banner Road. Brother Bethune showed an incredulous face, on which the old nose, dark as a fig in its withering days, dangled over a mouth as wide-open as a man's who was hearing this told in a story. An instant later he'd brought his heels together and fired his gun. Glistening, the snake appeared for a moment at the heart of the dust that played like a whirly-wind at their feet, and kept playing.

Rocketing hooves seemed to cover all the countryside at the same time, and the figure of Vaughn appeared as if flying upright above the top of the bank opposite. He was standing up in the wagon and driving Bet as if all their lives depended on it. He whipped the mule down the farm track and jumped her and the rocking wagon over the ditch and only brought them to a halt halfway down the hill on Banner Road.

Brother Bethune, his finger and thumb both rainbow-colored with tobacco stain, pared away at the well-toothed brim of his hat. He reloaded. "Now bring on the next one," he told Lady May. "You know they ranges in pairs."

Lady May had not shut her wide-open mouth. She sat on Gloria's arm staring at him.

Here came Vaughn running straight to the snake. "I'll carry that man back with me to show to Granny!" he shouted, plunging his arm in and holding up the running, perhaps headless, coils.

106

"It's an old story to Granny," said Jack. "No call for you to go carrying 'em home anything but Brother Bethune by himself."

"Didn't first catch on he's a rattler, sir!" Vaughn shouted.

Brother Bethune laid on his shoulder a hand that appeared weighty enough to sink him. "All poisonous snakes you can tell 'em because they crawls waverly, son. If a snake ain't coming with the idea to kill you, he crawls straight."

"In my judgment, you all ought to see the rattlesnakes at Parchman before you jump to a verdict," said Jack. "Throw that thing clear away from here, Vaughn. Anywhere but our ditch."

Vaughn squatted down, picked up the snake afresh with both hands under it, as if it were a fainting woman, and bore it slowly to the jumping-off place and threw it over the drop.

"Banner Top looks very natural," observed Brother Bethune. He pivoted. "And round, Baptist faces even more so. Many another one waiting on my words at your reunion."

"What lost you your bearings, sir?" asked Jack kindly.

"I'd like to tell you," said Brother Bethune. "A great big pleasure car in a cloud of dust and pine cones like to hit me right in the middle of the road, and that's what spooked my mule. Stranger asked me what road could he take to get him to Alliance and not have to cross the river on Banner bridge. He talked a little uncomplimentary about it."

"Brother Bethune, I'd love to know what answer you had for him," Jack said.

"Told him to turn around the first chance he got and go back to Halfway Forks and try it all over. 'Don't waver,' I told him, 'just keep to the straight and narrow, every opportunity comes along,' I told him, 'and you'll get to Grinders Mill in a little while, and see a bridge. Or there used to be one when I was taken there as a boy.' He didn't look too well pleased. But listen, Tiny—he spooked my mule," said Brother Bethune into Lady May's still horrified gaze. "Oh, what a day for upsets, Baby Child! I'll tell you where I hope my mule's gone—home."

"Thank you, Brother Bethune," said Jack.

"You're welcome, Prodigal Son."

"Now Vaughn," said Jack, "if you're cleaned off good, carry Brother Bethune on up to the reunion. Why didn't you bring Grandpa's buggy?"

"That mule can't learn Grandpa's buggy," said Vaughn. "She hitches to the wagon."

"See that Brother Bethune don't spill another time," said Jack. "And tell Mama to keep holding dinner—Brother Bethune's sent Judge Moody to Grinders Mill for me."

"*Is* that who that was!" said Brother Bethune over his gun shoulder as Vaughn took him by the trigger finger and led him down the bank to the wagon. "I declare it to be a small world." He set his foot in its high-topped shoe into Vaughn's hands and took the boost onto the wagon seat. He drew into his lungs a sweet, suspiring smell.

"I reckon you know you been breaking the Sabbath, son," said the old man, with one long-legged maneuver transferring himself to the nest of new hay in the bed behind. As the wagon rattled up the home road, he raised his gun high, and Lady May broke her silence and let out a shriek at it.

"Brother Bethune's going to drive all the snakes out of this end of Boone County if he don't slow down," said Jack. "Poor old chicken snake—I reckon he lived around here pretty close and was just paying his ordinary call for a sip of water."

"Why can Judge Moody be trying to seek out Alliance?" wondered Gloria.

"Well, he'll never start across at Grinders," said Jack. "Not if he knows anything about a bridge at all. And if he's gone all the way to Grinders on that road, he'll reason it out: any road that looks like it's working that hard against nature, it must have *somewhere* better to go than Grinders. He'll take the fork that brings him on around and back into Banner Road by keeping up with Panther Creek every switch of the way, if he's smart. I'm as sure as I am of anything in this world, Gloria, he'll roll right past here about forty miles further on from now."

Holding her hand, he had been leading her back toward the jumping-off place. Now he drew his finger down through the bow of her sash, and the whole dress stood away from her like a put-up tent. The sash itself slid down to her shoes. His arm went around her waist, and with her holding the baby they all sat down together.

Here in the best patch of shade, an apron of old cedar roots, long exposed to the elements and rubbed smooth as horn, was spread out under them.

Lady May had lost her hat, but she still had her little shoes on. "Carry Jack a secret," said Gloria. She whispered into the baby's ear and sent her tiptoeing. Lady May wrapped Jack's head in her arms and made humming sounds into his ear.

"I got it! Take Mama this'n from me!" he cried.

But when Lady May came to blow in her ear, Gloria reached for her, took her on her lap, and opened her own bodice.

Jack jumped to his feet, then suddenly crashed to the ground again as though the baby had tripped him.

"Possum, that's the last thing in the world I was picturing you doing," he broke out.

"Maybe it'll do you good."

"She's got teeth!"

"That's to show you how long you stayed gone. And let me tell you she's proud of those little teeth, too, every single one."

"Holy Moses!" He propped up on one elbow and looked at Gloria's sweetly lowered face. She raised her eyes and appraised him back.

"Get used to being a father, please kindly."

"She could eat a plateful, the same as you and me. Why, she's going to wear you out. She's a little pig, ain't she?"

"When you got your first look at her this morning, you weren't scared of a baby."

"Then, she made me feel right at home. She cannonballed in like a little version of Mama."

"And you stood on your head for her."

He couldn't take his eyes away. "She's such a sweet, helpful little thing, now ain't she!" he exclaimed. Lady May set a sidelong gaze on him while she held Gloria's breast in both hands, like a little horn blower whose hoots and peeps were given mainly with the eyes. "I reckon she can do everything in the world, next to talking."

"Don't criticize her!" cried Gloria. "If she could talk now, she would tell you you can't just prance back like this and take it for granted that all you have to do is come home—and life will go on like before, or even better."

"Trust your dad," he told the baby.

"The system you're trying won't work," Gloria said. "I wouldn't need to bring you down to earth if I wasn't your wife."

He smiled at her.

"I feel like you missed my last letter by coming home today," Gloria said.

"That's all right—you already had all the other letter writers in the world licked."

"I'm glad for you and sorry for the rest of the prisoners going deprived."

"Never mind about them. What they had was family coming to beg for 'em," he said, fanning her and the baby with his shirt-tails.

"Beg for 'em?"

"The smartest they had, the pick of their family. That's who'd be elected to come to Parchman and beg. Or else how would the poor lonesome fools ever get out of there? Renfros and Beechams and Comforts relied a hundred percent on me and Aycock's own behavior to turn the trick. Now that's the slow way."

"How could I have got myself to Parchman?" she cried.

"They call it Visiting Day."

"Coming afoot? All the way to Parchman?" Gloria cried.

"You could've brought me a bottle of Banner water. And a pinch of home dirt—I could have carried that around in my shoe. I'd be looking for you on Visiting Day. Uncle Homer's got the surest transportation, but he wouldn't have begged for me as hard as you. You got to beg pretty wholehearted before old Parchman will listen."

"I didn't know Parchman would behave like that," said Gloria.

"You got to aggravate 'em until they do." He fanned them.

"I had a baby. That's exactly what I was doing!"

He looked at her over the baby's little crop of hair. "And I wouldn't have had you set your little foot in a place like Parchman for all you'd give me! You know that, Beautiful. I was trying to make you smile. Where I'm proud and glad to have you is right here at home in Banner, exactly the way you are."

"Then why do you tease me?" she whispered.

"Honey, Judge Moody's gone to Grinder's Mill."

"You went farther than Grinders Mill."

"I'm back."

"And look what you're doing first thing."

"Is she satisfied now?" he loudly answered her, for the baby just then dodged from her mother to complete a yawn. He jumped up. "I believe she's sleepy. How sound does our baby sleep?"

Lady May's little hand dropped like a falling star. More slowly, her eyelids fell.

"She goes to the Gates of Beyond, just like you," whispered Gloria.

He took the shirt off his back and folded it and took up the limp baby in it and walked to where the shadow of the tree reached into the feathery plum bushes. He laid her down and wrapped her lightly in his sleeves, and saw that she had a little canopy of light boughs, with a plum hanging as if it might fall in her mouth.

He turned, and Gloria darted. Once more they were running as hard as they could go, Gloria in front, rounding the bank its whole way around, swiftly past the piecrust edge, streaking by the peephole, clicking across the limestone, bounding over the hummocks, taking the hollow places skip by skip without a miss, threading serpentine through the plum bushes, softly around the baby, and back to the tree, where he reached with both hands and had her. Catching her weight as though he'd trapped it, he lowered her into the seat that looked out over the drop and got in with her.

The tree trunk, as high up as the hitching limb, was well carved; it was wound up in strings and knots of names and initials as if in a clover chain. In the upper gloom of branches, two doves like two stars flew in, then flew out again, out over the unseen river.

"When will we move to ourselves?" Gloria whispered.

"I believe that's what you was saying to me the last thing before I left home for the courthouse."

"Our wedding day. It was those very words."

"They sound a familiar tune."

"And I wrote you the same words too, didn't let you forget 'em all the time you were gone."

"I so much rather hear your sweet voice saying 'em," he gasped, and taking her by the hand he laid his mouth over hers.

When she could speak, she said, "Stop. What is the most important thing in all the world?"

"I reckon what we need right now is a scout," he said without pulling his face off hers. "Now Vaughn would come if I'd give him another holler. Little fellow just sits there listening."

"No, I want Vaughn to remember you later as a good example."

"Or Aycock. Aycock'd do anything for me and I'd do anything for him. He'd keep a lookout—"

"Jack, I want you to give him up."

"Give up *Aycock?*"

"He's good-for-nothing and spineless. And now he's back home with a prison record besides."

"He's an old Banner boy! He just ain't had all the good things

I have—has no daddy at home, no mama able to keep on the subject, no sisters and brothers to call on—no wife! Not to mention a sweet, helpful little girl-baby."

"I wouldn't let Aycock touch the hem of her garment," she said. "If it wasn't for all the other people around us, our life would be different this minute."

"Who wants it different?" he whispered.

"Your wife."

He rolled closer.

"And here you are, going right back down in the road to more trouble, the minute you let go of me," she said, as he clasped her close.

"Just because something may give me a little bit of trouble, you don't see me go backing away from it, do you?" He rubbed his cheek against hers. "I'm beholden to the reunion to keep it running on a smooth track today, for Granny's birthday to be worth her living to see. For Mama's chickens not to go wasted, and for all of 'em that's travelled through dust not to go home disappointed. It's up to me to meet that Judge, Possum, sing him my name out loud and clear, and leave him in as good a ditch as the one he had before I saved him. That's all."

"Then it's up to your wife to pit her common sense against you, Jack," she said, catching her breath.

"Honey, Judge Moody's gone to Grinders. And our baby's lying safe where we can see her, in the Land of Nod." His arms reached all the way around her.

"Oh, Jack, I ought to've hit you over the head with your mother's cornbread irons, back when you first began! Beat you back over to your side of my desk with the blackboard eraser! Never kept you in after school to learn 'Abou Ben Adhem' by heart!"

"I like to never did learn it."

"I couldn't forget a word if I tried."

"Don't say it now," he begged, short-breathed. "I doubt if they come any longer."

Her face with a thousand freckles on it was moving from side to side like a tiger lily trying not to give out perfume.

"Possum!" he croaked.

She skinned loose from the knot of his arms and for a minute sat up over him. She brought down the sides of her fists on his naked chest as if it were solid oak, and his heart seemed to jump out of it, almost into visibility.

"Do you still think you're going to pick up living right where you left off?" she asked fast.

"Did something put the idea in your precious little head I can't?"

"This is the time I've been guarding myself against for a year, six months and a day," she gasped, but if he heard more than the first words he didn't show it, for the whole weight of his head rammed upward, blundered against her neck, and then moved in a blind way up her face, his cheek hot as a stove on hers, something hotter splashing between them that could have been tears.

"Oh Jack, Jack, Jack, Jack—now you've bumped my head on something hard—"

He had rolled over with her and stopped breathing. Without stopping to be sorry for her head he crammed kisses in her mouth, and she wound her arms up around his own drenched head and returned him kiss for kiss.

ᴥ§

But almost at once three or four nervous hounds began licking the back of Jack's neck and the sole of Gloria's foot that lay outside its shoe.

"Boo!" said a sober young man who came stalking up onto Banner Top with a guitar under his arm. Jack and Gloria sprang apart.

"Aycock! Seems like it was a hundred years ago when I last saw you!" said Jack. "How did you find your little mama?"

"Mad at me. What did they say when you come walking in?"

"They seemed to think it was right well timed," said Jack. "They had a big welcome on their faces. Then the news started trickling from 'em."

"Bet you had a sizable amount to listen to."

"Grandpa Vaughn is gone, Aycock, been laid in the ground while they had me off yonder where I didn't know it."

"Well, at least you know where he is," said Aycock. "Not like my dad. We don't know what's become of him at all."

**113**

"He didn't even take anybody with him? Your Uncle Earl?"

"Uncle Earl would rather do anything than leave Banner," said Aycock. He had such a short face that all his life he must have looked as he did now, ready to cry. His hair was the rust of a cedar bush winter-killed, even had the bush's shape and crinkly texture.

"Somebody watched me coming through the peephole. It was a red-headed baby," said Aycock.

"If she hasn't waked up and worked her way clear out of her harness!" Jack jumped up and ran to meet the baby, welcomed her, and swung her down in front of Aycock.

"Goodness-a-life. Which is it?" Aycock said.

"A girl! Wearing a dress to prove it!" Gloria said.

"Goodness-a-life." Aycock folded down into a squat. "Whose big shoe are you carrying?"

"I wonder if Aycock brought one good excuse along for coming up here," said Gloria.

"Mama said she heard gunfire overhead. So I come to see if you was still living, Jack," said Aycock. "While you was hearing the bad news, did you hear anything about Poison Ivy Moody?"

"I was just fixing to break it to you!" Jack cried.

"How long did it take you to find it out?"

"Uncle Homer told me. He made it in right behind me," Jack said. "Who told you?"

"I looked," Aycock admitted.

"You sound like you was expecting to see him! If you was on the watch for a judge on your way home from the pen, Aycock, I wasn't!" said Jack. "And when Mr. Willy Trimble merrily turned in front of his Buick and down he went, if that didn't give him first marks of being a stranger! And I took him for one."

"He looked the same to me as he done in Ludlow courthouse," said Aycock. "Like a sinner, more or less."

"Well, all I got to do now is shoo him back in a ditch just as good as he was in, and call it evens," Jack said, buttoning on his shirt.

"Don't one ditch satisfy 'em at home?"

"No, Aycock, he managed that much by himself. And I didn't have the sense or stamina to leave him floundering!" said Jack. "My family is just about on the verge of having a fit over it."

"How many you got up there today?"

"It's the whole reunion!"

"Has that already come around again?"

"My little granny's birthday come around again, and now it's my welcome home. It's going on right now."

"They waiting dinner on you?"

"How could they eat till I get back?"

"Always glad I ain't you," said Aycock.

"They'll wait," said Jack. "For one thing, Uncle Nathan's still got to come, from who only knows how far!"

"Jack, didn't you see what's right in your face? You bumped my head on it," said Gloria. She pointed back to a little wooden sign staked low to the ground not far from the jumping-off place. Its black letters were still running with bright fishtails of paint.

" 'Destruction Is At Hand,' " Jack read off affectionately. "Bless Uncle Nathan's heart, he *has* made it in!"

"They'll soon be gobbling, Jack," said Aycock. "I wouldn't mind being one at the table."

Lady May was creeping close on him, where he still squatted there. Tipping his sassafras-colored head to one side, Aycock laid the guitar over his knee. At the first chord he squinted an eye upward and his voice became a tenor.

> *"Bought me a chicken and my chicken pleased me*
> *And I tied my chicken be-hind a tree*
> *And my chicken said 'Coo-coo, coo-coo, coooo!'*
> *Anybody that feeds his chickens,*
> *Feed my chicken too."*

Lady May opened her own mouth wide, held her breath. Her eyes followed Aycock's sideburns moving with his singing—they were long as cat-scratches.

> *"Bought me a hen and my hen pleased me—"*

"Aycock, you made her cry," said Jack.

"Then Great Scots-a-life! Are you planning to try running that Judge in a ditch with a crying baby *girl* to be your partner?"

"She was having the time of her little life till Aycock Comfort came along," said Gloria. She put up her arms, lifted her hair high to the crown and tied it furiously tight but didn't bind it, so it flared from the ribbon like the petals of a flower. Her head was glary as a

**115**

trumpet flower against the hot green cedar shade. Aycock didn't look straight at her. His eyes went sleepy and even his ears turned gold.

With both hands, Jack worked the slipper back onto Gloria's slick, hot little foot. "I don't believe that shoe was ever *made* for serious hopping," he said. "I'm proud my wife and baby got nothing more to do than sit in the shade and watch me." Then he jumped up by Aycock. "Son, if what you're trying to do is come in on it, I better save time and invite you now."

"Jack!" Gloria cried out.

"Would make it seem like olden times, Jack," said Aycock. "But you got a majority on it?"

"She's my wife!" protested Jack. "How could Gloria be sitting here at my feet and not be for whatever I do?" And up she jumped.

"Then all we got to worry about is him. We can't get old Poison Ivy by wishing. He's got to come along, Jack," said Aycock.

"He's trying to get across the river to Alliance, that's his aim," Jack told him. "What his story is, I don't know."

"If he's using Banner Road, ain't nothing going to stop him. It throws him right on the bridge."

"He don't overly care for the looks of our bridge," said Jack.

"That could be why he run up in our yard, skinned around the martin houses, and gone again like a lost soul," said Aycock. "He was just using us to turn around."

"In your very yard?" cried Jack. "What did your mother say?"

"She complained of the dust. Next thing, she complained of gunfire up over her head."

"She heard Brother Bethune delivering judgment on a chicken snake. Before that, he talked Judge Moody into going all the way to Grinders Mill in the hope of a better-looking bridge. But he's going to find that old covered bridge at Grinders is going without a floor. I don't believe even the mill still calls itself in commission."

"Jack, where did you learn so much about Grinders Mill?" Gloria objected.

"Parchman. Ask me about anywhere! I reckon for every spot there is, there's somebody in the pen going homesick for it. Old trusty told me every inch of Grinders, the same as I told him Banner." said Jack. "I only hope now there isn't one of his kin standing there with little enough to do to tell Judge Moody he could bump three miles further on and be poled across the river at Wisdom's Point. Aycock'll guarantee that."

"Be ready for a shock," Aycock told him. "The ferry at Wisdom ties up on Sunday now. Uncle Joe Wisdom has been converted and spends the whole day in church shouting repentence. I'll bring you that much from Mama."

"Thank her for the best news she could have sent me. Now, unless they teach a Buick to swim, it's Banner bridge or nothing for Judge Moody. And he's going to make up his mind to it. He'll come puffing along again, any time now, gritting his teeth for it. He's more or less like me, not the kind to give up in the face of a little hardship," said Jack.

"Jack, I hope you're wrong," said Gloria, while he capered to the front of the bank and hung over the road.

"We'll land him in my own ditch kissing the mailbox!"

"That's bringing it close to home," said Aycock at his shoulder.

"It's not a bad ditch, Aycock. It's the ditch the school bus has deepened out for itself by eternally trying to get up out of our road and go to school."

"But you know what?" said Aycock. "If it's the second time he's run in a ditch in one day, he might think it was being done on purpose with him in mind."

"But that's the whole blooming idea, Aycock! That's the beauty of it," said Jack. "That's when I announce myself to him, the minute the dust starts clearing and he puts his head up!" He sprang onto Aycock's back, the guitar wobbled in the air, and the boys began leapfrogging.

"Well, old Poison Ivy ain't going to love me and you a bit the better for it," said Aycock, tumbling and rolling over.

"Love us!" Jack cried, sitting on him. "Aycock, I'm going to a heap of trouble just to blooming well keep him from it!"

"A man as out-of-patience as the Judge might for all I know send me and you both back to Parchman for it! First thing Monday morning!"

"I ain't ever going anywhere that flat again, and that's all there is to it. Shinny up the tree, Aycock, and watch till you see him coming."

"She's beating me to it," Aycock pointed. "Which one was that?"

A Robin-Hood patterned dress was already halfway up to the

first limb of the tree, with rosy arms reaching, sunburned feet tucking up behind.

"They've grown, every one of 'em," said Jack. "Etoyle looks as broad as Ella Fay now, sitting on that hitching limb."

"I'm here to see the look on Judge Moody's face!" Etoyle sang.

"Well, you've got more society here than a little bit. And all girls," said Aycock in polite tones. "Will I have time to enjoy my first sip of Banner water?"

"My eyes see dust!" sang Etoyle from the tree. "Somebody's a-coming!"

Gloria snatched up the baby and followed Jack and Aycock to where the front of the bank overlooked the road. It dropped away on both sides below them, like a sash picked up in the middle on a stick. The ditch ran with it, sometimes on one side and sometimes on the other. Then both ends of the road went out of sight in identical blind curves.

"Banner Road is just plain beautiful," said Jack. Then a puff of dust showed along the next ridge over, as though a match had been laid to a string in Freewill whose other end was here at Banner Top. "That's him. He's coming the long way round."

For a few minutes, a buzzard flying slow as a fence-walker along the rim of trees seemed to be in a bigger hurry. Then the dust was a growing cloud. Presently there came a sound from the road itself, thin as that of a veil being parted.

"He's passing the supervisor's house. I hear the gravel," said Aycock. Thoughts seemed to chase one another up and down his forehead, rippling it like a squirrel's tail.

"Is it fair for me to warn him?" Etoyle called.

"Want me to send you back to help Mama?" shouted Jack. "Keep count of the Dry Creek bridges, and when it's six, holler! Gloria! Hold our baby high out of the dust! Aycock! At the last minute you're hanging onto my britches!"

"Not everybody goes rushing into trouble as headlong as you, Jack!"

"Man alive, let go of my britches! Want me to come away and leave 'em?" Jack yelled. "We got to charge down fast and shoo him in! He ain't going to wait on us!"

"I changed my mind," said Aycock.

Jack's pants gave a rip, Aycock let him go, and Gloria handed him his baby.

"If you can't be a better example to Lady May—*hold* her!" Gloria's arm circled up in a teacher's best gesture, and it threw her off balance. She staggered backwards, and as her skirt blew up at the edge of the bank, spread, shone like a pearl, she wheeled and her shoes started sliding with her down toward the road.

Jack spun on Aycock. "Hold the baby!"

"You hold it."

"You hold it! I got to catch Gloria!"

"I don't know how to hold no baby! I just got back from the pen a while ago—I'm like to drop it!"

"Take hold of her and she takes hold of you!"

"Six!" sang Etoyle from the tree.

Jack held out the baby to Aycock, he parried with his guitar. Lady May gave a shriek. She turned herself around and plastered herself to Jack's chest, legs like a frog's. Binding him around the neck with her arms, ramming her head into his croaking throat, she pumped out soft, anticipatory cries on her own little bellows.

Jack's eyes bulged. His toes suddenly turned unnaturally outwards.

"Stop, Jack, stop, Jack, S-T-O-P stop!" Gloria's voice called from below, fading while it spelled. "Lady May hates downhill!"

A mockingbird threw down two or three hard notes on him like a blacksmith driving in nails, and he went rigid. Hugging Lady May to him, taking short, frantic steps as though he'd been caught naked, he hopped over the edge into Gloria's dust and went down, rigid and upright, first at a zigzag and then, shuddering on his heels, straight down a washboard of clay. He yelled, but the baby now made no sound at all except for clapping together the soles of her bare feet just above his belt-buckle. At the skin of his chest her little mouth nibbled—it might have been everything feminine laughing at him. He landed in a bed of yellow cosmos. On his face a wide, frantic smile of paternity flashed on and off again, as he raised the baby in his arms like a bunch of flowers for Gloria.

She had not been able to stop until she went down on both knees into the ditch at the foot of the mailbox, with her arms around it.

Lady May's hot little foot slammed Jack across the windpipe.

She slid down him, left him with his breath cut off and both feet ploughed out in front of him, while she set forth across the road. Each bare foot hopped from the heat of the dust. She had the crow of a tattletale. She hooked onto her mother, made sounds at her ear, then started back, hopping for Jack. This was the moment the car came thundering for the top of the hill, a sunset of red dust fanning into high air, bank to bank.

Jack staggered to his feet. Gloria sprang to hers, ran after the baby, collided with Jack, who was spun around so hard that he fell backwards into his own ditch this time, and she captured the baby by throwing herself down on top of her, and lay flat there in the middle of Banner Road as if she waited in the path of a cyclone.

The car took the only way left open and charged up Banner Top in a bombardment of pink clods like thrown roses. Aycock appeared in its train of dust. He was running after it, waving his guitar. He caught hold and was borne on up as if by some large, not local, bird. The car never stopped. The dogs streaked with it, barking it further off the road. Dust solid as a waterfall poured over the bank along whose roof the car rolled on, tossing a fence post, mowing down plum bushes. There was a shriek out of Etoyle, a blow, a scraping sound, a crack, then silence, even from the dogs.

Jack picked up his family. He stood holding Gloria's face between his hands, while Lady May stood spread-eagled against his legs, then he gathered the baby up fast and hugged her and Gloria together.

What looked like big Buicks of dust hung stalled in the air until they slowly turned pink and then gauzy. The cedar tree with Etoyle standing at the top emerged first. Then the car emerged; it was still there, standing still, in a position right beyond the tree. It couldn't be anywhere but on the jumping-off place. Then the dogs came to life and tried to bark it on over as fast as possible.

Jack lunged to go.

"Jack! Don't desert me!" Gloria cried.

"He saved my wife and baby!" he yelled, as she grabbed him. "Stay with 'em!"

"But I got to be quick if I'm in time to catch him!"

"I see his face!" called Etoyle.

The driver's door had opened, and Judge Oscar Moody climbed out of the car. He stood coated, hulking in seersucker, a middle-aged man in a little sea of plum bushes. In a voice hoarse from dust he called, "Young lady!"

"We're still living! You still living?" hollered Jack.

Then the door on the passenger side of the car opened, and somebody else got out. Judge Moody came around the tree to get to the other side of the car, and then came leading forward a middle-aged lady. Through the scarves of dust she appeared dressed for church. She was all in white, wearing a wide-brimmed hat, carrying a purse the size of a plum bucket. Judge Moody took her arm and they came, wobbling a little, across Banner Top.

"Here Judge Moody comes," said Etoyle, hunkering down and sliding down the face of the bank into the road. "And his mother with him."

"His wife," Gloria cried.

Jack said, "His what? I never had a notion there *was* a Mrs. Judge Moody! What's she doing along?"

Judge Moody set his foot on the bottom wire of the fence where it was still standing, and the lady came through headfirst, like a novice.

"Jack, try to make up your mind there's a wife for everybody," said Gloria in a voice that trembled.

"Sister Gloria, you scraped one knee," said Etoyle. "It's losing blood. But what if they'd aimed a little sharper at my tree?"

Gloria let out a short scream. Jack squatted, kissed the blood off her knee, and brushed her skirt in modest places until the pink dust re-formed and put up a gauze screen around them for a minute. He rose, put his lips to her ear, and whispered, "Face 'em, from now on. Your dress is tore behind."

Gloria took the handkerchief from her pocket, cleared away a coating of dust and tears from the baby's face, set her on her feet, and then cleared her own face. "And my baby's lost her little new shoes!"

"He saved you! And I reckon his wife was sitting there to help him," said Jack and more resolutely still she worked on his face.

"And now here they both come to eat us up," said Gloria.

The Moodys reached the road and started for them. Judge Moody had tied a handkerchief over his mouth and nose, and Mrs. Moody carried his Panama hat along with her purse.

Judge Moody in a strong, slow voice called through his hand-kerchief the same words. "Young lady!"

"That's you, Gloria," said Etoyle. "Maybe he'll march you to jail."

"You were right in front of my wheels. I might have run over you and killed you. Are you harmed?" called Judge Moody.

"No sir, only bleeding a little," answered Gloria.

"We could have run right smack dab into you! And that one was blocking off that other little road, the only way we could turn," said Mrs. Moody, pointing her finger at Jack. "And there was another one, scooting through the bushes—brandishing something! Everywhere you looked there was another one."

"And there was one in the tree," said Etoyle. "I wasn't scared."

"I saw you first, girl." Mrs. Moody pointed at Gloria. "Clinging to that mailbox like Rock of Ages. And the next minute you were streaking across the road! Yes, you *think* nobody lives on a lonesome road like this," she complained, "and then out of the middle of nowhere some little somebody jumps out at you, runs you off the road before you know it—"

"Little somebody? That's my wife you saved!" cried Jack, his face glowing at the Moodys.

Lady May lifted one foot and wailed.

"Good Lord! And where did that infant come from?" asked Judge Moody, as Jack scooped her triumphantly into his arms.

"Yes sir, here is our first," Jack said, holding up Lady May with a grip around her knees. She swayed, wandlike.

"Didn't you see her, Oscar? That baby just streaked across!" said Mrs. Moody. "And then this girl came from right yonder and threw herself down on her like one possessed. Spang in the middle of the road."

"I'm going to tell a lot of people on you," Etoyle told Gloria.

"Is that infant harmed?" asked Judge Moody.

"No sir, I was right on top of her," said Gloria.

Judge Moody groaned.

"But you saved 'em both!" cried Jack.

Gloria put her hand on his sleeve. "I don't want my husband too quickly blamed for the way he let his baby slide out of his grasp," she told Judge Moody. "This is the first time he's ever been anywhere in her company in his life, or hers, your honor."

"Girl, how in the world do you know who we are?" Mrs. Moody exclaimed.

"We are still within my circuit, Maud Eva. I suppose I'm pretty well known wherever I go," said Judge Moody.

"Well, thank goodness for small favors," she said. "I'm glad somebody knows *you,* because I certainly don't even know where I am."

"Where you are now," came the slow voice of Aycock, and everybody hushed—only his dogs barked with him, "is called Banner Top around here. Others call it Lover's Leap. It's the highest known spot in the Banner community."

"Aycock beat all of you. He got *in* the car," said Etoyle.

"The car! Look at the *car!*" yelled Jack, and he hurled himself straight up the clay wall.

Out on the shelf of clay that was the jumping-off place, the five-passenger sedan sat shining in its original paint, all but one fender still undented, its windshield and back window still unstarred, its back bumper flashing dusty light at them from below the spare tire. The tree was behind it. The Buick had skinned past the trunk, the tree had creaked back into place as if after a gust of wind, and now the old cedar stood guard just behind the left rear fender.

Jack pounded toward it.

"Buick ended up better than the way you first had it figured, Jack." Aycock was sitting up in the middle of the back seat.

"I got to figure again pretty fast," said Jack.

"It's like I told you. A ditch for the second time in a row wouldn't have made us popular at all."

"Shut up, Pete! Shut up, Queenie and Slider!"

This time when the dogs stopped barking, everybody cried out, Aycock along with the rest. The sound that made itself heard was unmistakable, though soft as a teakettle singing beyond the boil: the Moodys had climbed out and gone off and left the Buick with its engine running.

Aycock's foot, shorn of its shoe now and arched as if in fastidiousness, appeared over the rear door.

"Keep your foot!" shouted Jack. "Stay where you are till you hear from me! Aycock! This Buick couldn't be in a much sweeter fix had you been the driver!" He put out his hand and laid it with care against the side of the hood. "Like she's wondering if she can go ahead and fly," he said, looking respectful. "Well, she's going to find out in another two shakes, if she ain't real careful."

"Young man!" Judge Moody called through his dust protector. "I don't think that car needs much more encouragement before it'll go over—stand back!" He put out a foot.

All Aycock's dogs rushed down the bank and started barking at him. Mrs. Moody was already saying, "Oscar Moody, come back here. You're fifty-five years old, had a warning about your blood pressure, suffer from dust and hay fever, and insisted on wearing your best seersucker today. You stay put—you hear me? You can give those boys directions—"

"Stand back!" called Judge Moody. "Away from that car!"

"Grab it!" shrieked Mrs. Moody.

Jack bent his head studiously toward the hood, put his ear next to it. "Nothing to worry about here!" he called. "It's her own original sweet-singing engine this Buick's travelling on, and not much hotter than I am."

Wrapping his new shirt-tail over his hand, he reached for the radiator cap. The Buick responded by rocking back to front, as if the back and the front end were on the two pans of a balance scale.

"Show that car a trifle more respect!" Mrs. Moody protested.

When Jack took a step back from it, it kept rocking.

"I'm humanly certain I pulled that emergency brake," Judge Moody said. "If I'm not a complete ass, I pulled it."

"Judge Moody, you didn't pull it. And she's still in gear," Jack now called back. "But no harm done—your wheels is a hundred percent off the ground."

"Come back, you heard me. I don't want to lose you *and* the car! I don't know where I am or how I'd get home," Mrs. Moody cried to her husband, while the dogs barked in front of him.

"She didn't stop for the tree—what's holding her?" Jack shouted. He dropped to the ground and rolled fast underneath the Buick. He rolled out again and scrambled to his feet. "Let's all hope he's planted that one there to stay. Judge Moody, you're resting on top of the hickory sign my Uncle Nathan's drove in the ground and donated to the passing public just in time—the paint's still wet! Well, that was *one* way to stop!" He came trotting to face the road. "I'm ready with my verdict. Here it is. If one living soul adds on to the driving end of that car, or if another living soul is taken away from the hind end—" He raced back to the car, stuck his head in, and said, "Aycock, I got word for you: you can't get out."

124

"Can I sit up to the wheel?" asked Aycock.

"Ride where you are! *Lean back!*" Jack hollered.

"But that leaves us hanging over *nothing!*" Mrs. Moody cried in her husband's face.

"Well," said Judge Moody. "One thing sure. A good garage-man had better be sent for *now,* to bring that car down before something more happens to it."

"But you got a Good Samaritan right here!" Jack called.

"I'm not asking for a Good Samaritan, I'm asking for a man with some know-how," called Judge Moody. "And a good piece of road equipment."

"But you saved my wife and baby!" cried Jack, running to lean over the bank above him. "I can't let some stranger shove his way in and help your car off Banner Top, not while I'm living, no sir!"

"I want that car off of there," said Judge Moody.

"And in the road! In the road!" cried Mrs. Moody. "And listen! It's my car, I'll have you all know!"

"It's her car," said Jack hoarsely to Aycock. He pleaded down to her, "Mrs. Judge, don't have a fit. If you won't, I'll hop to the wheel and back this Buick off Banner Top like such a streak of lightning she won't even know what's grabbed her."

"Jack!" cried Gloria, but Mrs. Moody wildly cried over her, "All right! I don't care who does it, just so you do it in time and don't get a scratch on the finish! I only want to see that car down in the road!"

"Headed which way?" asked Jack.

"Young man!" said Judge Moody. "I'd like to point out something. There is a tree behind that car. It isn't going to get up out of the ground and walk off for you."

"All I need is a inch—I can *make* a inch! Just to give myself one inch to cut the wheel! It'll be over before you know it, Aycock," said Jack, running to the Buick and setting his hand on the door.

"I reckon I better go on up there and put the quietus on that boy," Judge Moody said. "Young lady, you are not the only member of your family who's too precipitous." As he spoke through the handkerchief, the baby leaned from Gloria's arms to watch it talk.

"Oscar! If you won't consider your blood pressure, consider mine. You stay down here where I've got you," said Mrs. Moody.

"Don't set your foot an inch up that bank, or I'll tell Dr. Carruthers on you the minute we get home."

"All it needs is one good push," said Judge Moody, and the baby showed her mirth.

"Girl, *you* go. Can't you talk your husband out of trying to rescue my car, till my husband thinks of something better?" Mrs. Moody asked Gloria. "If you can't, I'll have to tie Judge Moody up."

"If you will kindly hold my baby, I'll see how well I can discourage him," Gloria said, and she went lightly up the diagonal toe-holds, the way she would have shown off the staircase in her own imaginary house.

When she tripped to the car, Jack was wiping the dust off the windshield, using the sleeve of his shirt.

"Jack, I don't know which is worse," said Gloria. "What you thought you were going to do, or what you're ending up doing. For the sake of the reunion you were willing to run Judge Moody in the ditch. Now for his sake you are just as willing to break your neck."

"I'll be all through in a minute—now that I can see out through the glass where I'm going."

"Here I come!" Aycock suddenly piped in falsetto.

Jack jumped backwards and one foot slipped off the edge. He saved himself. One hollow root, broken off short, was trained onto space like the barrel of a cannon, and he grabbed it. One leg thrashed for a place on another root that plunged downward like a mermaid's tail. He fought his way back over the top.

"Hey, Aycock," he said, "I bet if you and me could be down on the Bywy fishing, this Buick'd look like a peanut balanced on the end of a nose!"

Gloria clasped Jack and pressed her dizzy head against his throbbing shoulder. "Jack, I've come just in time to put a limit on you."

"What's that you say, Possum?"

"I'll let you be a Good Samaritan one last time. But providing you use some of my common sense. I'm not letting you to the steering wheel!" she cried.

"But honey," he said, "who knows better than you what a good driver I am?"

"That's driving the school bus down Banner Road with me sitting right at your back," she said. "That's not backing Judge and

**126**

Mrs. Moody's polished Buick sedan down Lover's Leap with me watching—and breaking your neck!"

He stared. "I reckon you know that means find a slow way, Possum," he brought out.

"The slower the better," she said. She took one step toward the car. Aycock, at the side window, sat in profile, leaning back. Because of the way it grew, his hair looked like a sofa pillow with small tassels at the corners, worn pitched low on the forehead.

"Aycock Comfort, don't you holler 'Here I come' once more till you've got solid ground in front of you. I'll be listening," she said.

"Yes ma'am."

Jack handed Gloria down to the road, looking fondly as ever in all directions over the tall red lumps of clay and the yellow-fringed clambering road and the ditch that kept up with it, and the flower-hugged syrup stand and the Uncle Sam mailbox and the home track, falling between its own rosy banks and buckled like a little hearth in firelight.

"Never mind, Lady May! Nothing about it's got your daddy licked, not as long as he can tackle it on home grounds," he said.

"Young man, have you been made to understand to keep hands off of that car?" Judge Moody asked.

"Yes sir," Jack said. "My wife's done passed a law."

"Not any too soon. You almost went over all by yourself," said Mrs. Moody. "You've started looking to me like the kind who might scratch the finish. That car's been mighty lovingly cared for. I don't want to see it getting in any more trouble today than it's in already."

"Trouble!" Jack cried. "That's one thing I never look for. Ask my wife!" He turned to the Judge. "But if it suits your wife and my wife any better, I'll go up real easy behind the Buick, hitch to the spare with the best puller I can find, and pull her down, hind-end foremost. Mrs. Judge didn't let you start out without rope and tackle, did she, sir?"

"The rope and tackle, and all the tools," intoned the Judge, "are inside the car, safely stowed under the back seat."

"Aycock, hear what you're setting on?" Jack called, and then said, "Never mind, Mrs. Judge. I never seen the fix yet there wasn't some way out of."

"But I want to hear it first," said Judge Moody.

"My system is be ready for what comes to me in a good strong flash!" said Jack.

Judge Moody said, "But the way I prefer to do it is calling up my own garageman, even if we have to wait a little longer on him."

"Seek an outsider?" cried Jack. He gave Gloria and the baby a stricken look.

"Now there ought to be a store, reasonably there's some little store at a crossroads nearby with a telephone in it," Judge Moody said.

Up on Banner Top, Aycock laughed.

"You mean Banner! Curly Stovall closes up on Sunday, sir," Jack told Judge Moody.

"Get your storekeeper to open up, if that's the only phone there is," said Judge Moody.

"Yes, you could pull him out of church," agreed Mrs. Moody. "I'm sure he's no more than a Baptist."

"Old Curly uses Sunday to go fishing," said Jack. "He's floating down the Bywy, no question about it. But his store's shut just as tight as if he's a Christian in good standing. The old bench is pulled just as solid across the door."

"Who's got a phone in the house?" asked Judge Moody. "The nearest."

"Miss Pet Hanks."

"Where does the lady live?"

"Medley. That's five miles going the other way—you passed her house coming. She's who rings two longs and a short in Curly's store when somebody wants to talk to Banner."

"You might just as well go back to Ludlow," Mrs. Moody told her husband. "And use the one in your den."

"Then the store at the *next* benighted crossroads!" Judge Moody cried.

"Everywhere it's the same story, Judge: shut tight," Jack said. "Everything but the Foxtown icehouse is keeping Sunday."

"Where's that singing?" Mrs. Moody sharply inquired.

"When the wind veers just a little bit to the west, and it's First Sunday, you'll hear the Methodists letting off from Banner," said Jack.

" 'Throw out the life line! Throw out the life line!' " sang the Methodists. " 'Someone is sinking today.' "

"Then what are we supposed to do?" Mrs. Moody asked. "Stand here together and wait for the first person to come along?"

"Mrs. Judge, generally the first ones to come along the road ain't exactly the ones you'd have picked," said Jack. "Now, all I need to do is holler. There's a hundred up there just waiting." Taking in a barrelful of air, he squared his mouth to holler. But Gloria shook her head at him, and he swallowed it.

"I thought till today I knew any cranny of the county you might try to show me," said the Judge to his wife. "But where's any hundred people along this road?"

"It's the gathering of his family," Gloria told the Moodys. "I don't think it's more than fifty, but that's the way they count." She told Jack, "The way your family loves to tell stories, they wouldn't hear the Crack of Doom by this time. You'll have to send up there and pull one of 'em loose by the hand."

"All right, Etoyle," said Jack.

"Hooray!" she yelled.

"Without doing the St. Vitus Dance, just tell 'em I miscalculated a shaving on what I'd be running into," said Jack. "You might give 'em the idea I could use a rope. And some of their strength."

"But don't embroider!" Gloria called after the whooping child.

" 'Miscalculated' will tell my family all they need to know," Jack said. "So don't be downhearted, Mrs. Judge! Help'll come fast. All I need 'em to bring is the equal of your car to pull with. Uncle Homer's up there with a pretty good answer."

"Uncle Homer!" Gloria exclaimed.

"Well, some day he can be expected to improve—he's been married into the family for a good long while," said Jack. "Why wouldn't this be the day? Judge and Mrs. Judge, there's seats right behind you where you can fit right into the shade."

Straddling the ditch in the shade of a mulberry tree, some planks were nailed between two-by-fours to make Jack's roadside stand. The dust was on each plank like a runner of figured pink velvet.

"I'll stay right here on my own two feet. I'm not going to make myself comfortable till I see what happens to my car, thank you," Mrs. Moody said. "And that goes for my husband too."

Footing the bank along the ditch now there was a carpet-runner of shadow. Judge Moody walked it, to stare up the farm track that came cutting down through the bank, its clay walls, like its floor, scarred as if by battle. Dust lay in the old winter-made ruts, deep as ashes on an unraked hearth; it was dust sifted times over, quiescent now. At the foot of the track, where the wooden Uncle Sam stood as high as the Judge's waist, Judge Moody reached inside his coat to his breast pocket, as if to make sure that what he carried himself was comparatively safe.

"This is not where *I* come from," Gloria assured Mrs. Moody as the two of them stood together under the mulberry tree. "When I started out as a teacher, they handed me Banner School."

"A teacher? Well, you're just talking to another one," said Mrs. Moody, her eyes not leaving her car. "I taught nine years before Judge Moody came galloping along. I don't suppose there's a Mississippi girl alive that hasn't taken her turn teaching some lonesome school—but that serves as no excuse to me for jumping out of the bushes unannounced, dressed like a country bride, and scaring people that have cars off the road."

On Banner Top, Jack stood guard by the Buick, his arms folded and his legs crossed. The tree's shadow draped him there like a piece of sacking with holes through it. Everywhere else, the light drenched all that side of the road from top to bottom.

"Well, here we are," said Aycock. "I reckon Sir Poison Ivy is wishing him and his car was a mile away from here."

"And I'm going to do my best to get him started," said Jack.

"Let him stew a little while, Jack. I got me a seat in a pleasure car, riding here free, and I kind of hate to give it up."

"Aycock, you may not be in a hurry, but Judge Moody is. And it's still his car. Or his wife's, that's the same thing. I'm going to get it back on the road for him if it's the last thing I do," said Jack. "That's for saving my wife and baby like he did."

"He ain't done nothing for me yet," said Aycock. "Glad I don't owe him nothing."

"I'm trying to count up how many Uncle Homer will come bringing," said Jack. "For all I know, leaving the ladies out, it'll be the whole reunion. And I couldn't begrudge 'em if they want to help pull." He shoved out an arm and tried it against the tree.

"This here tree's been hitched to and carved on and chased around and climbed up and shot at so many times already," said Aycock, "if much more was to happen around this tree, it might not even stand for it."

"It's been a good old tree," said Jack. "And I aim to take care of it."

The cedar had suffered from the weather, and was set with the pegs of many lost branches; some of the stumps were onion-shaped, as though the branches had been twisted off by teasing boys whose names a good teacher could call right now. The upper trunk was punctured like a flute to give entry to woodpeckers or owls.

"Old-timers hung a rascal from this tree, my grandmaw used to tell. Jack, it wouldn't hold the rascal now," said Aycock.

"What I'm going to ask it to do is a little less than that," said Jack. "All you got to do is lean back and wait."

"Shall We Gather at the River" rose and faded on the air, and the stitching sound of the Buick's motor played on the midday silence. Then the distant sound of a pick-axe travelled to them, slow blows falling on dry ground somewhere below, spaced out with hollers of protest in between.

"That digs like my Uncle Earl," remarked Aycock. "On Sunday, too. Wonder who's played a joke on him?"

"I just want the world to know," Mrs. Moody raised her voice and called to the surrounding hills, "I wouldn't have budged from my cool house in Ludlow this morning except to go to Sunday School if I hadn't had my husband's conscience to contend with. And look where that's brought me."

"Could we possibly get rid of these dogs?" asked Judge Moody. As he paced, Queenie, Pete, and Slider were weaving hot circles around him.

"They won't bite, sir," said Jack. "They're just asking you what you want with Aycock."

Mrs. Moody suddenly exclaimed, "Where did those people spring from?"

A line of grown men and boys was coming over the crest of the road headed in the Banner direction. They kept the same distance apart from one another, and might have all been mounted on a single platform, some creeping flatcar, that moved them upgrade as a body by a pulley under them. They were all eating watermelon, their eyes raised to Banner Top.

"*They're* not bringing any help," said Mrs. Moody.

"The Broadwees are still living!" said Jack, and at his wave they made a rush for the roadside stand, where the first-comers took seats as if their names were on them.

**131**

"Hey, Jack. Hey, Aycock. Where you been!" the various ones began in hooting voices.

"Well, look whose car that is!" said the biggest Broadwee. "How about a good push, Jack? What you studying about?"

"There's a sample. There's what's wrong with this end of Boone County, *right there*," said Mrs. Moody, pointing her finger along the double row of Broadwees.

"Watch what you're saying, boys," Jack called. "There's ladies present."

"Hey, Teacher," cried one to Gloria. Then "Boo!" they all said at once to the baby, who had anticipated their greeting by starting to cry.

"You all be careful around my baby, it's a girl. She don't take to seeing roughnecks or hearing slang language," said Jack.

"Boo! Boo! Boo!" the Broadwees called systematically and in unison at the baby, like some form of encouragement practiced in their family.

"If you-all got nothing to do but sit and wait, start showing some manners!" Jack shouted. "And look out for your feet in front! Somebody may come out of my road in a bigger hurry than you are."

"A bite on the hook already, Jack," called Aycock. "Somebody's putting dust in your road."

"It's Uncle Homer for sure! He's yielding to the day!" Jack came scudding down the bank. "Judge Moody, here comes Uncle Homer and a load of helpers!"

Gloria caught him by the hand. "Uncle Homer's never come to your help yet," she said. "If he comes now, I'll have to take back my opinion of him."

Dust like a flapping blanket appeared back among the trees. A wall of dust rose on the farm track and toppled downward, there was a bang at the ditch, and a light delivery van came into view struggling to get up into the road.

"Am I to be towed by that?" asked Judge Moody.

"And just as church would be letting out at home!" cried his wife.

The van, as it pulled up its last wheel and turned toward Halfway Forks, showed its panel side painted with a big chicken dressed up in a straw hat, bow tie, and cane, while down over its head swung an axe of Pilgrim Father's size. It skidded, something was thrown out, and it ripped past them all. So empty of a load was it that its rear half danced all the way down the road, dust rising like a series of camp tents going up on the zigzag behind it. Tied onto its back doors, like an apron on backwards, there'd been a strip of oilcloth lettered "Let Homer Do It. There Is No Substitute for Experience."

"Didn't even wait to bring his own dog," said Jack. "Something about the way he handles himself makes you believe he'd be part-willing to take the joy out of life. Well, there's only one of Uncle Homer."

"I was right about him, anyway," said Gloria.

"Not a hundred percent," said Jack. He picked up what Uncle Homer had thrown at them—a length of chain, a little shorter than the length of Jack's arm. He held it up, to the Broadwees' cackle.

"Well, this means they know. That's how I read this chain," said Jack. "So help is still forthcoming, somewhere behind."

"They're all up there just sitting and listening to 'emselves talk, Jack," said Gloria.

"Recounting for Granny some tale or another about me?" he wondered.

"This is going to be another one if you aren't careful."

"There's another cloud of dust coming from the other way," said Mrs. Moody.

"And a whopper!" said Jack. "What that means is Better Friendship has turned 'em loose and a lot of hungry Methodists are headed home for dinner."

"Church people! Now they'll be my answer," said Mrs. Moody. "They'll stop and help." She composed a long face and moved forward.

"Watch out for your feet, Mrs. Judge," cautioned Jack.

Mrs. Moody raised Judge Moody's hat and started to wave it at the line coming, buggies and some wagons and a clacking Ford coupe all in one cloud of dust.

"What are your Methodists *like?*" Mrs. Moody cried, as one after the other they went driving past her.

"Well, Aycock is one," said Jack.

"Why won't they stop for a fellow worshipper, at least?" she cried, still waving Judge Moody's Panama.

"His attendance has been middling-poor," Jack answered. "For the last year and a half it's been down to nothing. His church may have forgotten what he looks like."

"I'd just like to see a bunch of Presbyterians try to get by me that fast!" said Mrs. Moody.

"There went Preacher Dollarhide, I believe. He must have worked up a fairly decent appetite," observed Jack, as the Ford coupe rushed the length of Jack's ditch and got past a buggy.

"Why, you didn't even help me make 'em stop!" Mrs. Moody exclaimed. "I believe you waved 'em on by!"

"It's my wife and baby Judge Moody saved, Mrs. Judge," Jack told her gravely. "And I feel right particular about my help."

"Now watch out—there's something else coming down that funny little road," warned Mrs. Moody.

Something that resembled a fat moon drawn in pink chalk had popped up on the rise of the farm track. It just sat there for the moment, as if waiting to be believed. It was the Banner school bus with the dust of all summer on it. It looked empty. Then Elvie's little face could be made out, framed in the lower half of the steering wheel.

Judge Moody jabbed a finger. "That child going for help?"

"It's her opinion she *is* the help!" said Jack.

"I object to being at the mercy of a school bus fully as much as my husband objects to a chicken wagon," Mrs. Moody said, as it waited there above them, with its jawless face, every metal part below the headlight sockets gone. "Now that's just not going to tow me."

"Not towed! Not with the Buick still trying so hard to go the other way!" cried Jack. "You're about to be one end of the best tug-o'-war ever seen around Banner!"

"Under no circumstances!" exclaimed Judge Moody.

"Judge Moody, I ain't going to hear No!" cried Jack. "Ears Broadwee, you and Emmett get up and give Judge and Mrs. Moody your seats on my syrup stand. Show some manners! You forgotten all you know while I been gone?"

They scrambled to their feet, strung themselves out along the foot of the bank, elbowing their way in with the cosmos.

"Judge Moody, they wouldn't make school buses if they couldn't stand their share of punishment," said Jack. "Take heart, because this is the one I used to drive myself." He hollered, "Let 'er come!"

"Clear the way or be run over," came Elvie's serious voice, and the school bus came dropping toward them, not running on its engine. It came like an owl on the glide, not quite touching the banks on either side. Scraped-up and bulging like the Ark, it slammed into the ditch, then on one bounce was elevated onto Banner Road, in perfect starting position to go to school. "I coasted!" she shrieked at Judge Moody, who sank to a seat on the stand to let her coast on past him, headed down the hill. Queenie, Pete, and Slider tore after it barking, Queenie on her way frisking wildly around a Broadwee, nipping him and then running off with his cut of watermelon.

"Keep a hold, Elvie!" Jack was running alongside. "Begin thinking where you'll stop."

"It's a relic, that's all it is!" called Mrs. Moody after all of them.

"Elvie Renfro, *can* you stop?" called Gloria, and the bus swerved at last and gave a big crack as it put itself back in the ditch again nearly at the bottom of the hill. The signal arm flipped out and, bright as a bunch of nasturtiums, rusty water spurted from the capless radiator.

Elvie sprang out into Jack's arms, carrying her water bucket.

"Oh, I always said I was going to drive one of them things before I died," said Elvie, raised in the air. "I wisht it'd been full of all the little girls I know, that's all."

"That was real sisterly, Elvie. Thank you," said Jack. "Who give you the first push?"

"Nobody. I pulled out the chunk and run for it," she said. "Say, will it crank?"

Jack had scrambled into the driver's seat. His foot beat the floor.

"What you fixing to do with it?" called Elvie adoringly. "Give Moody a last push?"

"Whoa, Elvie! I'm fixing to save him!"

She shrieked and ran for home.

The engine turned over once and died. Stomp as he would, Jack got no more sign out of it. "One more vacation has ruined one more battery," he said. "Every year, this old bus needs a little more encouragement to go. I feel sorry for this year's driver."

"Then feel sorry for your own brother," said Gloria.

"Vaughn Renfro?" he yelled.

"Instead of the most popular, the best speller gets it now," Gloria said.

"Well, he's already let a seven-year-old girl get the thing away from him!" Jack cried.

"I hate to see the next piece of help that comes out of *that* little road," said Mrs. Moody.

"You're about to see it now," called Aycock.

There was a clopping and a jingling, and Etoyle came riding down the track astride the mule, bareback, loaded with trace chains. She was barefooted, sawing Bet's ribs with her heels. When she fetched out onto the road, she bent over in a fit of laughter, and everybody could see her little flat chest ridgy as a church palm-fan, naked and quivering inside her dress.

"What's the word from home?" Jack greeted her over the barking.

" 'Don't let that baby fall.' "

"Ain't they been brought more up to date than that?" He took the chains, helped giggling Etoyle to the ground, then he sat up sideways on Bet and scratched her forehead. The mule wagged him up the road and onto the path up Banner Top, between fallen fence posts, through the plum bushes onto the clicking limestone. His shoulders were jolted as if by hard sobs, but when Bet turned him around at the tree they could see his face shining with pleasure.

He dropped to the ground and went fast to work with the chains. Bet posed sideways to the road; her markings were like the brown velour swag that goes over the top of a Sunday School piano. Then he slid astride her.

"Come on, Jack boy! Now!" shouted one of the Broadwees.

"What's the matter with Ren-fro?
He's all right!"

the Broadwees sang.

"Jack's not playing basketball any longer," Gloria broke out. "He's got his diploma."

"He's hitched that chain around that tree and the car, yes. But when the unknown quantity starts to pulling?" Judge Moody stood up.

"That tree's gonna give," chanted the Broadwees, and Mrs. Moody turned and commanded them: "Suppose you just pray."

Jack spoke into Bet's ear. But, drooping a long, kid-white, white-lashed eyelid, she balked.

"You want me to swap you for a chain-saw?" cried Jack.

There was an explosion, and he all at once sat on empty air. The trace chains flew in two as Bet shot, in a rippling cloud of pink,

**136**

madly down to the road. Jack pounded down the face of the bank to head her off. The Moodys rose to the plank of the syrup stand, where they stood with uncertain footing, and the Broadwees had already scattered. Gloria hugged Lady May tightly and hid the baby's face, while Jack ran to throw out his arms to guard them, and Bet went picking her way up the home track, as if to tell her story.

"Did you hear that bang?" Mrs. Moody asked her husband. "It sounded almost like a blowout."

"The one thing it couldn't be," he said.

"Yes sir," Jack called when he returned to the car. "Mrs. Moody's right. A blowout—that's what Bet was objecting to. It was your spare."

The baby, hearing the Broadwees laugh, wailed very loud, and the Broadwees helped her by bellowing, "Boo, boo, boo!"

"Just keep on," Gloria addressed them. "Boo some more. I want you to show our visitors just how ill-behaved Banner can be. Do your most, Emmett, Joe, VanCleave, Wayne, T.T., and Ears Broadwee. I expect it of you."

"Sorry, Teacher. Sorry, we're sorry," they said, drooping.

"All right, boy, when're you going to start getting the kind of help that'll do us some good?" Mrs. Moody asked Jack, pointing her finger at him.

"Don't be downhearted, Mrs. Judge! I've got a full reunion still to draw on!"

"And not one is going to do you a bit more good than your little seven-year-old crybaby sister," cried Gloria.

He scudded down to the road. "Sweetheart!"

"The most they ever do for you is brag on you."

He bent to search her face, while the baby placed a tear-covered hand against his cheek and patted it.

"Gloria," he said gently. "You know all the books, But about what's at home, there's still a little bit left for you to find out. Not all of 'em brag so foolish—here comes Papa right now."

"Well, I rather your papa than your mama," called Aycock.

Mr. Renfro had come into sight on the farm track. Elvie came with him, singing:

> *"Yield*
> *not to temp-*
> *ta-*
> *tion*

*for*
*yielding is*
*sin,"*

as she came down the steep track. Giving one skip to either side, she kept time to the homesick, falling tune in a sweet voice like plucking strings. Little by little, like a pigeon stepping down a barn roof, Mr. Renfro stepped his way behind her, then together they made the high step out of the ditch onto the road.

Mr. Renfro lifted his old felt hat to Mrs. Moody and Gloria, acknowledged Lady May's stare of recognition with one of his own, then came in a Sunday manner up to the Judge.

"Old man, are you connected to the telephone?" asked Judge Moody before he could begin. "Excuse me, but I believe I'm in a bigger hurry than you are."

With his drill shirt and pants Mr. Renfro had put on a mended dark blue suit coat, tight on his body as a boy's or even a girl's jacket. His shirt was still buttoned tight to his Adam's apple, and a pinch of traveller's joy had been freshly poked into his lapel.

"There's a telephone down to what's known as Stovall's store in Banner if anybody's getting ready to have a fit," he said.

"Then you can just go back, old man," Mrs. Moody exclaimed. "We know enough about that already."

"Why, this is Mr. Renfro," he said. "I reside right up that road." He turned to Judge Moody, who still wore the handkerchief across his lower face. "Been carrying Mrs. Moody for her Sunday ride? I hope she's fairly well. You seen anything lately of my son?" He gave a formal scan of the road.

"Take a peep over your head, sir," said Elvie, giggling.

Mr. Renfro glanced up Banner Top, then whistled.

"Papa!" said Jack, as he came running from the well, bringing him a glass of water. "You didn't need to be the one to come. What brought you forth?"

"Sensed undue commotion," said Mr. Renfro after he had drunk. "Nobody that left the house come back, and the mule come back by herself." He pointed at Banner Top. "I don't right exactly know how you managed it."

"I can't take the full credit, sir," Jack said, as Gloria blushed. "We all kind of managed it together."

"I'm glad to hear you admit it, son. You couldn't bring something like that to pass just by trying," Mr. Renfro said. "But I don't see how you could hardly improve on it for showing how to go about a thing the wrong way." He handed Jack the glass and struck out across the road and set his good foot on the bank that ran straight up.

"Papa, it don't need you!" Jack said, catching up with him and stopping him, giving an earnest look into his face.

"Mr. Renfro," Gloria said, "what the rest of us are busy doing is finding a way to bring the car down in the road again without letting Jack drive it."

"Well, I kind of wonder, now, which one of you's been giving the other more trouble," said Mr. Renfro, eyes bright, looking from Jack to Judge Moody. "It's a good thing for everybody I come along."

"Papa," said Jack, "there's no call for you to be in a rush about it."

"Why, there most certainly is a call," said Mrs. Moody.

"The old cedar tree is your drawback," said Mr. Renfro. "That's plain to see from right here. Yes, and that's a pretty stubborn old cedar. I'd like to up it out of your way for you."

"Oh yes, and scar the finish of my automobile!" exclaimed Mrs. Moody. "You're not going to come chopping around my car with any old axe."

"Papa, that Buick got where it is by cheating its way around that tree. We got to pull it back the same way—that's the answer."

"May be your answer, son. I got a more seasoned one," said Mr. Renfro. He tilted back his head and ran his gaze up the tree. "Good people, I can tell you pretty quick what's called for, and that is to spring it."

"What do you mean, spring it?" Mrs. Moody asked.

"Well, talking won't bring it down," he said kindly.

"Just a minute, mister," Judge Moody said. "I'd better talk to you next, and quick, I think."

"Let's you and me go up there," said Mr. Renfro, giving him a sudden grin of conspiracy. "We ain't too old for a little sortie to the top, are we? I reckon you're about my age."

"Papa, Mrs. Judge would have a fit," Jack stammered out.

"My son thinks his dad may be a speck out of practice. But I think if you asked enough of the right people, you'd find I'm pretty well known around Banner for the results I get," said Mr. Renfro to the Moodys.

"I'd like to point something out!" Judge Moody was saying.

"Mr. Renfro, we've got Aycock sitting *in* the car," Gloria said.

"Now I wouldn't a-done that either," he said instantly.

"It's his fault," Mrs. Moody cried.

"Well, now," said Mr. Renfro. "That changes the picture. It means going a little less heavy on the charge than I was first inclined."

"Charge?" asked Mrs. Moody, while the Judge could be heard breathing.

"Plain, common old dynamite, it's the reliable," said Mr. Renfro quietly.

"Preposterous!" said Judge Moody. The baby, who had been growing restless, smiled as his new word came popping through the handkerchief.

"I can just see visions of that! To be saved from falling to the bottom of nowhere by getting blown sky-high with a stick of dynamite!" said Mrs. Moody. "Honestly!"

"I'd have to send home for the materials, that's all. I've got bringers," said Mr. Renfro. "Sunday don't put a stop to me a minute, not when it's a need of setting my son a little straighter."

Jack laid both his hands on his father's shoulders, and Gloria spoke. "Mr. Renfro, Jack doesn't need you to rally up your dynamite for him. All he needs is a wife's common sense, and he's got that right here."

Mr. Renfro gave her the same kind of little bow that he often gave Miss Beulah.

"That's right," said Jack. "I could've already jumped that Buick around that tree and backed her down in a cloud of fiery dust in her own tracks, but Gloria run in too quick with her common sense."

"And here's a piece of mine: I'm not going to let any old man go lighting a stick of dynamite under my car, Oscar," said Mrs. Moody. "I warn you."

"Under the tree," Mr. Renfro corrected her gently. "Well, sir, we all have to stop doing what our good ladies tells us not to, and try to make out with doing what's left," he said to Judge Moody, the light going out of his eyes. "If you rather get Stovall, and for what Stovall charges, I won't be mad at you. Now what he'll come up with is a pair of oxen. Just as set on mischief as they can be, both of 'em, as you'll know if you can read the glints in their eyes right well. And you ain't going to like Stovall's work or be crazy about his behavior or his oxens' behavior. And I'm not promising that after he's had his go at you, you won't all run crying back to me." Mr. Renfro put his hat back on. "And now I must plead company. The good ladies is about to make use of some tables spread under the trees. Jack," he turned to his son and said, "it's dinner time."

"Thank you, Papa. Tell Mama to please keep holding it."

"Papa's feelings is hurt," said Elvie, patting her father's hand.

"Papa, Elvie let the school bus run right smack dab in the ditch," said Etoyle, popping down off the syrup stand.

"Why, come back to me, Elvie. Can't you show respect for your family any better than that? That's Vaughn's bus." Mr. Renfro pointed at Banner Top as though nothing unusual attached to it any longer. "Growing up there you'll find a crop of switches. Bring me one."

"Papa, me and Etoyle ain't allowed to go up there, we're too little! That's for sweethearts!"

"Prance."

Frantically, Elvie climbed up and hopped back down. Mr. Renfro took a switch, the lightest of the three she offered, and gave her legs the least brief stinging. Then he dropped the switch, lifted his hat, sent a reserved glance all the way around him, then whistled to the baby once like a far-away train, and mounted his road. Elvie passed him, speeding home to start her crying ahead of him.

The baby, looking over her mother's arm, peep-eyed at Judge Moody with the puff of her sleeve.

"That infant ought to be home," he fumed. "The help of babies and old men is getting us nowhere."

"Of course none of these people have any idea of how to get that car down. They're all one family!" said Mrs. Moody.

"Judge and Mrs. Judge, don't be downhearted. Banner is still my realm," Jack said.

"It doesn't sound like your realm to me," said Mrs. Moody. "If you don't have the phone or the team of oxen or any way to get visitors out of here."

"We got people," said Jack. "The best thing in the world."

"I don't need anything but a single piece of machinery in good working order and a tow line," said Judge Moody.

"And a driver," said Jack. "If you'd just waited and tried us about next Saturday, you'd had it all—me and my truck and a tow rope all ready for your holler."

"All I hope is by that time we're not still up there teetering!" Mrs. Moody cried.

Around the legs of both Moodys, Aycock's bony hounds endlessly darted and shied, loudly sniffing, like ladies being unjustly accused.

"Could we possibly get rid of these dogs?" asked Judge Moody.

"Can I whistle 'em inside with me?" Aycock called.

"No!" everybody cried, and Jack said, "They'd be in the driver's seat in no time."

There was another explosion. Jack charged up the bank.

"That was your right front!" he called in a moment. "A good old Firestone tire with the tread still on it. I believe they're overheating. One way to stop 'em is let the air out of the others before they start copying!"

"Keep your hands off—they're safer just blowing out," said Judge Moody. "Dear," he said to his wife, "how much air did you have put in our tires?"

"The maximum," she said. "I always order the maximum when I get anything for you."

"The maximum air? Then just give the others time," said Judge Moody. He looked at the car and gave a short bark of laughter.

"Now cut it out, Oscar. You're about to start feeling sorry for yourself. I'll tell you one thing," Mrs. Moody said. "If that car hasn't fallen to its destruction before much else happens, it wasn't intended to fall."

"How much longer do you think Providence is prepared to go on operating on our behalf?" the Judge asked her.

"Keep talking like that and it'll fall right now!" she exclaimed. "Oscar, instead of tempting Providence, you'd do better to head on down this road to that store that's all locked up. And if you don't see the man around, climb in through the window."

"And you know what somebody'd pop up and call it? Trespassing," said Jack.

"Yes, I'd call it that," said Judge Moody. "But if we knew where this man was to be found—if we had his ear in this—"

"He's safe out in a rowboat," cried Jack. "Though if he only knew what you wanted with him, he'd be right there to say No!

And I'd tackle him for you on the spot, and while you cranked up Miss Pet Hanks, I'd be setting on his chest where I could pound some willingness in him."

"There's not too much wrong with any of that, that I can see," said Mrs. Moody in a piteous voice. "Not if it allows you to use the telephone, Oscar."

"Direct me instead to the man with those oxen," Judge Moody told Jack.

"Still out floating in a boat, still the same scoundrel," said Jack. "And anything else you want to think of, that you'd like to have, old Curly's the one that's got it."

"If we had nothing but a good solid truck!" stormed Judge Moody.

"He's got it. He's got mine!" Jack told him. "With no right in the world to a single bolt of it. Before I got the last lick on it, he got ahold of it and they tell me it's down there inside his old iron shed with the iron shutter rung down on it and the padlock staring at you! Laying in a few more pieces now than it was when it's ornamenting my front yard, from the benefit of the trip! I bet you a penny he wishes he hadn't done it."

"Somebody might have to walk all the way to Foxtown," Judge Moody said to his wife. "And call from that icehouse."

"They haven't got a phone. They don't need a phone," said Jack. "But outside help—even if you could try 'em, ain't they shut? It's Sunday in the courthouse too, ain't it?"

"Then what is the answer, in all the sovereign State of Mississippi?" demanded the Judge of his wife.

"You've still got to prove it to me you want to *get* where you're going," said Mrs. Moody. "I see plenty of misgivings in your face."

"Right through the handkerchief?" asked Etoyle curiously.

"Right through the handkerchief," said Mrs. Moody.

When he gave a hapless swing of the arms, she walked up to him. "All right, dear." She put his hat on him. She took him by the shoulders and said, "March. To the ends of the earth if need be. Only bring me back somebody with the wherewithal and the gumption to get it back for me."

"Just so he keeps in hollering distance of Banner Top," said Jack. "We don't want Judge Moody to get lost."

"Lost? What do you think he is now?" said Mrs. Moody.

Judge Moody stood still a moment longer, then faced in the direction away from Banner.

"If you come to anybody with some boiled peanuts, I could go through a pack of 'em right now!" Aycock called down.

"Buster, you pay attention to *your* job!" cried Mrs. Moody.

"In what manner and at exactly what moment did he ever get *in* that car?" Judge Moody paused to ask her. "Did you see him do it?"

"No, dear. I was too busy trying to steer you," she said.

✑

But it was getting hotter everywhere before they were faced with another red cloud of dust, travelling from the direction of Halfway Forks. Coming out of it was a grinding noise.

Gloria clutched Jack by his belt. He was holding Lady May, and her little face rose just above his like a head-lamp, where she had wrestled her way up his neck and now clamped his ears with her elbows. "Jack, there's something I haven't told you."

"Save it till after dinner," Jack urged Gloria.

"Here it is. There's somebody in the world, and not very far away, that could pull that car down in a second, if he wanted to."

"Then he's got to have something with more power than a dozen mules he can pull *with!*" he cried.

"He has," she said. Closer now a chirping as from a load of baby chicks was added to the grinding.

"My truck! Or I'll eat it! I can just look in your face and read how right I am!" he gasped. "Curly's got it on the road without me!"

"Life don't just stop!" she cried.

"Holy Moses!" he yelled, and the baby clapped her hands over his mouth, opening her own wide.

At first only two yellowed globes, that caught light from the sun, could be seen through the dust, set like the eyes of a locust in the roof. Then a pair of oxhorns could be made out pushing up the road toward them, with a spread wider than the fenders behind them, all but scraping the banks.

"Why, here comes the very thing!" Mrs. Moody exclaimed.

**144**

"Like it sprung right out of the ground! Providence sent that. My husband only had to turn his back."

Jack pulled Lady May over his head as he would pull off a tight undershirt and set her on the ground, and staggered for a minute.

"I hated to break it to you—I waited till it was the last minute, before you'd find it out for yourself," Gloria said.

"You was just being the best little wife you knew how," he agreed in a painful voice. Then all of a sudden he shouted, "Mrs. Judge! Now I'm going to save your car by hook or by crook! Honey, you and Lady May get back from the road, about as far as the well," he cried to Gloria.

"But Jack, you know what we are here for!"

"Then put your heads down!"

"To think you would ask me to hide," she said sadly, going behind the syrup stand into the goldenrod and cosmos and down on mulberry leaves with her baby.

"Go home, Queenie! Go home, Pete and Slider! Go ask Aycock's mama for your bone. There ain't going to be nothing here for you!" Jack told the dogs. They skidded in their tracks, then turned and loped off down the road. Gloria from her hiding place let out a cry—in Queenie's mouth were both of Lady May's shoes. "And you lean back, Aycock, just look straight ahead where you're going! Old Curly's rolling right here in my truck, never dreaming." He whirled and disappeared up the farm track.

Mrs. Moody was already advancing into the center of Banner Road. She stood waving her purse, as steadily as a train brakeman with a lantern, guiding the truck to a stop. Strips of adhesive tape rayed sunset style from a hole in the middle of the windshield, but a large red face showed itself around it and advanced out the window and held itself there cheek up, as if waiting for a kiss. It was slick and jowled as a big vine-ripe bell pepper.

"Lady," said the thin voice of a fat man, "is that your car gone through the fence up there?"

"Of course it's mine!" she said. "Can't you see me flagging you down?"

"Then what's it doing on Banner Top? Can't you read? Every one of those signs along that fence says 'Keep Off.' You're trespassing."

"Trespassing! On as wild and forsaken a spot on earth for a

hot and breathless Sunday as I ever saw in my wildest dreams?" she cried. "Don't make me indignant!"

"Who told you you could run a pleasure car up yonder and leave it, lady? That's a spot just waiting to give trouble. Full of temptations of all kinds. You know what that car's asking for?"

"Listen here, I want to talk business with you, mister," said Mrs. Moody. "Do you know who I am?"

A head of cosmos wagged, and Jack came down the home track with his spring-heeled walk.

"Can you tell a stranger which is the quickest way to Banner?" he asked.

"Huh?" Then the deacony voice changed into a roar. A two-hundred-pound man in the prime of life rocked out of the cab, his boot heels striking the road and reviving the dust. He threw out both red arms. Jack at the same moment charged on him, and they began pumping on each other's backs.

"Thought you wasn't due till hog-killing time!"

"Trying to run off with my truck, you skunk!" Jack cried. "Giving her the last lick behind my back!" He scooped up a chunk from the ditch and ran to lay it under a front wheel.

Curly Stovall's curls were stacked like three-pound scale weights across the breadth of his forehead; they bounced with his laughter. Behind him, the truck's hood, fenders, and the railings around its bed all jumped too under their thatches of dust with the commotion of the motor. Some fishing canes lashed to the cab roof sawed on one another, and the open door danced on its single hinge.

"Yeah, I did that truck a favor, Jack!"

"She sure stuttered hard enough getting up this hill," said Jack, and ran up the hood. The engine stormed in all their ears.

"I want to talk business," Mrs. Moody called, raising her voice against it.

"Curly, I'm holding my judgment till I see her tested!" cried Jack.

"Wait till you see her going down," said Curly Stovall. "I'm on my way home now."

"How's Miss Ora, and how did you get away from her?" asked Jack. "How's the old store? Falling to pieces?"

"Jack, times is no better since you left. Nearly all my trade's trying to get me to starve to death, I can't get a bit of satisfaction.

Ain't hardly a Banner soul going to make a crop again."

"Whose troubles am I here to listen to? Yours or mine?" called Mrs. Moody, standing close.

"There wasn't but one answer, Jack. Run for office," said Curly.

"I hate for poor, hard-working Miss Ora to see how bad you'll get beat," said Jack.

"By Homer and that rattle-trap, shimmy-tail chicken wagon of his? Wait for Tuesday's explosion! This truck is my answer to Homer. A solid-built, all-round, A-one, do-all truck!" Curly Stovall's voice rose to a tenor yell over the clamorous motor. "It's ready for anything and everything, you name it—from hauling in their hay for 'em to pulling 'em out when they get stuck, before they go out of sight in Banner mud. Any act of neighborly kindness a justice of the peace can offer will be furnished cheap at the price."

Mrs. Moody pinched each one of them by his shirtsleeve. "Look at my car!" she cried.

"That's where I been this morning, doing a few little neighborly acts of kindness. I been to see the bedridden," said Curly Stovall. "And the shut-ins. Promised 'em I'm coming back on Tuesday and carry 'em every one to the polls. Old Mr. Hugg clapped his hands!"

"What you fixing to do right now, Curly?" asked Jack.

"It's a big all-out fish-fry on the sandbar! It's my last Sunday and I'm showing my hospitality."

"Look at my car!" Mrs. Moody cried, shaking her purse at him.

"Go a step further and you're going to be in badder trouble," he said.

"I have no intention of going a step further!" she cried.

"Why, do look at that car up there. Like a ladybug on a red rose!" said Jack. "How did a lady driver ever find her way up by herself?"

Curly Stovall squinted, then suddenly pointed his finger. "Not by herself! She's got another one in that car right now. Yonder's a man's head." He raised his prim voice another octave. "Hey, blooming idiot! This is the law! We discourage fools from riding up there on dangerous ground, you hear me? Bring that Buick back down here and set it in the road!"

Aycock was now holding an imaginary steering wheel in front of him, giving it some fast spins.

"Curly, squint harder. That fellow's in the *back* seat. He's nothing but just a harmless passenger," said Jack. "Don't let him fool you."

Curly turned to Mrs. Moody. In a voice beginning to sound almost respectful he asked, "How long a while you had that Buick and him up there, lady?"

"Forever is what it seems like!" she cried.

"Well, tell your blooming passenger to step up front and grab the wheel and pitch on down here," Curly Stovall cried. "We don't tolerate showing off like this from the passing public."

"Now listen," Mrs. Moody said with spirit. "It's my car. That idiot or any other idiot is not to touch that wheel, not for love or money."

"Then I got something to tell you. If you don't make him drive it off there in a pretty big hurry and of your own sweet accord, lady, I'm going to go up there and *haul* it down *for* you. Tied to the tail of my truck," Curly Stovall said primly, as Jack slapped both knees.

"The very thing I wanted!" cried Mrs. Moody. "If men would ever stop long enough to heed what's being told 'em! Now hurry! Before my husband gets back, hear? Wait till he finds I stayed right in one place and and without budging accomplished twice as much as he could."

"It'll be a dollar," said Curly Stovall. "In cash."

"Now wait, are you somebody reliable?" she asked at the same time.

"Reliable?" cried Jack. "Lady, this is old Curly Stovall. Everybody knows him! He's the storekeeper in Banner and he's a rascal and a greedy hog and a few more things—you can rely on him for all of 'em. Go ahead and show her, Curly—start riding!" He slammed down the hood of the truck. When he muffled the motor as he did, the soft lisp of the Buick engine went floating over their heads.

A thin little cry came from Curly Stovall's deacony mouth. "You trying to tell me that car's sitting out on the edge of nowhere with nobody to the wheel and nothing in front to stop it, and running on its engine?"

"Just breaking its heart to go over," said Jack.

"Then what's it waiting on! What's been holding it back?" Curly shouted at him.

"The Lord is looking after me and my husband," said Mrs. Moody in a sharp voice. "That's what's been holding it back! Now, then!"

"Cut that engine!" cried Curly Stovall.

"The fellow's arms ain't long enough, unless he grows 'em longer, waiting on your help," said Jack. "You heard this lady pass the law he can't move from where he's riding."

"Let him try budging one inch," said Mrs. Moody.

"Oh, I know better than budge," said Aycock at once.

"Wait," Curly said. "That voice had a Banner ring."

"Open them coon eyes a little wider," said Jack. "Ain't there the least little bit about that pumpkinhead to remind you of somebody you know?"

Aycock screwed his head clear around and grinned out the back window like a Jack-o'-lantern.

"Aycock Comfort!" Curly Stovall yelled. "What're you doing home and in a Buick car on Banner Top?"

"Just sitting," said Aycock.

"You didn't get there by yourself!" Curly whirled on Jack. The curls rolled down on his forehead as he lowered his head and said, "*Now* things is taking on the complexion of the rest of your tricks, Jack Renfro. Now it's starting to look natural and sound natural and feel natural around Banner! I feel like I just had a good dose of tonic! All right, what's been your hand in this?"

"I'm the Good Samaritan! And I've been it just about all day!" Jack hollered.

"You run this lady's car up on Banner Top yourself and for my benefit, didn't you, and just waited till I come along?"

"Honestly!" cried Mrs. Moody.

"Curly, I be dog if I did!" said Jack. "And this poor lady, I'd had her down long ago and she knows it, only I got the news broke to me this morning that even before you stole my truck you already went off with my horse!"

"How did your mule handle it?"

"About the way you reckon!"

"I wouldn't have your mule for all you'd pay me!"

"Is anybody listening to me?" cried Mrs. Moody.

"Lady, I just went up a dollar on you," said Curly Stovall, not moving from where he stood, gazing upward.

"As long as that Buick's holding to the same spot, Curly, she'll behave," Jack told him. "She's reposing in the sweetest balance you ever saw in your life, with her frame sitting right on a hickory sign donated to Banner Top by my Uncle Nathan, and not a minute too soon."

"I wouldn't trust any of his work, he lives without a penny," said Curly Stovall.

"You just wouldn't hardly believe what's the case up there. You wouldn't hardly believe the balance she's in, without giving her a little rock to test her yourself," said Jack. "There she sits, singing along, good as gold, fighting along against the laws of gravity, and just daring you to come near her. But the lady wants her down and you want her down—"

Curly Stovall leaned back against the truck, his purpled arm resting on the cab window. "Jack, I swear I don't know what I been doing without you."

"I'd been here the whole time, had the sayso been mine."

"No sir, there ain't nobody upped to start a blessed thing under my nose, not since you been gone. Banner just as well been dead!"

"It won't take long to wake it up now!" Jack said. "Me, you, and Aycock all doing our part!"

"Start, then!" cried Mrs. Moody. "Get busy! And remember! Don't get on the inside of my car, don't scratch the outside finish, and don't be in too big a rush coming down and tip over my chocolate cake—"

There came a loud report from the Buick.

"What was that?" asked Curly Stovall in a thin voice.

"Blowout number three," Jack told him. "I'm betting it's the other front wheel."

"Hurry, mister!" Mrs. Moody cried, as Curly made a lunge toward Jack and put up a fist. They both began weaving with their feet.

"Lady, how Jack prevailed on you to run your own car up there to start with, I still ain't made up my mind. How Aycock's keeping it from taking off the ground, it's a little early to ask him. All I got to tell you is Jack Renfro's home again and it's starting to get away too natural around Banner!"

"But aren't you going to keep your word?" Mrs. Moody cried.

"You ain't caught me as easy as you think, lady," said Curly, dancing on his toes. "Because listen to me—I don't do Sunday business! 'Tain't the law and 'tain't Christian!"

"And that's all I'm waiting for!" Jack shouted, and made a leap for the open cab door.

Curly was ready for him, spun him around, and climbed up and rammed himself in behind the steering wheel.

"Have I spoken of Providence too soon?" Mrs. Moody cried.

"Hitch over! Either move your carcass or get out!" Jack yelled.

"What're you trying to do now, steal my truck?" Curly yelled back. The engine was still pounding, the sheaf of fishing canes arching above the cab roof and hanging over the sides quivered their length like the whiskers of some oversized store cat.

"I'm taking the wheel! I'm going up and get this lady's suffering Buick down, what do you reckon?" yelled Jack. "I'm going to fire up this truck and save that Buick right in front of your eyes!"

"Oh, is that the case!" said Curly. "First you coaxed that car up Banner Top, by ways best known to you, planted Aycock inside, and you rigged up a trap for me so pretty I nearly fell in. All I had to do was rebuild the truck and pump in three gallons of gas and drive it past the right place at the right time, and turn it over to you to save one more lady. All right, I'm going to tell you what *is* the case! *I'm* going to go ahead and save her while you watch, and not charge you a dime for the privilege or your daddy a dime. I'll just charge the lady."

"Hurrah!" Mrs. Moody cried to Heaven. "He's giving in!"

"And you want to know why I'm treating you like a son, Jack? It's because old Curly Stovall is sorry for you!" Curly hollered.

"Jack! Jack, you're going right pale!" cried Gloria, running out from behind the syrup stand with the crumbles of mulberry leaves pressed into her flashing legs. She set Lady May down on her own little feet and tried to help Jack rise.

"Well, hello, Peaches!" said Curly Stovall.

"*Sorry* for me? Did you hear Curly say it? Nobody ever dared in his whole life to be sorry for Jack Renfro! Nobody in Banner or nowhere else ever so much as threatened to be sorry for me!" said Jack, holding onto Gloria.

"That's the way it used to be, but it ain't that way no longer!" Curly hollered. "It's time you had your eyes opened, Jack—you come home to be pitied!"

Jack staggered where he stood. Gloria fanned his face with little bats of both hands. Lady May held to her mother's knees and wailed.

"Curly don't know what he's talking about, Lady May," said Jack, and she wailed louder. He took a running jump and landed with both feet on the running board.

"Jack, you ain't got a prayer of getting this truck away from me, don't you know it?" said Curly, inside.

"When it's mine already? Something I made out of nothing, using about a ton of my own sweat?" Jack wrenched at the vibrating door against Curly's pull. "Man alive, I'm taking what belongs to me!"

Curly Stovall leaned out the window into Jack's face, his small mouth stretching into a grin. "Then ask your daddy! What do you think he give me to pay for that new tin roof? To keep folks from feeling sorry for your whole family?"

Jack tumbled backwards and sat down in the road. Lady May shrieked and Gloria ran and threw herself at him. "Lady May means she never loved you worse than now—seeing you so crestfallen," she whispered, clutching him.

Curly blew the horn on the truck, adding to the racket a sound like the buzzing of a hundred flies.

"Come back here!" cried Mrs. Moody, as he raised the throttle.

"Didn't you hear me say I was on my way to a fish-fry I'm giving myself?" he called out the window.

"But you're who Providence sent, you big bully!" Mrs. Moody cried.

"I can't be late to my own fish-fry, can I? The sandbar's load-ing up with voters now. I got a lot of brethren waiting on me," said Curly. "And my *ice* is melting!"

"With a lady in trouble like mine, you're going off and *eat?*" she cried.

"Ladies tells Jack Renfro what to do, but they ain't got me by the nose," said Curly, as Jack got himself to his feet. "You all can try looking for me after milking time in the morning. I'll come back and see what story the night has told."

"Serve you right if by milking time in the morning there's nothing here left for you to save!" Mrs. Moody cried as the wheels passed over the chunk and the truck started rolling down Banner

Road. "Oh, why wasn't my husband here to take charge of that man? I doubt if he even realized who I was."

The truck plunged.

"Curly, that was a close call you had, a close call!" Jack yelled as he ran to keep up with it. "You nearly got yourself in a fix you couldn't even get out of by tomorrow, didn't you?"

"Drop back, you're licked!" called Curly. "Go on home and tell 'em! While I wind up my campaign in a blaze of glory!" Then there was a volley of backfire.

"We'll see who gets the glory!" Jack yelled into it. He stood still in the road, his back to the others, looking after the truck. Bales of dust tumbled behind it, then it made the blind curve and went out of sight. "I still, I *still* don't see how he ever got the thing on the road without me—his *or* mine," he said. "So far as I could tell, those horns is the extent of everything he thought of that I hadn't thought of first."

Gloria ran to him, brought him the baby.

"Gloria! What would you rather most of all I'd do to that skunk now?" he begged her to tell him.

"Give him up!" she cried.

"I'm on your side now, Gloria," said Etoyle. "Know why? Because you're the one that's bleeding."

"I should hope I am!" cried Gloria.

At the same time, there came a second clattering up the road from the direction of Halfway Forks. As wheels rattled to a stop, and an axle creaked, dust went up like a big revival tent with the flaps popping.

"Oscar!" Mrs. Moody cried when the white triangle of handkerchief emerged. Then, as the rest smoked into view, she said, "You've brought me nothing but another old man, with a team that looks about ready to fall down."

Halted at the start of the downgrade, Mr. Willy Trimble's mules with forefeet splayed might have just alighted from the upper air and struck Banner clay too hard.

"I expect it's the other way round, Mrs. Judge, and Mr. Willy found *him*," Jack told her. "He lives in the road. Good evening, Mr. Willy, the world treating you all right?"

"Ready for me to hitch my rope to your circus and give it a pull?" asked Mr. Willy, squinting up from under his hat brim at Banner Top.

"No sir, we still ain't reached that point yet," said Jack.

"Not saying I would if you's to ask me. Looks like it might be liable to hurt my reputation to touch it," said Mr. Willy.

Judge Moody was climbing down from the wagon still wrapped like a burglar against the dust. "I reckon I got fooled at the forks," he began.

"You ought to have stayed here! I managed to get hold of a great big truck!" said Mrs. Moody. "But there's strings tied to it."

"No Sunday business?" Judge Moody sighed.

"First the man *threatened* me with bringing down my car. Then he discovered that's what I wanted. So he said no Sunday business. I offered him everything in your pants pocket, but he went off to a fish-fry! At the last minute he said he'd come back here in the morning, and I consider I'm lucky just to be here—you might have had to bail me out of jail for trespassing!"

"Did you get his name?" asked Judge Moody.

"Oh, it's the same one, the storekeeper," she said. "He did have a truck after all—I'll spare you what I had to stand here and listen to!"

"You did a better job than I did, Maud Eva. I got to a forks. I could see just one house. In the teeth of a dozen dogs I pounded, but nobody came."

"That was the Broadwees' house, sir. Even the women don't stay home on Sunday," said Jack.

"I found him drooping, and carried him back to you, lady. Told him better to stay put with who he's with," said Mr. Willy. "Stand still: your answer always comes along."

"Yes indeed, I've seen just about every sample of it, counting you! And now I doubt if there's anybody left at this end of the world *to* come," Mrs. Moody said with indignation in her voice. "Just take a look at the emptiness of this road."

There were only the claybanks and themselves. Where the Broadwees had been standing there was a newly gouged-out "B" like a cat sitting on its tail, and the two halves of a watermelon, eaten out, had been left beside the syrup stand like a pair of shoes beside a bed.

"It's dinner time," said Jack. "And even the Broadwees has bowed out. I reckon they're down at the fish-fry."

"Oscar," Mrs. Moody said, "you are to shanghai the next thing on wheels that dares to come along here and make 'em carry you back to civilization where you can beat somebody over the head till they come and haul us."

"Cock your ears right now!" Etoyle cried.

Something came quaking over a Dry Creek bridge. Then a confused noise moved toward them up the road, again toward Banner, a rumble and creaking accompanied by a full register of women's voices.

"Shanghai that!" said Mrs. Moody. A short broad bus, painted blue, came over the rise.

"Why, that's a church bus, Mrs. Judge, and it's headed the other way—he can't turn *them* around," said Jack. "And it's packed tight. I wonder where it's coming from and where it's going so late."

The bus sagged sideways, behind Mr. Willy Trimble's wagon, then stopped. Out of every paneless window an excited face appeared.

"Gloria Short!" one of them cried, and then a smiling middle-aged lady in white hat and white dress leaned out of a forward window as far as her waist. "Dressed up and waiting by the side of the road! You looking for a ride?"

"No, Miss Pet, I'm not dressed up like this to go travelling," said Gloria.

"You look like you're fixing to get married all over again. What did you do to get so skinny?" another one cried. "Well, I believe it's becoming to you."

Jack came and stood in the road beside Gloria, and rested his hand on her shoulder.

"I see now what you're dressed up for! You got your husband back," said the smiling lady, who had the voice of a tease.

"I got him back this morning, Miss Pet."

"And I hope you were ready for him!"

"Tried to be."

"How many ladies is it?" Jack wondered aloud.

"This is a busload of schoolteachers, all of them teachers but Miss Pet Hanks," Gloria told Jack. "It looks like all the teachers of the Consolidated School System of Boone County. This is the first time any of them's come to see me since I was married."

His lips moved to her ear. "Honey, ask those teachers what they want with you now."

"You got some mighty dressed-up friends, too," said Miss Pet. "You-all doing your visiting here in the road?"

"They're waiting to leave in their car. Try looking straight up over my head," said Gloria.

"Why, that's Lover's Leap," said Miss Pet Hanks with a wink. "As we used to call it. And yonder's somebody hugging somebody in the back of that car in broad, open daylight."

"It's not somebody, it's just a guitar he's hugging," said Etoyle, who had been running and skipping up and down, up and down the bank without attracting much notice.

"He'd do better to back up instead. I wouldn't give you two cents for where I think he's headed," said a teacher.

"Looks like he aimed for the moon and didn't quite get there. I rather they all stayed on the ground," said the flower-hatted driver.

"He's about to go off over the edge of doom and there's not much you and I can do about it, Mrs. Grierson. We're only teachers," said a cranky voice from nearer the back.

"Some of *your* work?" Miss Pet Hanks playfully pointed her finger out the window at Jack.

Gloria said, "Jack's here to help, he feels called on."

"Then I only hope you've been standing by to keep him from making any more mistakes," said Miss Pet.

"That's exactly what I'm doing," Gloria said.

Jack gripped her closer. "Honey, ask 'em what's the calamity," he whispered.

"I declare, Gloria, we picked a busy day to find you, didn't we?" teased Miss Pet Hanks.

"We're not sparing any effort," said Gloria. "It may be a long story yet, getting that car down without a scratch."

"Well, I daresay it was quite a story how it got up there," said the cranky voice.

"It'll fall, and solve your problems," two other voices said in unison and then everybody in the bus laughed and the two speakers made a wish on it.

"Aycock Comfort!" Miss Pet Hanks exclaimed, as his face turned full toward them. "Imagine you being where you are!"

"Is he kin to any *Mrs*. Comfort?" asked a new and timid voice from the crowded, benchlike seat at the back end of the bus. "Mrs. Comfort that lives in walking distance of Banner School and wants to board the teacher?"

"Sure! If that's all you ladies came for, just keep going," Jack

**156**

said. "Take the last chance you get to turn off before you start down to the bridge—you have to squeeze around a big old blackjack oak, but if the school bus can make it, you can."

"If there's one thing I was hoping I wouldn't get, up here, it was bad news," said Aycock in the car.

"Good-bye, then," said Jack to the teachers.

"Good-bye," said Gloria.

Leaning out of the windows, some of them standing and peeping over the others' shoulders, they looked down from the bus at Gloria. They themselves were rainbow-dressed in Teachers' Meeting dresses of spring crêpe, teachers' hats shading their rouge spots, and their voices competed together like sisters'.

"Gloria Short, we're going all the way to Alliance," Miss Pet Hanks called through the others. "Miss Julia Mortimer dropped dead this morning and I rounded up every teacher I could find and said, 'Let's all go!' "

Gloria stood as if she had been struck in the forehead by a stone out of a slingshot.

"She took a fall in her own home," said an old lady's voice. "Nobody with her. Somebody had to *find* her. Home's the most dangerous place after all, they say."

Jack was supporting Gloria—she looked ready to fall backwards.

"I spread the news, the minute somebody started trying to find her doctor. It went through me," said Miss Pet Hanks. "Gloria, I rung two longs and a short all morning long in Stovall's store and nobody ever came to the phone to take the message. Well! Some exchanges would give up, but that isn't my style." She laughed excitedly.

"Is Gloria crying? I don't think she's crying yet," said a voice farther back in the bus.

"The baby's crying," said another.

"And so," said Miss Pet Hanks, "as long as we could come by Banner as easy as any other way, and we still had one seat, I says, 'Let's pile in the new teacher that goes to Banner School and dump her where she boards, and let's hunt up Gloria Short on Banner Road—and she can have Myrtle Ruth's seat and ride with us the rest of the way to Alliance.' I says, 'Kill two birds with one stone! Be inexcusable to go all that way with an empty seat.' "

As if on signal, the door of the bus swung open and the breath of the engine and the smell of candy mints spread out into the road.

"Come ride with a whole load of teachers and me! All going to pay tribute!" cried Miss Pet.

"She's quaking a little. Maybe she's going to have a fit," said a teacher.

"No she ain't," said Jack. He clamped Gloria to him.

"The reason I'm one of the bunch is somebody had to be smart enough to think up the trip," said Miss Pet. "We've got 'em from Gowdy, Roundtree, Stonewall, Medley, Foxtown, Flowery Branch, Freewill. And you're the last on the line."

"We started the minute church let out," said one of the other voices. "We borrowed the Presbyterian bus because it stays the hardest-scrubbed—it's from Stonewall. Isn't it the luckiest thing it's a Sunday she picked? Suppose it had been a school day, like tomorrow. We'd been cooped up."

"I'm never cooped up. I never consider myself cooped up," said Miss Pet Hanks, turning her head from side to side. "I'm a free soul, I am."

"Come on. You're still one of us, Gloria Short. Even though you didn't wear too well or last as long as we did," said the driver. "You can come without a hat—join the ride."

"Because remember all you owe her," said the old voice from back within.

"Owes her even more than we do. Owes her the most of all," said another voice.

"The most of all!" they chorused.

"Besides owing her part of your education, you were just an orphan!" said Miss Pet Hanks. "I reckon I know how you begun!"

"She loved you the best and prized you the most—*you* started out with three strikes against you," said the strict voice.

"What was the third strike?" asked Etoyle, with a pull on Gloria's sash.

Gloria handed her Lady May, then slowly tears ran down both cheeks.

"It was my inspiration to pick you up and carry you just the way we found you!" cried Miss Pet.

"You certainly made yourself easy enough to find, Gloria," said the driver. "We couldn't have missed you."

"And you aren't glad after all to see some fellow teachers again?" asked one. "Don't you appreciate still being counted?"

"Does your baby cry like that all the time?" the new teacher's tiny voice asked.

"She's crying for me." Gloria turned her face into Jack's shoulder and he patted her a little faster.

"All this happening to you on one pretty Sunday, I *wanted* to come hunting you and find out how you'd take it. I *wanted* to say 'Come ride with us' to see how quick you'd jump in," said Miss Pet Hanks, turning her rose face in its wide-brimmed hat from side to side again, as if to accept praise from all corners of the world. Judge and Mrs. Moody stood as still as the Uncle Sam by the road. Judge Moody with his head sunk.

"You wanted to kill two birds with one stone," Etoyle reminded Miss Pet Hanks. "Now I see the other bird. I see the new teacher's face staring, the one we're going to get tomorrow, oh-oh!"

"Raise your head, Possum. I'm here," Jack told Gloria.

"No, let her cry," voices said. "It's good for her. Good if she could cry a little harder."

"Listen at her now," said a teacher to the others. "Makes you wonder how often she's cried when there's nobody to hear her."

"Sure is lonesome up Banner way. I'd forgotten how lonesome," said another.

"This is getting close to Miss Julia's old stamping grounds, right here," said Miss Pet Hanks.

"Yes'm, another five miles or so further on, and at the bottom of the hill just before you get to that bridge. There's Banner School, if it hasn't blown away," the driver said.

"And how many tracked here once, going to school to Miss Julia? I did!" cried Miss Pet.

"Trudged! We didn't have a bus like that one yonder, did we? School buses! What they do best is get away from the driver," said the flower-hatted driver of the church bus. "Look at that one. Glad it's over in the ditch if *I've* got to pass it."

"When I was growing up close to Medley and trudging to school at Banner, the way there wasn't as forlorn-looking as it is today," said Miss Pet Hanks. "Not to me."

"Not to me either, young lady," said Mr. Trimble from his wagon. "Remember me, anybody? I'll try you, Thelma Grierson: '*Willy Trimble?—Hope Not!*' I sat behind you."

"Willy Trimble, you put my pigtail in your inkwell," replied the driver. "I remember you and I want you to hitch yourself a little closer to that ditch and hold onto those mules. Thirty ladies want to get by you."

"That's right—that dishpan full of chicken salad don't want to wait much longer. Try Gloria Short one more time, and if she won't jump in we'll go on without her, carrying a perfectly good empty seat across that bridge," said Miss Pet Hanks.

Jack said, "I'll speak for her. She ain't coming with you. I'm not letting her, that's why."

A black-bonneted, wrinkled face leaned out of a back window and the strict voice said, "Gloria Short, I'm as old as Julia myself. I think you just better find something to do with that husband of yours and climb on board and ride to Alliance while you get the chance. Or what's to keep you from being sorry in afteryears?"

Gloria put up her head and asked the busful, "What makes you think a mother would run off and leave her baby?"

"It's the other way round," said Etoyle, jumping up and down beside her, pointing her finger up. "Look in the peephole!"

Jack pounded down the road. In the upper wall of the bank where Banner Top rose straightest from the downslant of the road, the peephole faced them at this hour with a shadowless rim, showing the circle of sky no brighter than the clay around it, just a different color of the same substance, like a seal on a document. Lady May's face showed itself in it, peeped, went away. It reappeared, peeped, went away.

Jack was already clawing himself up the steep smooth wall below her, thrashing and swinging his body. In an instant he was halfway to the top, hanging spread-eagled to catch his first breath.

The baby's face went away and out poked her foot with its little shoe gone. From below, it looked white and airy as a waving handkerchief.

"Jack! Climb! Climb for your baby!" Gloria screamed.

Then Lady May's little leg and behind entered the hole and nearly came too far, like a too-small cork. At once she busied herself with trying to turn around in the hole, as if she meant all the time to take a seat there facing front, and all of a sudden she did it.

"Aycock! Jump! Run to my baby and catch her britches!" Jack hollered, while he scrambled, inches at a time.

"Come on in here with me, baby," Aycock called.

"She's just got herself too big a crowd," moaned Gloria.

"I'm praying," chattered Mrs. Moody, holding onto her husband.

"Don't let that baby fall!" cried Etoyle.

Judge Moody lurched forward, but Mrs. Moody pulled him back by his coattail. "You'll just scare her, make her fall quicker, that's what you're good for," she said, with her teeth chattering.

Lady May watched them all from where she sat in the hole as if she were at home in the automobile tire that hung in the tree, waiting to be swung from behind. Jack took a recovering step and balanced on an outcrop of goldenrod. The sun had moved; only above him was the wall still rose red. That below was in deep brown shade, as if a big wave had come up out of the Bywy and filled everything but where the baby was. Out of it reached his shirt-sleeves.

Lady May put up her arms and dropped to Jack's, straight into his chest, where he folded her in.

Mrs. Moody grabbed Judge Moody at the same time and cried, "Couldn't you kill both of 'em!"

"What a trip already! And we're not even to the bridge!" cried Miss Pet Hanks.

Jack was studiously backing down the bank with Lady May. Once they were at the bottom, she hollered, turned herself upside down in the fold of his arm, and drove her little heel straight into his eye.

"Well, I've got me a tomboy," announced Jack.

He walked up the road carrying her, smoothing back her hair, clearing her forehead, baring her ears, giving her a wan, older face. She looked back at him soberly now, flat-headed, as if water were streaming from her, as if she knew she'd been bodily snatched from something and was now beginning to wonder what it was.

"That little hidey-hole she found keeps the heat like Mama's oven," Jack told Gloria, giving the baby over. "No wonder she was ready to jump out like a little grain of popcorn."

Lady May with one hand knocked her mother's dress ajar and set a fist around the nipple inside. Her tuning-up sounds stopped abruptly. Gloria curved her arm around her and bent her head over her.

"This is going beyond the pale," Mrs. Moody said to her husband.

*161*

"Can't you understand?" Gloria asked the busload. "I've got my hands so full!"

"Oh. Of the living," said one of the voices, gone flat.

"Stay right where you are, Gloria," said the driver. "Seeing is believing."

"Bye-bye, Gloria! You're needed here. Your baby said it for you!" called Miss Pet Hanks. "And she looks exactly like you, congratulations. Mr. Willy Trimble, this is the first time I ever saw you but I know who you are: pull over further in that ditch and let thirty schoolteachers and a lady by, please kindly."

Mr. Willy pulled over, saying, "I do like it when I come across a please, no matter how late."

Jack spurted forward to give the bus a push, and the engine at length turned over, a tenor engine that sounded fighting mad. With all the teachers looking back, the bus went past them, went past the wagon and then the school bus. Shutting off the throttle, the driver took it to the bottom of the hill on the glide.

Mr. Willy Trimble took off his bonnety hat and leaned down from his wagon toward Gloria. "That's right, daughter. This morning it was," he said. "Down fell she. End of *her*. You're looking at the very one found her."

Judge Moody, out in the road, put his hands to his cheeks and rolled the tied-on handkerchief up into a ring around his forehead, and there was his naked face.

Lady May gave an outcry. Perhaps she had simply expected that under that handkerchief there was a face like Jack's, or Mr. Renfro's or Bet's, or even no face at all—but not one she had never seen before, not one more new hot red face. And with it all in view, and the long lines creasing it, his eyes seemed to everybody there to show for the first time, brown and sad.

"All right, Oscar. And now let me tell you something more," said Mrs. Moody. "That church bus would have let you jump in with them. They had a seat for you. Men are the rankest cowards!" She stood up too. "Now what?"

"Judge and Mrs. Judge," Jack said, "there ain't all the time there was. I ain't going to let anybody at all stand out on Banner Road, roofless and perishing, with the sun already started down the sky. Now your Buick's got seven or eight good inches of gas to go— she can purr right ahead without the benefit of you watching, just as

*162*

long as Aycock donates his weight to your balance. I invite you to come to our reunion."

"Jack!" Gloria cried out faintly.

"Nothing is too good for Judge Moody, he saved my wife and baby. If I hadn't been here for Lady May this time, he'd have had to save her again." He turned around and planted himself in front of the Judge. "But Judge Moody, before you start to thanking me, wait. Think back. Have you ever seen me before, sir?" Jack drove his face close and stared at him.

Judge Moody took a step back. From behind him Mrs. Moody suddenly exclaimed, "I have! I have! Oscar, I swear it."

"I believe you are getting to look a little bit familiar to me too," said Judge Moody. "Now from how long ago—?"

Jack stood closer, his eyes open to squares.

"This very morning!" Mrs. Moody cried at him. "Our car went in the ditch and the first one to come along was you."

Judge Moody groaned. "A good safe ditch. A perfectly good safe ditch. I have no doubt it was you, and you ought to have left us there."

"But who was that Good Samaritan?" asked Jack urgently. "Go back farther than the ditch, Judge Moody. My name is *Jack Jordan Renfro*. That's what I came here to tell you and it looks like I finally caught up with the chance. Jack Jordan Renfro, from Banner." He looked Judge Moody intently in the face and got his stare returned.

"Son, I bet you a nickel we've had you behind bars!" said Mrs. Moody in a sudden flash.

"For doing what?" challenged Etoyle.

Judge Moody had fixed him with his eye. "Are you the fellow that subjected me to the screeching mother bird in court? And corrected the court on the name of the bird?"

"That's right! It was a purple martin. Start with her and you may remember it all in a grand rush," said Jack.

"What was your case?" Judge Moody asked. "You tell me."

Gloria, still giving the baby her breast, said in a voice from which exhaustion was not now far away, "Your honor, I'm here to tell you Jack Renfro's case in two words—home ties. Jack Renfro has got family piled all over him."

"Proud of it," said Jack. "And they had 'em a sorry time of it,

**163**

Judge, while I was away ploughing Parchman."

"I expect so." Judge Moody sighed. "Though I'm also sure that the first time they showed up like this and put in a plea for you"—without really looking at Gloria and the baby he nodded their way—"Parchman turned you loose, didn't they? Don't tell this court about home ties, I'm entirely familiar with 'em. How long have you been out?"

"Got in this morning, sir, in time to get the reunion warmed up to a good start," said Jack. "I wish you could've seen my baby streak in to surprise me."

"I saw her try it on me. What did I sentence you for?" asked Judge Moody, as if he barely could hold back a coming groan.

"Aggravated battery," said Jack. "And I might just as well have held my blow, sir—he's the same old Curly today."

"The same storekeeper that's going to bring the truck—when he feels like it?"

"There ain't but one!" said Jack.

"They're all in this together," said Mrs. Moody.

"And your partner?" Judge Moody looked up at the car. "Back from Parchman?"

"Fresh back from Parchman, sir, ain't had his dinner yet either, any more than you or I. But there's a plenty of everything where you and Mrs. Judge are invited if you hurry right now. They're only waiting on sight of me to sit down," Jack said.

The air rang as if all the pots and pans had dropped at once onto the iron top of a kitchen range somewhere. Gradually the reverberations died down.

"What was that?" Mrs. Moody asked, her hand on Judge Moody.

"That was good old Banner bridge," Jack said. "The church bus has just made it to the other side." He jumped to Mr. Willy's team and took hold of the white mule's bridle. "You could carry these folks to my house, couldn't you, Mr. Willy?"

"Don't approve of Sunday pleasure riders. And I ain't going to carry no crying baby anywhere—anything I do hate, it's baby-crying."

"You don't hear Lady May. She's sound asleep now," Gloria said in a whisper.

"All right, let 'em climb on and see if I will," said Mr. Willy. He spoke to the mules, and after they each took a juicy bite of cosmos they brought the wagon up out of the ditch and waited there.

"Look at your old wagon coming apart, Mr. Willy," said Etoyle as she skinned up the side and peeped in.

The high sides, like a skimpily mended fence, had missing places as wide as windows between some of the uprights. Scraps of lumber were visible lying on the floor by a pile of quilts, and a quota of chairs stood in a double row. The wagon gave off a smell like a busy sawmill's.

"Other people won't give me a chance to fix my own, girlie," said Mr. Willy. "They just won't leave me alone." He turned sideways on the seat and said to the Judge, "I'll sharpen your plough-point, mend your harness, fix your wife's sewing machine, and the rest of it. Banner's my home. Try me." His hat, that he wore year-round, had its wintry, dust-packed brim pulled down like a black sunbonnet around his withered cheeks.

"Just a minute," said Mrs. Moody. "Just one minute!" She elbowed past her husband to go around and get a look at the wagon from behind. "Oscar, this is the very same old fellow that started our trouble this morning, and I said I hoped I was never going to see him again on my road."

Judge Moody stood beside her. "Well, you've hit on a fact," he said. "Old man, you wouldn't let my car pass you, I'd have had to go in the ditch—"

"Well, to let you pass me, *I'd* had to go in the ditch," said Mr. Willy. "Figure it out."

"—and finally you turned right across the road in front of me, and forced me—"

"Thought everybody knew that's where I lived," said Mr. Willy. Only Etoyle, scampering over the wagon, laughed.

"Well, Maud Eva, and here we are in the heat of sun," said Judge Moody. "Now that you know the worst, do you think you can bring yourself to mounting this wagon and getting under the shelter of this boy's roof, and leaving the car where it is?"

"Oh, the car's not going to fall now. It's certainly been given every opportunity there is to fall," said Mrs. Moody in a surprised and almost offended tone of voice. "If the Lord had intended my car to fall, don't you think He'd have gone ahead and seen about it before all this came along? I do."

Judge Moody turned around, plodded to the foot of the bank and called in a hoarse voice up to Aycock. "Now I expect to find this car right in the same place when I get back. And you still in it. Is that understood?"

"Are you-all saying good-bye?" Aycock called.

"Can I trust you?"

"Yes sir, you can trust me," called down Aycock. "Anybody that wants to is welcome to trust me."

"Sure you can, sir. Aycock's the best friend I got and my closest neighbor," Jack said. "I only hope your Buick was listening as well as he was to what you said."

"Speaking of excuses nobody in their right minds would believe," said Mrs. Moody, pointing up at the Buick, "if you'd tried to *make up* an excuse for not getting where you were going, Oscar, you couldn't have beat that."

"I'm not much on making excuses, Maud Eva—"

"It's the last thing they'd believe," she said, still pointing. "The real excuse doesn't ever carry weight at all. It's just as well you're not going to get the chance to offer it."

Judge Moody was leading her to the wagon. The nailed-on ladder came down the wagon side nearly to the road. Mrs. Moody put her foot up. "All right, Oscar, but just remember this was *your* decision."

"Is this your ice, Mr. Willy?" Down in the bed of the wagon, Etoyle lifted the quilt from what it was covering. "Who's that for?" she asked as she jumped from the high board side into Jack's arms.

"Nobody from Banner," Jack told her with a pat on the head, and she danced away.

"Oscar, do you see what I see?" Mrs. Moody bumped back against the Judge. "Honestly!"

It was a new pine coffin, still a little rough-looking—the source of the medicinal smell that had kept coming out of the wagon while it waited in the road.

"I'm the artist," said Mr. Willy Trimble. "Got the lining to fit it with, and plane it some more. I'm just going down to the old sawmill." He nodded toward Banner. "There's still a whole raft of cedar boards back in yonder from Dearman's time, laying in that wilderness of honeysuckle. Pretty well seasoned by now. Any fellow can go stepping in there and help himself to some sound timber if he ain't afeared of snakes. Nobody to tell him halt. I'm finishing up this one special for a present. Aim to carry it across the river to Alliance." He took his hat off and folded it to point with into the distance ahead.

"Well, sir, you can just carry it *right on*," said Mrs. Moody. "Go right on to Alliance, and without benefit of the Moodys' company. Go on, shoo!" She stamped her foot in the road. "Get up, horse!" she cried to the mules.

Mr. Willy put his hat back on. A wasp staggered from its brim, then, carrying its legs like a basket, took off swinging into the air. He brought out into Banner Road and rattled off down it and disappeared around the blind curve, leaving them his dust.

"You didn't really hurt his feelings," Etoyle told Mrs. Moody. "Mama says it can't be done, no matter how hard you might try."

At the same time, another clatter filled their ears. A whirlwind of dust was rising on the home track. The same as the other time, Vaughn came at them driving the mule from a stand on the seat of the wagon as though all their lives depended on him. Bet jumped the ditch and the wagon seemed for a moment to fly to pieces, but before it could turn over, Jack got the mule halted.

"What does Mama say?" he asked Vaughn, picking him up from the road and setting him back on the seat.

"Said even if the world was coming to an end here, the reunion was ready to sit down."

"All right, Vaughn. I believe we're as ready as they are. But who you're carrying to the table is Judge and Mrs. Judge Moody."

Vaughn opened his mouth. Jack helped Mrs. Moody and the Judge up onto the spring seat beside him.

"What word do I take Mama along with 'em?" Vaughn broke out.

"Mama knows what to do," Jack said. "Just keep down to a trot and don't spill 'em. The rest of us will walk it and get there the same time as you," he told the Moodys.

"The school bus!" yelled Vaughn, in the minute between when his old dust faded and his new dust was still to be raised. "Look where you put the Banner School bus!"

"You got it to keep up with for a whole year, Vaughn. You ought to've started sooner," said Jack. He gave Bet a spank.

At the last minute, Etoyle sprang and made a jump into the wagon. She dropped down into the hay behind the Moodys and smiled at them.

*167*

"No, Mischief, you can't hold my baby again," Gloria said, as Etoyle held out her arms from the moving wagon. "She didn't get up Lover's Leap all by herself."

"And here *we* go up this funny little road," said Mrs. Moody.

As though he needed to wring out something, Judge Moody wrung out his handkerchief, then scraped it over his cheeks and brow and tied it on again.

When the dust began to rise behind the wagon, Etoyle stood and waved at the only one she could still see above it, Aycock. "Sweet dreams!" she called. The smile of pure happiness on her face was the same one she'd welcomed Jack home with this morning.

◄§

"How late is it drawing on to be?" Aycock called.

"Don't fret. One of my sisters'll find her way back to pitch you a chicken leg," said Jack.

"Stop her. I want a can of sardines and a can of Vyenna sausages and a pick to punch it open. And the kind of pickles Miss Ora Stovall knows so well how to cure," he called. "Those're what I been homesick for."

"Save 'em for Saturday," Jack advised.

"Can I keep Queenie? She'll be good, she's the mother dog."

"She took off, leading those two other scampers. They'll get home without you. But I'll run tell your mama you're safe and sound before she sets in to calling you," said Jack.

Now he and Gloria and the sleeping baby were the only ones in the road, and the sound of all wheels had faded. He set his hands in place around her waist and asked, "Ready for home?"

They started up the track, and Jack steered them toward the well. Its smell came to meet them, like that of a teakettle that has been steaming away, out of mind, on the back of the stove all day. Under the big pine was Gloria's satchel lying forgotten, already velvety pink. The wooden cover over the well had the heat of a platter under the Sunday hen. Through Jack's hands the rope ran down in a long coarse stocking of red, and then he drew the bucket up on its shrieking pulley. They shared the glassful. Then Jack, looking at Gloria's face, poured her another glassful and handed it to her.

"You can count on one thing, Gloria," he told her. "Before the day's out I'm going to see that you get your good-byes said to your Miss Julia Mortimer."

She spilled the water and dropped the glass. "Jack!"

"You needn't have worried—I wasn't going to let you get carried off by a gaggle of geese," he said, brushing the drops off her skirt, chasing the glass. "We ain't that bad off yet, that my wife has to be *come after* in time of trouble. We still got a wagon and mule to our names."

"Are you sending me back where I came from?" she cried.

"I'm carrying you. I'm going with you, not letting you go anywhere by yourself, sweetheart."

"I don't want to go! I've *said* my good-byes to Miss Julia!"

"But she's the one who was good to you. Your main encourager."

"Then listen! Miss Julia Mortimer didn't encourage me to marry you, Jack!" cried Gloria.

"What?"

"She was against it and gave that out for her opinion."

The pupils of his shocked eyes nearly overflowed the blue. "*Why?*"

"She said it promised too well for future trouble."

"She came out with the bare naked words?"

"Trouble and hardship."

"Gloria, next to losing Grandpa, this is the worst news to welcome me yet," he said.

"And the only letter I ever did find in that mailbox for me was from her," said Gloria.

"What did it say? Get it out, honey," said Jack.

Gloria hugged the baby closer. "It said for me to come to Alliance and she'd tell me what would become of me. To my face," she whispered. "I never went!"

"Because how could you get there?" he said. "You couldn't even get to Parchman to beg for me."

" 'Don't marry in too big a hurry,' she said."

"Possum, then what would she have had you do?"

"Teach, teach, teach!" Gloria cried. "Till I dropped in harness! Like the rest of 'em!"

He gripped her.

"Do you blame me for keeping out of her sight?" she asked.

**169**

"But it was so remarkable of her," he said, staring. "She knew what would happen without even laying eyes on me. Didn't even know me."

"She knew *of* you."

He held her close to him, her face spangled with its freckles and beginning tears as if dragonfly wings were laid across it. "Don't cry. Don't cry about it now," he said, his cheek on hers.

"I waited so long on today! I thought I was ready for anything, if you'd just come—reunion or no reunion. Then first Judge Moody and now Miss Julia Mortimer! I blame them both for where we find ourselves right now."

"You can't blame who you love," he said.

"I can. I blame Miss Julia Mortimer."

"You can't blame somebody after they're dead," he said.

"I can."

As they stared at each other, he suddenly jumped her aside, for a wasp came swinging toward her temple, like a weight on a thread. He beat it off, beat the air all around her, stamped on the wasp, and brushed her carefully again, although nothing had touched her. Nothing had bothered the baby, who lay against Gloria's bosom, open-mouthed in sleep.

"*You* can't blame anybody *living*," she accused him.

"Now I can't blame Judge Moody. He saved—" He drew her near, stroking her forehead, pushing her dampening hair behind her ears.

"Sending for me to tell me what she thought of our future! An old maid, and a hundred and one years old!"

"Old people want to tell you what's on their mind, regardless of what it is or who wants very bad to know it," whispered Jack. He went on stroking her, as if she might have fallen and hurt herself, or the wasp had stung her after all. "And they pick the time when they want to tell it. It's always right now—they don't like to wait. You just got to expect it."

"I've hoped against hope she was wrong through and through!" Gloria's tears ran down the face he was kissing.

"Poor little old fat Possum," he whispered. "I see now what you've been doing all this time without me. Thinking. Broodering."

"The very last time I was over the bridge, she tried to talk me out of listening to you. That's when you were still my pupil."

"And when you took my side," he asked her, stroking her forehead where it was so hot, "wouldn't she pay regard to your common sense?"

"Jack, she pooh-poohed it. She laughed at me." Then every bit of her was ready to dissolve in tears. He sank to the ground along with her and the baby, and took them on his lap—onto his old torn pants, whitened and crumbling along the seams as though they'd been trimmed in crusts of bread.

"I'd wondered why she didn't come to our wedding," he said. "But I see now why she couldn't show her face."

"I wouldn't have told you she laughed. Only if I hadn't, you would have carried me straight to her wake," she whispered.

"Now you've had one to laugh at you, and I've had one to be sorry for me," said Jack.

She sobbed.

"Never mind, honey. I ain't ever going to laugh at you, and you ain't ever going to feel sorry for me. We're safe."

"That's being married," she agreed between sobs.

"And never mind, sweetheart, we're a family. We've still got the whole reunion solid behind us."

"Oh, if we just had a little house to ourselves, no bigger than our reach right now," she whispered. "And nobody could ever find us! But everybody finds us. Living or dead."

He cradled her flaming head against his shoulder. He held her in his arms and rocked her, baby and all, while she spent her tears. When the baby began to roll out of her failing arm, he caught her and tucked her into the pillow of the school satchel. Then he picked up Gloria and carried her the remaining few steps to that waiting bed of pinestraw.

◆§

When the sun had moved, Jack said, "And they're waiting dinner on us." They stood up together and Jack lifted Lady May—the limp child whose cheek had been pressed pink by a little buckle, whose feet were bare as a beggar's.

A flock of birds, feathers of that blue seen only in the loneliest places, flitted across the path that started home. From behind them, a string was plucked, then another—a tune.

"I reckon what Aycock spent his year, six months and a day

**171**

missing was his guitar," said Jack. "He's serenading himself now. I wonder what told him he was going to need that before he got back home this time."

"And now, Jack," said Gloria, when they were back on the short-cut, "the reunion sent you to get rid of Judge Moody and what you've done is invite him home with you. And his wife along with him. This time, they'll kill you."

He smiled at her.

"Or they'll just have to give up and cry," she promised him.

"Little chicken, before you stopped, you'd cried enough for all of 'em."

"Those tears were saved up, Jack. I had to get that crying done before I could go any further."

He gave a nod, as when she mentioned her common sense to him.

Dense mounds of blackberry bushes held their own through the sheets of dust, looking like giant iron cooking pots set the width of the home pasture. Above the trees on the last rise, the roof began to flash. They could already hear the great hum. Lady May began rubbing her eyes.

"All I ask is you let me wash my face first," said Gloria. "To be ready for 'em."

"That's my little wife," Jack said, tying her sash for her.

# Part 3

*T*he shade had circled around to the front yard. The tables appeared to have opened and bloomed. They reached in a jointed line from the bois d'arc tree all the way down the yard, almost as far as the post with the bell on it. Elvie solemnly drew apart the sacks and unveiled the ice.

Miss Beulah ran to the old lady's chair. "Granny, are you of a mind to let Brother Bethune use the Vaughn Bible today?" she asked.

"Not until he shows me his right to be here at all," said Granny. "Who went so far as to let him through the bars?"

"Brother Bethune's carrying a Bible of his own, Mother," said Mr. Renfro.

"He can pocket it," said Miss Beulah. "I wouldn't trust it to have everything it needs in it. Bring the Renfro Bible, Elvie, off the table in the company room. All right, Curtis, Dolphus—one two three!"

Rocker and all, Granny Vaughn was lifted high and carried through the crowd. Little clouds of fragrance seemed to go with her. The day had brought out the smell of her black dress, a smell of black, of her trunk and its brass lock, and there was a little vinegary smell that lasted longer, from the washing of the hand-worked lacy collar that went raying around her neck.

Elvie came back out of the house, the Renfro Bible the only thing showing above her prancing legs. As she dumped it into

Brother Bethune's lap, its lid banged, heavy as a table top, and let out a smell loaded as a kitchen cabinet's. Brother Bethune rose with it sprawled in his own arms and first led the company, then trailed them, as in long spreading scatters through the solid shade of the house and the floating shade of the trees they moved toward the tables, with Miss Beulah calling and pointing them out where to go, or taking them by the shoulders and steering them there.

Granny, transported to the head of the top table and given some dahlias to hold, sat with head cocked. Brother Bethune and his stand were wedged into the tree roots by her side, in between her and Grandpa's chair. A tub of lemonade was fitted in too, next to the stand, so strong-scented that it drew tears.

"Table looks almost too pretty to be molested!" Uncle Noah Webster hollered from the foot, sitting high on the sugar barrel. Granny's table was seated round with her grandchildren—the Beechams and their wives, and Mr. Renfro and his sisters. Beyond the tables, the overflow sat on the ground at the cloths and quilts spread in surrounding diamonds, and the edges of the crowd reached back up into the wagons.

Uncle Nathan remained standing at Granny's back, his hand on her chair, a fixture there from now on. He had hair streaked with white, tangled and falling to his shoulders. His old coat and pants had been patched again on top of last year's patches and, though neat, had been put on rough-dry. He gave off a steam that spoke of the river and now and then of tar. His face was brown and wrinkled as the meat of a Stuart pecan.

"You a bachelor?" asked Aunt Cleo.

"And the oldest Beecham boy," said Miss Beulah, stepping up beside him. "Nathan never fails us. If only we could keep him!"

Aunt Nanny still held a baby boy on her lap, and only stopped tickling him and gave him up when Brother Bethune made a sign. He threw open the Bible and flung back his hand, as if to show he could start on any page it wanted him to. Without a glance downward, he smiled.

"Well, look at me!" said Brother Bethune. "I'm proud I made it. The way it is lately, every year that's rolled around, there'd be a Bethune to go. For a while it looked like this year it was going to be me. But as precious friends will remember with me, the Lord took two others instead. Lowered Sister Viola in her grave in Banner

**176**

Cemetery and they was fixing to cover her. My oldest brother Mitchell says, 'Hand me the shovel, Earl Comfort, I want to just shovel a little dirt on her coffin, it's the last thing I'll ever get to do for her.' And he did and the next minute the shovel flew and dirt flew and Mitchell was down kicking on the ground! It was Sister all over again! I throwed my weight on him, that's what I did for Sister, but I couldn't help but see his face was already going black. Oh, I held a fast grip on him. But he threshed right ahead. Until he's gone like Sister, and gone before she's even covered." He crowed. "And listen, then they couldn't get *me* up! And I couldn't get myself up! Well, Mitchell he made two and I all but made three—three Bethunes to go in one year and pretty near all in one day. There you are now, match that."

"I wish Brother Bethune would reserve some of that story for use in the pulpit," came the voice of Aunt Birdie. "It's not all that much, and those not in the family can get tired of it."

"And so," Brother Bethune continued in a key a notch higher, "this beautiful old home, this happy family, the bounty of God's blessings and all His wonderful gifts to Man is making our hearts glad this evening. Now if you was to ask me what exactly in the Book it looks like to me this minute"—he snapped over a page in the Bible which cracked like a whip and flourished the smell of honeysuckle—"I'd answer you quick: Belshazzar's Feast. Miss Beulah may have even out-provided it! And I bet it's as good as it looks."

Miss Beulah edged near enough to warn him: "Grandpa Vaughn made himself wait. He got the blessing said and the history every bit delivered and the lesson of it through our heads before he even looked at the table."

"It's Belshazzar's Feast without no Handwriting on the Wall to mar it," Brother Bethune went smoothly on, "and no angel, so far, to come and take the glory and credit away."

"Is he coming to Jack fairly soon?" whispered Aunt Birdie among the *Menes* and *Tekels* of Brother Bethune. "And forgive him quick and get it over?"

"Birdie, Jack hasn't reached the table yet. Everything in its time," said Uncle Curtis.

"Though I hope Ralph Renfro's not planning on acting like Belshazzar's daddy—that's Nebuchadnezzar going out to eat grass,"

*177*

Brother Bethune said slyly. "I'd like you to show me enough grass around here would satisfy a rabbit, Ralph, unless you count what's took over your cotton. Lord, you sure need a rain." He got his laugh from the men. "All right, then! Bow your heads and hush your babies, I'm fixing to ask the blessing."

When Brother Bethune addressed the Lord, he threw his voice as far as the top of the bois d'arc tree over Granny's head. It was this big tree that at this hour had taken command of the yard. Its look was this: if disaster ever wants to strike around here, let it try it on this tree. The top had spread almost as wide as the roof, which it had shaded blue as a distant mountain. Its hard, pronged branches could never be well concealed by leaves so constantly stirring, shimmering without a breath of air. Brother Bethune had leaned his gun against the trunk.

"Know another who draws his prayers out to too great length," said Granny when Brother Bethune had finished. "I'm putting a stop to it."

Then quickly Miss Beulah, with Ella Fay and Elvie to help her, began garlanding movements around behind them, offering them more to eat before they started, and telling them right and left the only good way to eat it.

"And keep your eyes peeled for Jack!" Miss Beulah cried over their heads while they were reaching. "Sometimes taking the first juicy bite is all that's needed to bring him."

"Those children's just like little pigs—what one won't eat, the other will. Look at 'em go!" said Aunt Nanny behind her drumstick.

"We are fortunate to have Granny Vaughn still with us today and in her right mind. Her living grandchildren and great-grandchildren are making her happy and going to fill her lap with presents as soon as I let 'em at her. First I'll look out over your heads and tell you who I *don't* see," began Brother Bethune.

"Now that's not what I came to hear," said Aunt Birdie to the top table.

"Let Brother Bethune warm up a little bit for the rest of us. You ain't eaten the crust off one little wing yet," Uncle Dolphus told her.

"One who is living but not present is Homer Champion," Brother Bethune told them. "Homer Champion is ready to give his

**178**

soul to keep on being what he is now come Tuesday: justice of the peace. Well, I haven't heard his excuse yet, but you know something? I believe we got as many as we need without Homer."

"Jack is a different matter," Aunt Beck was saying, when Brother Bethune rattled a page of the Bible for attention.

"All right! Granny Vaughn is the Miss Thurzah Elvira Jordan that was, born right here in this house, known far and wide in the realms of the Baptists for the reach of her voice as a young lady. She is one of our oldest citizens today, beaten only by Captain Billy Bangs, who has reached to the age of ninety-four and still going to the polls. Granny is mighty pretty, she's kind and courageous, sweet, loving, faithful, frisky, and outspoken. It is said that Death loves a shining mark. So we had all best be careful of Granny, precious friends, and treat her nice for the year to come, because she's shining mighty hard. Ain't that so, Granny Vaughn?"

Granny's eye met his perfectly. She was sucking on a little chicken bone.

"I believe it is true that her eye can still see to thread her own needle, though we won't make her prove it at the table," Brother Bethune went on. "She still gets up at four in the morning, sees to her chickens—"

"As if I'd let her," said Miss Beulah, marching to her grandmother with platter piled high with the white pieces.

"She started in at an early age, reared a lovely young lady that's in the graveyard, and then she started all over again on that daughter's family. And here they are, all living but one! She has had her trials in this vale of tears and still, as all can see, she's never yet bowed her head. As I look out over that sweet old head and count 'em—raise your hands!—I see six living grandchildren, thirty-seven or thirty-eight living great-grandchildren—and others galore. I see faces from Banner, Deepstep, Harmony, Upright, Peerless, Morning Star, Mountain Creek, and one who makes the whole wide world his home." He flung out a hand at Uncle Nathan. "According to her years, she is about to live up her life here on earth, and may expect any day to be taken, but we hope she will be spared to bring her precious presence to one more reunion."

"When he gets as far as Jack, I'm going to tell him to slow down a little," said Aunt Birdie. "I want to listen to every word when he forgives that sweet mortal."

**179**

Aunt Beck said, "We want Jack to get to the table first, to *be* forgiven. And Gloria and the baby in their place beside him, so we can cry for all of 'em."

"Jack won't disappoint us," Aunt Nanny said. "By this time he wouldn't even know how."

"It's Brother Bethune that ain't measuring up like he ought to," said Aunt Birdie. "What he's reeling off is tailored to fit any reunion he's lucky enough to get invited to."

"He uses the same old thing on all the Baptists—I expected that," said Aunt Beck.

"You'd both take it worse if he was to come up and beat Grandpa, wouldn't you?" asked Mr. Renfro. "Give him a little rope, ladies."

"Granny's granddaddy built this house. Built it the year the stars fell," said Uncle Curtis, talking along with Brother Bethune and raising his voice a little over the preacher's. "Jacob Jordan was his name, Captain Jordan was the way he liked to be known. He perched him here in the thick of the Indians, overlooking the stage road that come threading through the canebrakes up to Tennessee. It's still the road that comes to the house." He turned to gaze up at it. "It's got a chimney stack inside that's five foot deep and five foot wide. And after Captain Jordan's son settled for a Carolina bride, Granny herself was born squalling in that very room, by the licking fire."

"In August?" Elvie cried. "On the first Sunday in August?"

Granny studied her through the long narrow slits of her eyes.

"Winter used to come early around these parts," said Uncle Percy. "Lots of old tales about those winters. I believe 'em."

Granny put down a crumb and raised her fist ready for the next sentence.

"And by the time old Grant come over the horizon and put a cannon ball in that chimney, she was big enough to scamper out in the yard in her little flounce and boots and shame 'im for it to his face!" said Uncle Curtis.

"Just wish she'd been a year older, she'd done better'n that," Granny said, looking amused.

"What happened to Captain Jordan?" some child prompted.

"Died brave. His son died brave. And there's one of those Jordans, Jack Jordan, they had to starve to death to kill him," Uncle Curtis told.

"Couldn't dent a crack in my chimney, send all the volleys you want to," said Granny, and she ate her crumb.

"Preacher Vaughn he grew up in Banner too," said Brother Bethune. "Spent his whole life here."

"Grandpa's daddy was the builder of the first house in the town of Banner," Uncle Curtis prompted him.

"And that's a good smart piece away from where he ended up here," said Brother Bethune.

"Banner's just a good holler. It's the road that's winding," said Mr. Renfro.

"I believe there's nothing left of the first Vaughn house today," said Brother Bethune. "Banner's getting along without it."

"Grandpa's daddy raised that house out of his own oaks, pines, and cedars, and then he raised the church. He'd preach in the church on Sunday and the rest of the week he could stand on his own front porch and have it to look at," said Uncle Curtis. "Old house burned. Though not within living memory of any except Granny."

"When I was a boy, there's still a chimney standing, looked big enough to roast an ox," said Mr. Renfro. "It was backed up to the river. Then the chimney went. Then the whole back end of the bank where it stood, that went. Tumbled and sunk itself in the river. Delivered itself to the Bywy. I always got the general idea that Grandpa Vaughn just didn't care for that at all."

"He still had his old horse switch. Right here," said Uncle Percy.

Granny raised her wavering finger as if it could find what to point at. It was the big bois d'arc tree, right behind her.

"Yes sir, old-timers used to call that tree Billy Vaughn's Switch," said Uncle Curtis. "He'd stick it in the ground when he got down from his horse, trotting up here to court Granny, and one night he forgot it. Come up a hard rain, and the next thing they knew, it'd sprouted."

The tree looked a veteran of all the old blows, a survivor. Old wounds on the main trunk had healed leaving scars as big as tubs or wagon wheels, and where the big lower branches had thrust out, layer under layer of living bark had split on the main trunk in a bloom of splinters, of a red nearly animal-like.

"Too late to pull it up now," said Granny, looking from one face to another, all around her table.

"Well, but there's bodocks and bodocks growing between here

and the road," said Elvie. "They're lining our way. They couldn't *all* be Grandpa Vaughn's horse switches from when he came riding to see Granny and get her to marry 'im."

"Who says they couldn't?" Granny said swiftly.

"Granny's good husband, Preacher Vaughn, came here to this beautiful old house to live on their wedding day, and I believe he'd just surrendered to the ministry too, both at the age of eighteen. Mr. Vaughn is the living example of a real, real Baptist," Brother Bethune was declaring, and he smiled as his hand went reaching over his face. "I wonder does he recall with me a little story. I was taken along with him as a little feller, for company, to a Methodist revival being held one August over to Better Friendship. All went well as long as he could enjoy good singing and sermons and the shade of their trees, but after that, they started up one thing he hadn't counted on, poor man. Infant baptism! Such heartfelt groans you never heard in your life as good Preacher Vaughn give out that day, with his head dropped down on the back of the bench in front of us— suffering for them poor little Methodist babies."

A humming began to come from all the aunts at the table. When they looked at Granny, Granny looked back at them without blinking, as if she'd long ago decided how much it was worth her while to set them right about anything.

"One of the babies was Clyde Comfort," mused Brother Bethune.

"Aycock's daddy? I believe if Grandpa could see Mr. Comfort today, he'd groan again," Mr. Renfro said.

"And if Mr. Comfort could see Grandpa in our midst right now, he'd turn tail another time," said Aunt Nanny, helplessly winking.

"Oh yes, you could hear Preacher Vaughn well above them Methodist babies and the way they was crying." Brother Bethune let out a bark of laughter. "Ain't that so, Preacher Vaughn?"

Aunt Beck cried out in panic.

"Brother Bethune, you jumped your track a little ways back down the line there," called up Uncle Curtis primly, while some of the young girls at the table below cackled out like old women. "You know we lost Grandpa Vaughn."

"I declare, Brother Bethune, your memory's come to be no longer than your little finger!" Aunt Nanny called admiringly.

"Get up to date!" shrieked Aunt Birdie.

"You're hanging right over the Vacant Chair, Brother Bethune!

You've left your hat in it! If it had teeth, it'd bite you!" cried Uncle Dolphus.

"Don't you know what happened to Grandpa?" screamed Miss Beulah, her arms around Granny. "Can you think of a single other reason on earth why you should find yourself standing here at the table and making the effort to take his place at the reunion?"

"You're right," said Brother Bethune in a congratulatory voice, "we lost him, he left us just about exactly a year ago, at the age of eighty-nine. Stopped speaking, didn't care any longer for earthly food, then couldn't lift up his head, then perished. With all these blesseds around him and pleading him to stay."

"Wasn't that way at all," said Miss Beulah.

"I'm sure those are just the same words he uses for everybody," said Aunt Beck. "I advise you to get rid of him, before the next reunion."

She whispered, but Granny looked back at her in a fixed manner. Something about her glittered—the silver watch pinned to her front, worn like the medal she'd won by Grandpa's dying first.

"And I'm sure Granny Vaughn will forgive me for the first slip I've made all evening, and agree it was a mean trick to play on the new preacher, to see how far he'd go. Wasn't it?"

"Last year's reunion I wish we all could have skipped," said Aunt Beck, letting out a sigh.

"Jack was gone from sight. Grandpa Vaughn was groaning so, I asked him if he couldn't allow himself to give the history and the sermon to us sitting down. If he had, it might have saved his life!" said Miss Beulah. "We might have kept him till today."

"He died at you-all's reunion?" cried Aunt Cleo, and biting her lip, turned for a fresh look at Granny.

"No, Sister Cleo, he waited till after good-nights was over and good-byes was said and we'd all gone home to bed," said Uncle Curtis.

"In the barn," said Uncle Percy in a whisper.

"When he didn't come to bed, and didn't come, Granny went out there all by herself and found him, with a lantern. He'd fell over from his knees. But he had a nice sweet bed of hay under him," said Miss Beulah fiercely.

"I'll never forget Grandpa at that last reunion," said Uncle Curtis. "Oh, he thundered! He preached at us from Romans and sent us all home still quaking for our sins."

"We didn't know, till Mr. Renfro rode the horse into the day-light to tell us, how shortly he lasted after 'Blest Be the Tie,'" said Uncle Percy in a whisper.

They all stole glances at Granny. Her fingers reached for Grandpa's watch on her dress front. She opened it for a look, quick as she'd open a biscuit to make sure it was buttered, and shut it again.

"I think we're brave to keep coming, times like these," said Aunt Beck. "All of us, plain brave."

"I let my thoughts dwell for a minute on harvest time in Heaven," Brother Bethune called, passing behind her. He'd inter-rupted himself to line up with the children before the cake of ice. Dense with ammonia, like fifty cents' worth of the moon, it stood melting in its blackening bed of sawdust. He chipped some off into his cup to cool his lemonade, and came striding back talking.

"Granny Vaughn and Grandpa Vaughn—oh, they was David and Jonathan," Brother Bethune went gleefully on. "After Grandpa left this sorry old world, Granny appeared for a while to be trailing a wing. Yes sir, we in Banner told one another, he will soon have the old lady wooed upward. We know he's been hungry for her! I ex-pect while we set around her here today, Grandpa in Heaven is busy wondering why in the world she don't pick up her foot and track on up there with him. But I expect she's got her answer ready."

"Suppose you try taking a seat," Granny was heard to say. "Go over there in the corner." She pointed to the old cedar log.

"And behind him in the world Preacher Vaughn left five living grandsons, and only one keeping on with the Lord's work today—and then it's pretty much where and when he feels it coming over him." Brother Bethune right-faced toward Uncle Nathan.

Uncle Nathan, back of Granny's chair, inclined his gypsy head in acknowledgment.

Aunt Cleo pointed at him with a pie-shaped wedge of corn-bread. "You all got one in the family? Then why did you invite an-other one to do the preaching?" she asked them.

Miss Beulah said promptly, "Nathan's too modest, Sister Cleo, to think he could take Grandpa's place. Most everybody knows better than to try it."

"Why don't he eat, then?" asked Aunt Cleo. "If he won't preach, why don't he eat?"

"Sister Cleo, he didn't come to eat either. Just make up your

184

mind you don't always know what a man's come for," Miss Beulah advised her. "And some I'd think twice before I'd ask."

"There was only one Beecham daughter, there was Miss Beulah alone!" cried Brother Bethune. "And Miss Beulah Beecham she will ever be. And I want her to save me back some of those chicken gizzards she's provided such a plenty of, I want to carry 'em home for my supper—does she hear me? Miss Beulah, who ain't going to let no one in the world go hungry as long as she can trot, took for loving husband Mr. Ralph Renfro, who is yet with us today. He's here somewhere, trying to keep up with his children and stay alive!" Brother Bethune laughed. "Beulah and Ralph all their lives has worked right in harness together, raised a nice set of girls with a boy at each end. The girls is unclaimed as yet, but the oldest one is liable to surprise us any minute." He paused to let Ella Fay, wherever she was, stamp her foot.

"And *that's* making a mistake," Miss Beulah said, running around with the platter. "One day, Brother Bethune is going off the track and he'll stay off."

"I'm getting downright impatient listening for him to forgive Jack and get the hard part over," Aunt Birdie said as Brother Bethune lifted his voice and veered away into the Renfros.

"He can't do his forgiving till Jack gets here, unless he's willing to waste it," said Uncle Curtis.

"Grandpa Vaughn would have done it either first, or last, if he was going to do it at all," Aunt Nanny said. "Not just slip it in some-where."

Uncle Curtis said, "He wouldn't have done it at all."

⁢⁤ড়

"Papa," said Elvie, standing at her father's ear, "peep behind you. Here's them."

At the same moment, Etoyle seized her skirt and cracked it like a whip to get the dust out, and came rushing into the yard. She butted her head into Miss Beulah's side and embraced her.

"Lady May jumped through the peephole! Jack caught her! But he couldn't miss, she came like a basketball!" she cried.

"Oh, it's not so. But what's this?" And Miss Beulah was march-

**185**

ing toward the wagon. Judge Moody, wincing as if his bones creaked, got down and held his hand for his wife.

"Is somebody dead up here? I never did see so many," exclaimed Mrs. Moody.

"You see exactly how many we've got, with three more to be counted," Miss Beulah cried. "And if you came here expecting to find a bunch of mourners, you're in the wrong camp." Now she and Judge Moody stood eye to eye over the heaped-up platter she was carrying. "I bet you a pretty I can tell you who you had to thank for your invitation. What have you done with my oldest boy this time? I can tell that's your wife," she went on. "And I can see you're famished, parched and famished, in another minute you'll drop. Trot after me. Might as well shuck off your coat, Judge Moody, and don't dawdle."

"He's kept his coat on before me through it all this far—he can keep it on for the rest of the time, thank you," said Mrs. Moody.

"Vaughn! It's time for that spare on the porch!" yelled Miss Beulah, and Vaughn came bringing the school chair. It was a heavy oak piece with a hole bored clean through its back, the seat notched, the desk-arm cut like a piecrust all around and initialed all over. As Vaughn strong-armed it over his head, the deathless amber deposits of old chewing gum were exposed underneath.

"All right, sir. That gives you a little table all to yourself," said Miss Beulah.

"Mama, who is that? Is that the Booger?" asked a little child from the crowd as Judge Moody wedged himself in under the desk arm, and Brother Bethune caught his eye and waved at him.

"Mrs. Judge, Mr. Renfro is busy offering you his chair—slide in. And where are *your* children? How many've you got and what have you done with 'em?" Miss Beulah asked, coming at Mrs. Moody's heels.

"I was never intended to have any," said Mrs. Moody, looking out from under the brim of her hat as she squeezed in between Aunt Miss Lexie Renfro and Aunt Birdie and sat on a hide-bottomed chair.

Miss Beulah forked two crusty wings from her platter down before her. "You-all can start at the beginning and I reckon by trying you may be able to catch up," she said. "Yonder's my grandmother at the head of this table, she's ninety years old today. Try not to have her object to you. She's getting all the excitement she needs the way it is, and still got a while to wait to blow out her candles."

Granny's eyes hadn't left her plate, but Uncle Nathan, behind her, slowly raised his arm to hail the newcomers.

"Who's that familiar-looking old man doing the talking?" asked Mrs. Moody, and just then Brother Bethune waved his hand at her.

"And so here we all are, with very few skips and some surprises." Brother Bethune was keeping right on, in the argumentative voice of one who habitually brings comfort to others. His words ran on over Granny's bobbing head and down her table, over the rest of the tables and the sitters on the ground, went scaling up into the leaves, lighting on the chimney with a mockingbird, skimming down to the lemonade. Every now and then his eyes went to the cake of ice, as they might have gone to a clock-face. "They have journeyed over long distances and perilous ways to get here. Won't it be sorrowful if they don't all get home tonight! Let us hope they do—without losing their way or swallowing too many clouds of dust or having their horses scared out from under 'em or their buggies upsetting and falling in the river." He spread his arms. "Or meeting with the Devil in Banner Road."

"How long will this go on?" Mrs. Moody turned and whispered over her shoulder to Judge Moody behind her.

The school chair he sat in was crowded up against the althea bush. Mr. Renfro had hitched a keg up close to his other side, and sat just behind Judge Moody's elbow, eating off his lap. A little black and white dog came trotting up, lay at the Judge's feet, and began licking his shoe.

"Just eat like everybody else, Maud Eva. It can't be helped," he said, and set his teeth into a big chicken back.

"You let the children beat you to the finish, Brother Bethune— here's the birthday cake coming!" Miss Beulah cried. She caught Brother Bethune by his suspenders, turned him around, and pointed for him.

Coming out of the passage and around the cactus to cross the porch, and down the steps and over the yard, winding in and out among the sitters on the ground, Miss Beulah's and Mr. Renfro's three girls were joined in parade. Their dresses had been starched so stiff that they kept time now with their marching legs, like a set of little snare-drums. Elvie at the rear looked almost too small to keep up. Etoyle had splashed her face clean, and along with her shoes she had added her school-band coat, emerald green. Epaulettes the size of sunflowers crowded onto her shoulders and poked her dress out in front. The cake was carried by Ella Fay at the head of them, with twelve candles alight, their flames laid back like ears. In a hush that was almost secrecy, it was set on the table in front of Granny's eyes. For a moment nothing broke the silence except a bird shuffling about in the althea bush like somebody looking through a bureau drawer where something had been put away.

Then Granny rose to her feet, her own crackling petticoats giving way to quiet the way kindling does when the fire catches. She stood only by her own head taller than her cake with its candles and its now erect, fierce flames. With one full blow from her blue lips, breath riding out on a seashell of pink and blue flame, Granny blew the candles out.

"She'll get her wish!" cried a chorus of voices.

"Yes sir, Mis' Vaughn is right remarkable," said Brother Bethune, looking at her from the drawn-back face of caution.

Granny accepted the knife Miss Beulah offered, she placed the blade and sank it in. The cake cut like cream.

"I made it in the biggest pan I had," said Granny. "If it don't go round, I'll have to stir up another one."

While the birthday cake and its companion cakes went on their rounds, all sank back in a murmuring soft as a nest. Then suddenly Jack's dogs tore loose from their holdings and streaked through the reunion, turning over one or two sitters on the ground, their voices pealing. Shouts and cheers rose up on the edge of the crowd, then spread, and the dogs poured up the front steps and clamored on the porch.

Jack, Gloria, and the baby burst shining out of the passage.

"They set down without us," gasped Jack.

"I see the Moodys, first thing," Gloria said. "Their faces stick out of the crowd at me like four-leafs in a clover patch. Now see what kind of welcome you get."

Jack, washed and curried and with his shirt buttoned together, though it was tucked into the same ragged pants, went leaping into the reunion. Miss Beulah, with her arms open, clapped him against her.

"Son, what will you bring home to your mother next?" she cried, hugging him tight.

**188**

"Bring yourself forward, Jack! Fight your way in, and take your place at the table! Here comes the bashful boy!" roared Uncle Noah Webster, as they made a path for him to Granny. Behind him walked Gloria, gleaming and carrying Lady May, who was wide-awake with both clean little feet stuck out.

Jack bent to kiss the old lady, her mouth busy with coconut. She gave him a nod. She put out her hand and found Lady May's little washed foot and clasped it, as if to learn who else had come. Then she let them by.

"Uncle Nathan!" Jack cried. "When I see your face, I know Jack Frost is coming not far behind! I want you to know that's a good strong sign you planted on Banner Top."

"What did that one say?" asked Uncle Nathan in a modest voice, but just then Lady May's little feet, like two pistols, were stuck right in his chest, and he drew back.

Other arms reached for Jack, more hands pulled him along, and he made his way down Granny's table kissing and being kissed by the aunts, being pounded on by the uncles, with Gloria coming along behind him with a crowing Lady May.

"Jack, you got here in time for it," Aunt Beck told him.

"Though I don't exactly approve of Moody being here for everything," said Aunt Birdie.

"Never mind, Jack, we know you just can't help it," said Aunt Beck. "I'm not blaming you. I'm just glad to see you still alive. And ready for what's coming."

"We are all pleased and proud to welcome the oldest son of the house back into our midst—Jack Renfro!" Brother Bethune was calling out in competition. "He has been away and dwelling among strangers for the best part of two years! Though Jack has been away from our beck and call, we are sure without needing to be told that he's back here today the same as he ever was, and will be just as good a boy after getting home as he was before he went. Jack is just a good Renfro boy of the Banner community that we have all knowed since birth. Ain't that right, precious friends?"

Some shouts of approval could be heard through the noise, and Brother Bethune continued in rising shouts of his own. "Jack was getting to be one of the best-known farmers of this end of the ridge! He raised all his folks' cotton and corn, sorghum, hay and peas, peanuts, potatoes, and watermelons! And all needing him as bad as I ever saw crop needing man! He'd grind him his cane at the

right time and sell his syrup to the public!" As Jack made his way
down the table, Brother Bethune's tongue got faster and faster.
"Cuts him and sells him his wood in winter, and all of it goes to
Curly Stovall—the Renfros don't even get the sawdust! Ha! Ha! Ha!
Slops him a pig or two! Concerned in raising him a herd of milkers!
And his daddy's still got two left for him to start over with! Best of
all, he helps his father and mother by living with 'em! And now!
Now that he's come through all his trials and troubles unscathed and
is about to take up where he left off and get everybody back to as
good as before—all right, then! Today, the one that gets the baby-
kiss for coming the farthest is—Jack Renfro! How do you like that
for a change, Brother Nathan? All right, Jack!" shouted Brother
Bethune, though he could scarcely have been heard by now over the
other shouts, the teasing, and the dog-barking. "You wasn't a lick
too soon!"

A baby, like something coming on wings, was shoved into
Jack's face. It was still Lady May, in Aunt Nanny's hands.

"Haul yourself off the sugar barrel, Noah Webster—that's
Jack's," said Miss Beulah, and he had to bring up a stepladder for
himself and wedge it in on the other side of Aunt Cleo, almost in
Miss Lexie Renfro's lap. Miss Beulah pushed Jack onto the barrel
there at the foot of the table, where he and Granny could face each
other, and cried, "Now, start catching up!" as she turned a dozen
pieces of chicken onto a platter in front of him. "All right, Gloria,"
she said. "Now you. I saved you the baby-rocker."

Gloria lowered herself and slid in. The rocker, there below
Jack's barrel, was slick as a butter paddle and so low to the ground
that her chin was barely on a level with the edge of her plate. The
baby sat on her lap; only her little cockscomb could have been visible
to those up and down the table.

"Did Brother Bethune forgive Jack? Or not?" Aunt Birdie was
asking the other aunts.

"If forgiving Jack was what he was doing, I'd hate to think that's
his best effort," said Aunt Beck.

"Judge Moody and Mrs. Moody! I hope your appetite is proving equal to the occasion," Jack was saying, while the pickled
peaches and the pear relish, the five kinds of bread, the sausages and
ham—fried and boiled—and the four or five kinds of salad, and
the fresh crocks of milk and butter that had been pulled up out of the
well, were all being set within his reach. And then Aunt Beck's

chicken pie was set down spouting and boiling hot right under his nose. "Mama'll take it pretty hard if you go away leaving a scrap on your plate," he told the Moodys.

Brother Bethune had come down to the World War. "All the Beecham boys but the youngest and the oldest went over with me to the trenches and ever' last one of 'em but the youngest got back like me with their hides on. I don't know how they did it, exactly, but I do know it's a good deal more like the Beechams than it is like the Bethunes. A few scratches here and a few medals there to be put away and buried with 'em, but they come back the same old Beecham boys they always was, and just the good old Beecham boys we still know 'em to be. Like they'd never been gone."

"If we go German-hunting again, I say don't let's us leave even a nit over there this time!" shouted Uncle Noah Webster. Laughter spilled out of his mouth like the cake crumbs.

"They say the next time, them Germans is coming over here after us," whispered Uncle Percy.

"Let 'em come try!" shouted Uncle Dolphus.

"Will we arm ourselves as did the knights of old? Or will we turn and run, like that jack rabbit I see yonder?" asked Brother Bethune, arm shooting out to point, as every head turned to follow. Then came the laugh.

"Brother Bethune, I declare, you might get somewhere yet," Uncle Dolphus declared, and Uncle Curtis said, "You're not Grandpa Vaughn, but at least you know better now than try to be."

Brother Bethune cleared his throat and looked all about him. "The old homestead here looks very natural," he said, wearing the face of good news. He wheeled back to them so fast that he might have been expecting to find somebody already gone.

"Crops not what they used to be," said Uncle Curtis, as though Brother Bethune needed prompting.

He went on in soothing tones. "I don't reckon good old Mississippi's ever been any poorer than she is right now, 'cept when we lost. And in all our glorious state I can't think of any county likelier to take the cake for being the poorest and generally the hardest-suffering than dear old Boone." Sighs of leisure and praise rose to encourage him, and Brother Bethune paused to suck up some lemonade. Then his smile broke. "Looks like some not too far from the sound of my voice is going to have to go on *relief* for the first time. Ha! Ha!"

"Not Ralph Renfro," Mr. Renfro promised him shortly. He was at the lemonade tub too. He filled his cup and sat down again beside Judge Moody, so as to take pleasure in him.

"I believe we might even do a little material complaining around Banner, if we try right hard," said Brother Bethune, managing to dip up a little more for himself by tilting the tub against his knee. "Floods all spring and drought all summer. We stand *some* chance of getting *about* as close to starvation this winter as we come yet. The least crop around here it would be possible for any man to make, I believe Mr. Ralph Renfro is going to make it this year."

"Good old Brother Bethune," somebody was murmuring out in the crowd, "he's warming up now."

"No corn in our cribs, no meal in our barrel, no feed and no shoes and no clothing—tra la la la!" he sang to the littlest one he could see, a baby tied in the wheelbarrow. "No credit except for the kind of rates nobody is inclined to pay. Pigs is eating on the watermelons. All you people without any watermelons come on over to my house. Too cheap to haul from the field this year! And yet! It'd be a mighty hard stunt to starve a bunch like us." He spread his teasing smile over them all. "I reckon we'll all, or nearly all, hold out for one more round." As they cheered him on he called over them, "We got hay made and in the barn, we'll soon have some fresh meat, the good ladies has stocked the closet shelf with what garden we saved by hauling water. We got milk and butter and eggs, and maybe even after today's slaughter there'll be a few chickens left. And if we must needs accept them old commodities again from Uncle Sam, come about Christmas time, here's hoping he will have the preferences of Boone County better in mind than he did last year and leave out his wormy apples, ha ha! I expect he's found out by now we can be a little more particular here than the next fella!"

"Tell us some more!" the men cried, their voices aching with laughter the same as his, while Miss Beulah behind Jack's shoulder cried, "Ready for your next plateful? Here's the sausage I saved you from last year's hog! Here's some more home-cured ham, make room for more chicken. Elvie! Buttermilk! This time bring him the whole pitcher!"

"I would like to draw you a picture of Banner today," said Brother Bethune, gazing upwards, with his lips smacking over the name just as they smacked over "Bethune." But when he finished— "In Stovall's cornfield, only this morning, I saw a snake so long it was laying over seven and a half hills of corn. I didn't get him, either, precious friends! There was the other one coming, and I stood there torn between 'em, let the pair of 'em get away. There's a lesson in that!"—Aunt Cleo said, "He almost makes me glad I don't live here."

"That's because you've listened to the wrong preacher," said Aunt Beck.

"Now *I* didn't *recognize* Banner," claimed Aunt Birdie, pointing her finger at Brother Bethune. "And I was a Lovat and grew up right there, with the river right under my door. If that was Banner, I certainly wasn't hearing any compliments for it."

"I don't think that's high enough praise you've given the neighborhood, Brother Bethune," said Aunt Beck. "I miss something in your words. Can't you make that church rivalry sound a little stronger?"

Brother Bethune only looked down at them all from Grandpa's old place. "Banner is better known today for what ain't there than what is," he said. "I can truthfully say it hasn't growed one inch since I been preaching."

"It's been growing, but like the cow's tail, down instead of up!" cried Uncle Noah Webster. "Cleo, the old place here was plum stocked with squirrel when we was boys. It was overrun with quail. And if you never saw the deer running in here, I saw 'em. It was filled—it was filled!—with every kind of good thing, this old dwelling, when me and the rest of us Beecham boys grew up here under Granny and Grandpa Vaughn's strict raising. It's got everlasting springs, a well with water as sweet as you could find in this world, and a pond and a creek both. But you're seeing it today in dry summer."

"It's parched," said Uncle Dolphus. "Just like mine. So dry the snakes is coming up in my yard to drink with the chickens."

"And it's a shame and a crime about them web worms, too," said Aunt Nanny, looking to the other end of the yard where the majestic pecan tree rose, full of years. The caterpillar nets that infested it gave it the surface of some big old clouded mirror.

"It's loaded, though," said Mr. Renfro. "If you doubt that, Nanny, all you got to do is make a climb up there and count what's coming."

"I've about decided that nothing's going to kill some bearers," said Aunt Birdie. "Regardless of treatment."

"And won't you be glad when those little hard nuts start raining down," said Aunt Beck. "They're the sweetest, juiciest kind. The hardest to crack always is."

"None of you have much, do you?" said Aunt Cleo.

"Farming is what we do. What we was raised for," said Uncle Curtis in a formal manner, from there at Granny's right.

"Farmers still and evermore will be," said Uncle Dolphus, farther around on her left.

"We're relying on Jack now. He'll haul us out of our misery, and we thought he was going to haul us with that do-all truck." Uncle Curtis's long face cracked open into its first smile. "Since all my boys done up and left my farm."

"Mine too. That's only the way of it," whispered Uncle Percy.

"But all nine of mine," said Uncle Curtis, turning in his chair to gaze around at the crowd. "The only chance I get to see 'em, over and beyond the Sundays when their wives can drive 'em to church, is the reunion."

"What did they leave home for? Wasn't there enough to go round?" teased Aunt Cleo.

"It's the same old story," said Uncle Dolphus. "It's the fault of the land going back on us, treating us the wrong way. There's been too much of the substance washed away to grow enough to eat any more."

"Now well's run dry and river's about to run dry. Around here there ain't nothing running no more but snakes on the ground and candidates for office. And snakes and them both could do that in their sleep," said Uncle Dolphus.

"Too bad we boys had to ever leave Grandpa and Granny and the old farm," Uncle Curtis said. "All we boys had to come away and leave the old place so as to get by. We all tried not to take ourselves too far."

"I was the last of Granny's boys to go. I stayed to be the last one, didn't I, Granny?" Uncle Noah Webster asked from his ladder.

"Benedict Arnold," she said.

"How come everybody moved away?" Aunt Cleo teased. "Hungry?"

"There's only so much of everything," Aunt Nanny said.

"Takes a lot of doing without," Aunt Beck said serenely.

"Well," said Mr. Renfro, "we was never going to move, me and

**194**

Beulah. Granny's got us. And now, Jack and his family—we got them."

Everybody looked at Jack and Gloria, as they pulled a wishbone between them.

There came a louder report. Kneeling on the ground, Mr. Renfro had split open the first watermelon. He rose with the long halves facing outward from his arms, like the tablets of the Ten Commandments. He served Granny first, then around he started, cracking his melons, making his bows, putting down a half at each place.

Brother Bethune was going on, too, telling of the wanderings of his father and the one time he got help from an angel on Banner Road.

Aunt Birdie, unable to contain herself any longer, put her head around and said, "Jack boy, when Judge Moody finishes his dinner, you reckon he'll arrest you? Is that his idea, you reckon?"

"Well, it couldn't have been his idea when he started out, Aunt Birdie," said Jack. Over his watermelon he gave a smile at Judge Moody. "He'd sentenced me himself and he can count. He'd know I wasn't even due back here till tomorrow."

"Explain a little something right quick to Judge Moody, son," directed Miss Beulah, who was following Mr. Renfro, taking around the salt. "He looks like he's getting ready to lay down his knife and go home."

"I don't want to hear any further," Judge Moody said to Jack.

"Our reunion is one that don't wait, sir," Jack said at the same time. "Nobody, not even my wife, would have forgiven me for the rest of my life if I hadn't showed up today."

"You escaped?" Gloria cried out.

"Horrors!" cried Mrs. Moody.

"It was up to me," Jack said. "What good would it have done anybody for me to get back here tomorrow?"

Aunt Nanny was already laughing. "How'd you get rid of your stripes, darlin'?" she called out. "Ain't you supposed to wear striped britches? I don't see any!"

"Sh!" came from Uncle Curtis.

"Scaled the wall, I suppose, then fell off like Humpty Dumpty," Aunt Birdie said. "Or did you scoot right quick through the fence?"

"Out of Parchman? You couldn't find a fence," said Jack.

**195**

"Aunt Birdie, Parchman is too big to fence. There's just no end to it, that's all."

"You didn't just walk out of Parchman," muttered Judge Moody.

Jack said, "I come out on Dexter."

"I don't follow," said Judge Moody.

"Get up on a horse and just *ride* him out of there on a Sunday morning, while it's still cool—that seemed reasonable, and it was reasonable," said Jack. "I rode Dexter. He knows me. There's a overseer that rides him every day but Sunday. The kind of horse Dexter is, he's almost an overseer himself. He took me overseeing all over those acres, and finally he conducted me out onto a little road that meant business."

"Was Aycock riding on behind you?"

"Aunt Birdie, riding double could have caused somebody to look twice. Aycock come along behind the horse's tail, crouching lower than the cotton."

"Jack, you ought to have kept that a dim secret," Gloria whispered to him. "But you don't know how—somebody's got to keep your secrets for you."

"Roped my shirt and tied him to a shady cottonwood and talked to him and left him, and now if you're ready to laugh, Aunt Nanny," said Jack, "I don't even know whose pants these are I jumped into." She shrieked. "I traded with a clothesline. At first we couldn't find but one pair of pants. Aycock nearabout had to wear a bedspread. But we persevered, and the first preacher that came pitching down the road, we jumped in the car with him. And the story he told us, to get us to Winona! How somebody'd burnt down our courthouse!"

"Well, you can just go and change those pants instead of telling it here," said Miss Beulah.

"Keep on the pants you've got, Jack," Aunt Birdie begged him. "We're used to 'em now. Tell us the rest, do, please!"

"He just rode a plough horse out of Parchman," said Judge Moody to his wife, who was looking at him.

"Being church time, the roads was fairly well packed with Good Samaritans. Judge Moody was one and didn't know it." Jack turned to the Judge. "For about as long as it takes to tell it, I was riding behind on your spare, sir, and so was Aycock. Then we all went in together into Mr. Willy's ditch."

196

Judge Moody sat with a fixed expression on his face, while Mr. Renfro looked at him with enjoyment.

"Reckon they might come after him yet—using bloodhounds? It's a good thing we've got their equals!" Aunt Birdie squealed.

"I believe they'll let well enough alone," Mr. Renfro said to Judge Moody.

"If I was Parchman, I would," Mrs. Moody vowed, while the Judge just looked at her.

"I missed getting my good-bye present of new shoes," Jack told Gloria a little apologetically. "But I'll donate those whole-hearted to whoever would rather say good-bye to the pen tomorrow than today. I had to get me back for Granny's birthday Sunday!"

Aunt Birdie again shook her spoon at Judge Moody. "What was *he* doing on Banner Road, then?"

"Now we won't ask him for his story," said Miss Beulah. "The man's been tackling our roads, and at the first little bump and skirmish he lands himself in a ditch, and here he is. I think that'll do."

"Why, it won't do at all," Mrs. Moody began, but Etoyle set down her melon, joined her hands at her breast, and cried, "In the ditch? Judge Moody's car's gone straight up Banner Top!"

"'Tisn't so!" said Miss Beulah fiercely to Mr. Renfro, who sat there at Judge Moody's elbow with pleasure in his face.

"On Banner Top? Out on the flirting edge of nowhere? Is that right?" Aunt Nanny cried to the Moodys. "And don't know how to get down?" She shook with laughter.

Mrs. Moody pointed her finger across the table at Gloria's bright crown. "Give credit where credit is due," she said. "She's the one ran out of the bushes and right under our wheels, calling us by name. She's the one drove us right up that wall!"

Mrs. Moody said more but it was drowned out in the cheering that rose from the table.

"Look who's set here quiet as a mouse for two years! Bless your heart!" Uncle Noah Webster jumped off the stepladder and kissed Gloria, leaving cake-crumbs on her face.

"Gloria Short! I declare but you're turning out to be a little question mark! I'm wondering what you'll do next!" cried Aunt Birdie.

Aunt Nanny cried, "Now that's what I call trying to make yourself a member of the family. Stopped 'em right in their tracks? Sent 'em skywards?"

"Don't! Please don't brag on me," Gloria begged them. "Or at least, if you're going to start, don't brag on me for the wrong thing."

"I've been telling Gloria she should've stayed home with the ladies, but I eat my words this minute," said Aunt Beck, rising and coming to kiss her as if to make amends in public.

"Just let 'em have a little pleasure out of it, honey," Jack bent and said into her ear.

"She only gets the credit for not knowing no other way to stop. She had up too much steam!" cried Etoyle.

"I fell on my knees! I'm ashamed of what happened," Gloria cried, with her face almost as flaming as her hair.

"First time that young lady ever said she done anything to be ashamed of in her life, ain't it?" exclaimed Aunt Nanny with a broad smile.

"And I've listened," agreed Miss Beulah.

"I might have been killed! And my baby in my arms!" cried Gloria.

"And who saved you from it? Jack Renfro," said Miss Beulah, leading a chorus of answerers, some of whom were still trying to reach Gloria to hug and spank her.

"I was doing my best to *save Jack,*" Gloria corrected them as she worked free.

They laughed, loud with affection, at Jack. He'd risen up still holding his watermelon to his cheek, harmonicalike. He had eaten it down so close to the rind that the light of the sky shone through it now. "You *what,* honey?"

"That was what I started out to do!" Gloria cried. "I was going to save him! From everybody I see this minute!"

"Miss Gloria! I believe you're getting to be a little bit more of a handful than this family had bargained on!" Uncle Noah Webster sang out in pure hilarity.

"I'm keeping on trying! I'll save him yet!" she cried. "I don't give up easy!"

Aunt Beck said, "You know, I reckon there's nothing too much for a schoolteacher to try."

Jack shouted, "It's thanks to Judge Moody we still got her! He saved my wife and baby!"

"How in the wide world did you come to let Judge Moody save your wife and baby for you?" Miss Beulah cried. "With all this saving, where were *you?*"

"I was making such haste after Lady May that I sent Jack spinning in the ditch," said Gloria. "But if Judge Moody hadn't come along just at that minute, we would all have been all right and jumped right back on our feet."

Jack bent his brow on her.

"It was Judge Moody's own fault he had to save us," Gloria told them all clearly.

Judge Moody was heard saying to his wife, "The real culprit is that baby, of course. She ran between them—she was a moving target."

"That's right, blame a little suckling babe," said Mrs. Moody.

Miss Beulah blazed, "There's nothing you can say about that baby that's any fault of her own."

"But this is the first I realized that *all* plans has miscarried," said Auntie Fay Champion.

"And the car sitting this minute on Banner Top. You just come off and left it, Judge Moody, at the first crook of the finger?"

"I don't believe it's still there, Beulah," said Uncle Dolphus consolingly. "And I ain't going to take a hot walk yonder to prove it, either."

"I took the walk, saw it for myself," said Mr. Renfro. "And as far as the car goes, the car's up there and running in pretty good tune."

"And it's got somebody in it to hold it down! One guess! Aycock!" Etoyle screamed.

"Oh, for a minute I thought you was going to say 'Jack' once more," gasped Aunt Birdie.

"Aycock Comfort's deposited in your car and still behaving himself?" Miss Lexie Renfro asked Judge Moody coolly, speaking to him for the first time. "Well, I'm gratified to hear it. I expect Parchman did Aycock that much good. I wish you could find and send his daddy."

"Mama, as long as Aycock stays put, he's safe as we are," Etoyle said. "Jack says so."

"And if he budges, he's a gone gander. What about the rest of it?" screamed Miss Beulah. "These boys, these men, they don't realize anything!"

"Realize what, Mother?" Mr. Renfro asked her.

"What makes you think that's the end of the story? Somebody's still going to have to coax that car *down*. Suppose you never thought of that, any of you?" Miss Beulah cried. "What goes up has got to come down! Regardless! I declare there's no end sometimes! So you're elected, Jack."

"The home team might want me, all right," Jack said. "But the last I heard, Judge and Mrs. Judge are holding out together for old Curly."

"Curly Stovall and that brace of wore-out oxen? I declare, Judge Moody, that booger'll find a way to horn in on all you've got," said Miss Beulah.

&#x2766;

"That baby may still be baby enough for what she's up to, but if she's old enough to wear pockets!" exclaimed Aunt Cleo.

Gloria, down low as she was, almost too low for it to be seen across the table, had opened her dress behind the screen of one hand.

"All the same, that baby's had some little threads of white meat, some crumbles of hard-boiled egg, a spoonful of cornbread soaked in buttermilk, and a pickle," said Aunt Nanny. "From her father. And I saw her waving his drumstick in her little fist."

"Give us some more, Brother Bethune," called Uncle Noah Webster. "You can't give up yet."

Brother Bethune called that the prize for being the oldest here today went to Granny Vaughn. "Now the prize for the youngest!" he called, and up was rolled this year's new baby, lying bound around the middle to a pillow in a wheelbarrow, hands and feet batting like two sets of wings. "Now the prize for having the most descendants after Miss Granny Vaughn herself—stand up, Curtis Beecham!" Aunt Cleo was named the prize winner for being the newest bride, Uncle Percy for being the thinnest, Aunt Nanny for being the fattest.

"Grandpa never gave a prize in his life for being fat," said Miss Beulah. "You had to *do* right. And if you *did* right, you were considered having prize enough already. Weren't you, Granny?"

The old lady's head drove back from her plate for a minute, as though buggy wheels had started rolling under her chair.

"And now poor Jack! Judge Moody comes along Banner Road and right on time for him to put that truck to proof. And no truck," said Aunt Nanny.

"Yes, Judge Moody, we all know better'n you do what you

stand in need of," said Uncle Percy in his whisper. "Too bad you picked the wrong day to get it."

"If Jack ever gets through today alive, then gets back that truck and makes it go, I hope I for one am still on earth that day and with the eyesight left to see it perform," Uncle Dolphus said. "Jack's all but convinced his family it could even plough."

"What ever happened to bust it in the first place?" asked Aunt Cleo. "Running over some fool in the road? I don't think Jack's too careful with what's his." She looked at him with his second half of melon.

"Until it was busted, it never got to be Jack's," said Aunt Nanny, winking.

"Has there been something wrong with it?" asked Mrs. Moody.

"It started away from Curly's store in Banner on a Saturday morning, and the Nashville Rocket comes up the track. We was sitting there on the store porch, telling each other our woes, when there comes quite a crack," said Uncle Dolphus.

"It got hit by a train?" cried Mrs. Moody.

"It stopped the Nashville Rocket on the crossing, yes'm."

"This truck is something that had to be picked up out of the cinders of the railroad track?" asked Mrs. Moody.

"Jack picked it up. Had to wade to get it. There's a river of hot Coca-Cola and a mountain of broken glass trying to stop him— it was a Coca-Cola truck," said Aunt Birdie.

"Jack could have sliced an artery and no woman the wiser at home," said Aunt Beck.

"The only Cokes left standing for a mile around was the ones old Ears Broadwee had just finished delivering to Curly," Uncle Percy whispered.

"That was one sticky cow-catcher," said Uncle Dolphus.

"I'm surprised at the Coca-Cola people. It sounds to me like one more case of a careless driver," said Mrs. Moody to her husband.

"Watch out! That's my kin," said Aunt Nanny.

"I reckon there wasn't enough left of him for you-all to pick up and bury," said Aunt Cleo. "Have his funeral with a sealed coffin?"

"Didn't get a scratch. That was Ears Broadwee. He'd just been in the store, swapping yarns with Jack and Curly and the boys. Claims he ain't heard that train yet," said Aunt Nanny. "Ears was glad to be furnished an excuse to find him a job that would keep him nearer home. He's still looking, you-all. He may have to go to the CC Camp if something more to his liking don't come along."

"His touch is pure destruction, all right," said Uncle Noah Webster. "That truck wasn't much better than a chicken crate that's been waltzed around by a cyclone. The Nashville Rocket was right on time."

"The Coca-Cola people were a good deal put out. They sent one fellow here from Alabama to look at it. He just turned around and went back," said Uncle Dolphus. "Well, they can afford it."

"So it's pretty well scattered there on Curly's store yard, laying on his property. 'Who you reckon's going to make me the right offer for that International truck, Jack?' Curly says. 'Look there, not a part in it is over a year old.' Well, that got 'em all to drooling."

"It still looks to me like Curly ought to have thanked Jack for just hauling it this far off his premises," said Aunt Birdie. "Instead of charging him out of his corncrib. Hear, Jack?"

"Jack's trying to eat! He's got to catch up with you, not listen to you," said Miss Beulah. "To make a long story short, that truck, or what was left of it, ended up right here in our yard. Jack didn't ask his mother first, just started bringing it. Scrap!"

"Well, Mother, there's the old forge down yonder in the back," said Mr. Renfro. "And there's a raft of lumber standing on end in the barn, well seasoned, waiting on somebody to find good use for it. I told Jack what I'd do, faced with his problem, was finish taking it to pieces first. And start from scratch."

"How did Jack get the thing up to the house from the store yard? Did it have a steering wheel?" asked Aunt Cleo.

"Sister Cleo, he pounded him a sled together and loaded on and drug up this part and that part, Dan and Bet both pulling. And it all went right over yonder," said Miss Beulah, turning around to point with her long horn-handled fork. "There was four young pines growing just right to suit him. He chopped 'em off equal and mounted the frame of that truck with its corners sitting where you could see the stumps, if anybody'd get up and move away for a minute. It was a sight!"

"It was beautiful to Jack," said Aunt Nanny, grinning. "Oh, Jack was in a big hurry for that truck."

"I still wonder what he needed it for. You-all are clear off the highway or even a good gravel road," said Aunt Cleo. "What did he have that was so much to haul? I haven't seen it yet."

"It was his dream to provide," said Aunt Beck, though her eye was still on Brother Bethune, who had announced he was preaching on the subject "Be Humble." "And then to get hauled away like that himself!"

"And wouldn't it have done a perfect job of carrying a load of us to church and not let our shoes get nasty? And all winter long, from where we lived in mud, he could've been picking us up and carrying us to see him play basketball for Banner! Tore away like he was, he couldn't even be on the team!"

"Don't, Birdie, you're making us feel so sorry for him," pleaded Aunt Beck, looking back and forth between Jack and Brother Bethune.

"And more than that, it would've carried us to the courthouse faster and in a lot more style than we had, when it came time for his trial," Aunt Birdie said to the Moodys. "We could've passed the whole string of 'em going, and let 'em eat our dust coming home too, after we got our hearts broken in Ludlow."

"But what was *his* hurry for?" asked Aunt Cleo. "It wasn't to go and be tried!"

"He's courting! Of course, he got married before he got the truck finished," said Aunt Nanny. "It was a race with Nature, and Nature run ahead of all the hammering he could do."

"Shining at the end of the rainbow was Gloria Short," said Aunt Beck ardently.

"Where? Where was that?" asked Aunt Cleo.

"Where? Right here in this house," said Miss Beulah repressively. "Not twenty feet from where she sits now. She was in our company room, when she wasn't out in the kitchen with me, ironing her blouses."

"The new schoolteacher, soft, green, and untried," Uncle Noah Webster reminded her, smiling.

"Jack didn't think he ought to ask her to marry him if he couldn't even invite her to go riding on Sunday in something besides the school bus," said Aunt Nanny.

"Gloria's so much of a one to like nice things and nice ways and sitting up out of the dust to ride where you're going," said Aunt Birdie. "Two on horseback's not much her style. You'd never suppose that where she got to be Lady Clara Vere de Vere was in the Ludlow Orphan Asylum."

"Well, as school drew to a close, things got to growing mighty serious," said Uncle Noah Webster. "Jack was prepared to hand over a decent billy goat to Curly for what Curly's still got of the truck. It was trade-as-you-go right straight along, need I say!"

"And what was still Curly's?" asked Aunt Cleo.

"A whole heap of the engine," said Aunt Birdie, quick, like a good guesser.

"Be humble!" shouted Brother Bethune.

"That's right, Birdie," said Uncle Noah Webster. "Where the running parts was supposed to be, it still looked like a mule had taken a healthy bite right out of the middle. What Curly held onto till the last thing was the engine."

"Then it sounds to me like somebody went out of their way to trade Jack something that was looks only," said Aunt Cleo, and she gave a laugh. "Well, I'd say the fault was Jack's for not getting the engine part first."

"Jack thinks the other fellow is as honest and true as he is!" cried Miss Beulah furiously, still patrolling. "Even the hogs in this world! Keep going, Brother Bethune!" she cried. "Some people have still got the grace to listen."

"Curly mounted that engine on the post out in front of the store like a curiosity," Uncle Curtis said.

"And it was a freak to look at!" cried Aunt Nanny to Mrs. Moody. "You ever see one? It looks like some crawler you tie on the other end of your fishing line. Every time you tried to go in Curly's store to so much as wish for something, you had to duck for that engine."

"I hate to think that's what makes 'em go," said Aunt Beck.

"Why didn't Jack just swipe it?" Auntie Fay asked.

"Too honest. Too honest and too busy! When Jack wasn't driving the school bus and getting his cotton up and fighting General Green in the corn and tending to the last of his education, he was courting strong," said Aunt Birdie.

"Never anybody but the same schoolteacher?" Aunt Cleo asked.

"R-r-ruff!" Aunt Nanny growled. She grabbed Lady May over onto her lap, and growled at her like a wildcat and shook her. "That's right, Cleo."

"Well, Curly Stovall had Jack in a cleft stick with that engine."

"You're evermore right. Till finally he broke down and promised Curly the livest of his calves!" cried Uncle Noah Webster.

"Just for that dirty engine, a pretty little nuzzling calf with a white face," Miss Beulah said to Mrs. Moody, as she passed. "Ain't men fools?"

"Jack by that time was *dying* to get married," said Aunt Nanny, looking at him eat, and taking another bite with him.

"Do you wonder what Curly Stovall could still find to ask for, after he'd taken Jack's calf and staked it out along with his billy goat?" asked Aunt Birdie. "All right, he said the one thing Jack needed to do now so as to carry that engine home was talk the new teacher, Miss Gloria Short, into taking Miss Ora's seat in the boat and go floating with Curly on Sunday evening as far as Deepening Bend and watch him catch his supper!"

"Not a bad fight resulted," said Brother Bethune, aside.

"And there was no call for them to go to battle," said Gloria. "I'd already made my mind up what I thought of both of them, and was ready to put it in plain words if they'd only asked me."

All the uncles broke out in delighted laughter.

"That battle come close to taking the cake," said Uncle Curtis.

"Seldom seen one like it," said Uncle Dolphus.

"The last real good and worthwhile battle that's been fought for a worthwhile cause *in* the store," said Uncle Percy, "the last one before Jack was drug from us."

"Jack tied Curly up in the same old knots and trussed him in the same style?" Aunt Cleo asked.

"Well, this was the time that Jack got beat," said Uncle Curtis. "But it did us all so much good, because what it left us with, after Jack got hauled to the pen, was a peaceful feeling of having something to wait for. 'There'll be another Saturday,' says Jack, while we wrench on his good right arm and sink it back in the socket for him." He patted Jack's busy shoulder and turned and told Judge Moody, "Well, that's the Saturday we're waiting for now."

"And now Curly Stovall's got the whole shootingmatch back again?" Aunt Cleo said, laughing.

"That's right! Ain't it, Jack? Oh, I'm glad to see him go after that third melon with such appetite, but you'd think he hadn't had a bite of dinner at all," said Aunt Birdie.

"Yes'm, I suppose if Curly could finish the work it takes, he'd even start coming to church in that truck on Sunday. The hypocrite!" said Aunt Beck to Brother Bethune.

From Brother Bethune's side, Miss Beulah said, "Finish it? He wouldn't know which end to start. He can't even untie a knot in a little bit of clothesline, he can't get a store safe to stay locked."

"The truck is finished." Gloria stood up, appearing to them suddenly out of the low rocker. "We have seen it—Jack, Mrs. Moody, Lady May and me, Aycock, and all the churchgoing Methodists. Judge Moody came close to seeing it, but he missed it. It's going to pull the Moodys' car to the road, if it can."

"Jack's truck? It's riding?" shouted Uncle Noah Webster. "What kind of bad news is this you're bringing on a spotless fine day?"

"Foot! I can't believe Stovall had sense enough to know what it needed without Jack standing there to tell him," cried Miss Beulah.

"Must be something wrong with it. Surely now!" The uncles were all exclaiming to one another.

"Of course, nobody can promise you how far he'll get with it," said Mr. Renfro to Judge Moody. He had brought himself another glass of lemonade and sat down again close beside the Judge to watch him eat—Judge Moody was still no further along than chicken. "I'm just sorry to hear he's cranked it."

Uncle Noah Webster was shouting with delight into Judge Moody's face. "But *now* we've got something! *Now* we've got a war on that's like old times! Jack and Curly buttin' head-on again! And you in the middle! And old Aycock sitting holding his breath for everybody. Good old days has come back to Banner, Judge Moody! For a while I thought there wasn't much left for me to get homesick for."

"Poor old car," said Judge Moody to his wife.

"If nobody has any better idea tomorrow than they have today of what the word rescue even means!" said Mrs. Moody. "The very first fellow that came along today was sporting a chicken van, but would he stop? He sailed right by our signals of distress and went out of sight."

"He ain't too popular here at the reunion, either," said Miss Beulah grimly.

"Homer's got his own ideas," said Mr. Renfro, looking with interest at Judge Moody, who was still struggling with Miss Beulah's pickled peach. "I'll tell you how Homer's inclined, give you a little story. Now he used to make his syrup in my cane mill. The last time, he had Noah Webster to pull in the cane, while he's in the middle feeding it, and I was there to do the boiling, and our mule was grinding it. So Jack come along to get some skimmings, and somehow, someway, Jack put a scare in that mule. It was Bet with her blinders on. Bet commenced running away as fast as she could go," he said, smiling when the Judge looked up at him with a frown. "She had to go in a circle, it was the best she could do at the time, tied to the long arm of a cane mill. And old Homer's caught in the middle, ducking. Every time Bet come around, Homer tried to beat that pole and scramble out of the pit, and she wouldn't let him. His head would peek up, he'd start his foot, and here she come again, with the dogs giving very best encouragement. But as to Homer Champion, the family knows it, the world knows it, and Bet knows it—he just wasn't born to get out of a cane mill surrounded by a runaway mule. He's born to duck."

"I knew I ought to stopped Bet for him, Auntie Fay, but I just couldn't bring myself to get in a hurry about it," said Jack, a bite on the way to his lips.

"That was Homer's last batch," said Mr. Renfro. "And about the last batch our mule had anything to do with. It *was* the last. You couldn't persuade her to make any molasses for you today, Judge Moody. Although that was the smoothest-tasting that Bet ever made. Her last batch was her best, made for Homer."

"Oh, we've been at the mercy of that mule today too," said Mrs. Moody. "Only Providence got that truck ready for us."

"Stovall tied a string to the truck, didn't he? Said he'd make you wait till tomorrow to do business, didn't he?" challenged Miss Beulah. "And between 'em all, Judge and Mrs. Judge, they've left you high and dry with no place else to go, haven't they? I can tell by the downtrodden looks on both your faces."

"Give us some more, Brother Bethune! Don't let us think you're falling by the wayside!" The call floated up from the company.

"Don't you stop too soon, sir," said Aunt Beck.

"Well, let me welcome a surprise visitor to our midst!" Brother Bethune called. "Judge Oscar Moody, of our county seat of Ludlow! Let's all see him stand and take a bow! I know he's as happy as I am to see where he's found himself today. And the lady setting in front of him is none other than his good wife and helpmeet. Stand up, Mrs. Judge! I wasn't fixing to get me a wife till I finished hunting, and still without a wife to this day," he turned around and said to his gun.

"Why did we stand up?" Judge Moody asked his wife.

"I normally stand up when it's asked of me," she said. "Now, we can sit down." She sat.

But Brother Bethune became suddenly stern, as though he had had to pull the chair out from under Judge Moody. "Now sir! Now that you're here in our midst, Judge Moody, what you reckon we better do with you? I'm going to tell you." While they all, at last, hushed and waited, he waited with them. Then he addressed the Judge in the flat tones of inspiration. "We're going to forgive you."

"Forgive him?" cried Jack, with a leap to his feet, and Etoyle, turning loose from her swinging rope, performed, in the emerald coat, the jump she'd practiced for and alighted on his back. He staggered forward. All the faces, filled to bursting with the occasion, turned from the Judge to Jack, and back and forth.

"Brother Bethune! Brother Bethune! I wonder did you listen good to what you just finished saying?" Jack cried, though the re-union was already humming with fresh pleasure. "What's my family going to think of you?" Etoyle with a shout bounced to the ground and steadied his leg.

"Watch out, Oscar. You're blushing," said Mrs. Moody.

The color rose to his very forehead, as though he had prepared himself for the guilty part. "Forgive me? For what?" he asked.

"Don't try and forgive us for walking in on you. We were invited," Mrs. Moody warned everybody.

"That's plain hospitality," said Uncle Noah Webster, slapping Aunt Cleo on the back. "That ain't no guarantee you ain't going to be forgiven when you get there."

"No sign you are, either," Jack protested. "Brother Bethune! It seems to me like your memory comes and goes at a mighty fast trot today."

Judge Moody looked at his wife.

"Well, after all, you put my car where it is and then made me come off and leave it," she said.

"I'll forgive you for that," Aunt Birdie offered.

"A little forgiveness never hurt anybody," Mrs. Moody said.

"You think it's fitting and proper for them to make a clown of me?" Judge Moody asked her.

"I'll forgive you for bringing your wife," cried Aunt Nanny.

"That'll do, that's a plenty," cried Uncle Noah Webster, and the others began letting out cries and calls more and more hilarious at the sight of the Judge's face and of Jack's face, right together.

"Why is it necessary to forgive me?" Judge Moody demanded.

"That's what I want to know! Judge Moody, I got the same low opinion of it you got!" said Jack.

"Judge Moody, you do like the majority begs and *be* forgiven," Brother Bethune said with a spread of his great long arms. "Be forgiven for sweet forgiveness' sake, Judge Moody dear. Forgiveness would suit us all better than anything in this lonesome old world."

"And make this a perfect birthday for Granny!" said Uncle Percy, putting all his might into his voice.

"Oh, what's been let loose?" cried Miss Beulah. "It's the second time today I've had to ask this bunch of people that!"

"Well, I'm not going along with 'em, Mama," said Jack. "Not this time."

"What's a reunion for!" bellowed Uncle Noah Webster, while Aunt Birdie, charmed clear out of herself, threw open her arms and cried to the Judge, "I forgive you for livin'!"

Judge Moody again looked at his wife.

"That's about the limit," she told him, and he swung around from them all. "Cut it out, Oscar. You're just feeling sorry for yourself," she called, for he'd started away from his school chair, stumbling over some bright green bois d'arc fruits that rolled on the ground the size of heads. "Come on back here. You're not going to leave me sitting by myself! And you have nowhere to go."

"Come on back, Judge Moody," cried Brother Bethune in a voice of sweet invitation. "Don't you want to come back and hear yourself be forgiven?"

"No sir. I do not," said Judge Moody.

"Look! Jack's dog is *bringing* him back!" came laughing cries.

"I don't know why, but I never could teach that dog good sense!" cried Jack, as Sid ran with authority at Judge Moody's heels, driving him back, and as the Judge sank down again into the school chair, some hand rewarded the dog's jaws with birthday cake.

"What does this mean?" Judge Moody asked Jack.

"My family can't bring 'emselves to say it, Judge," Jack told him. "And not much wonder. They're trying to forgive you for sending me to the pen." He stared around him. "Judge Moody, I just don't hardly know what my poor family's thinking about."

"I'll forgive you for pronouncing judgment on Jack Renfro!"

cried Aunt Birdie, and she gave a clap of the hands, while Jack groaned.

"No!" said Judge Moody. "I wasn't feeling my way along that road to come to this—"

"He's where he is now because he's lost," said Mrs. Moody. "But can you show me a man anywhere that's got the fortitude to admit that for himself? No."

"I forgive you for being lost," said Aunt Beck.

"—and I don't want your forgiveness for being a fair judge at a trial. I don't deserve *that*."

"Judge Moody, me and you feel the same way about it!" cried Jack.

"Look at the boy, Judge Moody. Jack Renfro might just as well have been a boy was never heard of around here for the treatment he got from you in Ludlow. I don't believe his mother will ever get over it," said Uncle Curtis. "You need some pretty tall forgiving for that."

Miss Beulah marched up to Judge Moody with the cake plate and its crumbling remains held up in front of her chest to offer. "Don't tell me, sir, you have nothing to be forgiven for, I'm his mother."

"But the fact remains that whatever judgment I passed on this boy I'd be very apt to pass again, if the same case came to court," said Judge Moody.

"I knew it!" said Uncle Dolphus.

Brother Bethune was coming around the table and now he walked close to Judge Moody and linked arms with him. "I even forgive you myself for calling me 'old man,' but don't try it again very soon," he said. "Come with me—march one step further and you can take a bow," he coaxed the Judge. "I'm going to let you meet her. Mis' Vaughn, here's who's come forty-five miles to wish you happy birthday."

"In whose place? Who are you trying to fool?" Granny asked Judge Moody.

Miss Beulah ran to protect her, but she had already found the little wilted bunch of dahlias and swatted feebly at Judge Moody. He backed away, and Jack caught him, then guided him out of Granny's hearing.

"I'm sorry, Judge Moody—Granny's jealous of who tries to get in our family," Jack said. "But her shooing you off don't make me forgive you any the faster! Judge Moody, here you are because you and Mrs. Judge would be roofless in Banner and in danger of starving without us. And you're welcome to the table. And I owe you a raft of gratitude for veering and not killing my wife and baby. And I'm going to get your car back the way it was going in Banner Road. But I ain't going to forgive you for sending me to the pen! Because listen, Judge Moody, you caused all these you see here smiling to do without me for a year, six months and a day while I was ploughing Parchman. And I take it right hard, and it gives me right much of a shock on the day of my welcome home, to hear 'em all forgiving you for it—all but Granny." He gave Granny a look, and then cried, staring all around, "Is the whole rest of the reunion going to forgive him? Mama, Papa, sisters, brothers, aunts, uncles, cousins? Every last one except my wife?"

"I told you so," said Gloria.

"It's all part of the reunion. We got to live it out, son," said Mr. Renfro.

"No sir, I don't forgive you, Judge Moody," Jack told him. "Oh, I'm boiling for 'em still, for the way you deprived 'em. And *now* hear 'em!"

"Jack, make up your mind your family is always going to stay one jump ahead of you," said Gloria.

"I don't forgive you at all, sir," said Jack in a clear, loud voice.

"All right! Fine! I prefer it that way," Judge Moody said with some vigor. "Thank you."

"You're more than welcome," said Jack. He thrust out an arm, and he and Judge Moody shook hands.

"None of this would have happened if Grandpa Vaughn had had this reunion in charge," said Miss Beulah. "And least of all this headlong forgiving of the first craven soul that comes and offers. Oh, Grandpa Vaughn, I miss your presence!"

"We're just at the wrong end of Boone County!" Mrs. Moody burst out.

"Can I just tell *you* something?" interrupted Miss Beulah. "That coconut cake's so tender I advise you to eat it with a spoon."

"And now who wins for giving the biggest surprise?" Brother Bethune called, sweeping Lady May up out of her mother's lap and running with her back to his place, then setting her onto his gun shoulder. "It's a pretty little girl—the one you see raised at last above your heads. She answers to the name of Lady May."

"And if that ain't the longest upper lip in Boone County!" said Aunt Nanny.

Lady May, who had drawn a deep breath, took a look down at everybody, and then it came.

"And I want to take this opportunity to say," said Brother Bethune right over the baby's crying, almost crying himself, "that never have I seen any more of a family gathered together since the Bethunes started to go. There's been a Bethune and a Renfro to go every year, till this year somebody fooled us out of the Renfros. Wonder whose turn it'll be next time, Mr. Ralph?" Brother Bethune cranked his head around the baby's kicking legs and put it to him. He ripped out a bandanna, paused to mop his face, then the baby's, and drove on. "At no reunion the summer long have I enjoyed any better attention or seen any better behavior. The interruptions has been few and far between. And the boat—the boat this little baby, the youngest Renfro walking today, is travelling up on the river of life, I hope the oar of faith and the oar of works will row that little boat clear to the gates of Heaven."

He shut his mouth in a black line, put Lady May down on the ground, and from all around the yard the other babies all cried with her.

"And now, precious friends—if you think *this* is a big reunion! If you think *this* is a pretty full count and a brave showing! Wait! On the Day of Judgment and at the Sounding of the Trumpet—!"

"*I* can wait!" sang out Uncle Noah Webster.

"Why, Banner Cemetery is going to be throwed open like a hill of potatoes!" Brother Bethune cried. "All those loving kin who have gone before, there they'll all be—waiting for you and me! How will you start behaving *then*, precious friends? I'll tell you! You'll all be left without words. Without words! Can you believe it? Think about that!"

He threw out his arms and stood there, open-mouthed.

"Ain't we given him a splendid time?" Aunt Birdie exclaimed.

"Sometimes I think it was an old bachelor like Brother Bethune that thought up reunions in the first place," said Aunt Nanny.

"Three cheers for Brother Bethune!" shouted Uncle Noah Webster.

"Brother Bethune has not accepted many earthly titles," croaked Brother Bethune. "He is content to be one of God's chosen vessels."

"Three more cheers for Brother Bethune!"

"Never asked the church for a cent of money and never needed such. Without script or purse," he whispered, as the cheers died down.

"That's right, Brother Bethune. Sit down, Brother Bethune," several voices invited him.

"I may not have very many earthly descendants," Brother Bethune in an unmollified voice went on. "If you want to come right down to it, I ain't got a one. Now I *have* killed me a fairly large number of snakes. I have kept a count of my snakes I have killed in the last five years, and up to and including this Sunday morning, the grand sum total is four hundred and twenty-six."

They cheered.

"Brother Bethune holds the title of champion snake killer of this entire end of the county," contributed Uncle Curtis. "And I suppose he limits himself to the Bywy on this bank and five or six little branches of it. Is that so, Brother Bethune?"

"It is so so far," said Brother Bethune, still not sitting down.

"You use the old-time twelve-gauge shotgun, I believe," said Mr. Renfro. "That is your main weapon."

"It is my only weapon," said Brother Bethune. He threw out an arm for it, where it stood against the tree—as long as he was, its barrels silver-bright—and shook it at Uncle Nathan, who slowly saluted him back with his paint-stained hand.

Brother Bethune sat down with a groan. His eyes went first to the cake plate, where the last slice of birthday cake stood caving into its crumbs. With the flat of her knife, Granny rapped his reaching fingers.

But here ran Miss Beulah, who set a plate in front of Brother Bethune and rained down on it a collection of chicken gizzards, clattering like china doorknobs. She forked onto the plate the last pickled peach, so heavy it would hardly roll. Brother Bethune gave a hoarse sound of appreciation.

"Did Brother Bethune forgive Jack?" Aunt Birdie asked.

"No, he didn't. He was on the track, but he swerved," said Uncle Curtis.

Mr. Renfro split open seven or eight more watermelons and passed them around. Each time, he gave a different girl the bursting red heart to drown her face in. Each time, giggling, the girl accepted it.

"Listen, I want to know something," said Aunt Birdie. "If it wasn't to make trouble for our boy today, why did you come along Banner Road at all? Judge Moody, will you tell me?"

"My presence in this end of the county has nothing to do with him or the rest of this crowd," said Judge Moody. "I'm here on an errand of my own. I was doing my best to find a way across that river, that's all."

"But we didn't want to get up on that bridge," said Mrs. Moody.

"Shied at the bridge? Well, I don't entirely blame you," said Mr. Renfro.

"Why, of course they don't want to cross that," said Aunt Beck. "Neither do I. And I don't."

Miss Beulah said, "I reckon they must know the story."

"No," said Judge Moody warningly. "I just took a good look at it."

"That bridge is a bone of contention between two sets of supervisors, now that's one safe thing to say about it," said Mr. Renfro. "It's crossing the river between rival counties, you know. Boone on this side, Poindexter on the other."

"There's a sign hanging from the top saying 'Cross at Own Risk,' " said Judge Moody.

"With a skull and crossbones on it," said Mrs. Moody. "Do you argue with that?"

"And the same sign hangs for them on the other side," said the unexpected deep voice of Uncle Nathan.

"Boone and Poindexter, each one of 'em owns that bridge as far out as the middle," said Mr. Renfro. "Let something get the matter with it and the blame goes flying backwards and forwards, thick and fast. And that's about the end of it."

"I'd hate to hear the story," said Mrs. Moody accusingly.

"Clyde Comfort had been out gigging frogs that night, and was just pulling in," said Mr. Renfro, setting down his glass of lemonade. "And passing under the bridge in his boat, he chanced to look up. And he seen the three-quarter moon shining at him just like the bridge wasn't there. There's been a great big bite taken out of the floor of that bridge on the Boone County side, right where it leaves the bank at Banner, and the moon's peeping through at Clyde just like through a gap in the clouds. The first few rows of planks had give way and fell in, or somebody had carried 'em off out of meanness, nobody ever knew. If they'd been pitch pine, I wouldn't have put it past Clyde Comfort himself to run off with 'em, to feed the fire in his boat," he assured Judge Moody. "Well, while he sat there marvelling, he says, he heard a horse and buggy come tearing down the hill into Banner, lickety-split for the bridge. And it's still dark. The pine-knots burning down in Clyde's boat and the three-quarter moon in the sky, that's all the light there was anywhere. And about that same time, Clyde out of the other eye saw him a big fat frog, the kind he was looking for all night, just setting there waiting on him. What was Clyde going to do, hop out and skin up that bank to holler to 'em when he didn't know who—or not lose that frog? Well, he took the path of least resistance. Clyde liked to tell it longer than that, but that's the substance."

"Mr. Renfro, are you trying so hard to entertain Judge Moody that you'd give 'im that story from the other side?" cried Miss Beulah. "What that story is about is Mama and Papa Beecham being carried off young and at the same time, how that bridge flung 'em off and drowned 'em in that river one black morning when the Bywy was high, and afterwards being found wide apart."

"Oh, at least I've heard that one," protested Aunt Cleo.

"Our papa was a Methodist circuit rider, from over in Poindexter County," Miss Beulah began. "And he circuited around here for the declared purpose of finding himself a wife. Clapped his eyes *one time* on Ellen Vaughn stepping out of her father's church one pretty Sunday, and it was all over for Euclid Beecham."

"I wish I'd had a penny for every time I've listened to this one," Mr. Renfro told Judge Moody, but Miss Beulah drove on, and everybody listened except Gloria.

"She did more than marry Euclid Beecham, she made him give up being a Methodist too. And Granny and Grandpa took him in hand and made a pretty good farmer out of him, to boot. Oh, Ellen and Euclid's wedding! That's the one I wish I had a picture of!" she cried. "Rival preachers to marry 'em—Grandpa Vaughn and the Methodist. And the time of year when everything was all bowery. Wasn't it, Granny?"

"Time of locust bloom," Granny admitted.

"And it was two rings to that wedding," Miss Beulah went on. "She gave hers to him, he gave his to her."

"I reckon they did have a plenty more of everything in those days," said Uncle Percy in a whisper. "Long Hungry Ridge must have been a fair prospect then."

"And all this countryside hitched in the grove at Damascus Church and there was singing you could hear for a mile, and Mama and Papa was young and known to all around, and everybody said it was the prettiest couple ever to marry in Banner. Said they could hardly wait to see their children."

"Thick and fast we got here! Nathan the oldest, then Curtis, then Dolphus, then Percy, then me, then Beulah, and then Sam Dale the baby," said Uncle Noah Webster.

"Euclid got what he bargained for," said Mr. Renfro.

"And every last one of those children good as gold, bright and sweet-natured and well-mannered," continued Miss Beulah, still speaking as if from hearsay, or from beyond the grave.

"Well, we know what happened," said Aunt Cleo.

"Papa couldn't help it if he's good-looking beyond the ordinary," said Miss Beulah. "He couldn't help it if he's baptized in the cradle. Couldn't even help it if they named him Euclid, poor little old soul." Suddenly she folded her arms and cried, "I just wish he'd learned how to stop a runaway horse a little better! That's what I wish!"

"Maybe he'd done better if his wife hadn't been holding the reins," said Mr. Renfro.

"I'm going right ahead and tell it!" cried Miss Beulah. "You can't stop me. Now of all the children, Noah Webster was the one awake and was here on the spot to witness 'em go."

"*This* Noah Webster?" Aunt Cleo asked.

Miss Beulah raced on. "He run out when he heard the barn door open, run out in his little gown with a 'Stop, Papa and Mama! Wait a minute!' Almost catches onto the horse but just not high enough. So he just hollers 'Granny!' instead. Well, they was going right on, straight out to the gate, and Granny comes running to stop 'em and nearly got caught and mashed to pieces between the buggy shaft and the tree—" She jabbed her finger at the section of cedar down in the yard. "She run-run-run down the hill after 'em, calling 'em back here."

"Granny *running?*" Vaughn yelled out in horror.

"She jumped on her horse and whipped him up and followed behind 'em trot-a-trot, trot-a-trot, galloping, galloping, but her smart horse stopped dead at the bridge when he got her there. Because he smelled the danger and seen the hole, and there's the buggy-horse kicking down under, and the top of the buggy out in the water, standing up like a sail."

Uncle Curtis, Aunt Nanny, Uncle Percy, all but Uncle Nathan, with single accord flung up their arms in the air, and Uncle Noah Webster held his transfixed wide over his head.

"The beginning of the bridge was just a big hole, and nobody saw fit to tell 'em, and it throwed both of 'em out and drowned 'em in the Bywy River and left us orphans all in the twinkling of an eye," said Miss Beulah. "The Bywy was running high, was full that spring, and I don't know how far downstream they put up the struggle, or what may have tore 'em out of each other's arms. They wasn't found too almighty close together."

"Did they ever find the horse?" yelled Vaughn.

"He didn't manage to hit the water. Had to shoot him."

"Poor Noah Webster always tries to put in that he blames himself for that trouble. And it does look like there ought to been a wide-awake boy could have got his father and mother to hear him when he opened his mouth," said Miss Beulah, striking her own breast.

"Somebody was running away from us children, that's what I believed at the time and still believe," said Uncle Noah Webster. "If I hadn't believed it, I wouldn't have stationed myself in the road and waited for 'em. I'd have been in the bed, tumbled in with the rest of you. Because unless I dreamed it, I didn't know yet about the Bywy bridge getting a hole in it, didn't know any more than they did. I just knew I was in pretty bad danger of losing 'em."

"If they hadn't been who they was, his own mother and father, they might have done different. They only thought he was trying to go with 'em, I reckon. Didn't even turn their heads. If it'd been any-body but a Comfort out gigging on the river! And of course *Granny* couldn't do anything to stop 'em!" said Miss Beulah in anguish.

"Papa was fished out by evening, right where he went in. But where was Mama?" she cried at the company.

"I stood on Banner Top and watched 'em dynamite for her. Two days," said Mr. Renfro. "Old river was running by me faster than I could run, trailing its bubbles."

"But at Deepening Bend, she came up by herself, Mama did. Beulah's too little to remember it, she says," Uncle Dolphus said, sadly teasing.

"It's a wonder to me that river didn't swallow a whole lot of other people that morning who was behaving just as mule-headed," said Aunt Birdie, giving a deep sigh. "That's what still scares me."

"Old bridge has seen some progress. We keep the floor patched at *our* end, and keep driving spikes in the runners to hold 'em from flapping. But give it high water, or a little mischief, and it's still sure death," Uncle Curtis said to Judge Moody. "From my own bed, I've heard it sing all night and with nobody on it, when a north wind blows."

"Take me back to the bridge a minute. What errand was they both so bent on when they hitched and cut loose from the house so early and drove out of sight of Grandpa and Granny, children and all, that morning?" It was Aunt Beck with the gentle voice who prodded.

"Now that's a deep question," said Aunt Nanny.

"Beck, that part of the story's been lost to time," said Uncle Curtis, looking over at his wife. "I think most people just give up wondering, in the light of what happened to 'em on the way."

"Something between man and wife is the only answer, and it's what no other soul would have no way of knowing, Cousin Beck," said Mr. Renfro, and he climbed to his feet and made his way back to the lemonade tub.

"At any rate, by patience and waiting they was able to hold a double funeral," said Aunt Beck to Mrs. Moody. "That's always a comfort."

"At the double funeral," said Miss Beulah, her eyes burning at her grandmother, "it was the same church, with the same two rival preachers, but Grandpa Vaughn overpowering, and with all the little children lined up—that was us—bawling like calves in a row, I'll be bound, though I don't have a speck of recollection."

"So before it's too late," said Aunt Nanny, "those that's bringing comfort make up their minds to take one of them two rings off.

Not let 'em go in the ground taking just all there was of them. They taken Ellen's for the reason she was the most pitiful."

"And who got it?" asked Aunt Cleo.

Miss Beulah's warning hand came up and fixed itself in the air. The skin on her fingers was swollen and silvered until it was like loose, iridescent scales. Her own wedding band would never come off unless and until she lay helpless in her turn, for it was too deeply buried in the flesh.

"It went in Granny's Bible," whispered Aunt Beck, shaking her head.

"I thought it right to bury the ring with my daughter." Granny spoke, and their voices hushed for hers. "I thought it seeming. It was callers to the house saw fit to meddle. With Ellen in her coffin, they came circling round and stripped the ring from her finger. I never saw a one of 'em's face before."

Aunt Nanny winked once at the other aunts.

"That's it. That's the way of it, Granny," Aunt Beck said, and the women rose, came around Granny and said, "So often the way. The world outside don't respect your feelings, even to the last."

"And it's the ring Ella Fay carried to school that morning? Are we back around to that?" Aunt Cleo asked.

"It's the same gold ring, and all the one sad story," Miss Beulah said, patting Granny's shoulder, smoothing out the lace collar. "You didn't hear but the Renfro part this morning."

"Sit patient," Mr. Renfro said. "That's all you had to do."

"Oh, yes, it takes Ella Fay *one day of school* to come home crying without it. It'd take her a mighty long year to learn the way to scrub and hoe and milk and slop the pigs and the rest of it wearing a wedding band of her own and not lose it!" Miss Beulah laid her own ringed hand on the table. Aunt Beck and Aunt Birdie raced to lay their hands down with it and Aunt Nanny slapped hers down on top, and suddenly they all laughed through their tears.

"So to finish the story, Granny just tied on her apron, dusted off her cradle, and started in all over again with another set of children," Uncle Percy said.

"Yes, then it was our blessed little Granny that licked us all into shape," said Uncle Curtis. "With Grandpa towering nearby to pray over our failings. We would have been a poor sort today if we'd had to raise ourselves, wouldn't we, Granny?"

**219**

"We didn't believe in letting anybody go orphans in our family," said Miss Beulah.

"They might have even tried to separate us!" cried Uncle Noah Webster.

"That was surely acting a Christian twice in a lifetime!" Aunt Beck called to Granny. "Bringing all these up!"

"We was all fairly good children," said Miss Beulah. "Sam Dale was the best of all, being the baby."

"All except curly-headed Nathan," said Uncle Percy. "I can hear Grandpa saying it to Granny now, behind closed doors. 'Conquer that child! Stand over him, whip him till he's conquered!' Didn't he, Granny?"

"Come around from behind me," Granny said, "you who I'm guarding back there."

"This forty-pound melon is so good and sweet I believe even you could be tempted, this go-round, Brother Nathan," said Mr. Renfro. He stood offering him the heart on a fork.

"Don't be too hard on yourself, Nathan dear," said Miss Beulah. "You're here only one day and night in the year—all of us wish you wouldn't spend every minute of it standing up and not taking a bite at all."

Uncle Nathan put up his hand and said, "No, Brother Ralph, I'd be much obliged if you'd give it to one of the children."

"Hey!" Aunt Cleo cried. "Ain't that a play hand?"

Uncle Nathan's still uplifted right hand was lineless and smooth, pink as talcum. It had no articulation but looked caught forever in a pose of picking up a sugar lump out of the bowl. On its fourth, most elevated finger was a seal ring.

"How far up does it go?" asked Aunt Cleo.

"It's just exactly as far as what you see that ain't real," said Miss Beulah. "That hand come as a present from all his brothers, and his sister supplied him the ring for it. Both of 'em takes off together. Satisfied?"

"For now," Aunt Cleo said, as they all went back to their seats.

"I've just been to wake Sam Dale," said Granny. "He'll be along in a little bit."

Their faces were stilled for a moment, as though the big old bell standing over them in the yard had laid a stroke on the air.

"Who's Sam Dale?" asked Aunt Cleo.

"Jack's the nearest thing to Sam Dale we've got today," Miss Beulah said in a voice of urgent warning.

"Though Sam Dale left us before he ever got himself sent to the pen for something, I'll tell you that!" Aunt Birdie said in a voice helplessly gay. "If I hadn't married Dolphus, I'd *married* Sam Dale! I believe he was sweet on me."

"Yes, he was sweet on a plenty, but not as many as was sweet on him," said Miss Beulah. "Every girl in Banner was setting her cap for Sam Dale Beecham, and Jack went through the same hard experience."

"Sam Dale got out of marrying any of 'em—the hard way, though," said Mr. Renfro.

Then suddenly Miss Beulah folded her arms and said in a flat voice, "In all our number we didn't have but one with the looks to put your eyes right out, and that was our baby brother Sam Dale."

"Uh-oh," said Aunt Cleo. "Something happened to *him,* I bet."

"Will you try not to pull it out of us?" Miss Beulah cried, still standing with folded arms.

Aunt Beck said, "His is one story I wish we never had to tell."

"Handsome! Handsomer than Dolphus ever was, sunnier than Noah Webster, smarter than Percy, more home-loving than Curtis, more quiet-spoken than Nathan, and could let you have a tune quicker and truer than all the rest put together," said Miss Beulah.

"He sounds like he's dead," said Aunt Cleo.

The shade was deep and widespread now. The old bell hanging from its yoke on the locust post was the only thing in the yard still beyond shade's reach. The wisteria that grew there with it looked nearly as old as the bell; its trunk was like an old, folded, gray quilt packed up against the post, and the eaves made a feathery bonnet around the black, still, iron shape.

"He'd better come to the table in a hurry now, or miss his treat," Granny said, her finger trembling above the cake plate. "A fool for sweets ever since I put the drop of honey on his tongue to hush his first cry."

Uncle Noah Webster offered Aunt Cleo the dripping heart of his melon, and she took it in bites from the point of his knife, but still she said, "Are you all going to humor her? Just because she's old?"

Miss Beulah threw open her arms and brought her hands fast together in a clap. "Come, *children!*" she yelled.

Then an avalanche of the waiting children came down on Granny. "I'm not a baby," she said, putting out her little hands. One hand closed around a bag of red-hot-poker seed, and in the other was set a teacup quaking in its saucer. At the same time she was asked to unwrap a can of talcum powder.

"There's something you can make live through the winter!" "And that's something will bloom for you before you know it!" They all encouraged her.

Elvie came with the speckled puppy carried high to her cheek, his rump filling the cup of one careful hand, and with a sigh she gave him up, sank him into Granny's lap. "He'll run anything with fur on it. He'll retrieve anything with feathers on it," she said in the gruff voice of Uncle Dolphus. The puppy yawned into Granny's face. In the open pan of his muzzle a good-sized acorn would have fitted closely. "He'll do it all."

"Now what's that? It's that Christmas cactus coming around again," said Granny. "If there's one thing I'm ever tired of!"

"Then ain't these beautiful? And when Old Man Winter's at your door, how you'll love to eat on 'em," said Uncle Percy, coming himself to bring her a bottle of his own hot peppers steeping in vinegar and turned blue, red, and high purple. "Pretty as chicken gizzards to me."

The Champions' present, wrapped up like an owl, was an owl —in brown china, big as a churn, with potbelly, sunflower-yellow feet, and eyes wired to flash on and off.

"Like I didn't have enough of those outside without bringing one inside. Believe I'll like the next present better. I know what *this* is," Granny told them, as she took a box covered in yellowing holly paper from four children and clawed it open on her knee. She shook out the new piece-quilt. A hum of pleasure rose from every man's and woman's throat.

When the mire of the roads had permitted, the aunts and girl cousins had visited two and three together and pieced it on winter afternoons. It was in the pattern of "The Delectable Mountains" and measured eight feet square, the slanty red and white pieces running in to the eight-pointed star in the middle, with the called-for number of sheep spaced upon it. Then Aunt Beck had quilted it on her lap with her bent needle.

Granny's eyes tried to see into theirs while she shimmered it at them. She turned and held it the other way to show the sky-blue lining. Peering at them, she put it next to her cheek.

"Finished it last night. Took me just about all night," she said. "Pricked my finger a time or two."

"She'll be buried under that," said Aunt Beck softly.

"I'm going to be buried under 'Seek No Further,'" said Granny. "I've got more than one quilt to my name that'll bear close inspection."

The network of wrinkles in her face shifted a little, and deep within it for a moment her eyes shone blue as theirs. She bored her eyes into the nearest one there—it was Lady May.

"Look who's standing there for her!" said Aunt Nanny. "Don't she look like a little firecracker about to go off?"

The baby had come as close as she dared to all the presents, without having risked yet putting her hand on the puppy.

"What have you got for Granny, Lady May?" cried Aunt Birdie.

"I want a kiss," said Granny, leaning toward the baby. "I want lovingkindness."

Lady May bolted.

Miss Beulah threw back her head and in an unwavering note gave them the pitch. All their voices rose as one, with Uncle Noah Webster trailing his echoes in the bass.

> *"Gathering home! Gathering home!*
> *Never to sorrow more, never to roam!*
> *Gathering home! Gathering home!*
> *God's children are gathering home."*

As they sang, the tree over them, Billy Vaughn's Switch, with its ever-spinning leaves all light-points at this hour, looked bright as a river, and the tables might have been a little train of barges it was carrying with it, moving slowly downstream. Brother Bethune's gun, still resting against the trunk, was travelling too, and nothing at all was unmovable, or empowered to hold the scene still fixed or stake the reunion there.

# Part 4

*T*hey sang for a while longer, still in their chairs but settled back, some of them singing with their eyes closed. On the tables before them there were only the scraps and the bones, the boats of the eaten-out watermelons; yet still, now and again, a white chicken feather floated down from the sky and did a brief spin on the grass, or a curl of down landed on one of the tables.

"Why does she sing so old-timey?" Aunt Cleo asked. Granny was a jump ahead of everybody else with her fa-so-la, on up to the Amen of "Blessed Assurance."

"She sings it that way because that's the way she likes to hear it," Miss Beulah told her. "If that ain't the way you want it, my little granny's going to go you one better than you want."

By now the girls' and boys' baseball game had started again in the pasture. There was a board laid across the cedar trunk and little girls were seesawing.

"There's Gloria's perch those children are making free with," observed Miss Lexie.

"I don't need it any more, thank you," Gloria said.

She was coming out of the house now at Jack's shoulder; he was carrying a syrup bucket stuffed to the top.

"After Aycock gets his satisfaction out of this, I'll carry word to little Mis' Comfort where he is, so she can give up and go to bed," Jack told Granny's table.

"Is he going to eat it like a horse?" cried Miss Beulah.

"Promise me. Promise me when you get up there you won't try anything single-handed, young fellow," said Mrs. Moody.

"Yes, I'd like to have your word on that too," said Judge Moody.

"Single-handed—that ain't the way we do it around Banner," Jack told them. "And I already promised Curly the same thing. We're saving the Buick till in the morning."

He bounced kisses on Gloria's and his mother's cheeks and on Granny's chin, and walked away. There was nothing of the world to see any longer below their gate, only the low roof of dust lying over the road, fine-stretched and unbroken as skin, and Jack went down through that and out of sight.

"Don't like the way they keep sneaking in and out on me," said Granny.

"Never you fear," Miss Beulah said to her quickly. "He'll be back when we want him, he's not one to fail us."

"Seems to me you've let an awful lot hinge on Aycock. I wonder if you know a great deal about his appetite," Mr. Renfro said to Judge Moody. "I think of the time Jack got home from a little hunting and Aycock tagged along with him, and it was supper time." He hitched his keg a little closer to Judge Moody, there at his elbow, "Well, to let Aycock have a sample of what hospitality means around here, Beulah fried up Jack's squirrels along with the rest of supper, and she set those on a platter in front of Aycock's plate while he's eating. And remember, Mother, how one after the other he forked those over and et 'em all? Et fourteen squirrel? I counted, because that's how many times he apologized, once for each squirrel, saying he hadn't had a real solid meal since morning." Mr. Renfro sat looking into Judge Moody's face. "All them mouth-watering squirrels went into Aycock's mouth one by one, while we mostly just set and felt sorry for him," he said. "There don't seem to be nothing there to tell him when he's reached the point of enough."

"Jack can handle Aycock," said Miss Beulah.

"Then tomorrow there's Curly Stovall, and that tree to get around," said Mr. Renfro. "And it's a pretty stubborn old tree."

"Jack Renfro will find his own way," said Miss Beulah. "He's come along too splendid now to get himself licked in the morning."

"What a fellow's got to do is suit his strategy to the tree," Mr. Renfro said to Judge Moody. "I think now of a tree that must've been forty foot up to the first good branch when I come up against it. A honey tree that was, a poplar. You could hear those bees just boiling inside—oh, they was working heavy. So the way I licked it, I went and got me a good augur—inch-and-a-half, I reckon. Bored me a hole in the trunk and drove me in a peg and climbed up and stood on that. Drove me in the next one. Well, sir, I pegged me a ladder all the forty foot up that tree trunk, winding my way around it two or three times, and when I pulled up to that hollow limb, was it ever a-roaring around my ears! I hadn't climbed all that way without a saw at my belt. Sawed it through and let it down gentle on my rope, honey, bees, and all, the whole limb, until there, where she's standing down on the ground waiting, was Beulah's honey."

"Oh, *she* was the one making you," said Aunt Cleo.

"Beulah let it out some way—I managed to get it out of her— that however I could manage to reach it, she'd pretty dearly like to have it," said Mr. Renfro. "Truth is she'd been heartbroken going without it. Like Mrs. Moody'd be without her car, if my guess is any good."

"Can you see today where you went up, Papa?" asked Elvie from a branch of the bois d'arc.

"All healed over. Oh no, the tree's grown all over that now," he said. "If it's standing at all, that is."

"I wouldn't mind having another sample of that very honey," said Miss Beulah right behind him.

"I was a climbing fool," said Mr. Renfro to Judge Moody.

"We've got more company," called Etoyle up above Elvie. "Watch out, Gloria!"

The squeak of an axle cut through a song somewhere and the head of a white horse came swinging up through the dust, and its wagon with an old man driving it came past the seesawing children and tunnelled into the shade under the boughs. The dry yard, packed though it was with people, wagons, and cars, sounded hollow under the wheels like the floor of an empty barn.

"Willy Trimble, I'm always just on the point of forgetting about you!" Miss Beulah cried out like the best praise she had for him.

Mr. Willy saluted back by holding up his whip as if to crack it. Gloria jumped as if to get ready to run.

"What do you think you're doing here, Willy Trimble?" asked Miss Beulah. "We're holding our family reunion, or trying to, the best way we can."

"Happy birthday," Mr. Willy called down to Granny as he reined in.

"Go back where you came from," she suggested.

Mr. Willy got down from the wagon, gave them all a nod. "How're you, Lexie?"

"I'm livin'." That was the most that question ever got out of her.

Mr. Willy cocked his head at her. "And who's looking after your lady while you're gallivanting?"

"A nurse. One that's seven years old. I let him wear my Mother Hubbard tied up high around his neck. It's a little boy that can't know much," she said. "Lives down the road. And he don't know what Miss Julia Mortimer will do and Miss Julia Mortimer don't know what he'll do. So they're evens."

"And what are you going to have to give that little-old boy when you get back?" asked Aunt Cleo.

"A whipping if he breaks something!" cried Miss Lexie.

"Suppose she's played us all a trick," said Mr. Willy Trimble.

As Gloria's breath came fast, Miss Lexie said, "Now that I'm not there to soldier her, you couldn't surprise me with anything she'd try."

Miss Beulah hummed her high note with which she corrected the pitch of the congregation in church. "Let's not be served with any of your story today, Lexie," she said.

"Miss Julia took a tumble. And I'm the one found her," Mr. Willy Trimble said, his expression all self-amazement. "She'd made it down to the road, and pitched in the dust. I raised her up. Her face told its story."

"Now who's Miss Julia Mortimer?" asked Aunt Cleo into the sudden quiet.

"Hush up!" came a big chorus.

"Down fell she. End of *her*. And her cow was calling its head off," Mr. Willy Trimble said.

"It's not fair!" cried out Gloria.

Etoyle and Elvie jumped down from the tree. Locking knuckles they went spinning together around and around in a chicken fight, while the aunts gathered themselves to their feet.

"Gloria, sounds like it's your turn to go," said Aunt Nanny.

"That's right! You just better switch on over there the soonest

**230**

way you can," said Aunt Birdie. "There'll be work cut out for you to do, girlie."

"You owe her a debt of gratitude, Gloria," said Aunt Beck, coming to give her an embrace. "I'm sorry *for* you."

"Find somebody to take you, and go on. That's better than standing here crying," Aunt Nanny said, coming toward her. "There'll be ones there to cry with you."

"She's not crying yet," said Etoyle.

"Don't start tormenting her," said Aunt Beck. Now the aunts were passing her from one to the next to hug her and kiss her cheek. "I know you're being pulled two ways," she said to Gloria.

"Life's given to tricks like that," scoffed Miss Beulah at Granny's chair. "You just have to be equal to the pulling."

"It's not fair," Gloria was saying to each one who kissed her.

"I carried her in out of the sun, and then raised a good holler," Mr. Willy went on. " 'Anybody here?' And you know who it was? Little fellow from down the road, crying like he'd just took a whipping from somebody. I give him a drink of water and sent him home."

"And I'd like to know if any of this explains what you're doing *here,* Willy Trimble!" cried Miss Beulah.

"Well, do you know I just been run off from *there?*" Mr. Willy asked them all around. "I got it made to a T, a nice coffin, got all the way over there with it, and the crowd in the yard run me off. Like they'd never heard of such a thing or heard of me either. She's already fitted, they says. Don't need any present. I thought they'd be having a fit over it and welcome me with open arms. Seems like they opened up and got her one in Gilfoy. It's a Jew. They don't believe in Jesus—I reckon Sunday's just like any other day to him. When I went breaking the Sabbath for her! Then for it to get thrown back at me."

"I hope you didn't come bringing it here," warned Miss Beulah.

"I felt like I'd tailored my work to suit her," Mr. Willy said in a voice grown more and more proudly aggrieved. "I considered it dovetails correct, it's good good wood, there's not a thing cheap about it from one end to the other, or a thing shoddy about the way I fashioned it—squared off the ends and rabbitted them joints and the rest of it. I had full faith in it. For one thing, you know who taught me how to use a handsaw? She did."

"Exactly when?" asked Miss Lexie Renfro.

"Miss Julia Mortimer elected me every year I showed up at school to split up the wood for the potbelly stove, and I proved to her what I was good at. Oh, when I finally got my toolbox, time I was forty, I made her chicken coops a-plenty, flower-boxes, yard seats, porch swings, and till I got 'em right, too. She was ever the least bit hard to please. I don't believe, if she was still listening, she'd stop me from saying that. She was pretty smart, herself! She could have made her own coffin if she thought she had to. Of course, her *eye* was true, she couldn't help how true her eye was," apologized Mr. Willy. "As a child I recall her tacking up a crokersack over a busted school window on a snowy day. With a good ten or twenty tacks in her mouth all at one time, she'd *pp pp pp pp pp* not a miss. They all went in straight. And still hearing the history lesson. I told 'em my story in Alliance. It didn't budge 'em."

"Maybe it wasn't them to blame. Maybe it was you," said Miss Beulah.

" 'Why, I'm the one milks for her!' I says. 'I wanted to do something for her. She taught me to use hammer and saw when I was a shirt-tail lad, I've made many a coffin in Banner, and now I made hers. I made her a beauty.' They just went back in the house and left me with it."

"Willy Trimble, I'm going to tell you something, if you're all that anxious to find out," said Miss Beulah. "The main thing you know how to do is overstep. Just because you milk for a lady don't mean you're welcome, the next thing, to make her coffin. And until you get an invitation, you ought to stay home. "

"Well," he said, "she told me herself, when I was that shirt-tail lad, she thought I'd wind up making hers in the end, her coffin."

"Let me tell you right here and now, I don't want you making mine," said Miss Beulah. "And nobody else's you might have an eye on."

"I owed it to her, that's how I figured it," he went right on. "After she taught me just about everything I know. Once I got started, I just never looked back."

"Mr. Willy, between here and the schoolhouse I can count nine Uncle Sams, and they every one looks like you," said Etoyle.

"Well, I'm the artist," he said benevolently. "And it's all because she put a hammer in my hand. And it was for her I commenced writing my name with the question mark after it. 'Willy Trimble?' "

"She told you to?" asked Uncle Percy respectfully.

"Well, she told me not to. That's the way I'm down on the poll books today: 'Willy Trimble?' But she rammed a good deal down me, spelling, arithmetic—well, history's where she fell down," he said. "There's a heap of history I don't know, standing right here before you." He scraped his foot, gave them a bow. "But she knew it all. She had it by heart. There's just one thing Miss Julia come to find she couldn't do as well as I could, and that's to milk a cow. She got too old, and there wasn't anybody else, and she got me to do that for her." He turned and gave Gloria a bow to herself. "You want to climb on now?" he asked her. "I'll head back over. I ain't too proud to try anybody a second time. Maybe you could get *me* in."

"Pshaw!" said Miss Beulah.

"Gloria's staying right here! She don't want to leave the re-union!" cried Aunt Birdie. She put up a loyal fist. "We wouldn't *let* you go, you belong where you are, with us," she told Gloria.

"We had to tease you, just the first minute, because you was looking so found out, Gloria," said Aunt Nanny, poking her, and then pushing her back down into the baby rocker.

"Nobody's going over there with you, Willy Trimble," Miss Lexie Renfro said sharply.

"Then I reckon I'll just visit here a while, with some other folks that's left out," he said.

"*Left out?*" screamed Miss Beulah. "Mr. Willy, let's not have one of your jokes." She threw up her hands.

"I'll tell you one thing sure. I wouldn't go back over there unless I was sent for," said Miss Lexie Renfro.

"Lexie, you're supposed to be there now," said Aunt Nanny, with a wink at the table. "And I bet you was paid for it."

"I don't suppose you heard anybody over there call my name?" Miss Lexie asked, defying Mr. Willy, and he shook his head at her.

"But we can spare you," said Miss Beulah. "If that's what you want."

"There's others!" said Miss Lexie. "And people can always find you if they want you."

Aunt Beck said, "Well, I don't know about that. And I'm afraid, Lexie, you'd have a hard time persuading any of us to go with you."

"To the wake of somebody you don't know? I can't think of more than once or twice I've ever been persuaded," said Aunt Cleo.

"Somebody we don't know?" came a chorus from all around.

"You *all* know her?" asked Aunt Cleo.

"Know her?" a whole chorus cried. "Suffered under her!" cried Aunt Birdie.

"We all *had* her! She was our teacher, all the long way through Banner School," said Aunt Beck. "That's how well we know her, and so do a hundred other people born just as unlucky."

"Well, they know how to give you a hard time," Aunt Cleo said with an easy nod. "Whatever this one was like, though, I bet you I had one in Piney that would outshine her."

"Bet you a hundred silver dollars you didn't!" Uncle Noah Webster said.

"Mine was a regular hornet's nest to run up against," said Aunt Cleo. "I'm surprised the majority lived through mine. The only thing about mine is, I can't remember her name."

"You'd never forget the name of Miss Julia Mortimer," Aunt Beck said. "Or ever hope Miss Julia Mortimer would forget yours."

"She taught every single soul I see, leaving out three or four. Why, it's like coming back to school right here, as good as over there, gathered in her own house right now," said Mr. Willy, looking around him.

Brother Bethune excused himself and went off with his gun.

"How many's she got over yonder already?" asked Auntie Fay.

"She's got your husband, if that's what you're asking. Got all Alliance, half of Ludlow, and most of Foxtown. A little sprinkling from Freewill," said Mr. Willy. "It's as many as you got."

"That's as many as she taught, all right," said Miss Beulah. "Oh, and teach us she did. Here's one I bet she remembered right up to the end."

"She taught you, Mama?" Etoyle cried. "How could a teacher be as old as that?"

"She taught me," said Miss Beulah coolly. "She's responsible for a good deal I know right here today."

"Beulah, I want you to save and give her that compliment when you get to Heaven with her," said Uncle Curtis. "I bet she never expected to draw one out of you."

"Who do you suppose started the woman off? How do you suppose she'd get started teaching without having some Beechams to teach?" Miss Beulah asked Etoyle and Elvie, who stood with their arms wound around each other's waists.

"Miss Julia taught me, and that was back-breaking effort," said Uncle Noah Webster to the children. "But I reckon she about cut her teeth on Nathan. He was her shining light."

"She taught us every one. I can see her this minute while I tell it, thumping horseback to school, wrapped up in that red sweater," cried Aunt Birdie. "Red as a railroad lantern, of her own knitting. Ready to throw open school and light straight into us."

"I remember her waiting for us on the old doorstep, a-ringing that bell. She had more arm than any other woman alive," said Uncle Curtis. "That was her switching arm, too."

"She didn't scare the girls with her whistling switch. She scared 'em off by expecting a whole world *out* of 'em," said Aunt Beck.

"She used the same weapon on the boys," Uncle Dolphus argued. " 'Where's your ambition bump?' And she'd rub her chalky hand over our pore hot skulls."

"Though sometimes she'd only come and stand close while you sat trying. Like if she could just blow on you, you would know the right answer," said Aunt Beck.

"She had designs on everybody. She wanted a doctor and a lawyer and all else we might have to holler for some day, to come right out of Banner. So she'd get behind some barefooted boy and push," said Uncle Percy. "She put an end to good fishing."

"She'd follow you, right to your door!" Uncle Dolphus said.

"Taking over more'n her territory, that was her downfall," said Miss Beulah, nodding. "Made herself fair nuisance with the boys in particular. When these Beecham boys was shirt-tail lads, they was fairly high-spirited."

"Miss Julia Mortimer and her whistling switch put an end to their dreams," Aunt Nanny teased.

"That's right! Not many escaped her yardstick. Boys, she wanted us to learn something if it was to kill us," Uncle Percy said with ragged voice. He had started to whittle his stick of wood.

"She held that five months took out of our lives every year wasn't punishment enough. She had us commencing our schooling in August instead of November. And after planting time was over in spring she called us back and made us finish what we'd started, beginning at the very spot we'd left off," said Uncle Dolphus. "She was our bane."

"She drove what she could into us," said Miss Beulah. "But nobody could hold a Beecham boy down. Not if you was to kill yourself trying. Nobody could but Grandpa."

"Outside the home, we boys was more used to sitting on the bridge fishing than lining the recitation bench. Now she wanted that changed," said Uncle Curtis.

"She thought if she mortified you long enough, you might have hope of turning out something you wasn't!" cried Uncle Noah Webster.

"And then she'd take the credit!" cried Miss Beulah. "Where ninety percent of the time, the credit was owing to the splendid mothers at home!"

" 'Children never change,' she'd say. 'They come to school three kinds—good, bad, and hungry.' " said Miss Lexie, making a face like a hungry one.

"It appeared to be her notion nobody around here could give their children enough to eat at home," said Uncle Curtis, looking innocent. "Every Monday morning on her horse, she carted milk to school in a ten-gallon can—and give that milk to children at dinner time to wash their biscuit down with."

"Of course we had to pour ours right out on the ground," said Aunt Nanny. "Broadwees is as good as she is."

"She told us a time or two what her aim was! She wanted us to quit worshipping ourselves quite so wholehearted!" cried Miss Beulah, and set her hands on her hips.

"Maybe just about then is when we quit worshipping her," Uncle Curtis said.

"If I ever worshipped Miss Julia Mortimer, it was a pretty short romance!" shouted Uncle Dolphus.

"Deliver me from the schoolroom," said Aunt Birdie with finality. "I hate the very thought now of trying to teach anybody anything. If they came begging to me, I'd have to send 'em to you, Beck."

Auntie Fay primmed her lips. "Remember the day I got to be one of you?"

"Here goes Sissie. All right! Tell yours," said Miss Lexie sardonically.

"I wasn't but five years old that morning—and it all went dark, dark in the house, and I ran and got the door open. I says, 'Something's *coming!*' I heard it! 'Get out, Lexie! Run!' It was the *wind*

**236**

I heard. The air was too thick to see through. Too thick to breathe any of. Too strong to stand up in. And I went down on my hands and knees and I shut my eyes and crawled," said Auntie Fay. She was telling it with her eyes shut. "Blind crawled."

"Where was you going?" asked Aunt Cleo. "Did you think it would do you any good?"

"I was crossing the road to go to school but I didn't know it," said Auntie Fay.

"You went off and left me," said Miss Lexie.

"You was kept home from school with the chicken pox. I *called* you."

"The rest of us children was already right where we belonged, inside Banner School with Miss Julia Mortimer telling us it was the best place to be," said Miss Beulah with her straight-lipped smile. "She taught right ahead. We could perfectly well hear all outdoors fixing to come apart. I reckon most of Banner was trying to get loose and go flying. All of a sudden, the schoolhouse roof took off and went right up to the sky. The cyclone was on top of Banner School like a drove of cattle. There was our stove, waltzing around with our lunch pails, and the map flapping its wings and flying away, and our coats was galloping over our heads with Miss Julia's cape trying to catch 'em. And the wind shrieking like a bunch of rivals at us children! But Miss Julia makes herself heard all the same. 'Hold on! Hold onto each other! All hold onto me! We're in the best place right here!' Didn't she?" she cried to the others.

"I thought I saw her throw herself down on the dictionary once, when it tried to get away," said Aunt Birdie. "But I didn't believe my eyes."

"Where was *you?*" Aunt Cleo pointed at Auntie Fay. "You started this."

"I was out on the schoolhouse step, hollering 'Let me in!'" she said. "And it seemed to me like they was trying a good deal harder to keep me out. Till Miss Julia herself got the door open and grabbed for me. And the wind was trying its best to scoop me and her and all of 'em behind her out of the schoolhouse, but she didn't let it. She had me by the foot and pulled me in flat. She pulled against the wind and dragged me good, till I was a hundred percent inside that schoolhouse."

"Finally we got the door shut again, and Miss Julia got on her knees and leaned against it, and we all copied her, and we held the

237

schoolhouse up," said Aunt Birdie. "Every single one of us plastered with leaves!"

"And that chair—that's when this house was delivered that school chair, the one you're holding down this minute, Judge Moody. It blew here," said Miss Beulah, pointing at him. "And the tree caught it—Billy Vaughn's Switch did. If it hadn't, it might have come right in the house through that window into the company room. That chair's the only sample of the cyclone this house got. I reckon Grandpa was pretty strongly praying."

"What did it do to the store?" asked Aunt Cleo. "Stovall's store?"

"It was Papa's store then. Well, sir, the roof took off and it was just like you'd shaken a feather bolster and seen it come open at the seam," said Mr. Renfro. "I was watching the whole thing get away from Papa. Everything that'd been inside that store got outside. Blew away. And the majority of our house went right along to keep it company."

"What happened to the bridge?" asked Mrs. Moody.

Auntie Fay rattled her little tongue.

"No it didn't. It didn't even wiggle. I was paying it some mind, I was under it," said Mr. Renfro to his sister. "I was going a little tardy to school that morning, and when I heard the thing coming, the bridge is what I dove under. And it wasn't in the path, that bridge. No, the storm come up the river and it veered. The bridge stood still right where it was put, and a minute away, the rest of the world went right up in the air."

"It picked the Methodist Church up all in one piece and carried it through the air and set it down right next to the Baptist Church! Thank the Lord nobody was worshipping in either one," said Aunt Beck.

"I never heard of such a thing," said Mrs. Moody.

"Now you have. And those Methodists had to tear their own church down stick by stick so they could carry it back and put it together again on the side of the road where it belonged," said Miss Beulah. "A good many Baptists helped 'em."

"I'll tell you something as contrary as people are. Cyclones," said Mr. Renfro.

"It's a wonder we all wasn't carried off, killed with the horses and cows, and skinned alive like the chickens," said Uncle Curtis.

**238**

"Just got up and found each other, glad we was all still in the land of the living."

"You were spared for a purpose, of course," said Mrs. Moody.

"Everybody made it the best way they could till Banner got pieced back together. Grandpa Vaughn did a month's worth of preaching on destruction—it was all Banner but the Baptist Church. And if you want to count the bridge," said Uncle Curtis.

"It made another case of having to start over. You just don't quite know today how your old folks did it," said Mr. Renfro.

"Miss Julia was as wrong as you could ever hope about the best place to be," said Miss Beulah. "If it hadn't been for the children holding it up, that schoolhouse would have fallen right on top of 'em, and her too!"

"And in return, did we get a holiday out of that cyclone? Why, no," said Uncle Curtis. "That same day, and the first thing anybody knew, Miss Julia made all the fathers around here get together and give the schoolhouse the first new roof in Banner, made out of exactly what they could find. And she never quit holding school while they was overhead pounding. Rain or shine, she didn't let father or son miss a day. 'Every single day of your life counts,' she told 'em all alike. 'As long as I'm here, you aren't getting the chance to be cheated out of a one of 'em.' "

"Everybody went off that morning and left me," said Miss Lexie.

"Yes, Lexie elected to stay home by herself and the whole house blew away and left her in the frame of the front door, standing in her petticoat and all come out in spots. Wasn't that forlorn?" teased Aunt Birdie.

"Well, you've been going from one's house to another's ever since, Lexie," Miss Beulah pointed out. "You've made up for it now."

"I remember another time, when the river was high and Miss Julia Mortimer asked us how many in the room couldn't swim," said Uncle Curtis. "And at the show of hands she says, 'Every child needs to know how to swim. Stand at your desks.' And with us lined up behind her she taught us how to swim." Uncle Curtis flailed his arms. "The river was lapping pretty well at the doorstep at the time. The last thing she'd have thought of was send us home. When she thought we could swim, she went back to the history lesson."

"Foot. Nothing fazed her," said Aunt Nanny.

"She was ready to teach herself to death for you, you couldn't get away from that. Whether you wanted her to or not didn't make any difference. But my suspicion was she did want you to *deserve* it," Uncle Curtis stated.

"How did she last as long as she did?" marvelled Aunt Beck.

"She thought if she told people what they ought to know, and told 'em enough times, and finally beat it into their hides, they wouldn't forget it. Well, some of us still had her licked," said Uncle Dolphus.

" 'A state calling for improvement as loudly as ours? Mississippi standing at the foot of the ladder gives me that much more to work for,' she'd say. I don't dream it was so much palaver, either," said Miss Beulah. "She meant it entirely."

"That's what comes of reading, bet your boots," said Uncle Curtis.

"Full of books is what she was," said Aunt Beck.

"Oh, books! The woman read more books than you could shake a stick at," said Miss Beulah. "I don't know what she thought was going to get her if she didn't."

"She'd give out prizes for reading, at the end of school, but what would be the prizes? More books," said Aunt Birdie. "I dreaded to win."

"And memory work! Every single 'and' and 'but' in the right place. I'd like to know if her own memory lasted as long as she did," said Aunt Nanny.

Uncle Dolphus, tilting his chair back, crossed his legs at the knee. " 'Hark, hark the lark at Heaven's gate sings!' "

"Dolphus, you dog," they cried back at him.

"I love coffee, I love tea, I love the girls and the girls love me!" shouted Uncle Noah Webster as the handclapping stormed.

"If it was Miss Julia Mortimer taught you to recite that, I'm a billy goat," grinned Aunt Nanny.

"Yes'm, she taught the generations. She was our cross to bear," said Uncle Dolphus as the laughter died away. " 'Hark hark.' "

For the moment after, the only sound was that of Brother Bethune hitting the tobacco can he was shooting at somewhere behind the house.

"I'd got over there sooner, and found Miss Julia Mortimer sooner," Mr. Willy Trimble then said, "if she'd ever been persuaded to give a morning yell. I listen for Captain Billy Bangs, listen for Brother Bethune, and they listen for me—"

"What's a morning yell for?" interrupted Aunt Cleo.

"Mainly to show you're still alive after the night," he told her.

"You've got Noah Webster now," Miss Beulah told her. "You can afford to keep still."

"It's the time-honored around here, for us old folks left dwelling to ourselves. A chain of 'em—one hollering across to the next one. So then if somebody breaks it, we know what it is," said Mr. Willy, putting his tongue into the corner of his smile. " 'Sound travels over water,' I told Miss Julia. "You can holler 'cross the Bywy. I'll hear."

"She wasn't dwelling to herself, I was right there to watch her till this morning," said Miss Lexie. "But I didn't want to fail the reunion. I'd get myself talked about."

Mr. Willy did not cease regarding them. His eyes, where the whites showed above the rounds, were wary as a feeding rabbit's.

Aunt Nanny cocked her head. "Come on, tell it. There's some more. You found her: she hadn't drawn on her hose?"

"Did she speak to you?" Aunt Beck in a voice of dread asked.

"Yes'm. Before I got her picked up. She said, 'What was the trip for?' "

"The trip?" several of them chorused.

"But she hadn't been anywhere, had she?" asked Aunt Beck.

"We was equals. I didn't come with any answer," said Mr. Willy. "Well, she picked the wrong one to ask. It's the chance you are always taking as you journey through life. I just raised her up and carried her to her bed. But she didn't even know that. She was past it."

Granny was glaring up at him from the head of her table.

"And now they're all moving in on her and they'll set up with her all night," he told her.

"Granny's not scared of old Willy Trimble," said Miss Beulah, there at her side.

"She's sized him up," said Granny.

"Granny's not scared of Satan himself, is she?" cried Uncle Noah Webster.

"She's pretty venturesome," said Granny.

"And they'll bury her in the morning," Mr. Willy told them at large. "Want to go?" He smiled for them like a little girl. Then he pulled a chair quick under him and sat on it as if modesty had captured it for him. It was Brother Bethune's, only one chair away from Granny's own. "Now I didn't come to the table to catch your bites," he declared.

"Will you take a slice of cake in spite of yourself?" Miss Beulah cried at him, glaring. "Then take some of Lexie's pound cake that's going begging."

"I ain't choicy," he said, using both hands.

"Well, Gloria, if you hadn't changed your ways, an end like that was what might've been in store for you," said Aunt Birdie. "Glad you're married now?"

Aunt Cleo pointed at Gloria. "What makes me wonder is the school system. How'd it ever get ahold of *her?*"

"Gloria Short won the spelling match from over the whole state when they held it in Jackson and she was twelve years old. In the Hall of Representatives in the New Capitol. Schoolchildren against the Legislature—Miss Julia Mortimer's idea. And an orphan spelled down grown men. It gratified Miss Julia's soul, she said," recited Miss Lexie Renfro. "She coached that child so she could go to Alliance High School and keep up with ordinary children, till she got a diploma like they did, and she boarded her in her own home while she did it. She put her on the bus after that and sent her to Normal, headed to be a teacher. Miss Julia Mortimer was given to flights like that."

"How did she get to be so rich?" asked Aunt Cleo.

"A teacher? Not by teaching," said Mrs. Moody. "Ask one."

"She sure didn't have anything of her own? In that case she'd have quit," said Aunt Cleo.

They laughed at her. "Miss Julia Mortimer quit?"

"Taught to put herself through school in the first place," said Miss Lexie. "Just like anybody else."

"The year she boarded me and sent me to high school, she had Banner School to keep open herself. And she said she'd do that if she had to walk over the backs of forty supervisors. That's when she put some cows in the back and fenced her pasture," Gloria related. "And we milked them, before school and after."

"I never milked for her," said Miss Lexie, and Mr. Willy Trimble laughed. "Contending with a pasture full of cows takes about the same amount of strength out of you as teaching a schoolroom full of children, I'd judge. But she contended—because she was of the opinion nothing could lick her."

"Then she had fruit bushes and flower plants for sale, and good seed—vegetables. She had a big yard and plenty of fertilizer," said Gloria. "She'd sell through the mail. She wouldn't exchange. But she'd work just as hard trying to give some of her abundance away."

"Well, you have to trust people of the giving-stripe to give you the thing you want and not something they'd be just as happy to get rid of," said Miss Beulah.

"She put her lists in the Market Bulletin. She had letters and parcel post travelling all over Mississippi," Gloria said.

"I don't imagine she ever made her postman very happy," said Aunt Birdie. "Carrying on at that rate with that many poor souls makes work for others."

"One year, she sent out more little peach trees than you can count, sent them free," said Gloria, and they laughed.

"Her switches?" Uncle Noah Webster teased.

"These were rooted," said Gloria. "Came out of her orchard. She wanted to make everybody grow as satisfying an orchard as hers."

"I believe you. Listen! I got a peach tree from her, travelling through the mails. And so did everybody on my route get one. Didn't ask for it," said Uncle Percy. "Why'd she waste it on me? I'm not peach-crazy."

"I remember too. I only supposed it was from somebody running for office," said Aunt Birdie. "And voted accordingly."

"I give her peach tree room, and saw it get killed back the second spring. Didn't remember it was hers. Don't know how it would have eaten," said Uncle Curtis.

"It would have eaten good and sweet," said Gloria. "She wasn't fooling."

"I plain didn't plant mine," said Uncle Percy.

"Good ole blood-red Indian peach will ever remain my favorite," said Aunt Nanny. "I could eat one of mine right now."

"Did she keep you trotting?" asked Aunt Cleo of Gloria.

"She expected me to do my part," Gloria replied. "I hoed. And dug and divided her flowers and saved the seed, measured it in the old spotted spoon. Took the cuttings, wrapped the fresh-dug plants in fresh violet leaves and bread paper—"

"You sound homesick," said Aunt Beck. "Or something almost like it."

"And packed them moist in soda boxes and match boxes to mail away. I wrapped her directions around the peach trees and tied them with threads and bundled them for the postman."

"You was trying to keep on like Miss Julia herself? With those dreamy eyes? Honest?" asked Aunt Birdie.

"You copy who you love," Aunt Beck said.

"Unless you can get them to copy you," said Gloria. "But when I was young, Miss Julia filled me so full of inspiration, I even dreamed I'd pass her. I looked into the future and saw myself holding a State Normal diploma, taking the rostrum and teaching civics in high school," she told Judge Moody. "I'd keep on making the most of my summers, and finish as the principal. I always thought I'd wind up in Ludlow."

"Well, Jack wound up in Ludlow, and I can't say much for it," said Miss Beulah.

"Miss Julia undertook it, and she wanted me to undertake it after her—a teacher's life," said Gloria. She sat up as tall as she could in the middle of them, her face solemn as a tear drop, her head well aflame in the western light. "Her dearest wish was to pass on the torch to me."

"The torch?" asked Etoyle, dancing closer.

"What she taught me, I'd teach you, and on it would go. It's what teachers at the Spring Teachers' Meeting call passing the torch. She didn't ever doubt but that all worth preserving is going to be preserved, and all we had to do was keep it going, right from where we are, one teacher on down to the next."

"And the poor little children, they had to pay," said Aunt Nanny.

"Anybody at all that would come to her wanting to learn, she'd welcome a chance at them," said Gloria. "They didn't have to be a child."

"Who're you starting to take up for, girl?" Aunt Nanny cried, to tease her.

Uncle Noah Webster laughed. "Didn't there use to be a story that she even tried to teach Captain Billy Bangs? He come up like Granny in the bad years after the war, and in his case never got any schooling from his mother."

Gloria said, "She liked to say, 'If it's going to be a case of Saint George and the Dragon, I might as well battle it left, right, front, back, center and sideways.' "

"I'm glad Banner School didn't hear about that," said Miss Beulah. "Or me either, while I was one of her scholars. I'd had to run from a dragon, though that's about the only thing."

"She was Saint George," Gloria corrected her. "And Ignorance was the dragon."

"Well, if she sent you to high school and coached you in the meanwhiles, and was fighting your way to a diploma from Normal for you, she must have come mighty near to thinking you was worth it, Gloria," Aunt Beck said in comforting tones as she searched the young girl's face. "A heap of times, people sacrifice to the limit they can for nothing. But now and then there'll be a good excuse behind it."

"But the time came and I didn't want her sacrifice," Gloria said. "I'd rather have gone without it. And when the torch was about to be handed on to me for good, I didn't want to take it after all."

"For how long did you keep fooling yourself?" asked Aunt Cleo. "I don't see many lines across your brow."

"I finished Alliance High and crammed at Normal and studied in summer and took an exam and got my two-year certificate. Then I took Banner School to gain the experience to help earn the money to get back to Normal and win my diploma to keep on teaching—"

"And run bang into Jack Renfro," said Aunt Nanny, with a strong pinch at her from behind.

"Wait, wait, wait!" little Elvie cried. "What's Normal? Don't skip it! Tell it!"

"It's true, Gloria, you're the only one in sight that's been or is ever likely to go there," said Aunt Birdie. "Put it in a nutshell for us."

"Not enough of anything to go round, not enough room, not enough teachers, not enough money, not enough beds, not enough electric light bulbs, not enough books," said Gloria. "It wasn't too different from the orphanage."

"Was it pretty?" begged Elvie.

"Two towers round as rolling pins made out of brick. On top of the right-hand one was an iron bell. And right under that bell in the tip-top room was where they put me. Six iron beds all pointing to the middle, dividing it like a pie. When the bell rang, it shook us all like a poker in the grate," said Gloria. "I can hardly remember anything about Normal now, except the fire drills."

"Tell the fire drill!" cried Elvie.

"A black iron round thing four stories tall, like a tunnel standing on end, and a tin chute going round and round down through it," said Gloria. "You have to jump in, stick your legs around the one in front and sit on her skirt and the next one jumps in on yours, and you all go whirling like marbles on a string, spinning on your drawers—they grease it with soap—round and round and round— it's everybody holding on for dear life."

"Do you come out in a somersault?" asked Elvie.

"You pray all the way down somebody will catch you. Then you stand up and answer to roll call."

"I'm a-going," said Elvie.

"It's already too crowded," said Gloria. "Just us giving the history teacher the kings of England was liable to bring the roof down, and we practiced gym outdoors. When it rained, the piano had to be rolled like a big skate right into the post office, that was the basement. While you were trying to dance the Three Graces for the gym teacher, everybody else stood in your path reading out loud from their mother's letters and opening their food from home. We just had to dance around them."

"Do it now!" said Elvie.

"I said I hoped never to be asked to do that dance again."

"Didn't you appreciate a good education being handed to you on a silver platter?" asked Miss Lexie Renfro with a sharp laugh.

"There was too much racket," said Gloria. "Too big a crowd."

"Oh, but didn't you love it?" Mrs. Moody broke in. "A bunch of us in Ludlow still get in the car and go back there every spring to see 'em graduate."

"Come and see me!" Elvie invited her. "That's where I'm going. I'm going to come out a teacher like Sister Gloria."

"You've got a mile to go," Miss Lexie told her.

"Everybody was homesick, homesick, homesick," Gloria said.

"Who was *your* letters from?" asked Ella Fay.

"Miss Julia Mortimer, telling me to make the most of it, because it comes your way only once," said Gloria.

"That's a fact," said Mrs. Moody. "I majored in gym," she

went on. "Led the school-wide wand drill. I still have my Zouave cap." Judge Moody bent a surprised look on her. "*Ta-ta ta da!*" She gave him back a bar of the *Hungarian Rhapsody*. "Then I had to go forth and teach Beginning Physics. That's what they were all starved for."

"I can't hardly wait," said Elvie.

"For right now, you start getting busy with the fly swatter," Miss Beulah told her.

"So here came Gloria to take her turn at Banner School, and she run bang into Jack, only to have Miss Julia herself to face. I declare, Gloria!" Aunt Birdie exclaimed. "I wish you had the power of the Beechams to draw us a picture. I'd dearly loved to have been hiding behind the door the day you broke it to Miss Julia Mortimer you was leaving the schoolhouse and becoming a married woman."

Gloria rose to her feet from the baby-rocker. Aunt Nanny reached out and caught the baby.

"It's a sweet little story, I know," said Aunt Beck.

"Nobody's listening but we women," Aunt Nanny said. "The men are all about ready to fall asleep anyway, Curtis is nodding, and Percy is already whittling to his heart's content."

"Tell it. Maybe we can help you," said Aunt Birdie.

Uncle Noah Webster reached his hand up the neck of the banjo, as the other hand stole to the strings and began to pluck out softly "I Had a Little Donkey and Jacob Was His Name," without giving the tune its words.

"It was the last time I went across to see Miss Julia," said Gloria. "It was Sunday before my reports were due, the first reports after spring planting. Her bank going up the road to her house was a sheet of white, all irises and pheasant-eye. We had tender greens and spring onions with our chicken. The Silver Moon rose was already out, there at the windows—"

"It's about to pull the house down now," said Miss Lexie.

"The red rose too, that's trained up at the end of the porch—"

"That big west rose? It's taken over," nodded Miss Lexie.

"She'd filled the cut-glass bowl on the table," said Gloria. "With red and white."

"She didn't cut 'em any longer," Miss Lexie said, as if she were bragging on her. "The reds hung on the vine all over everything, and turned blue as bird-dog tongues."

"Leave the child alone, Lexie. Nobody asked you to help tell," said Aunt Birdie.

"I was sitting with her at the dining room table after dinner, under those frowning bookcases, and I had my report cards spread out all over the table, making them out."

"Skip those!" cried Aunt Nanny.

"And I spilled her ink," said Gloria. "And after we rescued the reports and mopped the table, I said, 'Miss Julia, listen. Before I go back to Banner, I've got something to tell you that'll bring you pain, and here it is. I may not ever be the wonderful teacher and lasting influence you are. There's a boy pretty well keeping after me.' And she said, 'A Banner boy? Well, give me his name and age and the year I taught him, and I'll see if I can point out an answer for you.' "

"Gloria, you've got her down perfect!" cried Aunt Birdie. "Go on!"

"So I handed her his report. 'Still a schoolboy?' she says. I told her he'd had to stay out of school and that's why he was coming so late, and she'd never got to teach him. I said *I* taught him and that was half my trouble, because I couldn't run from him. She said, 'I'm looking right now at who he is, and I see exactly your trouble. I'll go over a few questions with you.' "

"Poor Gloria!" breathed Aunt Beck.

"She said, 'In the first place, how did you get him to start back to school, once he was loose?' I told her, 'I let him be the one to drive the school bus.' She said, 'What way did you find to get him to study his lessons? Though it seems to have done little good.' I told her by asking him to run up my flag, cut and saw my wood, and keep up my stove so the whole school wouldn't either freeze us or burn us down, and watch my leaks and my windows and doors so we wouldn't have a chance to float out of sight or all get blown away. And he's studying between times before he knows it.' She said how did I keep him with open book on pretty days? I said, 'On pretty days, I might be driven to keeping him in after school.' I said, 'After he carries the children home to their mothers, he turns the bus around and sails back. He washes my boards and beats my erasers and sweeps my floor and cuts my switches and burns my trash and grinds my pencils and pours my ink, and takes down my flag—and all the time I'm right behind him, teaching him.' She says, 'After that, how do you make sure he doesn't forget it the minute you

**248**

finish?' I said, 'He carries me home. And I live at their house. We have all the evening,' I said."

"Go on," said Aunt Nanny. "Don't stop and dream on us."

"Miss Julia said, 'And what about now, after the seed's in the ground and before the crops are laid by? How far away from school is he now?' And I told her how even now he was still coming to run up my flag and salute it with me and coming back to help me home in the evenings. And on the days he missed all the recitations, I had that much more to catch him up on. When I saw the very most of Jack, I told her, it seemed like those were the same days when I had to take off from his attendance and mark him an absence from school. I told her the family was still trying to scrape a living from this old farm, the circle still unbroken, nine mouths to feed, and he's the oldest boy."

"Well, and just who is that, now, that you're making sound so pitiful?" cried Miss Beulah, still being everywhere at once, as if she'd be too busy to sit down to listen to foolish chatter.

"Did she say she'd love to meet him?" asked Aunt Beck.

"She didn't think that was necessary," Gloria said. "I tried telling her she'd never laid eyes on Jack. 'Scholastic average 72, attendance 60, and deportment 95 is a pretty clear picture to me of the two of you,' she said. 'You've awarded him a general average of 75 and two-thirds.' I said, 'And 75 is passing.' 'Passing so far,' she says. 'Is he going to be present on examination day and sit down and take those seventh-grade examinations? Remember, I'm the one who made those examinations out.' 'He'll take 'em if I have anything to do with it!' I told her. 'And win his diploma?' And I tell her I've already got his diploma filled out—all but for the Superintendent's signature and the gold seal. 'Miss Julia, I'm going to hang onto Jack and pull him through. And as soon as he gets his feet on solid ground, I'm going to marry him.' 'Marry him?' she said."

"Did she appear satisfied?" Aunt Birdie asked, nodding Gloria ahead. "And tell you to go on, keep a-courting?"

"Exactly the opposite," said Gloria. " 'Marry him! And leave Banner School without its teacher?' she says. And she jumped right up and it shook the china closet behind her, and said, 'Oh, you can't do that!' "

Aunt Nanny slapped her lap, on either side of the baby, and Aunt Birdie's high giggle led the laughing.

"She said, 'It's a thoroughly unteacherlike thing to do,' " Gloria went on. "She said, 'Instead of marrying your pupil, why can't you stick to your guns and turn yourself into a better teacher and do him and the world some good?' "

There was a fresh burst of womanly laughter, and along with that and the tickling notes of the banjo, one low groan from a man joined in—it could only have come from Judge Moody.

"I wonder what Miss Gloria *won't* decide to tell us," remarked Miss Beulah. "Something's happened somewhere to loosen her tongue."

"Keep on, Gloria! Gloria, I declare! After all the good excuse you'd put up!" cried Aunt Birdie. "Could you still go her one better?"

"I told her I wanted to give all my teaching to one," Gloria said. And as they sat silenced, she added, "That's when she laughed at me."

"You can't stand that," said Miss Beulah. "No, not from anybody, not you."

"Did you wilt?" asked Aunt Nanny.

Gloria's eyelids dropped shut and trembled. Then she went on. "Miss Julia said my story was one that had been heard of before now. She said I wasn't the first teacher in Creation to be struck down by tender feelings the first day I threw school open and saw one face above all the rest out in front of me. She said teachers falling in love with their first pupils was old at the Flood. But it didn't give them any certificate to stop teaching."

"Those words must still be in letters of fire on your poor brain," said Aunt Beck.

"What did you do? Laugh or cry?" said Aunt Nanny. "Tell you what I'd done—I'd run." As she hollered it, Lady May scampered down and ran from her.

"I argued as good as she did," Gloria said. "I asked her if she could give me just three good reasons right quick why I couldn't give up my teaching and marry that minute if I wanted to."

"Was she stumped?" asked Aunt Birdie eagerly.

"She thought she had them," said Gloria. "She told me, 'All right, Gloria. One: you're young and ignorant—each one of you as much as the other.' That wasn't so. 'Two: sitting and hanging your heels over Banner Top in the moonlight, you don't dream yet where strong feelings can lead you.' That wasn't so. 'And three: you need to give a little mind to the *family* you're getting tangled up with.' "

"For mercy's sakes! Only one of the biggest families there is!" cried Miss Beulah. "And one of the closest!"

"And it's exactly where they put me down with my valise," said Gloria.

"Well! Stacey Broadwee, Ora Stovall, and Mis' Comfort and me, we all drew straws for the teacher," said Miss Beulah to the company. "And who do you reckon got the little one?"

"Miss Julia didn't let up," said Gloria. " 'Here's reason four, for good measure: do you know who you are? Just who are you? You don't know,' she says. 'Before you jump headlong, ask yourself a few questions.' "

"And as if that wasn't our business more than hers!" said Miss Beulah. She added to Gloria with a show of sarcasm, "And I suppose she was ready with an answer for that too?"

While Uncle Noah Webster leaned toward her and picked at another chorus, Gloria was shaking her radiant head. "She said if only Mississippians had birth certificates and would be like other people! 'It wouldn't kill them,' she said. 'It's no insult to be asked to prove who you are. It wouldn't hurt a soul to be ready to furnish some proof of his existence at the right time. And nothing would be lost but a little fraction of the confusion.' "

In the disapproving quiet that came after her words, Judge Moody could be heard clearing his throat.

"There's a good long page, ain't there now, in everybody's family Bible for writing 'em down?" asked Uncle Curtis.

"For writing down ours. But Gloria's lacking in the ones to do the writing," Aunt Beck sadly reminded him.

"You're *here*, aren't you?" Aunt Birdie said with a scandalized laugh at Gloria.

"Miss Julia told me there was a dark thread, a dark thread running through my story somewhere," Gloria went on. "Or my mother wouldn't have made a mystery out of me. And I owed it to myself to find out the worst, and the quicker the better."

"The worst! And how did you like that?" grinned Aunt Nanny.

"I said it suited me all right kept dark the way it was. I didn't mind being a mystery—I was used to it. And if I was born a mystery, I'd be married a mystery."

"And die one?" prompted Aunt Beck.

"Miss Julia still wasn't satisfied?" asked Aunt Birdie, looking into Gloria's face. "I'd have been."

"She said it was a piece of unwisdom."

"Was that all?" asked several.

"No. 'Use your head,' she said. 'Find out who you are. And don't get married first,' she said. 'That's putting the cart before the horse.' "

"But you did that very thing, didn't you?" said Aunt Birdie sympathetically. "Don't blame you a solitary bit."

"She said, 'Go back to Banner School. Give out your reports tomorrow—and make those children work harder. Then teach out your year as you promised. And meantime, get your own eyes open. You're in the very best place to get a little light on yourself. Banner's the side of the river you surely were born on. You were found in Medley—that's in walking distance of Banner School. Get to work on yourself. And I'll work on you, too.' "

"Ouch!" cried Aunt Nanny.

"She said where there was a dark thread running, she hated to think of it being unravelled by unknowing hands, and after it's too late—when she couldn't be standing there to see it done right. She said every mystery had its right answer—we just had to find it. That's what mysteries were given to us for. And she didn't think mine would be too hard for a good brain."

"Poor Gloria!" murmured Aunt Beck. "I bet you wished mighty hard you hadn't got her started on you."

"You're lucky it didn't do her any good," said Aunt Birdie. "You're the same little question-mark as ever, ain't you?"

"How did you discourage her, Gloria?" asked Aunt Nanny.

"I snapped the elastic band around my reports, and took the roses she gave me with 'em, and went out of her house and into the spring, and took my road," said Gloria. "And Jack was there at the other end of the bridge, waiting for me. Whistling."

"Oh, I bet you skipped!" said Aunt Nanny.

"And never went back," said Miss Lexie, looking at her.

"And never give another thought to who you were," said Aunt Birdie stoutly. "And how would you have had the time, anyway, after that?"

"I didn't see how she could be right about the best place to look—about my beginnings being anywhere around here. I'd already seen all there was to Banner, the first day."

"Not grand enough for Miss Gloria?" Miss Lexie rocked back on her heels, giving her silent laugh.

"In my heart of hearts, I thought higher of myself than that."
Gloria lifted her chin and opened her eyes wide upon them. "I still do."

Granny's tiny voice spoke.

Uncle Noah Webster stopped his tune at once, everybody hushed talking and laughing, and Miss Beulah said, "What is it, what's that, Granny?"

She said, "Sojourner."

Miss Beulah went hurrying toward her chair. "Are you telling us something, Granny?"

"Prick up your ears. Once is all I'm going to tell it," Granny said. "Sojourner. That's your mother." She flicked her fan at Gloria. "Fox-headed Rachel."

All eyes travelled back to Gloria. She stood staring.

"Granny, Granny, wait a minute—I can't put my finger right quick on who Rachel Sojourner is!" cried Miss Beulah. "There's no Sojourners I know of!"

"Sure you know! Sure you remember!" said Aunt Nanny. "I do."

"Where'd they live?" asked Aunt Cleo. "In Banner, sure-enough?"

"Yes'm, clear to the bottom of the hill," Aunt Nanny said. "Lower than Aycock. They did! Nobody with the name left now." She slapped herself on her lap. "And Rachel is the one Miss Julia Mortimer taught sewing to—the little girl on the end of the recitation bench. Yes'm. Rachel couldn't learn to do mental arithmetic, so while the rest of us was firing off to beat the band, she sat like Puss—just pointing the tip of her little tongue out, and putting in a seam."

"Taught her to sew right here." Granny's voice came again. "Saw she's starving. Called her into my own house. 'You can help me with this brood, mending their stockings. At least you'll get fed.'"

"You're bringing her back to me," said Miss Beulah, in wary tones. "I don't see her face yet, but I'm beginning to hear just a little —hear the laughing. Yes, in this house, I'd hear the boys tease her, circling around her at the quilting frame, or the loom, maybe, tease her while she treadled. I can hear her laugh floating through the breezeway—and I can see her weak eyes now. She worked—or she laughed—till the coming tears would put her eyes right out. I'll remember two or three other failings about her too, in a minute," she added, her eyes moving to Gloria. "Yes, I'm about to see her pretty well."

"Tossing her mane," said Granny. "Fiery mane."

As Gloria let out a gasp of protest, Miss Beulah kept on. "And it was Nathan knew best how to make her cry."

"But was as still about her as that hunk of firewood going to waste down there in the yard," Granny said, looking around her and then up into Nathan's face.

"Couldn't help teasing Miss Rachel, Granny!" said Uncle Noah Webster. "I remember her for the very reason."

"But we had one she could count on. Sam Dale would never tease her," said Uncle Curtis, and instantly the tears stood in Miss Beulah's eyes.

Granny's head drove back against her chair as if it had started on its rockers to run off with her, like a buggy. "Mr. Vaughn put a stop to her foolishness, sent her on," she said. "Well, that's who you are. You're Rachel's."

"It's just because Granny is so old that you believe her," Gloria said in a rush to the company. "If she wasn't your granny, celebrating her birthday, you'd think she could be as wrong as anybody else."

"All I hope is Granny didn't hear that," Miss Beulah whispered.

"And you all believe her because *you're* old!"

"Gloria, you're showing yourself to be a handful today, whoever you got it from!" said Aunt Nanny, laughing.

"I'm not hers. I'm not Rachel's. I'm not one bit of hers," said Gloria.

"Well, where did she come from?" asked Aunt Cleo. "Gloria right here, I mean."

"Oh, that little story's fairly well known, as far as it goes," said Miss Beulah.

Aunt Nanny, shooing at a game of "Fox in the Morning, Geese in the Evening" which just then swept over the yard like a gust of wind, was already telling it. "The home demonstration agent of Boone County come out and found her new-born on her front porch one evening. In her swing. Tucked in a clean shoe box."

"You was tiny," Aunt Cleo told Gloria.

"She was red as a pomegranate, and mad. Waving her little fists, the story goes," said Aunt Nanny fondly. "So the home demonstration agent—that was Miss Pet Hanks's mother, and while she lived she's in the same house in Medley where Miss Pet's still answering the phone—Mis' Hanks, the minute she saw what she had, and even though it was her busy day, she planked that baby in her old tin Lizzie and bounced all the way to Ludlow. And it was dewberry time, ditches full of 'em, bushes just loaded, begging to be picked on both sides of the road all the way. Made her wish she had time to stop and enjoy 'em, while she could."

"Must have been shortly before our Easter Snap," said Aunt Beck.

"It was."

"What day do you call your birthday?" Aunt Cleo pointed at Gloria.

"April the first!" she said with defiance.

"I wish I'd known you was going begging!" Aunt Nanny cried to her through the others' laughter. "I'd opened both arms so fast! I always prayed for me a girl—though I'd have taken a boy either, if answer had ever been sent." She puffed on. "Mis' Hanks carried you straight to the orphan asylum and handed you in. 'Here's a treat for you,' she says to 'em. 'It's a girl. I even brought her named.' She named you after her trip to Ludlow. It was a glorious day and she was sorry she had to cut her visit so short. Gloria Short."

"It wasn't bad for a name for you either, Gloria—you was born with a glorious head of hair and you was short a father and a mother," said Aunt Birdie.

"It might be a sweeter name than you'd gotten from either one of them, for all you know, Gloria," said Aunt Beck.

"I would have named myself something different," said Gloria. "And not as common. There were three other Glorias all eating at my table."

"Considering who found you, be thankful you wasn't named Pet Hanks and been all by yourself," said Uncle Noah Webster.

"That's right. Now *they* know how to inflict you!" said Aunt Birdie. "The papas and mamas. Mama and Papa named me Virgil Homer, after the two doctors that succeeded in bringing me into the world. It wasn't till I tried saying it myself and it came out 'Birdie' that I ever got it any different."

"I named all mine a pretty name, every one of 'em," said Miss Beulah. "Give 'em a pretty name, say I, for it may be the only thing you *can* give 'em. I named all mine myself, including little Beulah, that didn't live but a day."

"I'm Renfro now," said Gloria.

"And in just no time!" said Miss Beulah. She studied Gloria with her head on one side. "Sojourner. That makes you kin to Aycock. And Captain Billy Bangs is stumping back there somewhere behind you. Reckon you'll be as long-lived as him?"

"I don't believe I'm Rachel's!" Gloria cried.

"It fits perfect," Miss Beulah said. "Only too perfect if you knew Rachel."

"But I was a secret," Gloria protested. "Whosoever I was, I was her secret." She jumped up, her head like a house afire.

"You might have been Rachel's *secret,* all right—but Rachel's story is a mighty old story around Banner, and now it comes crowding back in on me, the whole thing, coming like we'd called it," said Miss Beulah. "I reckon everybody and his brother heard that story once upon a time, and lived just about the right length of time to forget it."

"What about Rachel? Have you got *her* somewhere where you could corner her and ask her?" asked Aunt Cleo.

"You'll have to wait till you meet her in Heaven if you want to get it from Rachel," said Miss Beulah.

"Then how can you-all be so sure beforehand?" cried Gloria. "How do you know I'm Rachel's secret?"

"If Mis' Hanks was the only soul in Medley that Rachel Sojourner knew well enough to speak to, that's the one she'd give her baby to. Wouldn't she?" Aunt Birdie asked her.

"But Mis' Hanks might have known others going unmarried besides Rachel who had babies to give. She was the home demonstration agent, after all. Went countywide, pushed in everywhere," argued Aunt Beck for Gloria.

"But Rachel's baby has to be *somewhere,*" said Miss Beulah. "And I think with Granny that somewhere is right here."

"I'm not Rachel's," said Gloria. "The more you tell it, the less I believe it."

Aunt Nanny said, grinning, "Well, listen—mothers come different. Mama had two, and gave away both of 'em, me and my sister, when we was squallers, and she didn't need to at all—it just suited her better. She's up the road with Papa now, busy living to a ripe old age."

"But she was a Broadwee," Miss Beulah reminded her. "Tough as an old walnut."

"Old Man Sojourner, after Rachel had been laid in the ground, he reached in the chink of the chimney-piece and pulled all the money out that was being saved to bury he and his wife, and sold the cow to boot, all to put up a stone to Rachel's memory. It's still there—a lamb, and not very snowy," said Aunt Nanny. She reached out and gave Gloria a spank.

Gloria cried out, "It's the grave that looks ready to go slip-sliding down the hill and into the Bywy!"

"That's right," said Miss Beulah. "And by this time the whole tribe has pretty well followed suit and gone to the grave behind her. I reckon what keeps Captain Billy Bangs alive is purely and solely trying to outlive Granny." Then she took a step toward Gloria. "I ought to have known you on sight, girl. The minute you walked in my house with your valise and satchel and the little setting of eggs for the teacher's present, and unsnapped the elastic on your hat. You might have been poor, frail, headstrong little-old Rachel Sojourner all over again. Why didn't I just stop in my tracks long enough to think a minute?" She looked at Granny. "Why, that day, when Granny came in from the garden with a bushel of greens in her apron, she stopped in front of you and said, 'Aren't you under the wrong roof, little girl?' "

" 'No ma'am,' I told her. '*I* haven't made a mistake—I'm the teacher.' And her greens fell right down on the floor, for us to pick up," said Gloria.

Miss Beulah put a hand on the old lady's shoulder and told Gloria, "You might've been the very same, the one that used to come to this house and help sew and stay a week at a time in our company room, sleeping with the teacher. Maybe it was hoped Miss Julia Mortimer's head on the next pillow could talk some sense into her head!"

"Miss Julia Mortimer," Miss Lexie retorted to Gloria before she could speak, "is exactly who *found* Rachel Sojourner, when that girl was fixing to die. Quivering and shaking she was, on the Banner bridge. Miss Julia was driving across in her flivver, late leaving the schoolhouse, and it's changing—turning cold, and getting dark. There's Rachel! Her sewing pupil, that couldn't learn mental arithmetic. Miss Julia stopped and commanded her to halt right there and stop giving the appearance of being about to jump in the river and climb in the car instead, and backed all the way back across the bridge, turned around in the school yard, and headed for Ludlow, lickety-split. 'You're on your way to a doctor, girl,' she said. 'No time to waste sitting down and waiting for *him*. You're blue!' she said. 'Have you got any stockings on? What do you mean, walking out without stockings—it's icy!' The thermometer's dropped about forty degrees at a gallop—it's April. Miss Julia stopped the flivver in the middle of the road, tore off her own stockings, put them on Rachel struggling, and wrapped her up in her own cape too, I wouldn't put it past her, and rode her to Ludlow. By the time Miss Julia's blowing her horn at the doctor's front door, Rachel's an icicle. But Rachel tells the doctor, when she can chatter, 'I don't care if it kills me, I wouldn't be caught dead in Miss Julia's old yarn stockings.' She'd taken 'em right off again—using, I reckon, the last ounce of strength she had left. Then she went into a hard rigor. She wasn't going to wear Miss Julia Mortimer's old yarn stockings to Ludlow, and the cold got to her bones. That's how she got pneumonia. She died when her crisis came."

"I bet Miss Julia didn't even catch a cold out of it," said Aunt Birdie, shivering.

"Oh, she's iron," said Aunt Nanny.

All went quiet, except for those somewhere at the outer edges who were singing a round, "*. . . gently down the stream. Merrily merrily . . .*"

"Lexie, how is it you can furnish such a story?" asked Miss Beulah. "You must have picked that up from Miss Julia herself."

"On one of her sunny days, back when, when she had confidence in my nursing, she let me have it," said Miss Lexie. "But if there was a baby anywhere in it, she left it out for my benefit."

"Well, Rachel had already had the baby," Aunt Beck divined. "Do you reckon Rachel told Miss Julia some of her story on that long freezing ride?"

"No, not if she wouldn't wear her stockings," Aunt Birdie said.

"She'd just left her baby, and felt like it was a good time to come on home," said Aunt Beck. "She could stand, and no more, I feel sure. Just put one foot in front of the other. And when she got to Banner—"

"The Easter Snap got her," said Aunt Nanny, chopping at Beck with her hand.

"It dovetails perfect," Aunt Beck said to Gloria. "Just too perfect."

"I firmly believe the Sojourners wouldn't let Rachel back in the house when she tried 'em. That was one tale," said Aunt Birdie.

"Remember, now? What else drove her out on the bridge for Miss Julia's eagle eyes to find?"

"Old Man Sojourner, when they sent for him to come after her at the end of it, had to take his wagon all the way to Ludlow. And he had another long ride back to Banner, bringing her home to bury," said Miss Beulah. "That would have given him time to think."

"That's what brought forth the lamb," said Aunt Beck to Gloria.

"Well, she'd long since left our house, and good riddance!—Oh, she came back once. She came back once, I knew as soon as I'd got the words out of my mouth. To help Granny out when I was busy fixing to marry Mr. Renfro," said Miss Beulah. "Still sewing she was, then. Do you remember her being here, Mr. Renfro? I expect you don't—just the groom."

"Oh, without a question. I remember the dewberry-picking race," he said.

She gave a short laugh. "Oh, yes, that came to try our nerves," she said. "That was Rachel and one of these boys."

"That was Sam Dale Beecham," said Mr. Renfro. "Sam Dale and Rachel, each of 'em claimed in front of the whole table to be the best and fastest and most furious dewberry picker in the world. So nothing to do but for each to take a bucket and set on out to prove it. When each one's bucket got full, they'd scamper back to the house here, empty the buckets in the big washtub, then scamper out again. Every trip, they'd just meet each other again back at the tub. They picked from first thing in the morning till last thing in the evening, when it was still a tie—am I right?"

"Don't remind me of any more," said Miss Beulah.

"They filled the tub and every bucket on the farm, and Sam Dale finally had to hollow him out a poplar log and fill that and come carrying it in over his shoulder. And Rachel still showed her bucket full to match him."

"It must have been a plentiful year," said Aunt Nanny.

"It was more than that, it was a matter of each of 'em vowing they could beat the other and neither being willing to give in," said Aunt Birdie.

"They *called* it a tie," said Miss Lexie.

"Blessed Sam Dale let her tie him," said Aunt Beck sweetly.

"And where did all that carrying-on leave the rest of us?" Miss Beulah cried. "Poor Granny was back in the kitchen up to her el-

bows in dewberries. What was she going to do with so much blooming plenty, and with a wedding right at her heels? She put up forty-
nine quarts of dewberries that night before she give up and went to
bed. Or was it sixty-nine, or ninety-six?"

Granny replied with a nod to all these numbers.

"Well, it may have been a tie the way you tell it, but I think
Granny come out ahead," said Aunt Nanny.

"By the time you was ready to be born, Gloria, looks like the
dewberries had come around again," said Aunt Birdie.

Gloria cried, "I wish you-all wouldn't keep on. I know I'm
better than Rachel Sojourner and her lamb. Nobody here or anywhere else can make me believe I'm in the world on account of any
fault of hers." She threw back her mane.

"Oscar, can't you do 'em some good?" asked Mrs. Moody.
"That would make some of this worthwhile."

"Things that should be a matter of record in Boone County
just aren't," said Judge Moody. "I can't remedy that, Maud Eva."

"There ain't no more records. Not now, Judge Moody. They
went," said Mr. Renfro.

"I know about the courthouse fire," said Judge Moody drily.
"We're still holding court in the Primary Department of the First
Baptist Church."

"Squatting on Sunday School chairs," said Mrs. Moody, with
a short laugh for him in the chair that held him now.

"Yes. I didn't have to come to Banner to find out what happened in Ludlow," said Judge Moody. "But what about the doctor
who attended this girl? There'd be his record—or if that's thrown
away, he might come up with it out of his own memory, if he was
tantalized long enough."

"I think Rachel had that baby *by herself*," said Aunt Birdie,
with a storyteller's snubbing look. "Did the best she could, gave it
away to the one who'd know best what to do with it, and let the
good Lord take her."

"Oscar, you know full well they could never get a doctor to
plough his way up here," said Mrs. Moody. "You'd have to go
down on your knees to one and beg him!"

"Well," said Mr. Renfro, with a warm eye cocked on Judge
Moody, "I didn't know that, and so when we had one ready to be
born—" Miss Beulah gave a short laugh, and he went on. "I
hopped to the store and took the phone and asked 'em to put me in

touch with a doctor in Ludlow, and the doctor said all right, he'd come. 'Come to the old Jordan house,' I says. 'Everybody can tell you where that is.' Well, it was already darkening up considerable by the time I got back here, and I see there's a storm rising I never had quite seen the like of. I got a little anxious for fear a big tree might blow down right on the road and catch the doctor before he could get here. Lightning and thunder just flying! I was walking the gallery here, looking out for him. Never had seen the doctor and the doctor hadn't ever seen me, but I told Beulah when a man said he's coming he meant it, and for her just to hold on.

"Saw him coming, just burning the wind! He had a good horse under him, and the fire was just flying when the shoes hit down on those stones. First thing he did when he pulled up here was hand me down a great big gun he'd been carrying across his lap. I was the least bit surprised, I was half-expecting it to be his doctor bag, but that was the next thing he handed me. Then his saddlebags.

" 'You do a lot of hunting around here?' he says, hopping down, and he wasn't much older than I was, and I says, 'I sure do, Doctor.' 'Well,' he says. 'I thought this sounded like a real good part of the world to go out and get squirrel. So tomorrow,' he says, 'if it clears and all, tell you what—let's me and you go out and get us a bagful.'

"So the baby come that night, true to Beulah's prediction, and the next day was clear—beautiful!—and me and the doctor went hunting. And that doctor, he didn't go home for a week. Not till Grandpa invited him to come hear his sermon. He and I was out on the ridge every day of the world and we got all the squirrels your very own heart could wish for. Granny cooked all he could eat every night, and beyond that, when he finally told us good-bye, he had his saddlebags just loaded with pretty dressed squirrel. When he left me and Beulah and the baby and the old folks, he said he'd never had such a pleasant visit in his life. Carruthers was his name."

"Gerard Carruthers?" protested Mrs. Moody.

"How much did he charge?" asked Aunt Cleo. "Plenty?"

"I'm sure it wasn't too steep a bill for all he gave us," said Mr. Renfro. "I reckon he knew when he started how little well we'd be able to pay it."

"Grandpa Vaughn gave him something to put in his purse, I know," said Miss Beulah. "No, we weren't going to be thought beggars here!"

"So he's been up here too," said Judge Moody. "You got Gerard Carruthers too."

"That's Judge's doctor," cried Mrs. Moody. "Imagine getting him way up here!"

"It was some several years ago," said Mr. Renfro. "Jack was the baby."

"He even wanted to name the baby, on top of the rest of it," said Miss Beulah. "I wouldn't allow him. 'That's Jack Jordan Renfro,' I told him."

"Try and get him to pay a house call today," said Mrs. Moody.

"Lady May got here fine without a doctor," said Gloria. "And I didn't die either, like I might have, if I was a Sojourner."

"You had Granny," a chorus of voices rose to tell her.

"Beulah had Granny too," said Granny. "Good thing."

"But even Granny can't prove I'm Rachel's," said Gloria. "Nobody can."

"Then watch out—I can show you the proof right now," said Aunt Birdie with fresh glee. "It's coming right out to meet you this minute, and in front of our eyes."

From under the skirts of the tablecloth Lady May came crawling out on hands and knees. Somewhere down there she had found a bone. She gave her mother a shout, as though she'd beat her to it. The bone had a live jacket of tiny ants.

"Like mother, like daughter! Isn't that the old-timey rule? See there?" Aunt Birdie sang in a charmed voice.

Gloria opened her mouth but stood speechless.

"Go back, Red Roses," Aunt Beck warned Lady May.

"Come here, Britches!" cried Aunt Nanny, and with a red arm she swept the child up. "Yes, you was a pretty good little secret yourself, wasn't you?" she asked her.

"And don't you wish she was yours?" The other aunts stood up around Lady May, opening their arms. "Come be mine!" "Come be mine!" They took her bone.

"Gloria, we didn't come here to cry," Aunt Beck said. "If we'd wanted to do that, we could've just stayed home, couldn't we, everybody?"

"There's two now," said Aunt Nanny, as Lady May, from there in her lap, joined her mother in tears.

"There, let her go. I'll tell you who it is she likes, it's the men," said Aunt Birdie. "She'll grow up to be a heartbreaker too, just watch."

Lady May, down on her feet, ran past the uncles too, all sweeping their arms out to catch her, and saddled herself on Judge Moody's foot in its city shoe. At once it stopped swinging, though she belabored his silk-clad ankle with her little hand.

Miss Beulah had been raising her voice at the aunts. "Birdie Beecham, and every one of you, now I want you to know something: I taught my boys to do the right thing, do you hear me? Jack Renfro never gave Banner community the first cause for complaint! He'd treat a girl strictly the way he's been everlastingly told! And if something's wrong, *she's* to blame."

"I always told myself the same thing you do, Beulah," said Aunt Beck soothingly. "About my nine boys."

"Hey! You mean to tell me Gloria here jumped the gun?" exclaimed Aunt Cleo.

Gloria stood straight and defied them, the same as when she had had to tell them her birthday was April Fool's Day.

Aunt Nanny made a reach at Gloria and gave her a spank. "Stand up there, Gloria! In your skirt there, where the sash is trying to hide it—you got a rip. Been in the briar patch with it?"

"Gloria, peep behind you. Did you know you look like you just met up with a biting dog?" asked Aunt Birdie.

"Is that the only Sunday dress you got?" Aunt Cleo asked.

"My wedding dress!" said Gloria.

"Homemade?" asked Aunt Cleo.

"Yes ma'am."

"Bet you made it on yourself, with nobody to tell you how," Aunt Cleo said.

"Thank you. I did."

"But I'll tell you one thing about it: it don't fit you very perfect," said Aunt Cleo. "You work with a pattern?"

"I remember seeing you wear it on your wedding day," said Aunt Beck. "And you simply looked like all the brides that ever were."

"I believe it's that sash that makes it so old-timey-looking," Mrs. Moody now joined in.

"Yes'm, brought-in like that with a sash a mile high, she looks suffocated, " said Auntie Fay.

"But so many brides have the tendency," said Aunt Beck.

"She's wearing it as tight as Dick's hatband now," said Aunt Nanny, as she tested the sash.

"Pull it," said those around her.

Aunt Nanny drove her finger through the knot and the sash slipped, fell with the heaviness of an arm down the skirt to Gloria's feet.

"Lands! Will you look at the wealth of material she allowed herself in that skirt!" exclaimed Aunt Birdie. "Had to rope yourself in to be sure you was there, Gloria."

"Now wait a minute. I never noticed anything wrong with the *dress*," said Miss Beulah. "It just looks like a good many widths of material went into it. Takes an hour to iron it, but suppose you just call it a little roomy—that's better than one that'll pinch you after a while."

"I believe that sash by itself must've weighed a ton," said Aunt Nanny.

"It did," said Gloria, looking down where it made a gleam like water around her. "It's slipper satin." She gathered it up carefully and Aunt Nanny took it away from her.

"Holy Moses! Where'd a schoolteacher get hold of slipper satin!"

"She sacrificed," Aunt Beck said, as if that should be enough.

Aunt Birdie went on. "Yes, and look at that little vein of pink running along the edge of it there. That sash has been light-struck."

"It might be an old piece of goods," said Aunt Nanny.

"It is not!" Gloria cried. "No ma'am, I bought it new and paid for it. Nothing I have on is second-hand!" All the while, more of the aunts were coming to pat the dress at Gloria's shoulders and waist and here and there, as if trying to find her in it.

"It's swallowed her whole," said Aunt Nanny. "It's waiting on her to grow some."

"I don't see how she could have tracked around all day in a dress that's ten miles too big for her, and expected only compliments," said Aunt Cleo. She picked up the edge of the hem. "It don't even look very snowy to me."

"It was brand-new material! I'd spent my whole life wearing second-hand!" said Gloria. "And wishing for new! And I made me this."

"Gloria just considers she's made to look the bride regardless,"

**264**

teased Aunt Nanny. "Getting a head-start with those curls."

"Let her have it her way. But it's still a mighty good country saying—like mother, like daughter. She's Rachel's child, and yonder rides somebody to prove it," Aunt Birdie said, starting to giggle at Judge Moody with the baby on his foot.

"Who said it needs proving! I know she's Rachel's child!" insisted Miss Beulah. "All I needed to do was stop and look straight at her. But if Rachel's your mother, it's picking out your father that's going to be the uphill work," she told Gloria.

Gloria opened her mouth as if on the verge of shrieking.

"Rachel took to going Sunday-riding with call-him-a-Methodist," said Aunt Nanny, eyes glinting.

"Are you putting the blame for the father on the Methodist?" asked Aunt Cleo.

"Well, you know how Baptists stick together," said Aunt Beck. "They like to look far afield to find any sort of transgressor."

"Let's not go any further with it," said Miss Beulah urgently. "Let's stop before we get started. Let's perish the whole idea."

Gloria put one hand and then the other hand too on her mouth.

Granny's voice spoke. "Sam Dale Beecham. Sam Dale Beecham was going to marry fox-headed Rachel."

There was uproar at the table. Gloria's shriek came out and ran through the middle of it.

"Granny, you've got Sam Dale on the brain! Do you know what you're saying?" Miss Beulah cried out, running back to the old lady's chair.

Granny glared at the company. The rheumy blue eyes looked lit up as with fever.

"No, Granny dear. Sam Dale wouldn't have got a girl in trouble, and then gone off and left her," said Uncle Noah Webster. He put the banjo down, out of sight.

"Oh, if only he might have!" cried Miss Beulah in great agitation.

"No, Sam Dale was too good. Too plain good," Uncle Curtis stated. "Granny, all we boys know that."

"I don't think he had a single mean trick in him," said Uncle Noah Webster, shaking his head soberly. "Or even a mean thought about a one of us. Or about a soul in Banner, or the wide world if you want to carry it that far."

"Oh, I won't be a Beecham!" cried Gloria.

Granny was looking at the still silent Uncle Nathan. "Go get the Vaughn Bible, from under my lamp," she told him, her lifted forefinger pointing straight up.

But Elvie, too quick for Uncle Nathan, ran and came staggering back with it, carrying it between her legs, barely able to keep it off the ground. She just made it to Granny's lap. She knelt in front of Granny's knees, facing out, and bent her little back forward to help hold up the weight.

Granny fished in her pocket and brought up a pair of spectacles, fished again and brought up a blackened and silky dollar bill which she polished them with. With the spectacles on her nose, she raised the Bible's cover and turned to the first page.

She dwelt for a moment over the angel-decorated roster of births and deaths set down in various hands, then lifted and wet her finger and began turning systematically through her Bible—not as though she needed to hunt for what she wanted but as though she were coming to it in her own way. Those nearest her saw the lock of Ellen's hair when it went by in Chronicles, pale as silk. Deep in the crease of First Thessalonians lay Grandpa's spectacles. Granny poked them free and put them on top of hers. Here came the ribbon that had held Ellen's ring, like a pressed flower stem without its flower. Then she turned one more page and drew out what looked like a brownish postcard. It had lain in its place so long that it had printed the page brown too, with a pattern like moiré.

"Let 'em hear that and see how they like it," she told Uncle Nathan.

But Miss Beulah flew between them and seized it herself and brought it to her eyes, picture side up. "It's Sam Dale! It's Sam Dale Beecham in his soldier suit!" she cried. "I never saw him dressed in it except when we buried him."

"The message is spelled out on the other side," Uncle Curtis told her, but she could not take her eyes from the picture. They waited until at last she turned the card over and cried out again. " 'Dear Rachel'!" Her voice suddenly lost all its authority as she began to read aloud from the written words. In monotone, halting herself every few words, she read, " 'Dear Rachel. Here I am in—front of the—mess tent. Excuse me for—just wearing my'—something—'blouse but it is so hot in'—something—'in *Georgia*. Here is a—present for our—baby save it for when he gets here. Bought it with today's—pay and'—something—'*trust* it keeps good time. I miss one and all and wish I was in Banner.' Something—'Sincerely your husband Sam Dale Beecham.' "

Gloria cried out but didn't move. Miss Beulah bent and peered into her grandmother's face. "Sam Dale put the words on that but he never sent it. Did he?"

"It was bundled with his things. This and the watch. I got 'em when I got back Sam Dale," said Granny. "It's a likeness. I can peep at it, before I get my prayers said."

"Well, now, ain't that pitiful," Miss Beulah was murmuring. Then she cried in a loud voice of release and joy, "Ain't that pitiful! Oh, all these years!" She turned the card first to the faded handwriting, then to the picture, turned it back and forth faster and faster, as if trying through her tears to make the two sides one, bind them. "You held it in, kept it hid. Granny, what have you been saving this for?"

"Till I was a hundred years old and had my grandchildren and great-grandchildren all around me, all with ears pretty well cocked to hear it," Granny replied. She frisked the postcard out of Miss Beulah's fingers, returned it to her Bible, and shut up the Bible. Elvie sprang up and went hauling off with it.

"Fan me, Granny," Miss Beulah said, kneeling at the old lady's chair. "Oh, cool my forehead a little." She hugged Granny's knees and laid her cheek down on the ancient, unstirring lap. "Sam Dale got to be a father after all."

"He was not my father!" Gloria cried out.

"But he wasn't too good to be, he tells you right on the card he wasn't," said Aunt Birdie. "He must have had a reason mighty like you to want to marry little-old Rachel Sojourner."

"Oh, I believe he had, I believe he knew what he was saying!" Miss Beulah cried, as Granny laid on the crown of her head a dispassionate look.

"I hope Beulah ain't happy too soon," said Aunt Birdie.

"Beulah's got more fortitude than some," said Aunt Beck gently. "Yet, if the right story comes along at the right time, she'll be like the rest of us and believe what she wants to believe."

"I wish I'd known, I wish I'd been allowed to know," Miss Beulah said. "Then, when I could see the handwriting on the wall, I could have smiled to myself over this child and my boy Jack. Well,

I'd have thought, even this may turn out all right in the end, with Beecham blood on both sides." She suddenly climbed to her feet and threw open her arms to Gloria, who burst into tears.

"Rachel's the one you take after," Miss Beulah said, lifting the girl's convulsed, streaming face in her hand. "There's very little Beecham in your gaze. I don't see the first glimmer of Sam Dale. Yes, your face is Rachel's entirely, and with all the wild notions in it. Makes me remember how she used to vow she was going clear to Ludlow some day, and live in style."

"And the mane," said Granny.

"But never mind, Granny—she's here. Gloria's here, and she's proof, living proof! I didn't do hurt to my own, after all. I can die happy! Can't I?" Miss Beulah's voice rose exultant. Gloria wept. And Judge Moody, whose head with its long forehead, long nose, long upper lip and chin, and long, close-set ears had been tilted back as if out of reluctance to listen, made a melancholy sound in his throat. The cheers were coming from everybody else, drowning out all three.

"Well, Gloria! We told you, didn't we? We told you who you are. Ain't you going to say thank you?" asked Aunt Birdie with excitement, staggering up from her chair.

"I never heard Gloria say thank you for anything yet," said Miss Beulah. "But that won't stop me from hugging her now."

"You didn't need to find out for yourself, Gloria. You didn't need Miss Julia's helping hand. You had us," said Aunt Birdie. "I don't consider we had to go to too much trouble, to figure you out. Here's a kiss for you."

"Pull me up!" said Aunt Nanny, then came toward Gloria, walling up like a catalpa tree in full bloom. "Welcome into the family!"

The uncles were all rising too, laughing and pressing in, all but Uncle Nathan.

"I don't want to be a Beecham!" Gloria cried. "Now it's ten times worse! I won't be a Beecham—go back! Please don't squeeze me!"

Over their heads, the chimney swifts circled as if a crooking finger below held them on tight strings. As though in some evening accord with the birds, the aunts came circling in to Gloria, crowding Miss Beulah to one side—all the aunts and some of the girl cousins. They had Gloria out in the clear space in the middle of the yard, moving her along with them.

"*London Bridge is falling down,*" some voice sang, and a trap of arms came down over Gloria's head and brought her to the ground. Behind her came a crack like a firecracker—they had split open a melon.

She struggled wildly at first as she tried to push away the red hulk shoved down into her face, as big as a man's clayed shoe, swarming with seeds, warm with rain-thin juice.

They were all laughing. "Say Beecham!" they ordered her, close to her ear. They rolled her by the shoulders, pinned her flat, then buried her face under the flesh of the melon with its blood heat, its smell of evening flowers. Ribbons of juice crawled on her neck and circled it, as hands robbed of sex spread her jaws open.

"Can't you say Beecham? What's wrong with being Beecham?"

Lady May, as if catapulted into their midst, arrived and stood rooted, her mouth wide open and soundless, the way she'd watched Brother Bethune go bang with the gun. The next minute Miss Beulah snatched her up and carried her off.

"Jack!" called out Gloria. But they were ramming the sweet, breaking chunks inside her mouth. "Jack! Jack!"

"He went to take Aycock some bread and water." That was Aunt Beck's voice—one voice the same as ever, trying to bring comfort.

"Say Beecham!" screamed Aunt Nanny.

"Don't you like watermelon?" screamed Aunt Cleo. "Swallow, then! Swallow!"

"I declare," murmured the voice of Mrs. Moody to the side, "I haven't seen something like this in years and years."

"Say Beecham and we'll stop. Let's hear you say who's a Beecham!"

"*Fox in the morning!*" called some little girls playing in the distance. "*Geese in the evening!*" Up in the tree, Elvie passed to and fro in her swing and gave the scene below the deadly eye of a trapeze artist whose turn would come next. The chimney swifts ticked in the deepening sky overhead, going round and round, tilting, like taut little bows drawn with arrows ready. In her chair, Granny sat with the face of a cornshuck doll, a face so old and accomplished that it might allow her to sleep with her eyes open.

"Come on, sisters, help feed her! Let's cram it down her little red lane! Let's make her say Beecham! *We* did!" came the women's voices.

"What you so proud about?" Aunt Nanny held high a hunk of melon as generous as a helping at the table. They were crying with laughter now. "Say who's a Beecham! Then swallow it!"

Gloria tried to call Jack once more.

Somebody shouted, "Wash it down her crook!"

Elvie in her swing said, "If she swallows them seeds, she'll only grow another Tom Watson melon inside her stomach."

A melony hand forced warm, seed-filled hunks into Gloria's sagging mouth. "Why, you're just in the bosom of your own family," somebody's voice cried softly as if in condolence. Melon and fingers together went into her mouth. "Just swallow," said the voice. "*Everybody's* got *something* they could cry about."

"I think she's lost her breath now. She's just letting us sit on her," said a voice that sighed.

"Sometimes women is too deep for me. But I reckon it's only for the good reason that I never had any sisters," pronounced Miss Beulah from the porch, in the voice of lofty argument she used with Lady May.

The aunts were helping each other to their feet. Gloria lay flat, an arm across her face now, its unfreckled side exposed and as pale as the underpelt of a rabbit. The swifts were gone out of the sky, perhaps all down their chimney.

"Remember when she first come to Banner? She wasn't as determined then as she got to be later. She was scared as a little naked bird. Wonder why!" said Aunt Nanny.

"Far from what she knew," said Aunt Beck. "That's in her face again now."

"Got here and didn't even know how to pull mustard," said Aunt Birdie.

"Yes, she knew that. She was brought up an orphan, after all," Auntie Fay said.

"What do men see in 'em?" whispered Miss Lexie.

Miss Beulah came marching to Gloria and planted her feet beside her. "Gloria Beecham Renfro, what are you doing down on the dusty ground like that? Get up! Get up and join your family, for a change." Miss Beulah reached down, took Gloria by the arm, and pulled her to her feet.

"I still don't believe I'm a Beecham," she came up saying. The watermelon juice by now had chalked her face pink and stiffened her lips as it dried.

"Gloria," said Miss Beulah, "go back in the house and wash that face and get rid of some of that tangly hair, then shake that dress and come out again. Now that's the best thing I can tell you."

"No thank you, ma'am." She stood right there. "I'm standing my ground," she told everybody.

"And look at her," said Miss Lexie. "I guess you-all will make me be the one to fix her so we can stand the sight of her." She walked up to Gloria and clapped a hand on her shoulder as if she'd been empowered to arrest her. "You need a little trimming done on you. Gonna run?" Miss Lexie invited her. Her fingers made sure of the needle she carried in her collar. She threw out her hand at random, a thimble was tossed from among the aunts, and she cupped it to her breastbone to catch it. Then she threw forward her Buster Brown bob and pulled off over her head the ribbon that carried her scissors with her everywhere.

"Lexie, you always bite off more than you can chew," said Miss Beulah. "And this house never allowed sewing on Sunday."

"I'm not going to come out of my dress for anybody," said Gloria, arms clamped to her sides.

"We know you're modest," teased Aunt Nanny.

"You just stand still, and tell it to stay light," said Miss Lexie to Gloria. "The men ain't going to pay a sewing session a bit of attention, and Jack ain't here to worry about."

On her saying that, the uncles turned their chairs a little bit, and Mr. Renfro got up and hobbled away, as if to see how many more of his watermelons still waited in reserve under the porch. With a long sound like a stream of dry seed being poured into an empty bucket, the song of the locusts began.

⋅§

"I'll tell you one thing about that dress—you can't hurt it now! Not after the travelling it's done today," Aunt Nanny said gaily, "and the waltzing around it's had." She swung the sash she held.

"I found my patch ready-made," said Miss Lexie, ripping.

"Will you please spare my pocket?" cried Gloria.

"I've already got it," said Miss Lexie and slipped it wrong side out.

"No wedding dress I ever saw *had* a pocket," said Mrs. Moody.

**271**

"It was carrying my wedding handkerchief," said Gloria.

"Looks prettier if you hold it," said Miss Lexie, handing it up. "And you might want to drop some tears, who knows? Just for a change."

Miss Lexie began snipping at the hem of Gloria's dress. "I worshipped her! Worshipped Miss Julia Mortimer!" she suddenly declared from behind Gloria, close to her there near the ground. She brought out her words as loudly or as softly as she ripped, as if to keep up with her thread. "She lived and boarded with us, right across the road from the schoolhouse, and taught me as far as the seventh grade. She encouraged me too, when I was coming up. For all anybody here knows, I might have had my sights set too on stepping into her shoes." She paused to rock on her heels where she squatted, giving her silent laugh. "But they die," she said. "The ones who think highly of you. Or they change, or leave you behind, get married, flit, go crazy—"

"Lexie, has anybody asked you for your story?" Miss Beulah asked, still patrolling the yard, down as far as where some boy cousins were tinkering under two of the cars, keeping her eye on the whole scene.

"My memory reaches back to where she first came to Banner," said Miss Lexie, going after the thread. "But it was before that that Grandfather Renfro said, 'I've lived a long time and come a long way to find out there's a rushing river still left between my folks and something they ought to have on the other side. And I'm going to pray till I find a way for mine to get ahold of it.' He meant a good schooling. He'd had Papa and his two little sisters going to Alliance. It meant two of 'em riding the horse to a place up the river, and the little one hanging on behind to ride the horse back home. Then they rowed 'em across and walked the rest of the way."

"Where was the bridge?" Aunt Cleo was asking.

"Nobody'd dreamed yet we needed one," Miss Beulah said forbiddingly.

"Man would pole you across for the promise of a fat hen or a sack of potatoes," said Granny. "A fellow thought twice about it, then, whether he wanted quite as much as he thought he did to be on the other side."

"Grandfather took all this to the Lord," said Miss Lexie, "and the Lord told him it would be a lot better if they built a school on this side of the Bywy and let the *teacher* do the crossing. So as to save

272

time and trouble and to cheat the bad weather, she could board on the Banner side during the week. Well, then!"

"You mean to say we owe Banner School to a Renfro? Never dreamed that!" Aunt Nanny cried, and called, "Why, Mr. Renfro!"

"And Miss Julia Mortimer was the living answer to Old Preacher Renfro's prayer? I never knew that either!" cried Uncle Noah Webster.

"Well, not right directly," said Mr. Renfro. "There had to be a generation go by before something more come of it. They had to build the schoolhouse. And after it's built and standing there, there was a little breathing space while they could hope the teacher they prayed for'd never come."

"But here she came. Miss Julia Mortimer," said Miss Lexie, snipping and ripping, squatting her way around Gloria's skirt. "Solid as a rock and not one bit of nonsense, looking like the Presbyterian she started out to be. First thing, she clamped down on the men and made 'em fence the yard to keep us in and saw out more windows to see our lessons by, and she scrubbed it inside out and scoured it without any help, raised up a ladder and painted it herself inside and out. 'That's a good start, now,' she says when it's white and got a flagpole. 'And I'll keep lessons going till you find somebody better.' That's how she got herself in harness."

"Where did they even *find* her!" exclaimed Aunt Birdie.

"They didn't have to find her. She'd found them. Banner School was ready for a teacher, and that was all she needed," said Miss Lexie.

"How old was you then, Lexie?" asked Aunt Nanny. "How old are you *now?*"

"I'm old enough to remember the first morning," said Miss Lexie, "with a mind still clear. She steps to the front and says, 'Children of Banner School! It's the first day for both of us. I'm your teacher, Miss Julia Mortimer. Nothing in this world can measure up to the joy you'll bring me if you allow me to teach you something.' "

"And Banner was glad to get her!" Miss Beulah said. "Oh, yes, Grandpa offered up a prayer of thanks for her and asked the Lord to spare her."

"At first everybody must have been as happy as she was," said Miss Lexie. "Fell in love with each other! I've come to believe that's a bad sign. The next thing they knew, Miss Julia Mortimer was saying that poor attention and bad behavior on a Monday would always be punished on a Tuesday. On Tuesday, here came all the children to school and some leading their fathers. So Miss Julia said 'Good morning!' to all alike, and then she called up the pupils that hadn't behaved on Monday, like Earl Comfort, and one by one she gave 'em a little token of her meaning with her fresh-cut peach-tree switch. Then she says, 'Now. If any of these fathers who were so brave as to come to school this morning feel prompted to step up too, I'm ready for them now. Otherwise, they can all stay right there on the back bench and learn something.' And invited up old Levi Champion first —Homer's daddy."

"He run," said Mr. Renfro. He sat down by Judge Moody and smiled at him. "I know that without being there. She meant her words entirely, the lady did. Then and every other time she delivered herself."

"From that day on, she was a fixture at Banner School," said Miss Lexie. "She wouldn't have given it up for anybody. Now, *your* turn," she told Gloria. She went on. "Promptly, she nailed a shelf there under the front window and called it the library. She took her own money to fill up that shelf with books."

"She made salary, didn't she?" asked Aunt Cleo.

"The first month, the way the old folks remembered it, they paid her with seventeen silver dollars. But afterwards, they wasn't ever able to come up to that brave start," said Miss Beulah.

"They knew about warrants, even in the early days. Teachers just got a warrant," said Mr. Renfro. "And there come up Mr. Dearman—"

"Perish the name!" cried Miss Beulah.

"Well, he was going around the country buying up teachers' warrants at a discount," said Mr. Renfro. "That's telling the least of him, Mother."

"No matter how, Miss Julia got books and came bringing 'em. I bet you Banner School had a library as long as your arm," cried Aunt Birdie, as though she saw a snake.

"Then what happened to it? It was gone by the time I came along," said Auntie Fay.

"It got rained on, darlin'," said Aunt Nanny, letting her grin show. "I believe the teacher was young enough to cry."

"She only started it again. And kept her map of the world hanging up year in, year out," said Aunt Birdie. "And did it rattle on a March morning!"

**274**

"And we're not on it," said Miss Beulah. "Miss Julia said—"

" 'Put Banner on the map!' " came a chorus, the men joining in.

"We know the rest!" said Miss Beulah. "That'll do for her now, Lexie."

"I worshipped her as a child, though please don't ask me to find you the reason for it now, now that I've seen her go down," Miss Lexie said. "I cried when she had to leave our house for this one."

"Stayed with me first," said Granny, looking at them sideways out of the slits of her eyes.

"Don't start getting jealous, Granny!" Uncle Noah Webster said. "You didn't *want* the teacher, did you? Grandpa and us children filled up the house for you, didn't we?"

"Everybody had to have her. The Comforts, they had their crack at her too. Come the long winter evenings, they all had to crowd mighty close together in the room with the fire to both see and keep warm by. And she'd stand up and read to 'em! Made 'em mad as wet hens. They had to hush talking, else be called impolite," said Aunt Nanny. "I used to be there and in the same boat with 'em, because, you know, that's who Mama gave me to."

"*Read* to 'em? At *home?*" Aunt Birdie cried.

"It was her idea, not theirs," said Aunt Nanny. "*Old* Mis' Comfort says nobody'd ever know what her and the children suffered, with that teacher cooped in with us all winter. Old lady's dust now, but she one time heard Miss Julia out to the tag end of her piece in the reader, and then that old lady spit in the fire and told the teacher *and* her own daughter—who'd just had a baby without sign of wedding band—'Now be ashamed *both* of ye.' "

"That's enough," said Miss Beulah.

Miss Lexie said to Gloria, "If anybody's trying to cut under you, hold still." She looked up at the rest of them, from under her Buster Brown bangs, and said, "But I didn't come in that class. She *encouraged* me. She *made* me work."

"That's her case, all right," said Auntie Fay. "Lexie went charging through Banner School and got her diploma right on time. And she went and lived in Ludlow in a Baptist preacher's widow's boarding house, and in the afternoons and all day Saturday wrapped packages in the corner department store. We didn't think she was strong enough to go to high school too."

"I had my sights set," said Miss Lexie, squinting her eye now

**275**

at the scissors in her hand. "But it took more strength than I had—I fell down on Virgil, and wasn't shown any mercy."

"They was just trying to keep you out of State Normal," said Auntie Fay provocatively.

"I thought I could teach just as well without Virgil," said Miss Lexie. "And I could have, if they hadn't given me Banner right on top of Miss Julia. They'd put her out to pasture—against her will entirely and much to her surprise—it's nothing but a state law. And who would dare come after her? I tried holding 'em down. But my nerves weren't strong enough. I switched to caring for the sick."

"Uh-oh!" said Aunt Cleo.

"And then it came. The Presbyterian sisterhood in Alliance sent out a call on both sides of the river for a settled white Christian lady with no home ties."

"Oh, *those* are the scum of the earth!" Mrs. Moody burst out. "We had one of those for our preacher's widow! Got her the same way!"

"And I presented myself," Miss Lexie said. She was under Gloria's arm now, snipping higher, at the gathers of her waist. Gloria had to keep both arms raised while Miss Lexie went around her, smelling of sour starch. "I left Mr. Hugg for her. I thought the change would have to be for the better."

"I don't know about the rest of it, but it looks to me like you've got a few ties," remarked Mrs. Moody, as if a nerve still throbbed.

"The one thing I was sure of was I was the best she could do," said Miss Lexie. "And that's what I told her. You're supposed to turn when I punch you," she said to Gloria. "Have to get you from all sides. You would suppose she'd count it a blessing, getting for her nurse somebody she'd once put to work and encouraged. Somebody that knew her disposition and couldn't be surprised at her ways. Another teacher."

"Look where it's brought both of you," said Miss Beulah. "That's a good place to stop your story now, Lexie."

"For how long was she gracious?" asked Aunt Cleo with a short laugh.

"I wish I'd kept count of the few days," said Miss Lexie. "She was the same to everybody, though. The same to people in Alliance as she was to me, no favorites. All her callers fell off, little at a time, then thick and fast. She made short work of the sisterhood in Alliance."

"The very ones that went out of their way to bribe you to be her nurse?" asked Aunt Cleo, giving a nod.

"Miss Julia sent them packing when they came calling and told her the angels had sent me," said Miss Lexie. "When they told her she'd finished her appointed work on earth and the Lord was preparing to send for her and she ought to be grateful in the meantime. She clapped at 'em—they left backing away."

"She was a Presbyterian, and no hiding that. But was she deep-dyed?" asked Aunt Beck. "There's a whole lot of different grades of 'em, some of 'em aren't too far off from Baptists."

"I don't care to say," said Miss Lexie after a moment.

"I suppose they were right there again the next day, and the next," said Aunt Cleo, nodding. "The sisterhood."

"After Miss Julia Mortimer dismissed them?" Miss Lexie exclaimed. "No, nobody tried it again, and then she wondered what had happened to everybody. What had happened to *her?*"

"That's the ticket," said Aunt Cleo. "Well, whatever it was, it wasn't your fault."

"So they made me have her by myself. Sunday after Sunday we'd sit there and wait and nobody'd peep their heads in at all. 'Are they keeping absent on purpose to miss today's lesson?' she'd ask. And she'd struggle to her feet and walk to the front porch and ask, "Where's Gloria Short?' You were right in style when you didn't come," Miss Lexie said, close to Gloria's back. "There Miss Julia Mortimer and me would sit, getting older by the minute, both of us. Both foxed up for Sunday, I saw to that. Her on one side of the porch and me on the other, her in the wickerwork rocking chair and me in the oak swing. Pretty soon she'd stop rocking. 'And what're you doing here, then?' says Miss Julia to me. 'Suppose you take your presence out of here. How can I read with you in the house with me?' She'd put her foot right down. I'd put my foot down. She'd stamp: one. I'd stamp: one. After all, we'd both learned our tactics in the schoolroom. In my opinion it didn't matter all that much any longer who'd taught who or who'd started this contest. We'd stamp, stamp —and one-two-three she'd kilter."

"And where was you, Lexie?" cried Aunt Birdie.

"Right behind her!" Miss Lexie called, right behind Gloria.

"Don't!" Gloria cried.

"Don't, yourself. Stop quivering, because I'm fixing now to take a great big whack out of your skirt. I had to puff a little bit to catch Miss Julia. She was too used to charging off in a hurry. She was looking all at one time in the vegetable patch and in the shed where her car gathered dust and behind the peach trees and under the grape vine and even in the cow pasture, to see where the bad ones were hiding. There was I, chasing her over her flower yard, those tangly old beds, stumbling over 'em like graves where the bulbs were so many of 'em crowding up from down below—and on to the front, packed tight as a trunk with rosebushes, scratch you like the briar patch—and down into those old white flags spearing up through the vines all the way down her bank as far as the road, thick as teeth—and there in the empty road she'd even crack open her mailbox, and look inside!"

"How long did she keep it up, looking for company?" asked Aunt Cleo. "A week? A month?"

"Longer! If you could see today the trough her feet have worn under that old wickerwork chair in the yard—she had me lug it right off the porch to where she could sit and watch the road. Like children wear under a swing," said Miss Lexie. "I used to say, 'Miss Julia, you come on back inside the house. Hear? People aren't used to seeing you outside like this. They aren't coming visiting. Nobody's coming. And what if they did, and found you outside with your hair all streaming?' I'd say, 'Why are you turning so contrary? Why won't you just give up, Miss Julia, and come on in the cool house with me?' And when she was inside again, then she turned around and ran me out and dared me to come back in! 'Get out of here, old woman!' And she's full eleven years older than me!"

"She's a scrapper, all right." Granny was nodding her head. "Knew it the minute I got my first look at the girl, teaching her elders."

"She put up her fists next?" asked Aunt Cleo.

"If I got to the door and locked it first, she'd try to get out of her own house," Miss Lexie said. "Shake—she'd shake that big oak door! You ever see a spider shake his web when you lay a pine-straw in it just for meanness? She could shake her door like a web was all it was. I felt sometimes like just everything, not only her house but me in it, was about to go flying, and me no more'n a pine-straw myself, something in her way."

"I'm ready for you to stop," whispered Gloria.

"I tied her, that was the upshoot," said Miss Lexie. "Tied her in bed. I didn't want to, but anybody you'd ask would tell you the same: you may have to." Gloria tried to move, but Miss Lexie gripped her that moment by the ankle and said, "Don't shift your weight."

"If Lexie can find something to do the hard way, she'll do it," said Miss Beulah. "Setting a patch in that skirt, now, with the girl inside it!" She paced around them.

"It's a matter of being equal to circumstances," Miss Lexie asserted. "Every day, Miss Julia there in her bed called me to bring her her book. 'Which book?' I ask her. She said just bring her her book. I couldn't do that, I told her, 'because I don't know which book you mean. Which book do you mean?' Because she had more books than anything. I couldn't make her tell me which book she meant. So she didn't get any."

"Book! It looks like of all things she'd have been glad she was through with and thankful *not* to have brought her!" exclaimed Aunt Birdie.

"Bet Gloria could have picked one out," teased Aunt Nanny.

"Gloria, I think it was really you that must have disappointed her the most," said Aunt Beck, as though she offered a compliment. "She hoped so hard for something out of you."

Gloria cried out.

"Elvie, bring me a row of pins!—But no, you never came to see your old teacher, all the time she lay getting worse," said Miss Lexie. "She was peeping out for you, right straight along. First she'd say, 'Gloria Short will be here soon now. She knows it's for her own good to get here on time.' Even in bed, she'd lean close to her window, press her face to the glass even on rainy mornings, not to miss the first sight of Gloria coming."

"Where was you hiding, girl?" Aunt Cleo cried with a laugh.

"Hiding? I was having a baby," Gloria broke out. "That's what I was doing, and you can die from that."

"You can die from anything if you try good and hard," said Miss Beulah.

"I said, 'Oh, she's just forgotten you, Julia, like everybody else has,' " said Miss Lexie.

Granny had begun to look from one face to the next, her breath coming a little fast. Miss Beulah saw, and went to stand beside her.

"So the next thing, didn't she ask me for her bell. She wanted the school bell!" said Miss Lexie.

"Why, that's a heavy old thing," said Uncle Curtis. "Solid brass and a long handle—"

"She couldn't have raised it. Never at all. Never again in her life. And I told her so. 'And no matter if you could,' I reminded her, 'you haven't got the school bell. Banner School's got it! It doesn't belong to you,' I said. 'Banner School's got the bell and you've been put out to pasture—they're through with you.' I thought that would finish the subject. But 'Give me back my bell,' she'd say. And look at me, with living dread in her face."

"Dread?" scoffed Miss Beulah, staunch beside Granny.

"You're hurting me," whispered Gloria.

"It's not me, it's my scissors. I'd say, 'Julia'—I'd got to the point where I didn't call her anything but Julia—'what is it you *want* that bell for? Give me a good reason, then maybe I'll get it for you. You want to bring 'em, make 'em come? Or is this the way you're going to drive 'em off if they try? Make up your poor mind if the world is welcome or unwelcome. The world isn't going to let you have a thing both ways.' "

"You can't always easily fool 'em," said Aunt Cleo. "I'm a real nurse, *used* to all that, *used* to going in other people's houses, and just like today becoming one of the family. I've had a worlds of experience, now, just a worlds. And I could tell *you* tales, now."

Miss Lexie said, "And she looks me back in the face trying to think of an answer, and all she can think of to say, and she said it loud and clear, was 'Ding dong! Ding dong bell!' "

"But where was her mind?" cried Miss Beulah.

"I asked her, plenty of times," said Miss Lexie.

"But why wasn't Miss Julia content with her lot?" asked Aunt Beck in a low voice. "Like an ordinary Christian?"

"An ordinary Christian wouldn't want to wear her red sweater and keep her shoes on in bed," said Miss Lexie. "And if she didn't know what she was doing, any better than that, bed was right where she belonged. And I wasn't to touch her fingernails, either. They grew a mile long. She said she wanted to be ready for me."

"She must have put up some battle, for somebody that's part-paralyzed," said Aunt Birdie.

"She wasn't paralyzed anywhere. That would have made it easier."

"But I happen to know about a lady who wouldn't cut her own

**280**

toenails," Aunt Cleo said. "And she wasn't paralyzed, either. Until they crossed each other over all her toes and weaved back and forth over her feet sharp as knives, and she finally had to go with 'em to the hospital. The doctors said they'd met with a lot before, but not that. Her funeral was held with a sealed coffin."

"They could never have paralyzed Miss Julia Mortimer," said Miss Lexie. "I'd say, 'Why don't you quit fighting kind hands?' She'd say, 'Only way to keep myself alive!' Knocks my arm back with her weak little fist. 'I *love* you,' I says. 'You used to be my inspiration.' 'You get out of my house, old woman. Go home! If you've got a home,' she says."

"She hit the nail on the head when she said you didn't have elsewhere to go," said Miss Beulah. "Not unless you went back to Mr. Hugg, took care of him again." She patted Granny's bent shoulder.

"Then she quoted some poetry at me. I don't mean Scripture," said Miss Lexie.

"Sure-enough, Lexie, we didn't mean to ask you all that," said Aunt Birdie.

"Old Lexie's truly been stirring up the bottom," said Aunt Nanny.

"Lexie, you'd take all night long to sew up a little hole in your stockin'!" cried Miss Beulah.

"I take pains with all I do and I want my results to show it."

"You've got coming night to contend with now. I warned you," Miss Beulah said.

"Oh, I'm used to putting out my eyes! Here's where you climb up and stand on a chair for me," said Miss Lexie to Gloria. "I'm tacking your fresh hem in. Oh, she never forgot she had something to tell *you*."

Mr. Willy Trimble hopped to bring Miss Lexie up her own chair, and she took it and shooed him back. She drew a needle from her collar with a thread that was never seen, lost like the outlines of Gloria's dress now in the glow of evening that was all around them. She went to work on Gloria where she stood with arms slowly lifting, legs ladylike, feet one in front of the other on the rush seat.

"If it'd been me doing it, I wouldn't have used my scissors and cut my thread behind me. I'd have it now to put in over again," said Auntie Fay.

"Sissie, do you forget I'm the one taught you to sew?"

"How late in the game was it, Lexie, when Miss Julia took it in she'd met her match?" asked Aunt Nanny.

"If the news ever sunk in, she kept it a pretty good secret," said Miss Lexie. "I reckon what it amounted to was the two of us settling down finally to see which would be first to wear the other one out."

"There you give a perfect little picture of the battle of nursing," said Aunt Cleo.

"But it was only if I'd hold out her pencil to her that she'd come quiet."

"A pencil?" cried Aunt Birdie. "A common *pencil?*"

Gloria drew breath. She was turned to face the deep blush of distance, out of which the cows were coming in now, the three in a line. Their slow steps were not quite in time to the tinkling, as though their thin-worn bells rang for what was behind them, down the reach of their long, back-flung shadows, back over Vaughn's shoulder and his shadow as he drove them home.

"Yes'm, pencil! And you want to see the way she wrote?" asked Miss Lexie, and she showed them, while her hands went on sewing.

"Wrote with her tongue spreading out?"

Miss Lexie smacked her lips at them. "Like words, just words, was getting to be something good enough to eat. And nothing else was!"

"Lexie, you're about to ruin this reunion in spite of everything, giving out talk of death and disgrace around here," exclaimed Miss Beulah. She cried to the others, "Take away her needle, if that's what sewing brings on."

Granny's eyes raced from one face to another, as though here at her table she had somehow got ringed around by strangers. She breathed in shallow gasps, striving hard to hear the voices.

"I wouldn't have wanted to be shut up with Miss Julia Mortimer too long, myself. She might have brought up with something I wasn't inclined to hear," said Aunt Birdie.

"She was just doing harm to herself, wearing herself out like that," said Aunt Beck.

Miss Lexie cried out, "I didn't think just writing letters could hurt her! But reckless? She'd tell 'em! Let 'em know she's afraid of nothing! Speak out whatever's the worst thing she can think of! Holler to the nurse for tablet and pencil! Lick and push! Lick and push! Fold it and cram it in the envelope till it won't hold one word more! Bring up the stamp out of hiding! And say, 'Mail it, fool!' "

"Oh, were those real letters?" asked Aunt Beck.

"Is there some other kind?" asked Judge Moody from his same school chair. The ladies paused at his voice, and Gloria's hands let fall her handkerchief and reached up to her cheeks.

"I've heard that licking an indelible pencil was one sure way to die," Aunt Birdie said.

"I've seen her wetting that pencil a hundred times a day—it wasn't very sharp. Opened up that old Redbird school tablet and up would come her pencil and out would go her tongue and away she'd fly," said Miss Lexie. "And send that old purple pencil racing, racing, racing."

"Didn't you tell her it'd kill her?" asked Aunt Nanny.

"For the thanks I'd get?" Miss Lexie dipped back to laugh.

Gloria said over her head, "She wouldn't have quit writing just for your satisfaction. I've known her to correct arithmetic papers with a broken arm. But I never knew her to lick a pencil before."

"What'd you do with those letters, Lexie? Throw 'em in the pig pen?" cried Miss Beulah.

"I don't want to say."

"You threw 'em in the pig pen. So I guess it didn't make any difference who they was to."

"I said, 'Listen, Julia. If you've got something this bad to say about human nature,' I said, because I skimmed one or two of 'em over, 'why don't you go ahead and send it to the President of the United States? What do you want to waste it on us for?' "

"And I'd believe it of her! My, she was vain! Was vain!" Miss Beulah cried, in a voice of reluctant admiration. "To the end, I should say?" she asked Lexie.

Miss Lexie replied without a sound—only opened her mouth as for a big bite.

"Yet, the littler you wish to see of some people, the plainer you may come to remember 'em," said Miss Beulah, with some darkness. "Even against your will. I can't tell you why, so don't ask me. But I can see that old schoolteacher this minute plainer than I can see you, Lexie Renfro, after your back's turned."

"In the long run, I got her pencil away from her," said Miss Lexie, speaking faster. "I could pull harder than she could."

"What'd she do then?" asked a voice.

"She just wrote with her finger."

"What'd she use for ink, a little licking?"

"Yes'm, and wrote away on the bedsheet."

There was a stifled sound from Judge Moody. Aunt Beck said with a sigh, "I'm glad for you you couldn't tell so well by then what she was saying."

"And I pulled off the hot sheet and she wrote on, in the palm of her hand."

"Wrote what?"

"Fuss fuss fuss fuss fuss, I suppose," Miss Lexie cried.

The chorus of locusts came through the air in waves, in a beat like the brass school bell wielded with full long arm, all the way up to the yard, to the forgotten tables, to the house, to where the setting sun had spread its lap at that moment on the low barn roof.

"Lexie, will you please quit going around on your knees and with your tongue hanging out?" asked Miss Beulah. "There's some may not be able to appreciate that."

Even when it was Miss Beulah, Granny gave each speaker a bewildered look, her little head shaking as it turned from one to the other.

"I was tacking in my hem," said Miss Lexie, staggering to her feet.

"Well, we're all getting there, I suppose. And it won't be long before the baby of us all—!" Aunt Beck murmured.

"Oh, I could tell it wouldn't be long," said Miss Lexie. "I hid her pencil, and she said, 'Now I want to die.' I said, 'Well, why don't you go ahead and die, then?' She'd made me say it! And she said, 'Because I want to die by myself, you everpresent, everlasting old fool!'"

"She didn't know what she was saying," said Aunt Beck.

"That's just what she did know!" said Miss Lexie.

"Take away her needle," Miss Beulah commanded.

"Some things you don't let them make you say," said Miss Lexie. "And I don't care who they are."

"But does that mean it's better to just come off and leave 'em?" asked Aunt Beck, and slowly one of her hands went in front of her face to shield it.

"I had the reunion to come to, didn't I?" Miss Lexie retorted.

The barn was a gauzy pink, like a curtain just pulled across a window, and Vaughn was coming in now with the cows and the dogs. With the sun as low as where the cows swung their heads, the brass nubs on their horns sent a few last long rays flashing. Then all marched slowly into the folds of the curtain.

"One thing I didn't hear, if you told it," Aunt Cleo said. "I'd like to know what disease was eating of her. Did anybody ever find out, or did they tell?"

"Old age," said Miss Lexie. "That do?"

"Now are you satisfied, Lexie? Now will you set?" cried Miss Beulah.

"You don't get over it all that quick—what some of 'em make you do," returned Miss Lexie. "But I'm *through!*" she said to Gloria, as though the girl had cried out. She dipped her head close to Gloria's leg and bit off the thread. "It was nothing to hurt you, now was it?" She lifted the girl, roughly enough, and set her down on warm ground.

"At least we know who it is, can see who you are now, Gloria," said Aunt Birdie.

"Look at those skinny little legs, everybody, like a sparrow's," said Aunt Nanny, coming to tie on her sash.

"Petticoat shows now," said Auntie Fay.

"And remember from now on," Aunt Beck said, "every little move you make, Gloria, is still bound to show on that sash. Every little drop you spill. Every time you get up or down, it'll tell on you."

"Hey, Gloria," said Aunt Cleo. "With all those scraps and without half trying"—she pointed to them, organdie scraps as pale as the scraps of tin that still lay around from the roofing, ready to cut open a foot—"you could make Lady May a little play wedding dress, just like yours."

"*Where is my baby?*" Gloria cried.

Aunt Nanny barred Lady May's path with a big quick arm. She caught the child up and hugged her. "And you was a pretty good little secret yourself, wasn't you?" she asked her.

Lady May struggled, got free of her, ran from her and from her mother too, and vanished behind the althea bush with its hundreds of flowers already spindling, like messages already read and folded up.

Miss Lexie gathered up the scraps and balled them, to drop into her own gingham pocket.

"Last reunion, it was Mr. Hugg. And we had it all to hear about him," said Auntie Fay.

"I knew you'd say that, Sissie."

"Hugg? Thought he had the Ludlow jail," said Aunt Cleo.

"Jailer had a daddy, didn't he? This is his daddy," said Miss Lexie.

"Isn't *he* worse than *her?*"

"I sit there and he lays there, Fay. When I see his eyes fly open, I get ready for him."

"Sister Cleo, Lexie first took care of an old man in the bed named Jonas Hugg, kept house for him, fed him and his frizzly hen. And the old man'd just as soon pitch the plate of grits back in her face if she tried to get him to eat it," giggled Auntie Fay.

"Looking back, I don't mind Mr. Hugg one bit," warned Aunt Lexie. "I don't mind him any longer."

"And if she went for more grits, peed in the bed to pay her back for it."

"I'm above it," sang Miss Lexie. "I'm above it. Him and his money belt too. He's just exactly one hundred percent what he seems. Bad Boy."

"Why did you ever bother to leave him for her? They're all the same," Aunt Cleo told Miss Lexie.

"No. Mr. Hugg cries. And the *first* day, he clapped his hands together just to see me coming!" said Miss Lexie. "He was glad to see me at first and didn't hide it."

"The thing to remember is they change," said Aunt Cleo, with a nod toward Granny. "And you and me will do the same, I hate to tell you."

From the moving swing above them, Elvie pointed to far away, to the edge of what they could see. There stood the moon, like somebody at the door. One lop-side showing first, the way a rose opens, the moon was pushing up through the rose-dye of dust. The dust they'd breathed all day and tasted with every breath and bite and kiss was being partly taken from them by the rising of the full, freighted moon.

"When I first went to Miss Julia, I loved her more than Mr. Hugg, now I love Mr. Hugg more than her—wish I was back with him now! These are his socks," Miss Lexie said, cocking her ankle for them. "I'm still busy wearing out some of his socks for him."

A thrush was singing. As they all fell quiet, except for Miss

Lexie dragging her own chair back to the table, its evening song was heard.

Granny heard that out too. Then she whispered, and Miss Beulah put her head down.

"I'm ready to go home now."

Miss Beulah put her arms around her. Granny, as well as she was able, kept from being held. "Granny, you *are* home," said Miss Beulah, gazing into her grandmother's face.

"What's she getting scared of?" asked Aunt Birdie.

"Granny's not scared of anything."

"Afraid we'll all go off and leave her?" asked Aunt Beck.

"Please saddle my horse," Granny said. "I'd like you to fetch my whip."

"Granny, you're home now." Miss Beulah knelt down, not letting the old lady with her feeble little movements escape out of her arms. "Granny, it's the reunion! You're having your birthday Sunday, and we're all around you, celebrating it with you just like always."

"Then," said Granny, "I think I'd be right ready to accept a birthday present from somebody."

Miss Beulah moved a step back from Granny's chair, and there she sat where everybody could see her. Her lap was holding a new white cup and saucer, and on the ground around her rested everything else she had untied from its strings and unshucked from its wrappings, all their presents—a pillow of new goose feathers, a pint of fresh garden sass, a soda-box full of sage, a foot-tub full of fresh-dug, blooming-size hyacinth bulbs, three worked pincushions, an envelope full of blood-red Indian peach seeds, a prayer-plant that had by now folded its leaves, a Joseph's-coat, a double touch-me-not, a speckled geranium, and an Improved Boston fern wrapped in bread paper, a piece of cut-glass from the mail order house given by Uncle Noah Webster, a new apron, the owl lamp, and, chewing a hambone, the nine-month-old, already treeing, long-eared Bluetick coonhound pup that any of her great-grandchildren would come and take out hunting for her any time she was ready. And there behind her, spread over her chair and ready to cloak her, was "The Delectable Mountains."

"You've had your presents, Granny. You've already had every single one," said Miss Beulah softly.

Granny covered her eyes. Her fingers trembled, the backs of her hands showed their blotches like pansy faces pressed into the papery skin.

"Just look around you," said Miss Beulah. "And you've thanked everybody, too."

Then Granny dropped her hands, and she and Miss Beulah looked at each other, each face as grief-stricken as the other.

&

By now, the girls' and boys' softball game had gone on, it seemed, for hours. But now the teams trailed in, Ella Fay Renfro in front tossing a sweat-fraught pitcher's glove. Children too tired to sing or speak could still blow soap-bubbles through empty sewing spools, or hold out their arms and cry. Little boys raised a ring of dust around them too, galloping on cornstalk horses and firing a last round of shots from imaginary pistols over their heads. A hummingbird moved down the last colored thing, the wall of montbretias, as though it were writing on it in words.

At that moment the distant reports stopped. There was a sound like a woodpecker at work: Uncle Curtis snoring in his chair. In the school chair, Judge Moody sat very still too, with his hand over his eyes.

"I believe your husband's reached the Land of Nod, with my husband," Aunt Beck told Mrs. Moody. "Is that chair where he's going to sleep tonight?"

"And still I'd know him for a judge," said Miss Beulah, slowly turning around to her company again. "Look at that dewlap. I suppose a man like him goes right on judging in his sleep."

"He's not asleep," said Mrs. Moody. "Far from it."

&

"Oh, come—come—come—come," the bass voice of Uncle Noah Webster started off, and they came in with him, "Come to the church in the wild wood, oh come to the church in the dell." After that, Miss Beulah, with a churning fist, led them through "Will there be any stars, any stars in my crown when at evening the sun goeth down?"

Mr. Willy Trimble, who didn't sing, got to his feet and waited on them to finish.

"Well, I'll tell you a little something *I* know *they* don't know about," said Mr. Willy. "Goes clear back to early morning, when I carried Miss Julia up to her house and safe inside. Laying spang in the middle of the kitchen table, instead of a spoon-holder or a piece of flypaper or a nice pie, was this." He reached for his back pants pocket and brought out a narrow, stiff, blue-backed book, handling it like a little paddle.

"I'd know that a mile away," said Miss Beulah, coming and taking it out of his hands, then immediately thrusting it back. "It's the speller. Oh, how I could beat the world spelling! I could spell everybody in this reunion down right now," she offered. "Give me a word."

"Can't think of any," several immediately said.

"Extraordinary," said Miss Beulah. "E-x, ex, t-r-a, tra, extra, o-r, or, extraor, d-i, di, extraordi, n-a-r-y, nary, extraordinary. Does any of my sisters-in-law here present remember *that* spelling match?"

"You got it spelled but wet your britches," Aunt Nanny said, pointing a finger at her.

"Laugh, then! I spelled you all down with that word like a row of tin soldiers."

"One thing I can tell you: she kept that book by her and it's all she did keep by her, after she got like she was. Now what was it doing out on the kitchen table?" demanded Miss Lexie. "It lived under her pillow, with her hand over it. Once she had it, try and prize it loose. Finger by finger! You couldn't."

"Well, under her pillow's where it was," said Mr. Willy, sounding apologetic. "I didn't like to say where, but it was. I laid her down and trying to ease her fiery head, I jerked out what was so ungiving beneath it. She didn't say 'Put it back,' didn't say not to. She was past it."

Miss Lexie peeked, on tiptoe, over Mr. Willy's shoulder. "Look at the cover-boards," she said with an odd look of pride. "After I got her pencil hid, she did that work with a straight pin."

The white gouges in the dark blue, with faint-hyphenated scratches fraily joining them together, Miss Beulah followed from point to point with a slow-moving finger. "M-Y-W-I-L-L," she spelled out.

Judge Moody, sitting crammed in the school chair, lifted a face strained around the eyes, filling now with a martyred look, as though he might be sitting in Ludlow, back home in the courthouse again. "I'll take charge of that speller, if you please," he said. "I think there may be a document preserved inside it that was meant to be delivered to me."

Hands passed him the speller through the dumbfounded silence. Judge Moody lifted the speller and shook it. Nothing dropped out of the pages, though birds came down low into the althea bush behind him, as silent as petals shedding from a dark rose.

He laid the book down on the desk-arm and opened it, letting the pages riffle by, back to front. When he came to the flyleaf at the beginning, he sat back, drew with care from his breast pocket his spectacle case, and hooked the horn-rim spectacles on. They watched him study that narrow page. There was handwriting on both sides of it. Then, without raising his head, he began pounding with the flat of his hand on the desk-arm of his chair.

"Judge Moody." Miss Beulah ventured close. "I've heard you more than a time or two try to put a word in edgewise. Are you about to tell us you come into this story too?"

Judge Moody pulled himself out of the chair and climbed, heavy and rumpled-looking, to his feet.

"Mama," patiently asked the same child's voice that had asked it before, "is that the Booger?"

"I'm an old friend," he said. "Now this is written in her own hand, and my name is on it." He offered the open book to their unwilling gaze, exposed it there for a moment. Then he took it back under study. He began to frown, turning slowly ahead in the book, shifting its angle this way and that. "It's written right on the spelling pages," he muttered. "And the pencil's a little hard to read. Now, will you listen, please? This concerns you all."

Exclamations of dismay rose from the whole crowd.

"What's the substance of it?" Uncle Curtis asked. "Could you just give us that?"

Judge Moody took his eyes from the page and told them. "The substance? Yes. You're all mourners."

Miss Beulah even laid a hand behind her ear, as the groans gave way to a straining hush over all the reunion.

"You are every one going to attend her burial," Judge Moody said.

They cried out.

"We're invited, sir?" asked Mr. Renfro.

"Not invited. Told. You'd all just better good and well be there," said the Judge, reading on ahead to himself.

"The whole reunion? Is she counting me?" asked Aunt Cleo. "Well! I'm famous!"

"The reunion is still not quite everybody. She says everybody. I gather from her words if you ever went to school to Miss Julia Mortimer, you are now constituted her mourner," said Judge Moody.

"What's constituted?" the aunts asked one another, while some of the uncles rose to their feet.

"Whoa! Slow down a minute for us," said Uncle Noah Webster, trying to laugh.

" 'A plain coffin, no fuss . . . Father Stephen McRaven, if he remembers how hard I tried to teach him algebra, can try praying me into Eternity. St. Louis, Missouri, will find him . . .' Here," said Judge Moody. " 'The Banner School roll call is instructed to assemble in a body inside the school yard. The old, the blind, the crippled and ailing, and the congenital complainers may assemble inside the schoolhouse itself, so far as room may be found on the benches at the back. For the children, there is positively to be no holiday declared.' "

"Why do we have to go back to school? We've done with all that," said Uncle Curtis.

"And at the signal, we all go marching over the bridge in a long, long line to Alliance?" cried Uncle Dolphus. "She's not asking much!"

"May I have quiet restored?" said Judge Moody. "You won't need to go to her. She's coming to you."

"Whoa!" called Uncle Noah Webster again, and Uncle Curtis asked, "Judge Moody, are you certain-sure you know what that book's saying?"

The Judge's mouth had drawn down. He continued, " 'The mourners will keep good order among themselves and wait till I reach the schoolhouse. Good behavior is requested and advised on the part of one and all as I am lowered into my grave—' " He looked at what was coming and for a full minute stopped reading aloud. Then he went on—" 'already to have been dug beneath the mountain stone which constitutes the doorstep of Banner School. The stone is to be replaced at once after the grave is filled, so the children will be presented with no excuse for staying home from school. In case of rain, the order of events will proceed unchanged.' " Judge Moody closed the book with the sound of a crack of thunder, then gave them the last words. " 'And then, you fools—mourn me.' " He lifted to them a face that was long and lined.

" 'Whosoever shall say, Thou fool, shall be in danger of hell fire!' " said Brother Bethune, as he came and joined the table again. He sat down, giving off a smell of steaming Bible and gunpowder smoke.

"If this ain't keeping after us!" Uncle Dolphus cried. "Following us to our graves."

"You're following her," said Judge Moody.

"Well," said Miss Beulah, "she may be dead and waiting in her coffin, but she hasn't given up yet. I see that. Trying to regiment the reunion into being part of her funeral!"

"Well, you can't make people come to see you buried just by trying the same tricks you used on 'em when you was alive," said Aunt Nanny.

"Who's going to not mind her, and stay home? I'm just not too sure I can be in her parade. I'm going to have to ask Miss Julia's ghost to excuse me," said Aunt Birdie in a childlike voice, beginning to giggle.

"I've been in a heap of your dust today already," said Auntie Fay.

"How's she going to get us back home?" Uncle Noah Webster inquired. "She's burying herself and just leaving us standing in the school yard. I live in South Mississippi now!"

"As for me, I'm not a child," said Uncle Percy, whittling. "To be told."

"I'm not a child either," said Aunt Nanny.

"I'm a child," said Etoyle, hopping up among them. "And I like funerals."

"Well, listen to me. I ain't a-going," said Uncle Dolphus. "Now what's she going to do about it?"

"I might have gone back and pitched in today, if anybody'd asked or sent for me. But they didn't," said Miss Lexie. "And now, I'm not real sure I'll even go and swell their number to see her buried. I might ask myself first, who'll mourn *me?*"

"Well, you may wake up feeling more like charity in the morning, Sister Lexie," Brother Bethune said heavily. "Me and you both. Take it from me, Sunday can get too crowded."

"Miss Julia didn't stint herself when she called on everybody to be present!" said Aunt Nanny. "Greedy thing."

"But you go expecting too much out of other souls all your life and the day comes when you may have tried 'em too far," Miss Beulah said. She cocked her head at Judge Moody. "Well, I can say this much to you, sir: all it'd take to keep the whole nation away would be for you to stand up like she wanted you to and let 'em know they's whistled for."

"I wish she'd minded her own business and not ours," said Aunt Birdie.

"She never did that in her life. And so brag on her, brag on her all you want! But I'll tell you this when you've finished," Miss Beulah warned them all. "She never did learn how to please."

"No," said Uncle Curtis, "she never. You're right, Beulah, and you nearly always are." Miss Beulah nodded. "Knowing the way to please and pacify the public and pour oil on the waters was entirely left out when they was making her pattern."

"Maybe that wasn't what she was trying for," Aunt Beck said. "Since she was going about the other thing just as hard as a steam engine."

"Beck is always in danger of getting sorry for the other side," said Miss Beulah.

"Didn't even know how to please when she picked a day to die, to my notion!" cried Aunt Birdie loyally. "But she didn't damage our spirits much—howsoever she might have liked to. Not ours!"

" 'I am in school to learn.' That was her cry. To this day I can see Earl Comfort being sent to the board to write it a hundred times. And every single line of it going right downhill," said Uncle Dolphus.

"And if she's going in a grave down at the schoolhouse, it's old Earl himself will be the one has to dig it for her," said Uncle Noah Webster. "Don't imagine he's too pleased at her yet."

"And she couldn't beat time when she marched us," said Aunt Birdie. "She run ahead of us."

"No, she couldn't beat good time. And I say give me a teacher who can do it all. Or else don't let her even start trying," said Uncle Percy. "It's her fault, right now, we don't know as much as we might. Stay poor as Job's turkey all our lives. She ought to made us *stay* in school, and learn some profit."

"Yes siree. If she was all that smart, why couldn't she have done a little better work on you and I?" Uncle Curtis asked.

"She read in the daytime." Mr. Renfro's lips were judicious as he looked at Judge Moody. "When she boarded with us, she did. And that was a thing surpassing strange for a well woman to do."

"Well, I expect what happened to her was she put a little more of her own heart in it than she knew. And tried to make her teaching all there was," said Aunt Beck. "She was in love with Banner School." Awe and compassion together were in her voice.

"All she wanted was a teacher's life," Gloria said. "But it looked like past a certain point nobody was willing to let her have it."

"Well, it's too late to change it now," said Miss Beulah.

"When she could be sitting at the foot of Judgment this minute? I reckon it is too late!" said Aunt Birdie.

"She knows more than we do now," Aunt Beck reproached them gently.

"There was only one Miss Julia Mortimer, and I'm glad. But she didn't spare herself for that reason. She *once* was needed, and could tell herself that," Aunt Beck said. "She had that."

"Not in the end," Miss Lexie claimed. "That failed her in the end."

"What did she finally get like? Drawing to the end?" asked Aunt Cleo.

"She was getting a good deal like Mr. Hugg, or he's getting like her, take your pick. Old men and old women, they lose that too," said Miss Lexie, with what appeared to be contentment.

"Sister and ladies, she's dead and not even covered," said Mr. Renfro then, so softly that his voice barely made its tunnel through theirs. "Let's leave her lay. We've lived through it now."

"And Banner School makes just one more thing that's *happened* to me," Aunt Birdie confided to them. "It must've been pure poison while it lasted, but it didn't leave me any scars. I was so young, and it was so far-fetched. And I've gone a long ways ahead of it now!" She blew a kiss at Gloria. "And you will too!"

Uncle Nathan now broke his long silence to say, "Many a little schoolhouse I pass on the mountainside today is a sister to Banner, and I pass it wondering if I was to knock on the door wouldn't she come running out, all unchanged."

"I can still hear her, myself," said Uncle Noah Webster, gazing at his brother Nathan as he might at some passing spectacle. "Saying the multiplication table or some such rigmarole. Her voice! She had a might of sweetness and power locked up in her voice. To waste it on teaching was a sin."

"She spent her life in a draught!" said Aunt Birdie. "If I'd had to take her place for even a day, I'd have died of pneumonia."

"What other mortal would know the way to die like she did? Just met her end all by herself—what other mortal would succeed?" cried Aunt Beck. "Even if they wanted to, for some contrary reason."

"Going to meet it by herself in the road! Taking a chance of being found not even exactly decent. I can't hold with that or give it my understanding," Aunt Birdie said soberly.

"It seems to me like a right unkind thing to do unto others," Aunt Beck said as if unwillingly. "Getting 'em all to feel like traitors, or even worse."

But Miss Lexie said, "She was equal to it."

"I could have told you she was threatening the schoolhouse," said Auntie Fay. "Only it don't amount to a row of pins."

"Sissie, what do *you* know about her and the schoolhouse?" asked Miss Lexie.

"Homer says the board of supervisors got a letter from Miss Julia Mortimer—and that must have been through *your* fault, Lexie. Homer was tittering over it—said she told 'em like it was her royal due she wished to be buried right there by the schoolhouse when her time came. Those supervisors today, they were mostly boys of Banner School, and she just *told* 'em."

"The *bad* boys of Banner School," Miss Lexie amended. "That's why Homer Champion's so thick with 'em, he's another one."

"The supervisors didn't answer her letter and they voted her down," said Auntie Fay. "The supervisors said Nay."

"It don't sound highly Christian to me either," said Aunt Beck.

"Homer said the supervisors said that if you was to take the stone out of place for even long enough to sink her grave, the whole schoolhouse would give in and fall down in a heap," said Auntie Fay.

"I can easily picture it," said Miss Lexie. "I don't need any supervisors to tell me. Grandfather Renfro started with that stone when he built that schoolhouse, and he meant it to stay. He didn't mean it to come out for anybody. And didn't think to foresee any such mischief out of the teacher, I don't care how long she'd labored or how crazy it had run her. I'm only surprised that bunch of supervisors had the gumption to stand up for the schoolhouse against her."

"It was unanimous," said Auntie Fay. "Homer heard the same thing from all of 'em."

"Neither am I very happy about her wish," muttered Judge Moody. "About what I read between the lines." He took out his handkerchief and blotted his forehead.

"Can you be buried anywhere you want to?" Mrs. Moody asked him. "Just anywhere you want to?" She gave an abandoned wave of the hand.

"I don't know, as I stand here. The question has never come up in a form like this, not in my experience," he muttered. "At any rate, law or no law, she ought to have been talked out of it. She'd no business to humble herself—"

"Humble herself?" Miss Beulah laughed out loud. "She's about as humble as I am serving a grand dinner to a hundred!"

"It wasn't like her. It shows how poorly off she had gotten to be," he said.

"Well, I'll tell you what: I'm ashamed of her now," Miss Beulah said as she folded her arms. "That's the windup of her story for me, I'm ashamed *of* her and *for* her."

"She was so wrought," Aunt Beck said with a sigh.

"She ought to have married somebody," said Aunt Birdie. "Then what she wanted wouldn't mean a thing. She would be buried with him, and no questions asked."

"Where was Miss Julia Mortimer born, for pity's sakes?" asked Aunt Cleo. "Is there some reason why they can't go against her wishes and carry her back there?"

"Born in Ludlow! She sold her house behind her, to go on teaching. So, where she had left to go, when they put her to pasture, was across the river—the house her mother came from," said Miss Lexie. "But you can't miss it. She lives on Star Route, in sight of the Alliance water tank. The hot afternoons while she's asleep and I've walked to the Jew's store and back for a needle and thread for me and a fresh cake of soap for her! It's all of a mile and a half."

"She came out of Boone County, the same soil we did. What made her to be Miss Julia Mortimer, only the good Lord can tell you," said Uncle Curtis.

"You'll have to put her *somewhere*," said Aunt Cleo.

"Watch out, Oscar," said Mrs. Moody.

He stood there looking as if he'd found his hands too full, holding the speller, and he answered his wife by taking a step to lay it in her lap. His hand reached into the breast pocket of the coat he'd kept on all day, and he brought out an envelope, dusty, flattened, and bent. From this he pulled forth some folded sheets covered on both sides with handwriting.

"How'd you get *that?*" Miss Lexie sharply cried.

"It reached me through the U.S. Mail. It came to my post-office box in Ludlow," he said.

"Lexie, I thought you threw those letters in the pig pen," said Miss Beulah.

"I *mailed* 'em. I couldn't think to my soul what else to do with 'em!" cried out Miss Lexie. "I may not have mailed 'em right on the day she told me. I had more to do than go trotting to the mailbox every whipstitch."

"Don't read it to us!" cried more than one voice at Judge Moody.

It was almost too late to see to read. The world had turned the hyacinth-blue that eyes see behind their lids when closed against the sun. The moon was all above the horizon now. It looked as though it had been added to with a generous packing of Banner clay all around.

"I couldn't have imagined it this morning," Judge Moody said. "When I set out with this letter in my pocket, I couldn't have imagined ending up in circumstances under which I would share it with anybody. I hadn't even meant to show it to my wife." Abruptly he spread out the page. The paper was thin, unlined, not the kind that comes in a school tablet; even in the poor light it looked all but transparent. The high, precise steeples of handwriting, a degree up-hill on one side of the page and a degree downhill on the other, appeared one puzzle that crossed and locked in the middle.

"Looks like it's our fate to sit through one more lesson," protested Aunt Birdie. "Ain't we remembered enough about Miss Julia Mortimer?"

"Your memory's got a dozen holes in it. And some sad mistakes," said Judge Moody.

They sat stiffly, as though some homemade thing they'd all had a hand in, like the quilt, were being criticized.

" 'I have always pretty well known what I was doing.' "

At the opening words he read, they all shouted. He might have just flashed Miss Julia's face on the screen of the bois d'arc tree with a magic lantern. Even Aunt Beck laughed, putting a corner of her handkerchief to her eyes.

Judge Moody ignored them and read on. " 'All my life I've fought a hard war with ignorance. Except in those cases that you can count off on your fingers, I lost every battle. Year in, year out, my children at Banner School took up the cause of the other side and held the fort against me. We both fought faithfully and single-mindedly, bravely, maybe even fairly. Mostly I lost, they won. But as long as I was still young, I always thought if I could marshal strength enough of body and spirit and push with it, every ounce, I could change the future.' "

"I can't understand it when he reads it to us. Can't he just tell it?" complained Aunt Birdie.

"Come on, tell us what it says, Judge Moody," said Aunt Nanny. "Don't be so bashful."

Judge Moody with a rattle turned the page over and read on. " 'Oscar, it's only now, when I've come to lie flat of my back, that I've had it driven in on me—the reason I never could win for good is that both sides were using the same tactics. Very likely true of all wars. A teacher teaches and a pupil learns or fights against learning with the same force behind him. It's the survival instinct. It's a mighty power, it's an iron weapon while it lasts. It's the desperation of staying alive against all odds that keeps both sides encouraged. But the side that gets licked gets to the truth first. When the battle's over, something may dawn there—with no help from the teacher, no help from the pupil, no help from the book. After the lessons give out and the eyes give out, when memory's trying its best to cheat you—to lie and hide from you, and you know some day it could even run off and leave you, there's just one thing, one reliable thing, left.' "

"Wait," said Aunt Birdie. "I don't know what those long words are talking about."

"What long words?" said Judge Moody. He read on. " 'Oscar Moody, I'm going to admit something to you. What I live by is inspiration. I always did—I started out on nothing else but naked inspiration. Of course I had sense enough to know that doesn't get you anywhere all by itself.' " Judge Moody's mouth shut for a moment in a hard line. " 'Now that the effort it took has been put a stop to, and I can survey the years, I can see it all needs doing over, starting from the beginning. But even if Providence allowed us the second chance, doubling back on my tracks has never been my principle. Even if I can't see very far ahead of me now, that's where I'm going.' "

"I wish we didn't have to hear it," Aunt Beck said, sighing.

"I don't know how much time goes by in between the parts of her letter, when the writing gets worse," said Judge Moody under his breath, frowning at the page. " 'I'm alive as ever, on the brink of oblivion, and I caught myself once on the verge of disgrace. Things like this are put in your path to teach you. You can make use of them, they'll bring you one stage, one milestone, further along your road. You can go crawling next along the edge of madness, if that's where you've come to. There's a lesson in it. You can profit from knowing that you needn't be ashamed to crawl—to keep on crawling, to be proud to crawl to where you can't crawl any further. Then you can find yourself lying flat on your back—look what's carried you another mile. From flat on your back you may not be able to lick the world, but at least you can keep the world from licking you. I haven't spent a lifetime fighting my battle to give up now. I'm ready for all they send me. There's a measure of enjoyment in it.' "

"Now I know she's a crazy," Miss Beulah was interrupting. "We're getting it right out of her own mouth, by listening long enough."

" 'But I've come to a puzzler. Something walls me in, crowds me around, outwits me, dims my eyesight, loses the pencil I had in my hand. I don't trust this, I have my suspicions of it, I don't know what it is I've come to. I don't know any longer. They prattle around me of the nearness of Heaven. Is this Heaven, where you lie wide-open to the mercies of others who think they know better than you do what's best—what's true and what isn't? Contradictors, inter-ferers, and prevaricators—are those angels?' " Aunt Birdie gave out a little scream but Judge Moody didn't stop for it. " 'I think I'm in ignorance, not Heaven.' "

"How can you see any longer to give us those words?" Miss Beulah asked from where she stood stock-still at her grandmother's chair.

"I have read the letter to myself, before now," Judge Moody said. It was the rose-light from the sun already down that he read by. The moon did not yet give off light—it was only turned to the light, like a human head. He read on. " 'I'm right here on my old battleground, that's where I am. And there's something I want to impart to you, Oscar Moody. It's a warning.' "

"Oscar, listen to me," said Mrs. Moody. "I suggest you sit down."

" 'There's been one thing I never did take into account,' " he continued. " 'Most likely, neither did you. Watch out for innocence. Could you be tempted by it, Oscar—to your own mortification— and conspire with the ignorant and the lawless and the foolish and even the wicked, to *hold your tongue?*' " Judge Moody steered the sheet of paper around where a few more lines of writing ran under his eyes along the margin. " 'Oscar Moody, I want to see you here in Alliance at your earliest convenience. Bring your Mississippi law with you, but you'll have to hear the story. It leads to a child. If I'm finally to reach my undoing, I won't be surprised to meet it in a child. That's what I started with. You'd better get here fast.' " He stood still, lowering the letter in his hands.

"Is that all?" asked Granny dismissively.

"Listen at Gloria," Aunt Nanny said. "She's shedding tears."

"That's right, Gloria. Now's a good time," Aunt Beck said lovingly. "A few tears for somebody else, you can spare those."

"They're not for somebody else," wept Gloria.

Miss Lexie Renfro had stalked her way forward. She cried to the Judge, "When did that come?"

"The letter? I've been carrying the letter around in my coat pocket for the better part of a month," Judge Moody said in his hard voice.

"Let's see that envelope." Miss Lexie filched it out of his hand. "An old one she used over again—it's the one the light bill came in. *I* didn't mail that. Don't blame me. I wouldn't have wanted the mail rider to see it." She put it back into his hand.

"It's a wonder you ever opened such a thing after it got there, Oscar," said Mrs. Moody. "That paper it's written on has got a mighty suspicious gold edge. And those rounded corners. Don't tell me it's the flyleaf out of her Testament."

Judge Moody stood silent.

"You can make sure by smelling it," prompted Mrs. Moody, to no avail.

"I'll tell you how she must have put one over on me," said Miss Lexie. "It must have been still only July, for her to write it. I was getting overtired of always tying her sheet. She found her chance,

I reckon. Pulled up on the back of the chair till she could stand. Walked with the chair going in front of her, carrying the letter, out to the chicken house and robbed a nest. Walked back with her chair, carrying the letter plus the egg—she always had a pocket—down the hill to her mailbox, and put the letter there for the mail rider, along with the egg to pay him for the stamp. She learned one thing from the way it's done in Banner! Then she made it back with her chair to her bed. And I never knew I slept more than thirty minutes at a time."

"Can't trust yourself any longer," Aunt Nanny told her.

"Or I might even have been gone to town to pay the light bill," said Miss Lexie. "If I'd found *my* chance."

"The time, the effort, the trickery even, it cost that beleaguered woman to get this to me!" Judge Moody stared at Miss Lexie briefly and then widened his gaze to take in them all. "The complete and utter mortification of life! Of course," he said, "this required an answer in person."

"But here you are," said Mrs. Moody.

"Exactly," he said.

"You said 'Anything for Miss Julia!' " Mrs. Moody said.

"Look here, Judge Moody," interrupted Miss Beulah. She stopped her pacing. "I just this minute got a pretty good inspiration of what's the matter with you—you're kin to that woman!"

All cried out but the sleepers.

"Beulah, it's true! That's got to be it. That's his secret!" Aunt Birdie cried. "That's why he's so mad at everybody."

"Explains a whale of a lot!" Uncle Noah Webster cried.

"And so we've been allowed to talk about somebody who's kin to present company?" Miss Beulah moved in on Judge Moody. "While you set here in our midst and let us rake her up one side and down the other, and never once put claim on her? Never give out one peep you was armed with a letter from her till you got good and ready and thought it was a good time to spring it?" She drew up her hand and pointed a finger at him. "Treatment I wouldn't mete out to my worst enemy! Cheating on my hospitality like that!" She whirled on Mrs. Moody. "And you let him!"

Judge Moody had been holding up his hand toward her, palm flat. When he could be heard again, his voice was quiet. "Just a moment. I am not kin to Miss Julia—there are other ties."

"You wasn't *married* to her!" Uncle Noah Webster hollered

out. "You can't stand here and tell us that, not after you brought your wife along to hear you!"

"I wouldn't mind, when you're ready, hearing a little more about you and Miss Julia myself," said Mrs. Moody to her husband.

"There are other ties," Judge Moody repeated.

"We don't appreciate a comer like you getting up in our midst and making us listen to ourselves being criticized," said Uncle Percy in a whisper. "If she couldn't be kin I just wish anyway she'd taught you."

"So she did," said Judge Moody.

Aunt Nanny stamped her foot and hollered "Don't believe it!" over the clamor of his listeners.

"She coached me," said Judge Moody. "The house I grew up in in Ludlow was right across Main Street from hers."

"That old house with the stone dragons?" asked Mrs. Moody.

"Missionary stock," he said with a nod.

"Judge Moody's just one of her Ludlow pets," said Miss Lexie, and she tried her laugh.

"One summer," said Judge Moody. "Myself along with some other high school boys who aimed for college. She coached me in rhetoric, and I won first place in the Mississippi Field Meet."

"Oscar, your blood pressure," said Mrs. Moody as if in despair, but he deepened his voice and mocked himself. " 'Archimedes said: "Give me a standing place and I will move the world." ' "

"Never mind. If you lived across the street from her, you were in a dangerous enough place," said Miss Beulah.

"Then what?" asked Mr. Renfro to lead him on.

"When I came home to practice, and pretty soon was made district attorney, she climbed the stairs to my office one day to say she was proud of me."

"She was claiming you," said Miss Lexie. "Taking the credit for you."

Judge Moody was still.

"He don't know her the way we did," said Aunt Birdie. "See if you can tell us her horse's name," she challenged him.

"When she left Ludlow for good, to track across the county and give her life to Banner School, she was driving an automobile. A Ford coupe, a thank-you present from Senator Jarvis the year he went to Washington. I remember her style of backing out: she set the throttle, fixed her eyes straight ahead on the back wall of the garage, and erected a perpendicular on it," said Judge Moody. "She was teaching herself to drive. I used to wonder how many innocent bystanders she scattered without knowing it." He took out his handkerchief and wiped it over his face.

"So there was a time when *you* laughed at her too," Mrs. Moody told him.

"I don't suppose even a Ford could get over these roads, not in winter," he said.

"Was that good-bye?" asked Mr. Renfro.

"A little later on, at her request, I sold the house for her, the old Mortimer house," he said.

"That means she wrote to you before. She had the habit of writing to you," said Mrs. Moody.

"I handled things, acted for her once or twice," he sighed. "That little inheritance. Taxes."

"So you wrote to her."

"Yes," he said. "On occasion."

"So not only was she writing letters. She was getting 'em," said Aunt Beck mournfully.

"What did you do with the letters that came for her, Lexie?" asked Miss Beulah. "Throw 'em in the pig pen?"

"I don't care to say," said Miss Lexie.

"That's what you threw in the pig pen."

"Who was the best judge! She was too sick and bad off to be bothered with something she would have to give her mind to."

"Oscar, you're rocking on your feet," said Mrs. Moody. "Sit down, you're just feeling sorry for yourself, standing up."

"And then this morning," said Judge Moody, reaching again inside his coat and bringing out another rumpled envelope, "in my box I found this. The envelope is one of my own, used over again. No letter inside, only a map she'd drawn me, showing how to get from Ludlow to Alliance and where she lived. That's when I gave up and started."

"I mailed it when I could, and not before!" cried Miss Lexie.

"And it's a maze," he said, squinting down at the old bill on which a web of lines radiated from some cross-mark ploughed into the center. "Just a maze. There wasn't much right about her thinking any longer. I didn't try to go by it—but I lost my own way on Boone County roads for the first time I can remember. I could almost believe I'd been *maneuvered* here," he said in grieved, almost hopeless tones. "To the root of it all, like the roots of a bad tooth. The very pocket of ignorance." He raised his head suddenly. "What have I been thinking of? I came here and stood up and read her letter to you. And you," he turned and said to his wife. "I've broken her confidence."

"I think that was unlawyerlike," she told him.

Judge Moody was struggling to get the map and the letter back inside their envelopes. "All the same, in my judgment, this bunch had it coming," he said.

"I'd just like to hear now, Oscar," said Mrs. Moody, "what you were doing getting letters like that at the office, and I didn't even know about it."

"Maud Eva," he said. "Why, she felt free—"

"It irks the fire out of me!" Mrs. Moody exclaimed.

"Both of us wrote, occasionally," he said.

"You and a poor, lonesome, old maid schoolteacher?" asked Mrs. Moody.

"Not always—" He stared down at her. "Why, every young blade in Ludlow was wild about Miss Julia Mortimer at one time."

"When she was young?"

"When all of us were young."

"A country schoolteacher? Why, that's no more than I was," said Mrs. Moody, eyebrows very high. She asked, "And you did your full share of courting her?"

"Oh, no. There were plenty without me, from Ludlow and all around. Herman Dearman, even, from this neck of the woods and crude as they come—even he aspired to her, knowing no better. She didn't discourage him enough—perhaps didn't know how," said Judge Moody. "Perhaps was able to even see something in him."

"Aspired!" said Mrs. Moody.

"He came to a sorry end, I believe."

"Sorry is right," said Uncle Curtis.

"There, that's enough," said Miss Beulah.

"So did Gerard Carruthers," said Judge Moody.

"So did he what?" asked his wife.

"Aspire. He trotted off and worked himself to the bone in Pennsylvania Medical School to come home and set up a country practice, you know," said Judge Moody. "He had a fond allegiance to her. And he kept coming, didn't he, attending her?"

"He was a liquorite, now that was his trouble," Miss Lexie

**304**

replied. "He came. But in the end she dismissed him, and he went."

Judge Moody persisted. "She's made her a Superior Court judge, the best eye, ear, nose, and throat specialist in Kansas City, and a history professor somewhere—they're all scattered wide, of course. She could get them started, lick 'em into shape, but she couldn't get 'em to stay!"

"You stayed," said Mrs. Moody.

He sat down hard in the protesting chair.

"That irks the fire out of me," Mrs. Moody said again. "There's still something from way back somewhere that you haven't told me. I can tell by looking at the way your hair's all standing on end. What did you do, propose to her? To have her turn you down?" she pressed.

He put his hand over his eyes. "That's not it."

"Well, did she propose to you?" cried Aunt Nanny with a daring grin.

"Like you did to Percy?" a chorus called.

"It was owing to her I made the decision I did. That's right. She expressed her satisfaction that I hadn't chased off somewhere but was staying here, working with my own. In consequence, I never moved out of the state, or to a better part of the state."

"Oh, my! To think if only you had left!" Miss Beulah sighed.

"I had chances, you know, Maud Eva. I'm where I am today because she talked me into staying, doing what I could here at home, through the Boone County Courts." After a pause he said, "Well, and I never fully forgave her."

"Who did you take it out on?" Miss Beulah asked with a sage face.

Judge Moody turned again to his wife and seemed to repeat the question to her silently. As the company looked at him they could see his lined face glisten. He said, "Well, it's owing to her we're both here."

"Here? Right here?" asked Miss Beulah.

"Where I am on earth. Yes ma'am, here in the middle of you all right now. She's still the reason," Judge Moody said. "Mrs. Moody was shrewd—I wasn't anxious enough at all to see Miss Julia today, find out what had happened to her—I admit that, Maud Eva. I suffered an attack of cowardice, there on the road."

"I don't know why you keep addressing these complaints to me," said Mrs. Moody. "I made a six-egg cake, and piled on that icing, and skipped Sunday School too on account of your conscience, and I rode up front with you. I've been trying to get you there all day."

"I was already too late when I started," he said. "She said come and she meant *now*."

"She wouldn't have known you by the time you got there anyway," Mrs. Moody all at once told him. "Might not have known who she was herself, after you made the trip." She threw up her hands.

He struck at the breast pocket of his coat where the letters were. "She knew exactly who she was. And what she was. What she didn't know till she got to it was what would *happen* to what she was. Any more than any of us here know," he said. As she stared at him he added, "It could make you cry."

"All I know is we're all put into this world to serve a purpose," said Mrs. Moody.

"It could make a stone cry," said Judge Moody.

Around them the white tablecloths, clotted with shadows, still held the light, and so did old men's white shirts, and Sunday dresses with their skirts spread round or in points on the evening hill. The tables in their line appeared strung and hinged like the Big Dipper in the night sky, and the diamonds of the other cloths seemed to repeat themselves for a space far out on the deep blue of dust that now reached to Heaven. Now and then a flying child, calling a name, still streaked through everybody, and some of the die-hards turned themselves round and round or rolled themselves over and over down the long front hill, time after time, toward an exhaustion of joy.

Mrs. Moody still leaned toward her hubsand. "Yet you vow it was all platonic?"

Silence that was all one big question opened like a tunnel, long enough for all the birds in Boone County to have flown through in one long line going to roost.

"Don't try to read any secrets into this, Maud Eva," said Judge Moody then.

"Your real secrets are the ones you don't know you've got," said his wife, as if she'd been irked into knowing that, and she still waited on his answer.

"I'm not kin to her, was only once living nearby, only counted as a summer pupil, didn't try to propose to her, didn't do all my duty by her, she gave me advice I took and cherished against her, and when at the last she sent for me, I failed to get there: I was her friend, and she was mine."

"Well, she was older than you, you fool," said Mrs. Moody.

"Ten years," he said, staring as if aghast into the purple of first-dark.

"Then what's got wrong with you, after all this time?"

In a voice so still and so stubborn that he might have been speaking to himself alone, Judge Moody said, "Nothing wrong. Only I don't care quite the same about living as I did this morning."

"I feel like we've *been* to her wake," Mrs. Moody accused him.

"Watch out, everybody!" Elvie sang.

"Look! Granny's rising up out of her chair," said Uncle Percy hoarsely.

With the cup, the saucer, the pincushions tumbling, the quilt sliding down behind her, the little puppy sleepily following a few steps, Granny walked by herself into the middle and stood before them, at the height of a boy cousin. She lifted both little weightless hands. Miss Beulah started on the run toward her, then arrested herself.

Shoulders high, hands stiff but indicating the least little movement from side to side, Granny stood gathering herself, and then, in a quick, drumbeat voice just holding its own against the steady, directionless sound of crickets, she began to sing. Uncle Noah Webster rose, put his foot on the seat of a chair, and raised his banjo to his knee. Picking lightly, he fell in with her.

"Is it 'Frog Went A-Courting' or 'Wondrous Love'?" Aunt Birdie whispered. "Sounds like a little of both."

She knew every verse and was not sparing them one. When the verses were all sung, Granny, giving them calculating looks, kept on patting her foot. Uncle Noah Webster kept up with her, the banjo beat on, and as her left hand folded itself small as Elvie's against her hip, she gave a pat with her right foot and was lifted bodily straight up—Uncle Curtis was ready for her—to the top of her own table and set down carefully among the platters and what was left of everything. Uncle Noah Webster's hand came down sharp on the strings, and under its long skirt her foot, her whole leg, was lifted inches high to paddle the table in time to another chorus. The little black sliding-slipper with the silk-fuzz pompon on the toe must have been a dozen years old, though it was as good as new.

"With that little patting foot, she comes in right on time," said Uncle Dolphus. "Something she never showed us before."

"Just so we ain't seeing the last of Granny!" mourned Aunt Beck.

She danced in their faces.

"Mama, tell her it's Sunday," Elvie whispered.

"You got the brain of a bird? She's got track of what day this is better than you have, better than anybody here," said Miss Beulah fiercely, leaning forward and ready to spring. "Her own birthday."

Then Granny's old black hem began to trail and catch itself across the dishes behind her as she started to walk off the table.

"Catch-her-*Vaughn!*" screamed Miss Beulah in panic.

Electrified, the little boy opened his arms but like everybody else stood rooted where he was. It was Jack, racing in at that moment and flinging aside his empty bucket that rolled clang-clanging down the hill behind him, who got there and did the catching.

"Well. I've been *calling* ye times enough." In Granny's eyes gathered the helpless tears of the rescued. As he held her, she put up her arms to him. Her sleeves fell back. Moving like wands, her two little arms showed bare, strung and knotted with dark veins like long velvet Bible markers. Her hands reached for Jack's face. Then a faint cry came, and her face, right in his, broke all to pieces. "But you're not Sam Dale!"

Miss Beulah spread the birthday quilt over the chair and Jack carefully set her down within it.

"Granny, you just slipped back a generation there for a little," said Uncle Noah Webster fondly, bending over her.

"Put the blame right on Brother Bethune," urged Aunt Beck, fanning her.

"She's all right, Granny's all right," said Miss Beulah in a desperate voice.

The old lady still looked at Jack in a fixed manner. Dust as if from a long journey twinkled back at the moon from the high plush crown of her hat. "Who are you?" she asked finally.

He dropped to his knees there beside her and whispered to her the only answer there was. "It's Jack Jordan Renfro, Granny. Getting himself back home."

# Part 5

$T$he substance fine as dust that began to sift down upon the world, to pick out the new roof, the running ghost of a dog, the metal bell, was moonlight.

"Nightfall!" said Aunt Birdie. "When did that happen!"

"And they've started back to biting," said Aunt Nanny, spanking at her own arms and legs and at the invisible cloud of mosquitoes around her head.

"Let's get Granny's little soles off this ground!" cried Miss Beulah. "We don't want the dew to catch her!"

By Jack alone the old lady was lifted up in her chair and carried through the crowd back to the porch and to her old place at the head of the steps. The others began to follow more slowly. Groaning, carrying their chairs, they moved away from the tables and through the yard back again to the house. Those who could found the same places for their chairs that they had marked out this morning. As many others, who sat on the ground or lay with their heads in somebody's lap, elected to stay right where they were, not to move until they had to.

At Granny's back, with his wild gypsy hair pale in the moonlight, Uncle Nathan again took up his post with his hand on her chair. Judge Moody brought up his wife's chair and seated her, and when he brought the school chair up he placed it within the radius of Granny's rocker, where her small black figure in its little black hat waited perfectly still. He sat down there beside her.

"And we're sitting here in the dark, ain't we?" said somebody.

"If a stranger was to come along and find us like this, how could he tell who's the prettiest?" teased Aunt Birdie.

"Turn on them lights, then, Vaughn!" Uncle Dolphus called. "Why did you let 'em snake in here and hook you up to current for? For mercy's sakes let's shine!"

Suddenly the moonlit world was doused; lights hard as pick-axe blows drove down from every ceiling and the roof of the passage, cutting the house and all in it away, leaving them an island now on black earth, afloat in night, and nowhere, with only each other. In that first moment every face, white-lit but with its caves of mouth and eyes opened wide, black with the lonesomeness and hilarity of survival, showed its kinship to Uncle Nathan's, the face that floated over theirs. For the first time, all talk was cut off, and no baby offered to cry. Silence came travelling in on solid, man-made light.

"Now that's better," Mrs. Moody said. "Seems like we're back in civilization for the time being."

"Gloria!" Jack cried. "Where is our baby girl?"

He leaped back into the dark. They watched until they saw him come walking up out of it, carrying the baby. One of Lady May's arms hung over his shoulder, swinging lightly as a strand of hair.

"She had her a nest all made in the grass," Jack said as he came up the steps. He stopped before Granny in her chair and then rocked the baby downwards into the old lap. The baby was gone in sleep, where any nest is the same.

"Jack, I called and called you and you didn't come. Mr. Willy Trimble invited himself here and told the whole reunion on Miss Julia, how she died by herself and let him find her," cried Gloria. "Miss Julia and Judge Moody were two old cronies!"

He stopped her, his face struggling. "I was listening. I was standing to the back. I heard that teacher's life." Then he broke out, "That sounds about like the equal of getting put in the Hole! Kept in the dark, on bread and water, and nobody coming to get you out!"

"Jack—oh, don't let it spoil your welcome!" Miss Beulah said wildly.

**312**

"And she ain't calling you. They quit calling you after they're dead, son," said Uncle Dolphus.

"I'd rather have ploughed Parchman," said Jack to Judge Moody. Then he placed his hands on Gloria's shoulders. "I'm thankful I come along in time to save my wife from a life like hers."

"But were you here to see what your family did to *me?*" Gloria cried. "That's when I wanted you! That's when I called you. Listen to me—they pulled me down on dusty ground and got me in a watermelon fight!"

"I know you proved equal to that," Jack said, his voice soft again for her. They stood right under the naked light where it blazed the strongest, facing close; he was patting her on the shoulder.

"They didn't hesitate to wash my face in their sticky watermelon juice!"

"And you let 'em? What's happened to your old fight since morning?" he teased under his breath.

"They washed out my mouth with it! And I called 'Jack! Jack!' and you didn't come. They found the tear in my dress and Aunt Lexie sewed it right up on me in front of all, sticking her needle and scissors into my tender side. They all banded together against me!"

"Anyway, they've quit making company out of you, Possum," he said softly. "You're one of the family now."

"Oh, Jack," she said, all the more despairingly, "they say I'm your own cousin."

"Well, the sky hasn't fallen," he said, and smiled at her.

"May yet," said both Miss Lexie and Uncle Percy.

"They say Sam Dale Beecham's my daddy though he had no business being," Gloria rushed on.

"Uncle Sam Dale? Why, bless his mighty heart!" Jack cried, turning toward Granny. But she sat silent, looking straight ahead.

"And my mother was Rachel Sojourner, who never taught a day. They never had time to get married, they both of them died, all apart from each other, and here I am now. One way or the other, I'm kin to everybody in Banner," she said in a voice of despair.

"They'll be proud to hear it," Jack told her, and he stood back to hold her at arm's length as though never had she been more radiant.

"And my *baby* is kin to everybody," she mourned.

"This makes my welcome even better this time than it was this morning!" he cried.

"I might as well never have burned Miss Julia Mortimer's letter!"

"You got one too?" cried Aunt Nanny. "Glad it's gone!"

"It's still in words of fire on my brain. It said if I was going to marry who I threatened to marry, to stop right there. And come to see her—there were still things I needed to know," said Gloria. "She said she'd been delving into her own mind, and was still delving."

"Just to see what she could find?" cried Aunt Birdie.

"I was praying against her!" cried Gloria.

"What's delving?" Aunt Beck asked miserably, and Aunt Nanny asked, "Gloria, what did you *do?*"

"Tore up that letter. Put the pieces in the stove. Never answered. Never went. I got married!"

"Decided to fly in her face and go ahead with it anyway. Without telling no more than Jack himself, I bet a pretty penny, without telling the Beechams, without telling the Renfros, or Granny, or Grandpa, or the Man in the Moon. Pretty brave," said Aunt Birdie. "Or else pretty sneaky."

"I just try to mind my own business," said Gloria. "It hasn't been easy!" she cried to Mrs. Moody.

"Didn't you realize, young lady?" Judge Moody asked her. "Do you *ever* realize your danger?"

"But I didn't have to believe her just because she's Miss Julia!" Gloria said. "I had eyes of my own. And if I was an unmarried Banner girl's child, like she'd have me believe, all I had to do was take one look around the church at my own wedding, and see the whole population gathered, to know what family I was safe with. There was just one unmarried lady." Gloria turned and faced Miss Lexie. Shouts of appreciation rose up for a moment.

Gloria hushed them all with her pleading hand. "Miss Julia didn't tell me it was my *father* to be scared of. Or that my mother even had to be dead."

"She'd been saving the worst till she got you there," said Aunt Beck, shaking her head over at where she thought Alliance lay.

"I'd still like to know what Miss Julia Mortimer was so busy warning *you* for, Gloria!" cried Miss Beulah. "*You* did the only

314

safe thing in the world—married your own cousin and found a home."

"Not safe," said Judge Moody. He spoke from his same school chair but it was closer to them now, and his voice louder. "Not safe if that's what *has* happened, and supposing the State has any way to prove it."

"We proved it, right yonder at the table," said Miss Beulah.

"I don't think much of your proof—I listened, without being able to help myself," the Judge said, while the chair creaked under his weight. "In fact, there's not a particle of it I'd accept as evidence. Fishing back in old memories. Postcard from the dead. Wise sayings."

"But we settled it," cried Aunt Nanny from among the exclaiming aunts.

"By a watermelon fight. In court we settle problems a little differently."

"*I* didn't say I'd ever believe it! No matter how many tried to make me," Gloria said. "I go by what I feel in my heart of hearts."

"Feelings!" added Judge Moody.

"And what's your feelings now, Miss Gloria?" cried Miss Beulah.

"They don't change! That I'm one to myself, and nobody's kin, and my own boss, and nobody knows the one I am or where I came from," she said. "And all that counts in life is up ahead."

"You're an idiot," Judge Moody told her, not unkindly. "The fact is, you could be almost anybody and have sprung up almost anywhere."

"Why, Oscar," said Mrs. Moody. "That's strong words."

"I'm ready for 'em."

Jack grabbed hold of Gloria and drew her back and put himself in front of her.

But Gloria came around Jack and on toward the Judge. She told him with a musing face, "Why, at the first warning she gave—I thought I might even be *hers*."

"Miss Julia's?" There were gaping mouths all the way around the bright porch.

"My lands," said Aunt Birdie. "That's what I call using the unbridled imagination."

"Why else would I have ever thought I could be a teacher?" Gloria put it to them, and this time a louder groan rose out of Judge Moody. "That would have explained everything. If once *she'd* made a mistake—and had me."

"No hope. No, she's never made a mistake, on purpose or otherwise," said Miss Beulah. "And I think if she had, she'd stuck right to her guns, Gloria, and brought you up for the world to see and brag on. She wouldn't make a mystery out of you. Had no use for a mystery."

"And it takes two!" cried Aunt Nanny.

"But she saved me from the orphanage—even if it was just to enter me up at Normal," argued Gloria. "She encouraged me, she wanted me to rise."

"I don't suppose for a minute Miss Julia saw the danger ahead. I think she had all the blindness of a born schoolteacher," said Aunt Beck, a little pleadingly.

"What Miss Julia didn't figure out like she ought was a nameless orphan can turn out to be a raving beauty," said Aunt Birdie. "More than likely will."

"Judge Moody, you ain't got fault to find with anybody here but me, have you?" Jack asked.

Squinting and scowling in the light that beat down, the Judge looked at him. "Jack," he said, calling him by name for the first time, "the thing that strikes me strongest is that you didn't know you were marrying your cousin—if you *were* marrying your cousin."

"No sir," Jack stammered, "I wasn't worrying about who she used to be before I married her!"

"Jack, you didn't know?" Aunt Birdie asked.

"Jack? Jack know?" they chorused at her all around, as Miss Beulah gave a short laugh.

"No, but *she* did. *She* had knowledge," Miss Beulah said. "You didn't warn Jack away from you, even a word, did you, Miss Gloria?"

"But Judge Moody!" said Gloria. "Then Miss Julia let fly at me a second letter! She wrote and told me the wedding would be scratched off the books and Jack would have to go to the pen—"

"Well, Jack did!" Uncle Noah Webster said. "In his own way he managed it!"

"What came over her? What did she have against these two

sweethearts?" Aunt Birdie cried. "What was the woman thinking of?"

Judge Moody said, "The innocent. She thought of the child."

Gloria slowly bowed her head.

"Miss Julia was able to conjure up Lady May without even seeing her? Just laying over there in Alliance?" cried Aunt Nanny.

With one accord, everybody turned to Miss Lexie, who stared them down.

"That baby was never on my lips. Not with all I had to contend with! All I ever told Miss Julia Mortimer was I supposed Gloria had forgotten her, the same as everybody else had," Miss Lexie vowed.

"Did she ask you straight to your face, Lexie?" asked Auntie Fay.

"By the time that baby'd arrived in the world, I was making her right sure she didn't know anything but what went on inside her own head," said Miss Lexie.

Granny's little black shoulder started to tremble again. The baby in her lap never stirred but slept with her face turned up bared to the light, her lips parted.

" 'Baby'? Is that what her letter said, Gloria?" asked Aunt Beck. "The naked word?"

"The letter said a baby, if one was to get here, might be deaf and dumb."

They laughed all around but hushed on the instant.

"No. More than that. There's a worse danger than that," Judge Moody said, scowling down at Gloria.

"And my baby would go without a name," she said, not raising her head.

"With a name like Lady May?" Jack cried, looking aghast.

Even at the sound of her name, the baby didn't wake or stir.

"And what's wrong with a family any way you can get one?" cried Aunt Nanny.

"And all the while, when I was waiting on my husband, sitting apart from the others on my cedar log, quieting my baby, singing to her, all I could think of were the two words I'm scaredest of, null and void," Gloria cried out. "In Miss Julia's handwriting!"

"And the pen? Watch out, Jack, they could come after you again," said Uncle Curtis. "And run you back in for getting married."

"For marrying Gloria?" he cried.

"Catch him, Gloria, don't let him topple over on you!" cried Aunt Nanny.

But Jack had turned around to Judge Moody. "If I've done something wrong, I'd kind of like to be told about it, sir. I'd like to hear the reasoning, Judge Moody—hear it from you," he said. "Now it looks to me like the law'd do better to run me in if I hadn't."

"No. It was wrong to get married," Judge Moody said. "If you two young people are related within the prohibited degree, then you ran head-on into a piece of Mississippi legislation—I think they passed it about ten years ago. And I reckon they'd be in their rights if they arrested you for it. You could be tried—"

"Tried?" screamed Miss Beulah.

"And if convicted—"

"I'd be convicted all right! When I married Gloria I married her on purpose!" Jack cried. "All right. If they want two more years of my life for that, it's worth it. Here I am, sir."

"And if convicted," Judge Moody went on in spite of women's cries, "you'd get a fine or a ten-year sentence in the penitentiary—"

Gloria sank to the floor and wrapped her arms around one of Jack's legs, screaming "No!"

"—or both, and the marriage would be declared void. That's now State law."

"And Miss Julia Mortimer was the one who dug that up," Aunt Birdie marveled.

"And before this ever happened may have helped get the law passed," said Judge Moody briefly.

"Young people have 'em a hard time starting out always," pleaded Aunt Beck. "They're going to overcome this, aren't they?"

"This is different from me and you, Beck," said Miss Beulah. "All the time Jack took, all the load he shouldered, and all the trouble he went to, even blackening his name going to Parchman, was in order to marry his own cousin and have Judge Moody come back and open the door so Curly Stovall could walk in the house and arrest him all over again."

"I'd welcome Curly to try it!" Jack said, with some of his color returning. He lifted Gloria to her feet and they stood with their arms wrapped around each other's waists.

"I still think it's the sweetest thing in the world," said Aunt Beck.

"But Mississippi law is bound and determined it ain't going to let you drink or marry your own cousin!" shouted Uncle Noah Webster. "It's too pleasurable!"

Mrs. Moody said to Gloria, "You broke the law worse than that boy did."

"Ma'am?"

"Look what you made of that baby—"

"My baby!" Gloria ran a step, took the limp child into her arms. "She's speckless!" Then under the bright lights she saw the first freckle lying in the hollow of the baby's throat, like a spilled drop of honey.

"—and *knowing!* And *knowing!* Then, when this baby grows up and starts finding out a thing or two for herself—" Mrs. Moody shook her head at her.

"Couldn't she find it in her heart to forgive her own mother?" cried Gloria. "*I* did!"

Judge Moody in his melancholy voice remarked, "Forgiving seems the besetting sin of this house."

"With good reason!" said Mrs. Moody. "Though I wouldn't know any more about cousins marrying being wrong than they did," she confessed. "Somehow, I always thought it was the thing to do."

"Well, then we're lucky it wasn't what you did," Judge Moody told her.

"And now, lo, it's a sin!" said Mrs. Moody.

"Oh, I suppose it just aggravates whatever's already there, in human nature—the best and the worst, the strength and the weakness," Judge Moody said to his wife. "And of course human nature is dynamite to start with."

"Oh, when I'd thought, for a minute, that with Beecham blood on both sides the world would turn out all right!" Miss Beulah cried out, her imploring voice still going toward Granny, who sat fixed and silent.

"You ain't too well-schooled along the highways and byways of Mississippi law, Mother, that's all," said Mr. Renfro kindly. "But Judge Moody is, and he's setting right here to aim it at us."

"And *I* thought when I came to Banner to teach my first school, I was going forth into the world," said Gloria.

"Instead, you was coming right back to where you started from," said Aunt Birdie. "Just as dangerous as a little walking stick of dynamite."

"That's right! You come here danger personified," said Aunt Beck.

"Living danger. You come here and started waving your little red flag at Jack," teased Aunt Nanny.

"Waving a red flag? I was trying to save him!" Gloria cried. "I've been trying to save him since the day I saw him first. Protecting his poor head!"

"From what?" Miss Beulah demanded, both hands on hips.

"This mighty family! And you can't make me give up!" Gloria threw back her hair, and a few dried watermelon seeds flew out from it. "We'll live to ourselves one day yet, and do wonders. And raise all our children to be both good and smart—"

"And what is it you think *I've* done, right here?" Miss Beulah interrupted in a voice of astonishment.

"What are you trying to say, girl?" Aunt Birdie cried.

"I'm going to take Jack and Lady May and we're going to get clear away from *everybody,* move to ourselves."

"Where to? To the far ends of the earth?" cried Aunt Beck, as Jack stifled a sound in his throat.

"Carry me with you," begged Etoyle, jumping up.

"Carry me," begged Elvie.

"Carry me, carry me!" cried a chorus of sadly teasing uncles and one or two distant voices joining in.

"And just how do you think you're going?" Miss Beulah demanded to know.

"That's still for the future to say." And she looked out to see the distance, but beyond the bright porch she couldn't see anything at all.

"Poor Gloria," said Aunt Beck. "Given fair warning, she was. She knew she was risking Jack too. Honey, why did you marry our boy? I think you can tell it to us now."

There in blinding light Gloria cried out, "It's because I love him worse than any boy I'd ever seen in my life, much less taught!"

Jack turned the color of a cockscomb flower as he stood rigid by her side.

"There. That was tore out of her," said Miss Beulah.

"I didn't have to believe Miss Julia Mortimer if I didn't want to," Gloria repeated. Then she came headlong at Judge Moody, holding her baby bucketed, and Lady May's little legs stuck out pointed at his head like two guns even though she was asleep. "Is that what's at the end of your Sunday errand, sir? Did you come all the way to Banner to make Jack's baby and mine null and void, and take Jack away from me again?"

"My errand could be in no way so interpreted," he said drily.

"If you could just turn around, go back to Ludlow again and not do anything more to me and Jack. If you could just see your way. If you could just be that yielding, sir," said Gloria softly. "Then I'd forgive even her. Miss Julia."

"Forgive!" He did look ready to shake her. "You, whose fault it all is! You and your everlasting baby's!"

"Well, I would forgive her."

"It's just as wrong now as it was then, when she found out about what she was doing, isn't it, Oscar?" Mrs. Moody prodded her husband. "If they were first cousins on their wedding day, they'll be first cousins again in the morning."

"Yes. If," he said.

"Are they going to be hounded till they die?" Mr. Renfro asked Judge Moody, and Miss Beulah whirled on Mr. Renfro to say, "And I thought you knew what you was doing when you hammered a new roof on the house!"

"No, before that happens, they could pack up and take this infant with them and go live in Alabama," said Judge Moody.

"Alabama!" cried Jack, a chorus of horrified cries behind him. "Cross the state line? That's what Uncle Nathan's done!"

"It's not over a few dozen miles. Cousins may freely marry across the Alabama line and their offsprings are recognized," Judge Moody said.

"You want me and Gloria and Lady May to leave all we hold dear and all that holds us dear? Leave Granny and everybody else that's not getting any younger?" Jack's eyes raked across all their faces.

"There ain't no end, it looks like, to what you can lose and still go on living," Uncle Curtis pointed out.

"Why, it would put an end to the reunion," Jack said. Gloria, at the sight of his face, pressed herself and the baby close to him.

"There's the answer to your wish. Didn't it come in a hurry!" cried Aunt Nanny. "Ain't that what you been wishing for, Gloria, a good way to leave us?"

"Not by being driven!"

"So Miss Julia Mortimer couldn't stop you from marrying

Jack by fair means or foul," Aunt Birdie said to Gloria. "Just couldn't prevent you."

"And I wish I could let her know now," said Gloria softly.

Women's voices echoed peacefully around her. "Let her know what?"

"How wrong she was. How right I was. She only needed to see my baby. And I was going to carry her over there!" said Gloria. "I was only waiting till she could talk."

Again Judge Moody groaned.

"Judge, I believe you'll make up your mind to forget this blood-kin business," Mrs. Moody said.

"What? Now, just a minute, don't go so fast, Maud Eva!" he said. His face grew darker as the blood ran into it. "I would just like a little evidence. My kind of evidence." He scowled around at the family. "Though as far as that goes, there's very little of that left now for any of us—that we were ever born, were married, had children—that any of our family have died, where they're buried."

"You've got your family Bible, haven't you, with it all down on the page?" cried Miss Beulah.

"No deeds to say whose the land is. No tax receipts, no poll books. There's no written proof left that any of us at all are alive here tonight. We're all in the same boat."

"What kind of people would burn down a courthouse?" cried Mrs. Moody.

"Varmints," said Granny. "They're all around us."

"Well, go on from there," said his wife impatiently to the Judge.

"And here," he said, with his eye on her, "they've told a patched-together family story and succeeded in bringing out no more evidence than if their declared intention had been to conceal it. Now this cousin story may be fact, but where is the present proof of it?" he asked the company. As Miss Beulah started to speak, he shook his head at her. "I saw there was a postcard," he told her. "It was signed 'Your loving husband.' That could have been their manner of speaking, you know, calling themselves husband and wife, real enough to them—meaning to make it a lawful union when he got his soldier's leave. But a postcard isn't the same evidence as a license to marry, or a marriage certificate, and even that—"

"It's better! There's a whole lot more of Sam Dale in that post-card, if you know how to read it!" Miss Beulah cried. "And Granny saved it from destruction, kept it in her Bible, showed it to you! Granny's word is as good as gold, don't you believe it? She's better than any courthouse, anywhere on earth."

"Oh, yes. Yes ma'am, I believe her word," Judge Moody said, moving his weight a little, leaning forward to let Granny hear him. "But I'm not wholly persuaded that this lady is always saying exactly what you think she's saying. Be reminded it's her birthday. She's a privileged character."

Granny's eyes moved along their slits and fixed on him. She still didn't speak. The others looked at him too, except for Jack, Gloria, and the baby, who clung together all one.

"Look at 'em, all hugging. They's victims of justice, all three," Aunt Birdie said, pointing. "I love 'em more than ever. What's ever going to become of 'em?"

Miss Beulah glared at Judge Moody. "Well, you don't have long to enjoy your little bit of foolish hope, do you?" she said. "But we've got to look after that little scandalous, haven't we?" She came to meet Judge Moody eye to eye, just as when he came breaking in at the dinner's start. "And with you to listen, and Granny not moving to stop me, I guess I'm going to have to tell it. And save 'em myself."

"Now, Mother," said Mr. Renfro.

"I believe to my soul we're misjudging one, and him not here tonight to stand up for his own innocence, and that's Sam Dale Beecham. And so I'm just going to silence you, everybody!" said Miss Beulah.

"Mother, I believe I'm going and put up the evening bars," said Mr. Renfro, leaving them.

"I know good and well I punished the poor little fellow when he was in dresses and I was too little to know better how to watch over him!" cried Miss Beulah. "Judge Moody, Sam Dale wasn't no more likely than you are now to be responsible for Gloria being in the world."

"Don't, Beulah," Aunt Beck pleaded. "We didn't come here to cry, I keep on telling us."

"Something happened earlier than anything else to Sam Dale Beecham, and the main reason I'm in torment when I think about him is they all blame me. Yes sir, you do!" she cried to Granny, whose expression did not change.

"Mama," said Jack, "you wouldn't do harm to your own little brother. Now that's something you ain't going to make us believe."

"Then try listening," she said harshly. "Sam Dale's a little fellow sitting up close to the big hearth—still in dresses. I was supposed to be minding him but I don't know and can't ever remember what I was doing instead. Coal flew out of the fire and hit in his lap. Oh, it was a terrible thing! Granny called for some slippery elm for it and I said I'd go, I'd go! And instead of settling for the first elm I could find—instead of settling for the closest-to, I had to send myself farther and farther and farther, hunting for the *best!* For what's good enough to help what I'd done? They thought when I came running late with that slippery elm that I'd dawdled along the way."

"Wasn't all your fault, Beulah," said Aunt Beck, as the silence lengthened itself. "No big sister nor anybody else could tell a spark to keep from flying out of the fire."

"Grandpa whipped me himself. The only time in his life. Granny still lives to blame me," Miss Beulah told Judge Moody, bending forward to see into his averted face. "They had me to grow up in torment for little Sam Dale."

"Jack's stricken, Beulah. Jack can't stand to hear 'em cry," said Aunt Beck.

"Neither can Oscar," said Mrs. Moody.

"Beulah always feels like she has to tell some of that story to the old folks before she lets us go," Aunt Beck said, sighing. "But I never heard it come out sounding any sadder than today, now that she's given us all of it."

"Is it evidence?" Mrs. Moody asked her husband.

"Hearsay. Hearsay," Judge Moody's voice rumbled, and when it stopped there was a silence of fresh amazement.

"Well, I don't know what the whole *world's* hanging on by!" cried Aunt Birdie in a voice of indignation. "While it's waiting to get proved it's there according to Judge Moody!"

"This one's a sadder story. But not for that reason does it stand up any better as proof," said Judge Moody quietly to Miss Beulah. "They didn't have a doctor, I suppose," he said, and waited for what seemed a long time.

When Granny spoke, she said to Miss Beulah with shaking

lips, "They've just carried me the message. He didn't last through the crisis."

"God takes our jewels," came the soft response from the porchful.

Judge Moody said over them in a heavy voice, "Never mind any more. I've succeeded only in worrying another old lady."

Granny said, "Far from home. Under Georgia skies . . ."

"It's that baby. I think we'll have to close one eye over that everlasting baby," Judge Moody said in the same heavy voice. "You end up doing yourself the thing you hate most, the thing you've deplored the loudest and longest," he said to Uncle Nathan, the one who was looking at him now, with fixed eyes, over Granny's bowed head. "Here I am, taking the law into my own hands."

"Well," said Uncle Percy in a remote whisper, "that ain't such a poor idea. It's a whale of a lot better idea than going to Alabama."

"Take the law in your own hands? These people have never let it *out* of their own hands," Mrs. Moody said to her husband. "And I think that goes for your precious Miss Julia too. A tyrant, if there ever was one. Oh, for others' own good, of course!"

"Hush, everybody," Miss Beulah commanded. "Judge Moody's standing up again. I think this time he's going to do his part for the reunion."

For a moment he stood silenced. "It's that baby," he said. "I think we'll have to leave it that what's done is done. That there was no prior knowledge between the partners. And no crime."

"We can just bury it. With all else she knew," said Mr. Renfro, walking back from just within the passage and standing beside him. "The schoolteacher."

"Well, it's wonderful the way the Lord knows how to work things out," said Aunt Birdie brightly to Judge Moody.

"I hope that means the world's all right again! And that Jack can stay home a little longer this time!" cried Aunt Beck.

"I knew that's what you were going to have to do," Mrs. Moody said to her husband. "You'd have saved time and caused fewer tears to do it when I told you."

"I suppose, if I was the first of Miss Julia's protégés, this girl was her last," said Judge Moody with a sigh.

"She expected too much out of you too, Oscar," Mrs. Moody

said, and he all at once sat down. "*Now* what have I said wrong?"

"Are you going to say 'Thank you,' Gloria?" asked Aunt Beck anxiously.

Mrs. Moody was holding Gloria's eye. "You had a talent for spelling. And some early determination." She granted her two short nods. "And what did you have besides?"

"She was an orphan child with nothing in this world and nobody knew who she was—" began Aunt Birdie.

"Youth," Judge Moody said shortly. "Her life before her."

Lady May opened her mouth and let out a long, welling cry.

Gloria said, "Miss Julia saw *promise* in me," and opened her bodice.

"Poor little scrap of mischief!" Mrs. Moody broke out. "She can't satisfy nature like that. And honestly, if a child is old enough to wear *pockets*—"

"She eats at the table too!" Gloria cried back at her. "She gets common, ordinary food just as well as this. What I'm seeing to is she doesn't *starve!*"

Dead silence greeted her. Aunt Nanny grabbed Jack and seemed to hold him from falling. Miss Beulah came up to Gloria in measured steps. Then she said, "All I'm thankful for this late, Gloria, is that Grandpa Vaughn didn't last long enough to hear that. Has a soul in this household ever been allowed to starve yet?"

"And when Jack jumps out in those fields tomorrow, he'll resurrect something out of nothing. Don't you know he will?" cried Aunt Birdie.

Aunt Nanny said, "And Jack will butcher the hog. You'll tide yourselves over, one year more. And the cow will freshen—"

"I beg your pardon," Mrs. Moody said to Gloria.

"Granted," said Gloria, nursing.

"You see, Judge Moody, and Mrs. Moody, now that Jack has come home to stay, everything's going to look up. It'll all be on his shoulders," said Uncle Curtis. "Trust him."

"Young man!" cried Mrs. Moody. "Jack! Merciful fathers! Is my car still there where Judge left it?"

"Running in good tune," said Jack, standing with his hand on the baby's head. "Uncle Nathan's piece of work is still holding. I went down and apologized for Aycock to his mother, and when I told her where he's spending the night she gave the credit entirely to me. And Aycock says he enjoyed his dinner and the same thing again for supper would be all right."

"Then what took you so long?" cried Miss Beulah. "Too much tried to happen while you tarried!"

"I had to tell Aycock about the new teacher that's come to board at their house, Mama," said Jack. "Young, green, and untried, and just the right medicine for him. I'm going to get behind him and help him marry her."

"I forgot all about what was pitched on the edge of a forty-foot drop!" said Mrs. Moody. "And oh, Oscar, where are we going to lay our heads tonight?"

"I very much fear that by this time that question's been settled for us," Judge Moody said.

◄§

"I think it's about time for us to take a little prettier view of ourselves," said Miss Beulah. "Go bring out my wedding," she told Elvie. "Stand on a chair and reach careful."

Elvie trotted inside, then there came from the company room a shattering noise. It sounded like handclapping. She came hurrying back with something made out of thin cardboard that had rolled up tight from both ends. Miss Beulah took it carefully and opened it out as if she uncoiled a spring, then carried it over to Granny's chair to hold it where the old lady's eyes might fall on it and where the rest might stand to see. It was nearly two feet long, seven or eight inches high.

"The only picture that ever was made of our whole family," Miss Beulah said, while a crowd gathered behind her shoulders.

The earlier company had lined up three deep that day on the front porch and steps of this house where they themselves were now. They stood then in April light; the house stood dark, roof and all, as a woodsy mountain behind the water-splash of the bride.

"That's me," said Miss Beulah. "That's you, Granny. And there's Grandpa, Granny."

At the apex of the group stood a medium-tall, upright lady with black hair showing under her hat, with her hand over the arm of the

**327**

man standing in a preacher's stance; a crack in the surface had split his beard like lowered antlers.

The old lady didn't say a word.

"Remember, Mr. Renfro? The man on the mule that happened along to take the picture? Cranked it off, packed up and rode away, never saw him or his mule again. You fished out and paid that fellow I never knew what, and it was a month coming! Rolled like a calendar! I remember how hard it was for fingers to get it unrolled. It's been propped twenty-five years on its shelf with two flatirons to hold it, but it still likes to roll up on you—step on the wrong floorboard and see."

"I give him a silver dollar for it," said Mr. Renfro. "And never saw that man evermore."

"Just one of life's wayfarers, a picture-taker," said Miss Beulah. "You was up on crutches before that picture got back to us."

Mr. Renfro, the groom, was seated by the standing bride; he was in a chair with one of his legs offered to the forefront of the picture, set out on a cot like a loaf on a table; and the very bedspread on the cot was the one just inside the window on the company bed, visible now in the hot electric light.

"But you kept right on, Brother," said Miss Lexie.

"I had to come behind Dearman and get the stumps out for a mighty lot of people," Mr. Renfro said. "In those days I was called on here, thither, and yon."

"Be grateful you was on earth to be in the picture at all," said Miss Beulah. "Look, it's got all the Beecham boys together, standing shoulder to shoulder. There's precious Sam Dale, Granny!"

The old lady didn't give out a word.

"Did he have inkling?" asked Aunt Cleo.

"Does he look like it?" countered Miss Beulah. "Look at that face—there's nothing in it but plain goodness, goodness personified."

"But it's in twice," said Etoyle.

Evidently by racing the crank of the camera and running behind backs, Sam Dale had got in on both ends of the panorama, putting his face smack and smack again into the face of oblivion. Though too young and smooth to print itself dark enough not to fade, his face could not be mistaken; the hair stood straight up on his forehead, luxuriant as a spring crop of oats.

"Wasn't that a little mischief-making of him?" murmured Aunt Beck.

328

"That was being eighteen years old and fixing to march off to war," said Miss Beulah shortly.

"Only one of the boys was married yet," said Aunt Birdie. "So that only gave the right to Nanny to be in the picture."

"Look, oh look, in those days Percy was bigger than Nanny. Now it's the other way round," said Aunt Birdie. "I always forget what tricks time likes to play."

Aunt Nanny's finger flattened on the blur where someone had moved, and she asked, "Rachel Sojourner?"

"Oh, those slipping fingers!" cried Miss Beulah. "Don't bring back to me, please, how she tried to button me up in that dress— I thought those fingers'd never get to the foot of the row! Slipping, hurrying, and ice cold!" She pulled away Nanny's finger. "But what's she doing hiding in my wedding picture, and I never saw her before?"

"She's been in the company room with you all this time, Gloria," said Aunt Beck. "Your mother."

"I can't see what this girl looked like," said Gloria, coming at last to look at the picture with them.

"She didn't hold still. Beulah, this picture's filling up with the dead," said Aunt Beck. "After this year, let's not try taking it off its shelf any more."

"I'll hand you this much: looking at it today you get the notion there was nobody on earth but Renfros," said Miss Beulah. "And it was a big tribe to start with. They didn't ever outshine the Beechams, but they did threaten once to out-crop 'em. All them's Renfros! That's Mr. Renfro's father and mother, cocking their heads at each other. Dust these many years. All them's Renfros! That's Fay, with her finger in her mouth. And not a living man of 'em walking around today but the bridegroom I took for my husband."

Mr. Renfro made her a bow.

"What kind of a dandy is this?" asked Aunt Cleo, whose finger was moving behind theirs, more slowly. "Walking cane! And a straw hat with a stripey band on it. A flowing tie! Is that Noah Webster?"

"That's Nathan!" a chorus cried full of glee.

"Well, he's got both hands," Aunt Cleo challenged them. "Was he born like you and I?"

"That picture was taken before he surrendered to the Lord," said Miss Beulah. "That's enough of the picture. Carry it back in the house and stand it back on the shelf with my switches."

"They didn't have many pretty ones," Aunt Cleo said, her

finger still moving slowly across the picture, across Miss Lexie's face, then stopping. "I'd have to give the prize to that one."

"Pull back your finger!" said Miss Beulah, pulling it back for her. "That's not Vaughn, not Beecham, not even Renfro, that's no kin to anybody here, and to my mind hadn't much business here at my wedding. Grandpa and Granny Vaughn was boarding her here at the time of the big occasion. Now who's the answer?"

She was standing the last one on the back row, her head turned away from the crowd and ignoring the camera, looking off from this porch here as from her own promontory to survey the world. The full throat, firm long cheek, long-focused eye, the tall sweep of black hair laid with a rosebud that looked like a small diploma tied up in its ribbon, the very way the head was held, all said that the prospect was serious.

"Miss Julia Percival Mortimer," Judge Moody said, standing with them, looking down.

"She'll never git it all on one tombstone," said Aunt Cleo. "Just what I've been telling Noah Webster Beecham."

Mrs. Moody remarked, "It doesn't sound to me like she's even very sure of a grave."

"Where was I?" Elvie asked, her eyes still fixed on the photograph.

"Lucky for you, you was nowhere on earth yet!" said Miss Beulah. "Now that you're here, put this picture back where it belongs. Granny dear, don't you want to see it? Just one more time before it goes?"

Granny waved it away. Elvie skipped.

&

"Look-a-there! Look at our light!" cried Etoyle, and some of the aunts involuntarily shielded their eyes.

Within the opening of the passage, the bright bulb on its cord rose up toward the ceiling, slowly, then dropped in fits and starts, then zoomed up with the speed of a moth. Close to the ceiling, into which its cord disappeared, the bulb clung for a minute, then dropped and danced to a standstill.

"Well, now you're haunted," said Miss Lexie.

"It's starting afresh!" said Elvie.

"Jack!" yelled Miss Beulah, as the cord moved like a fishing line with a bite on it.

"I think now that whoever said ghosts is right, not that I ever held with ghosts. I'm a pretty good Presbyterian, back home," Mrs. Moody said.

"Jack! Jack! Ever out of sight when most needed. Vaughn, you climb a piece of the way up under the roof, take a poker, and just poke for a second at what's doing that," said Miss Beulah. "Come back and tell us what we've got there. I bet you a pretty it's alive, now."

"Who's going to wait on me like that when I get old?" crowed Miss Lexie, as Vaughn slowly went. "Not a soul, not a blessed soul!"

"You'll have to go to the poor farm," Aunt Cleo told her without taking her eyes from the ceiling. "If they still got room for you."

"I'll come wait on you, Aunt Lexie," cried Elvie, jumping up and down to watch the ceiling. "As long as I ain't too busy school-teaching. And if I don't get married or have children before I know it. Look!"

"Ha ha ha!" Etoyle cawed out. Now the light was being let down on its cord, jerky as a school flag down its mast.

Then all the lights went out. It seemed a midnight moment before the moonlight gathered its wave and rolled back in.

"Well, that's one more system that today's put out of commission," said Uncle Curtis, as if with favor.

In a moment they heard Vaughn come running up the passage, and now they made him out—he came cradling something alive. All around, the dogs put up a clamor.

"Here's who it was, Mama. Playing with us all from over our heads."

"Uh-*huh,*" said Miss Beulah. "What did I tell you!"

"Horrors," said Mrs. Moody. "Is that a monkey?"

"Don't try to put him in my lap," said Aunt Cleo. "I mean it."

"Hey, Coony!" cried the little girls.

"He was just tantalizing you, Mama," said Vaughn pleadingly.

"Eternal, everlasting mischief!" stormed Miss Beulah. "There's always *that* you can count on! I said I wasn't going to have coon or possum under my roof and I'm not," she went on, with repeated pokes testing the coon's needly teeth on her finger. "Yes sir, and you're one little scrap of mischief I mean to send right back where it started from."

While the boy cousins tried to keep back a battery of hounds, two enormous yellow globes moved out of the passage. Etoyle had gone for the oil lamps, even while Miss Beulah was calling over the frenzied barking of the held-back, straining dogs, "Bring the lamps! Don't leave your great-grandmother sitting in the dark!" Etoyle brought the lamps to the coon.

The coon, circular-eyed, lamp-eyed itself, fluffed up and drew one long breath, hoarse and male.

Then it got itself thrust into the lap of Ella Fay, who hollered, "Jack!"

"Hold him, Ella Fay, hold him!" shouted the uncles. "That's not the way! He's scrambling!"

"Don't let him run off with anything belonging to me," said Aunt Cleo. "Oh, they're great for thieving."

"Oscar, I want to go home," said Mrs. Moody piteously.

Held up by Elvie, Lady May was shaken awake again to see the coon. When she saw it, her eyes went three-cornered and her cheeks went plump as two Duchess roses on a stem.

"Look at that smile. There it comes! And it's her mother's. And looks like you're going to have to work just as hard to get it," Aunt Birdie said.

"Mama, I believe he knows you're the cook," pleaded Vaughn. "See how he wants to follow you. Let's keep him, let's keep him! When I get him chained up and you bring him some food in a saucer, he'll quit his monkeying. I want to name him Parchman."

"He'll go!" said Miss Beulah. "And I don't want to have any coon-and-dog battle on the premises. Boys! Tighten up on those visiting dogs! Come here to me, Sid."

Little Sid, to their laughter, ran at even draw with the head of the pack as the coon streaked straight to meet them. In the moonlight Sid showed his teeth like a row of lace.

"I give the coon fifty-fifty and the dogs fifty-fifty," said Uncle Curtis in leisurely tones.

"There's a little more racket out there than I like to hear," moaned Miss Beulah.

The dogs' tails, white and moonlit and all beating at once, disappeared last, speeding down the hill towards joy. But a boy cousin came plodding back into view to tell them, "He got away. Coony got away. It looked like he was heading for Banner Top."

"That coon didn't put up the fight those dogs expected of him," said Uncle Dolphus. "He'd been suffocating under that roof too long, that might have been his trouble. Better luck next time!"

◆§

The moon shone now at full power. The front gallery seemed to spread away and take the surrounding hills and gullies all into its apron. Banner Top seemed right in their laps. Banner itself all but showed itself over the rim, as though the only reason why anything on earth was still invisible tonight was that it had taken the right steps to make itself so.

"You know, I can hear that thing running from here," said Aunt Beck. "Mrs. Judge, your motor sounds to me like the old courthouse clock trying to strike again, and not making it."

"You sure are stranded here," said Mrs. Moody. "Mercy, what a long way off from everything!"

"Long way off? They're right in the thick," cried Aunt Birdie. "This is where I wish I was when I get hungry to see something happen."

"In my young days," said Brother Bethune, "I incurred the wrath of the law-abiding, one sweet summer's night."

"Brother Bethune!" the aunts turned slightly in their chairs to exclaim. "Never dreamed that," said one.

"Are you trying to tell us you got yourself marched off to jail?" Miss Beulah asked.

"I'm trying to tell you I incurred the wrath of the law-abiding. There was at one time a little whiskey-making going on in and around these peaceful moonlight hills. And I supplied 'em the sugar."

"Brother Bethune!"

"Every last one of us got caught. Yes, in my day revenuers roamed these moonlight roads as thick as thieves. But I was the only one arrested that they let run back in his house a minute. They said I could gather up my Bible."

"They owed you at least that much!" hollered Uncle Noah Webster. "What happened to the makings? They drink it up then and there?"

"I went on out through the back window," said Brother Bethune. "Into the moonlight."

"Well, it done you good to come out and tell us, didn't it?"

said Aunt Birdie. "Now we know at least one thing *you're* sorry for."

"Brother Bethune, I think you might go back to it," Miss Beulah broke out. "Go back to making your moonshine. There's less chance of mistakes than there is in trying to preach the Lord's Word. Grandpa's turned in his grave more than once or twice today."

"Beulah! Do you know what you're saying?" Uncle Curtis asked her.

"I was young and untried," said Brother Bethune. "Needing to be shown the way, that's all."

◆§

"Well, the Lord only knows how I'm going to get home, even if I live till morning," Mrs. Moody said.

"Mrs. Judge, you and Judge Moody's welcome to our company room," Mr. Renfro said immediately. "Where's my wife? Hear it polite from her."

"My car sitting up on the edge of nowhere, with nobody but a booby in it," Mrs. Moody went on. "I guess before morning he'll find my chocolate cake, and just sink his teeth in it."

"Well, sir, I'll be looking in next week's *Boone County Vindicator* to read what's the outcome. Ora Stovall is the Banner correspondent, she'll get it all in. If the worst should happen to your car, most readers will say it served Curly just about right," said Uncle Dolphus.

"What about the way it'll serve me?" asked Judge Moody.

"It won't be that bad," Uncle Noah Webster promised him.

"Mother, hurry to invite 'em," said Mr. Renfro, looking about for her. "Or they'll go!"

"If you still got no place to be till morning, Judge and Mrs. Moody," said Miss Beulah finally, "we got our company room. I'll just move Gloria and the baby out of it before Jack gets in it, and now that Jack's home, I'll move Elvie out of it too and put Elvie on Vaughn's cot on the back porch, since Lexie's in with the other two girls, and Vaughn can sleep where he's inclined."

"Well, if that's not any trouble," said Mrs. Moody, while Elvie cried.

"But you'll have to wait on it," Miss Beulah said. "You can't

**334**

even see your way in till some of this company starts saying good-night and takes babies and hats and all away from the bed."

❦

All the women and nearly all the men sat with some child's arm hanging a loop around them. Other children, still wide enough awake, ran stealthily behind the chairs, tickling their elders with hen feathers. Sleeping babies had been laid on the company bed long ago, there were sleepers on pallets in the passage, and others slept more companionably among the chair-legs and the human feet on the gallery floor, like rabbits in burrows, or they lay unbudging across laps.

"Well, you're visiting an old part of the country here," said Mr. Renfro. "If you was to go up Banner Top and hunt around, Judge Moody, you'd find little hollows here and there where the Bywy Indians used to pound their corn, and keep a signal fire going, and the rest of it. But there ain't too much of their story left lying around. I'm afraid you could call them peace-loving."

"Indian Leap," said Granny.

"That's the name my grandmother called it too. Blue Knob is another old-timey name for it," said Aunt Beck.

"There's nothing blue about Banner Top," laughed Aunt Nanny. "It's pure barefaced red."

"You ever seen it in the evening from Mountain Creek?" asked Aunt Beck. "I was born in Mountain Creek. And from there Banner Top is as blue as that little throbbing vein in Granny's forehead."

"The Indians jumped off from there into the river and drowned 'emselves rather than leave their homes and go where they'd be more wanted. That's Granny's tale," said Uncle Curtis.

"There's a better name than any, and that's the one it got christened by those that walked it here all the way from Carolina in early times and ought to knowed what they was talking about," Mr. Renfro said to Judge Moody. "Renfros, that is. They called the whole parcel of it Long Hungry Ridge."

"If tonight was as much as a hundred or more years ago," Uncle Curtis said, addressing the Moodys, "you might not have had such an easy time finding us. There was just the thin little road, what you might call a trail, mighty faint, going along here through the standing forest. So dim and hard to find in the trees that they thought it would be the best judgment in the long run to ring a bell to let the travelers know where they was. Once an hour they had to remember to ring it, and regular, or the woods would have been full of lost travellers, stumbling on one another's heels. That was back in the days when there was more travelling through here than lately—folks was in a greater hurry to get somewhere, you know, while the country's new."

"There it is," said Miss Beulah. "Straight ahead of your noses."

The black iron bell hung from its yoke mounted on a black locust post that stood to itself. The leaves of a wisteria climbing there made a feathery moonlit bonnet around the bell.

"I've read somewhere about a bell like that on the Old Grenada Trail," Judge Moody said to his wife. "Doubt if that one still exists."

"That's the Wayfarer's Bell," said Miss Beulah. "And it was here before any of the rest, I reckon. Before Granny was born."

"I rang it this morning, a little before sunup," said Granny.

"Yes, Granny dear," said Uncle Percy, his voice nearly as much of a whisper as hers.

She nodded to either side of her. "Brought you running, didn't it?"

◦⑤

"You missed things," called Auntie Fay serenely, as the Champions' chicken van bounced into the yard and stopped under a moonstruck fall of dust. "Gloria's born a Beecham, she's Sam Dale's child— that's the best surprise that was brought us. She's here tonight as one of the family twice over.—Oh no she isn't!—Well, believe what you want to."

"Well, chickens come home to roost," said Uncle Homer, stumbling once on the steps, the bright hearth of moonlight.

"We got a little extra company as usual," Auntie Fay kept on. "Two that turned up with no place to sleep."

Uncle Homer came on into the lamplight. "Judge Moody! What's that man doing in this house?"

"He's spending the night," said Auntie Fay. "Beulah's just asked him in spite of herself."

"Judge Moody, you was asked for over at Miss Julia Mortimer's

**336**

all evening long!" cried Uncle Homer. "Doc Carruthers was about to go hunting the roads to see if you'd fell in somewhere. I had to rake up a dozen excuses for you."

"*You* did? You're the very fellow rode right by us this morning and left us to languish!" Mrs. Moody said. "And my car clinging to the edge of nowhere. If clinging it still is."

"It is," said Uncle Homer. "It evermore is, ma'am. Still clinging. I'm glad to be able to bring you the comforting word. I saw it again on my way back, just passed it."

"Possum," said Jack, low, "don't tell Mama, but Uncle Homer's back here the worse for wear. We ought to have been over yonder for the family in place of him. Paying respects is not Uncle Homer's long suit."

"I don't suppose you heard anybody over there call my name, Homer Champion?" Miss Lexie said, coughing from her dry throat.

"I don't believe the splendid name of Renfro ever came up," he said.

"I would have gone back and pitched in today, if anybody'd asked for me and sent after me. But they didn't," said Miss Lexie. "I listened hard to be asked for and I wasn't."

"Lexie, are you working up for a crying spell at this late hour?" Miss Beulah asked.

Miss Lexie raised her voice. "I can get my feelings hurt, the same as anybody else!"

"When I cry, I go off somewhere and cry by myself," Miss Beulah said, taking a step away from her high on tiptoe to show her, "and I don't come back till I'm good and over it. But if her crowd adds up to more than we've got here, Homer Champion, I'll eat that table out there—I promise you!"

"If she's got a crowd now, they didn't come paying her any attention while she's sick, any more than this crowd here," said Miss Lexie.

"Well, darlin', maybe all of 'em was waiting for now," Aunt Beck said in consoling tones.

"That whole house is busy filling up with big shots! They're everywhere, with hardly room left for the homefolks to sit down," Uncle Homer was saying. "It ain't just Boone County that's over there. I saw tags tonight on cars from three or four different counties, and that ain't all—they're here from Alabama, Georgia, Carolina, and even places up North!"

**337**

"Found their way all right," said Mrs. Moody, with a glance toward her husband.

"A Willys-Knight from Missouri liked-to crowded me off my own road! And Father Somebody-Something, that's who's going to preach her funeral, and he wears a skirt. He's a big shot from somewhere too, just don't ask me where," said Uncle Homer.

"That's no Presbyterian!" flashed Mrs. Moody. "No *Southern* Presbyterian!"

"The nearest one he reminds me of is Judge Moody," said Uncle Homer.

"What bridge were all these crossing on?" Judge Moody asked.

"Dear old Banner bridge is the one I use. And you know who sent a telegram he wishes he was coming to the funeral tomorrow? Governor Somebody from I forgot to listen where! Getting telegrams is pretty high style," said Uncle Homer.

"All right for high style. But the way we've been told, Miss Julia herself is still going without a place to be buried," said Auntie Fay.

"That's a false charge," said Uncle Homer, holding up his hand. "When Miss Julia Mortimer's letter came down on the supervisors to give her right-of-way to a grave under the schoolhouse doorstep and they said Nay, I went to work on it myself—until I got her a site in dear Banner Cemetery. That's hitting it pretty close to her mark, ain't it?"

"In Banner Cemetery? Homer Champion! You're bringing her right smack in our midst?" cried Miss Beulah wildly. "She's going to be buried with us?"

"Beulah, I got the site from Earl Comfort in return for a Comfort site and a Jersey cow. He said he couldn't afford to turn it down, and little Mis' Comfort could milk her for him. Mr. Comfort's got to be buried in Ludlow among strangers for his brother's pains, and little care I. Getting Miss Julia buried to Banner's credit is worth a heap to me," said Uncle Homer. "I can always point to it."

"Well, old Earl come just about as close to digging his own grave as a man could get, and still tell it," said Mr. Renfro. "Eh, Willy Trimble?"

But Mr. Willy Trimble sat there very papery, still as a finished fly in a web, his eyes shut.

"Homer Champion is not ungrateful," said Uncle Homer. "Let

338

that never be told against him. Miss Julia Mortimer made me what I am today, and you could have heard me declaring so tonight if you'd been there. I grew up only a poor Banner boy, penniless, ignorant, and barefoot, and today I live in Foxtown in a brick veneer home on a gravel road, got water in the kitchen, four hundred chickens, and filling an office of public trust, asking only—"

"I'm never a particle surprised at you, Homer," said Miss Beulah. "You'd find a platform anywhere at all."

"So she'll be going in in the morning," Uncle Homer went on, clapping Brother Bethune on the shoulder. "And you can have your whack at her. I think you can look for a good crowd."

But Brother Bethune now slept too, with his head thrown back and his mouth open. They had a glimpse of his old wrong tongue, shining like a little pocket-mirror back there. It was reflecting the moon.

"Damascus Church don't even have an organ," said Aunt Beck.

"The best sounding-board in the world! That's all!" exclaimed Miss Beulah. "And voices do the rest. When Damascus lights into a hymn, the countryside will know what it's in praise of!"

"The funeral won't be ours. Just the burial, Sister Beulah," said Uncle Homer. "Wait till Brother Bethune sees him coming— his rival in the skirt. Boys, they're having 'em a high old time over yonder, let me tell you."

"How much of a one have *you* had?" Aunt Cleo asked. "Let me get a good look at your eyes."

"Besides the rest, Mr. Ike Goldman of Goldman's Store brought in a trayload of eats you never seen the like of," said Uncle Homer. "And decorating a silver tray was a bottle of something— the bought kind—and some little glasses the size of a lady's thimble! Some of those Presbyterians made out like they'd rather go home, but there was plenty of the other kind that helped themselves."

"If you'd rather be celebrating at her house than mine, just turn around and go back over there, Homer," said Miss Beulah to his face. "A hundred to one they haven't started missing you yet."

"Is it going on all over her house?" Aunt Beck asked.

"It's Bedlam," said Uncle Homer, as though satisfied. "It's pure unadulterated Bedlam over there. Cigars!"

"Well, Homer," said Miss Beulah, "you may have gained yourself a margin of votes today by racing off from your own family and rubbing shoulders with a crowd of mourners—but no further stars in your crown, not if I had any say-so about it. And I doubt if the eats could come up to mine—they had pretty short notice."

"Chicken predominated," said Uncle Homer. "Chicken predominated." Suddenly he sat down.

···

Again quiet threatened. Only a few children still had their eyes open. Wild with asking a riddle one minute, they would be stopped by sleep the next, as though a cup were being passed around the company, and having tasted what was in it they fell back open-lipped one after the other, even the most stubborn. Now their elders had their own silence left to them.

"And on moonlight nights like tonight," said Granny, "they'd mount 'em the same steed and ride 'em up the road and down the road, then hitch the bridle to the tree. That's after I was safe under the covers and Mr. Vaughn had left off his praying and settled in to snore."

"Who, Granny?" the aunts were all asking her.

"Just told you. The schoolteacher. Ain't that who you're trying to bury?" she asked.

"Miss Julia Mortimer? Granny!" Uncle Percy, Uncle Curtis, and Uncle Dolphus all exclaimed at her in shocked voices. Uncle Noah Webster asked, "Granny dear, are you telling us about Miss Julia Mortimer and a sweetheart?"

"Call him Dearman. That's his moniker," said Granny.

The laugh that rose and fell around her was one of dismay.

"Who can believe that?" challenged Miss Beulah. "Well, I'm not saying I can't. A rascal like him's just the kind that some over-smart old maid would take a shine to."

"Some did consider her beautiful of face as a girl. Haven't you ever marvelled to hear that?" said Aunt Birdie.

"Miss Julia Mortimer had ears set close to her head, little ears that run up in points—like Judge Moody's and mine," said Mr. Renfro in candid vanity.

"If she'd married Dearman! It would have been a different kettle of fish," said Aunt Nanny.

340

"We would have escaped from a lot," agreed Aunt Beck. "But would *she* have been as satisfied, with only a husband to fuss over instead of a whole nation of ignorant, squirming schoolchildren?"

"Watch out, Beck. Watch out for your sympathies," said Aunt Birdie.

"Don't talk about Dearman around here," said Miss Beulah.

"What's his story? Ain't he the one you come home from German-hunting and found in charge of your store?" Aunt Cleo asked Mr. Renfro. "Oho-oho."

"I didn't go German-hunting," Mr. Renfro replied.

"He managed to blow himself up right here at home," said Miss Beulah.

"I didn't have a bit of excuse in the world, I was right here in Banner, and watching him, and lost it to him. Mr. Dearman," Mr. Renfro said. "The store I had from my daddy."

"Shucks," said Aunt Cleo.

"I was *out* of the store some, blowing stumps, cleaning up after him—he needed somebody knowing how to do that," said Mr. Renfro. "And hunting some. And he all at once had my business. There ain't hardly what you could call a story to it."

"It's your story. Not Dearman's. You don't know your own story when you hear it," Miss Beulah said. She whirled on Aunt Cleo. "All right. Dearman is who showed up full-grown around here, took over some of the country, brought niggers in here, cut down every tree within forty miles, and run it shrieking through a saw-mill."

"Did he cut your trees?" Aunt Cleo asked.

"Did you see any giants left, coming?"

"Went through our hills and stripped 'em naked, that's all!" Aunt Nanny cried. "I kept asking how he got in here and found us!"

"Followed the tracks. The railroad had already come cutting through the woods and just barely missed some of us. Yes'm, he put up a sawmill where he found the prettiest trees on earth. Lived with men in a boxcar and drank liquor. Pretty soon the tallest trees was all gone."

"Reckon you-all got something for 'em," said Aunt Cleo.

"By then we was owing to Dearman," said Mr. Renfro.

"We didn't even get the sawdust!" cried Uncle Noah Webster to his wife.

"It was a tearing ambition he had to make all he could out of us. And even some of our girls listened to his spiel and was sweet on him," said Uncle Percy. "I hated that."

"What he left us was a nation of stumps," said Mr. Renfro.

Granny put out both hands in an amazingly swift predatory gesture.

"That's him!" said Miss Beulah. "Just a great big grabber, that's what Dearman was."

"Well, that's the way to get something," said Aunt Cleo, grinning at them.

"I believe down your way was exactly where he come from, Sister Cleo," Uncle Curtis said.

"He did. Manifest, Mississippi, is where he sprung from," said Miss Beulah.

"That's a familiar-sounding name, Dearman," said Aunt Cleo.

"He's what levelled Piney!" Uncle Noah Webster told her. "Why, I've learned that since I've been living in your house and going to the barber shop. Those forest pines he took right in his maw. And when he first showed up there he didn't have but two goats."

"And when he left it he had all the money he needed and a gang to go with him and they just started up the railroad track," said Uncle Dolphus.

"Then after the store he took my house away from me," Mr. Renfro went on. "I had a little bad luck just at the perfect time to suit his needs, and he put me out and moved himself in. Thinking he was going to dwell in it forever, I reckon, and lord it over Banner forever and aye. He didn't get to do that."

"That's enough!" warned Miss Beulah. "He was just a glorified Stovall. Now will everybody please forget about him?"

"I don't know what Beulah could have married me for, after that. Unless she did it just to show she felt sorry for me," Mr. Renfro said.

"Go to grass," said Miss Beulah. "And now you've told more than enough, haven't you?"

"What happened to Dearman?" asked Aunt Cleo.

"I sent him home," said Granny.

A long sigh travelled over the company, like the first intimations of departure.

"Poor Brother Bethune. His memory has tried to serve him one time too many, look at him," said Aunt Nanny.

"He may last. May last another go-round. May not last," said Aunt Birdie. "Poor Brother Bethune. I'm a little inclined to pinch him."

"Wake him up and see if he knows who's got him!" said Aunt Nanny.

"No, Mr. Willy Trimble's just as sound asleep as he is. Tilted right together, look at the picture. Foreheads kissing like something could run right out of one head and into the other one."

"And wouldn't it surprise them both if it did!"

"Nathan, what're you fixing to do to start us home? Blow or pray?" Uncle Noah Webster called.

Uncle Nathan slowly walked out from behind Granny's chair, where she sat all motionless. He raised his right hand. Then his arm jerked aside. His nose darkened the center of his face.

"Uh-oh," said Aunt Cleo. "He's fixing to go."

"He's fixing to go, right now!" cried Brother Bethune, jumping out of his sleep and coming as if to pounce.

Miss Beulah was ahead of him. Running, she caught hold of her eldest brother under his arms and let his head tumble into her breast. She planted her feet and stood propping him up.

"Don't try to speak a word," she said between her teeth. "Now don't be foolish. I've got you."

He jerked back his head and jerked open his mouth longways at her, but no sound came out. Neither did he seem to draw breath. Presently he leaned forward again and coughed.

"Do I see blood on his shirt?" asked Aunt Lexie.

"A little bite of watermelon," said Miss Beulah fiercely. "Get back if you don't know the difference." Moving her hand like one feeling her way, Miss Beulah patted Uncle Nathan on his great head of springing, doglike hair. Presently he raised his head and looked at her, gray-faced.

"Now what came over you?" she asked calmly. "You be quiet like I said. Don't jabber."

"Well, what's *he* got to hide?" asked a voice.

"Sister Cleo, I don't know what in the world ever guides your tongue into asking the questions it does!" Miss Beulah cried. "By

**343**

now you ought to know this is a strict, law-abiding, God-fearing, close-knit family, and everybody in it has always struggled the best he knew how and we've all just tried to last as long as we can by sticking together."

Now Jack came up and put an arm around his uncle. "Every word Mama's saying is true, Uncle Nathan. You're back with us. You can feel comforted like I do." He looked into the old, dark-burned, age-stained face. "Some day, Uncle Nathan, I wish you'd tell it," he broke out. "What ever caused you to go off like that among strangers, and never stay still, and only let us see you at reunion time. You make me wonder tonight if what you had to do was as bad as aggravated battery."

"Whatever that is," said Miss Beulah in strong, prohibitive tones.

Uncle Nathan moved; he turned his shaggy head toward Jack and spoke. "Son, there's not but one bad thing either you or I or anybody else can do. And I already done it. That's kill a man. I killed Mr. Dearman with a stone to his head, and let 'em hang a sawmill nigger for it. After that, Jesus had to hold my hand."

"Now what did you want to tell that for?" said Miss Beulah shortly, her voice the only sound that was heard. "We could've got through one more reunion without that, couldn't we? Without you punishing yourself?"

But Uncle Nathan's face shone. It looked back at them like a dusty lantern lighted.

"Don't show us the stump! Don't show us that," came voices.

But he did. He took off his hand and showed them the stump. There was good moonlight to see it by, white and clean with its puckered stitching like a flour sack's.

"Is that the hand that did it?" asked Miss Lexie behind his back. "Didn't he ever tell it before, Beulah? Didn't anybody know besides just you, you and Granny?"

"Lexie Renfro, he told Miss Julia Mortimer. And she told him, and I heard her: 'Nathan, even when there's nothing left to hope for, you can start again from there, and go your way and *be good*.' He took her exactly at her word. He's seen the world. And I'm not so sure it was good for him," said Miss Beulah.

Brother Bethune with a shocked face asked Uncle Nathan, "Why didn't you break down and tell the preacher, if you sinned that bad?"

"The preacher was Grandpa," said Uncle Nathan. Then he stalked back and stood in his place again, behind Granny's chair.

"Did it for Sam Dale," said Granny. She turned her head around and looked Uncle Nathan in the face.

Judge Moody, his face fixed, had watched him in dead silence. Uncle Nathan now returned his look but it was a moment before he seemed to place the Judge.

"You're journeying to Alliance," he said then. "I left Alliance this morning and walked *here*. I believe in the old method of travelling."

Miss Beulah took a step back and asked in horror, "Did you try to pay her one of your breakfast-time visits this morning, dear? Miss Julia Mortimer?"

"Jesus Lord told me not to," he said.

"You see a good reason why I told you not to harp on Dearman, Mr. Renfro?" Miss Beulah broke out.

But Mr. Renfro in his chair gave no answer. The only sound coming out of his open mouth was like dry seed being poured between two buckets, back and forth.

"Never said Sam Dale was the father," said Granny. She gave a minute nod at Judge Moody. "Going to marry the girl, I said. Think Sam Dale was pulling her out of a pickle."

"Granny!" Miss Beulah ran to the old lady. She picked up a church fan and fanned her.

"Granny, you're playing with us now, ain't you? With your grandchildren and all? With the reunion that's gathered round to celebrate the day with you?" Uncle Curtis stood and asked her.

"Hush. She wouldn't play with us about Sam Dale," said Miss Beulah. "She's saying things the way they come back to her at their own sweet will. Maybe she's not right in step with the rest of us any longer—that's all."

"Think he's pulling her out of a pickle," said Granny.

"Granny, which would you rather? Keep Sam Dale perfect, or let him be a father after all?" Miss Beulah asked, her voice pleading.

"It's not a matter we can settle by which we'd rather," said Judge Moody down a long sigh. "You can't change what's happened by taking a voice vote on it."

Miss Beulah begged. "Granny, you can't have Sam Dale both ways."

"And carry him a generous slice of my cake," Granny ordered her.

"Hey, don't she know the difference yet? Who's alive and who's dead?" asked Aunt Cleo in a nurse's whisper.

"She knows we're all part of it together, or ought to be!" Miss Beulah cried, turning on her. "That's more than some other people appear to have found out."

"You could be anybody's," said Mrs. Moody to Gloria. "My husband was speaking truer than he knew."

Gloria turned toward Granny.

"Don't make an ell's worth of difference, does it? If you're not Sam Dale's," said Granny, waving her away.

Jack held his arms out. He clasped Gloria as she threw herself against him. "She's Mrs. J. J. Renfro, that's who she is," he told the reunion. "Grandpa married us in Damascus Church and she's my wife, for good and all. And that's the long and the short of it."

He turned with her and they walked the short way down the steps into the yard and sat on the old cedar log in the moonlight and began looking at each other.

"There was a time, some years back, when I didn't deplore her presence here." Granny was speaking. "Mr. Vaughn is so much given to going out of sight to do his praying before we blow out the lamp. And she and I could set and catch our breath when the day's over, and confab a little about the state the world was in. She picked up a good deal from me."

"Who's that? Miss Julia Mortimer for the last time, Granny?" asked Aunt Birdie.

"Too bad she wasn't able to put two and two together," Granny said. "Like I did."

"But all that happened a mighty long time ago," Aunt Birdie objected during the hush that followed.

"You forget feelings, Birdie! Feelings don't get old!" Aunt Beck said, with all the night's agitation. "We do, but they don't. They go on."

In her soft yellow lamplight, Granny smiled, showing her teeth like a spoonful of honeycomb. "She was young herself once. And if she was, I was. Put that in your pipe and smoke it."

Uncle Nathan stepped down from them and went to his pack, which was still under the tree where he had dropped it. Groping in it, he brought up his cornet and readied it.

"Play 'Poor Wayfaring Stranger'!" came a call.

"Play 'Sweet and Low' for me!"

When they all stopped asking, he played them "Let the Lower Lights Be Burning." He needed nothing but his good left hand.

"Makes the hair of my skin stand on end. Like I was pulling okra," said Aunt Nanny. "To hear him reach with his horn like that."

"That's right, that's the way. Blow 'er over Jordan, Nathan," called Uncle Noah Webster. "Blow Miss Julia Mortimer over Jordan."

Uncle Nathan held the last note. He held it till none of them listening had any breath of their own left—then he ceased. Miss Beulah looked at Granny. So did they all. Though the hills were ringing still, Granny nodded in her chair.

Miss Beulah drew the lamp away from her face. One bit of brightness still gleamed about her—the silver wire of Grandpa's spectacles she had put away in her lap. There behind her, spread over her chair and ready to cloak her, was "The Delectable Mountains," known to be green and red and covered with its ninety-and-nine white sheep, but now a piece and puzzle of the dark.

❧

Jack and Gloria sat side by side on the old cedar log, close together, their backs to the crowd. Around them, though they appeared not to know it, the girl cousins as if with one accord began stirring about, cleaning up after the day. They cleared off the tables, carried platters and watermelon plates and cloths back to the kitchen or the back porch. The cake of ice had disappeared, the lemonade tub had nothing left but hanging crusts of sugar and a pavement of seeds. From the complaint they made, there had been little left to feed the company dogs. The cows were calling, taking turns.

Presently Uncle Nathan passed close by the porch, going down into the yard carrying upright a hoe with rags draped about the blade in a sort of helmet. There was a cutting smell of coal oil where he walked. After a moment, a red torch shot up fire, moved; then an

oval, cottony glow, like utterly soft sound, appeared in the dark—
how close, how far, how high up or low down, was not easy for the
eye to make sure. Then it went out, and appeared almost at once in a
new place.

"We've lost him, I know, to the Book of Revelation," said Miss
Beulah. "But once a year I feel like he still belongs to us. Right now,
he's burning the caterpillar nets to finish up the day for the children."

Their eyes as they watched all reflected the fiery nests in dancing points.

"And at the same time, it's a hundred thousand bad little worms
that's curled up and turned black for every touch he gives," said
Aunt Birdie. "You can be thankful for that much deliverance."

Uncle Nathan carried his torch past Jack and Gloria as though
he didn't see them. Neither did Jack and Gloria seem to know he
went by. They sat without moving, kissing each other.

"Mr. Renfro, do you dream at all of what's coming next?"
cried Miss Beulah.

He didn't move. Only, while they looked, the wilted snippet of
traveller's joy slid out of his shirt pocket and dropped to the floor.

Granny, the moment she was touched, put up her head warily.

"The joining-of-hands!" Miss Beulah at her side put out the
cry. "Everybody stand! It's time for the joining-of-hands!" She
threw out her arms. "Where's Jack? Sometimes just making your
circle will bring him in. Stand up, catch Granny, don't let her fall
now! Pull up Brother Bethune before he's slipped clear down out of
reach! Stand up! Judge Moody, stoop a little, catch hold of Elvie's
hand. Mrs. Judge, I've got you." She shook Mr. Renfro and got a
cry out of him. "Drag Nathan in where he belongs!" came her
urgent voice. "Now, are we a circle?"

By now the chairs were pushed back out of the way and as
many of the reunion as could worked themselves into a circle in the
expanded space of the porch. The rest of them carried the circle
down the steps and along the flower rows and around from tree to
tree, taking in the well-piece and the log seat and the althea bush
and the post with the Wayfarer's Bell on it, encompassing the tables
and the bois d'arc tree.

"Are we a circle?" cried Miss Beulah again, and she struck off
the note.

Then they had the singing of "Blest Be the Tie." There was
only one really mournful voice—Judge Moody's.

"And will you give us the benediction, Brother Bethune?" cried Miss Beulah. "Are you fully awake?"

For a moment Brother Bethune tottered, but Vaughn caught him and held him by the waist to steady him. His arm shot into the air and his voice exploded: "God go with us all!"

"Amen," said the voices around the circle.

"Now," said Miss Beulah warningly, "would anybody care for a further bite before starting on their road?"

"I couldn't get another bite in me if you was to stand before me with gun loaded, Beulah," Uncle Dolphus said, leading a chorus of No's.

Uncle Noah Webster and Uncle Dolphus gave a brotherly shout together. Unregarded, a flower had opened on the shadowy maze of the cactus there on the porch with them.

"Well, I reckon that's what you've all been waiting for," said Miss Beulah.

"We scared it into blooming after all," said Aunt Birdie, sashaying towards its tub. Little groups in turn looked down in a ring at the spectacle, the deep white flower, a star inside a star, that almost seemed to return their gaze, like a member of the reunion who didn't invariably come when called. The fragrance, Aunt Beck said, was ahead of the tuberose.

Only Granny sat and stared rigidly before her.

"Leave her alone," said Uncle Curtis.

"Granny's almost a hundred," whispered Uncle Percy, trying to tiptoe going by her.

"Granny heard the Battle of Iuka. Heard the volleys," said Uncle Dolphus, circling around.

"Talked back to General Grant. Remembers the conversation," said Aunt Beck, pausing at the still chair.

"Mrs. Moody thinks she wants to say something," Miss Beulah said.

"You've produced a night-blooming cereus!" repeated Mrs. Moody. "I haven't seen one of those in years."

"Yes'm, whatever in the nation you called it, it bloomed," said Miss Beulah. "Even if it never does us the favor again."

"Wait on it a little longer and there'll be another one," said Uncle Noah Webster. "I love 'em when they smell sweet."

"And not a drop of precious water did I ever spare it," said Miss Beulah. "I reckon it must have thrived on going famished."

Not a groan but a long expenditure of breath was heard.

"I think Judge Moody had best be excused to bed," said Miss Beulah to Mrs. Moody, and she took one of the lamps and started inside. "That man's ready to drop."

Uncle Homer threw out an arm to keep Judge Moody from passing. "Oh, we're going to tend to that road better—wait till I get to be supervisor," he said. "Roads—mosquitoes—our many cemeteries—mad dogs—floods—I'll get my hands on all of 'em. Some day we'll even do something about that bridge. Though no use us fixing our end any better till they fix theirs!"

"Oscar, just beat your way around him," said Mrs. Moody, as she herself went stepping over the sleeping twins who lay entwined on the threshold of the passage, their twin pea-shooters pressing crosses into their naked chests.

"Here's the company room—be careful how you step," Miss Beulah's voice came from inside. "And don't bump your head. The only thing I still haven't offered you is my nightgown—could I help you to it through the door? It's fresh and it's cool—I starched it this morning—and the only one to my name. It's going on eleven years old."

"You didn't suppose I would *undress,* did you?" exclaimed Mrs. Moody's voice.

"Do you want to let Judge Moody tell you goodnight, Granny? He's bowing to you," said Mr. Renfro at the old lady's chair. "You remember Judge Moody."

"Thought I sent him to Coventry," Granny said.

Judge Moody slipped around her and followed his wife inside. His voice came out saying, "But if that's to be our bed, I'd like this one last baby carried away from it." When Miss Beulah returned to the porch she was holding her—it was Lady May, still dressed, and sound asleep. Gloria took her and carried her to a shadowy corner, out of the glare of the moonlight, and sat down with her, to watch the reunion go.

Mr. Willy Trimble came up to Granny. "Then keep a close watch on this young lady, folks," he said, putting his long, joker's face down beside Granny's unblinking one. "If she starts to cutting up and you-all don't want her, send for me and I'll come back after her and have her for mine."

All at once, and at the very end of her day, Granny decided to take off her hat. Elvie received it from her—it sank heavy as a setting hen in her small arms. She ran into the house with it, blowing on it, as though in its dust lived a spark.

Granny was staying.

"Now I got far to go. And no mule. And Willy Trimble has whispered in my ear I still got to turn around and get me back to the cemetery in the morning," said Brother Bethune. "I'm just good enough to get her into the ground," he said, after he'd found his gun. "She's still being a schoolteacher about it, up in Heaven. I'm the one she couldn't bring to school."

"Now you're paying for it," said Aunt Birdie.

"She tried. But she just couldn't lure me inside the schoolhouse," Brother Bethune went on. "I went right along with my daddy where he's going and helped him preach. Sung the duets with him, standing on a chair. It was an outdoor life, and I don't see nothing wrong with it *yet*."

"All right. You gave us as good today as you knew how," Miss Beulah cried at him. "You can go if you want to."

"And I'll tell you what you can give me for coming. The surprise of a nice nanny goat tied to my front porch one moonlight night," Brother Bethune replied.

"Granny, when it comes around to your next birthday, do you want to invite Brother Bethune and give him another chance?" asked Miss Beulah.

"See him in Tophet first," said Granny.

"Granny's going to be my next girl," said Mr. Willy. "I lost me one girl this morning, but I believe I already found me another'n."

"Willy Trimble, if you come a step closer—!" cried Miss Beulah. "Didn't you feel your foot stepped on in 'Blest Be the Tie'?"

"And take that jade of yours off somewhere and leave her," Granny told him in dismissal. "She's been cropping my flowers."

Brother Bethune elected to keep Mr. Willy Trimble company. They rode off together with the gun pointing up like a mast on the wagon seat between them.

"And where do you think *you're* going?" Granny asked inside a circle of her grandsons. They bent above her, squatted before her, patted her knee, took her by the hand, tried to kiss her face.

"Are you trying to tell me you're leaving me too?" she asked.

"Granny, there's stock at home waiting to be fed, and bawling, no doubt," Uncle Curtis said gently.

"Then what are you running off for?" asked the old lady.

The great-grandchildren were already loading up the wagons and finally mended cars. "Love you a bushel and a peck, Granny. Many happy returns!" One by one her great-grandchildren began putting kisses on Granny's face. They walked off from her carrying their own children stretched out in their arms, or hauled up over their shoulders, arms and legs dangling, little girls' hair streaming silver. Children that had barely waked up carried children still asleep. The whistled-up dogs flowed at their heels.

"Who're you trying to get away from?" asked Granny. "Come back here."

"Go if you must, but you can't get away without these!" Miss Beulah shrieked.

At some moment during the day she had found time to run out and cut the remainder of her own flowers against their departure. She was ready to load everybody home. Here was the duplication of what they'd come bringing here—milk-and-wine lilies, zinnias, phlox, tuberoses.

"Who's running off with my posies?" asked Granny.

Now the uncles were shaking hands with each other and with Mr. Renfro, then Jack.

"Well, we brought you, Jack. We brought you back home," said Uncle Curtis.

"And my wife and I are much obliged to one and all," said Jack.

"I should say on the whole, Jack, we let you back in the ranks of the family pretty easy today. Didn't make it too hard on you," said Uncle Dolphus.

"If only he didn't have in-the-morning to go through with!" cried Aunt Birdie.

"He's young!" said Aunt Beck.

"Stay," Granny said.

"And little-old Gloria! We made you really and truly one of us today," said Aunt Birdie, kissing her good-bye. "You can always be grateful. and show it as well as you can."

"You're one of the family now, Gloria, tried and true. Do you know what that means? Never mind! You're just an old married woman, same as the rest of us now. So you don't have to answer to the outside any longer," Aunt Beck said, putting an arm around her.

"Just put that dress away more careful when you take it off tonight. They can bury you in it, child," said Aunt Birdie. "Put yours away like I did."

"If it'd been my dress, it'd stayed deep down in its trunk today! If I'd get my wedding dress out and try wearing it again in front of this crowd, I'd expect you all to fall into a hard fit of laughing," said Miss Beulah, trying to persuade Aunt Nanny down the steps.

"I'll tell you something," said Aunt Nanny with what looked like pride. "If my wedding dress could talk, I'd burn it."

"Reckon Lady May's got just one little word? One little word to say about it all before we go?" Aunt Birdie cried into the oblivious face.

"Nothing ever wakes her but the sun coming up and feeling the fresh pangs of hunger," said Gloria.

"I never said I wanted you to go," Granny said.

"Here's one that's staying till tomorrow," said Miss Lexie. "Because I want to see the behavior. I'd like to see 'em finish what they started today."

"And because starting with tonight you got nowhere to go," said Miss Beulah. "Unless you happen to worship sleeping between Ella Fay and Etoyle."

Miss Beulah stood accepting their thanks. "Fay, I was crazy about you at one time," she told her. "Because you weren't Lexie. And look what's happened to you. You're Homer's wife." They put their tired arms around each other.

"Miss, you must wear stockings on your arms when you work in the field," said Aunt Cleo, pinching Ella Fay's shoulder. "Or they'd never be white in the moonlight like that."

"That's one secret you guessed, Aunt Cleo," said Etoyle.

"How old is Ella Fay getting to be?"

"She'll be seventeen on Groundhog Day next year," said Miss Beulah.

"Why's she hanging back?"

"Now from what? I thought you were on your way!" cried Miss Beulah.

"Sister Beulah, let me inquire, have you ever been into the deep subject with Ella Fay?" Aunt Cleo kept on.

"Listen, will you tell us good-bye and crank up?"

"Truly I mean it. You've got a growing girl on your hands."

"I'd as soon start worrying over Vaughn!" said Miss Beulah violently.

"Her *feet* are growing," said Mr. Renfro.

"My mama never went into the deep subject with me. And you know what? I've always felt a little sorry for myself," remarked Auntie Fay, waiting now up inside the chicken van.

"But I haven't been told what the commotion is all about," said Granny. "What the headlong rush is for."

"Bless your heart, Granny Vaughn! Good-bye, good-bye, Jack! Brought you home by all of us working together, didn't we? Good-bye, Beulah, sweet dreams, Mr. Renfro. Ain't you growing faster than ever, Ella Fay?" Uncle Homer was hugging the Renfro girls. "I swear, Ella Fay, I wouldn't be surprised if we couldn't find a way when Tuesday dawns to let you vote."

"Hush up! She don't even want to," said Miss Beulah. "My children have learned to wait for everything till it's the right time for them to have it. Wish somebody'd taken the time and trouble to teach a few of their elders that lesson."

"Jack'll go on working the rest of his life to pay for that roof," said Uncle Noah Webster with a mighty slap of congratulation on Mr. Renfro's back. "You've got an acre of tin up there. It'll take it all the rest of the night to cool off." He gave Jack a fierce smile and wrung his hand as if he couldn't stop. Then he smacked Gloria's cheek with a last big kiss that smelled of watermelon. "Gloria, this has been a story on us all that never will be allowed to be forgotten," he said. "Long after you're an old lady without much further stretch to go, sitting back in the same rocking chair Granny's got her little self in now, you'll be hearing it told to Lady May and all her hovering brood. How we brought Jack Renfro back safe from the pen! How you contrived to send a court judge up Banner Top and caused him to sit at our table and pass a night with the family, wife along with him. The story of Jack making it home through thick and thin and into Granny's arms for her biggest and last celebration—for so I have a notion it is. Eh, Nathan?" He raised his arm high to salute the oldest brother. "I call this a reunion to remember, all!" he called through the clamoring goodnights. "Do you hear me, blessed sweethearts?" He swung over to Granny's chair and folded his arms around her, not letting her go, begging for a kiss, not getting it.

"Benedict Arnold," she whispered. Then as Aunt Cleo came to pull him away, Granny spoke to her too, and said, "But I'll give you a pretty not to take him."

"Remember, there's a South Mississippi too!" Uncle Noah Webster called when they were both up inside the cranked car. "It ain't all that far on a pretty day!" He leaned out and looked back at them while he drove away. They could see the gleam of his home-sick smile beneath the crossed-pistols mustache.

"Now we know that nothing in the world can change Noah Webster," said Miss Beulah. "Even the one he's picked."

"Oh, Grandpa Vaughn, if only you'd lived to see!" Aunt Birdie said, hugging Jack. "Jack, listen, when you went to the pen, it's just about what carried Grandpa off, precious!"

"Mr. Vaughn never knows when it's bedtime. Have to go out there with a lantern and prod him again," Granny said.

"Listen. Thunder," said Aunt Beck. "Did I hear distant thunder?"

"I don't believe it," said Uncle Dolphus bluntly. "By now I'm not ready to be fooled by any more of folks' imagination. It ain't ever going to rain." He shook hands with Mr. Renfro. "But your hay's just aching to be cut. You're about to realize you one crop in spite of yourself, Mr. Renfro." The horn of the pickup was bleating out there; all the children were packed back inside. He hugged Miss Beulah and bent to say goodnight to his grandmother.

"Now I once thought I had a *big* family," said Granny. "What's happening to 'em?"

"Come see us!" came calls as the pickup started off on its freshly patched tire to Harmony. "Come before Old Man Winter's broke loose and we all have to try to keep from going out of sight in mud!"

"Shame on ye. *Shame* on ye," said Granny, as their dust began to rise.

"I've still got a craving under my breastbone for a little more of that chicken pie, Beck," Aunt Nanny said as they parted.

"You'll have to wait for next year."

"Then good-bye, good-bye! Good-bye, Jack boy—kiss that baby for me. Good-bye, Beulah, and sweet dreams, Judge Moody in there! I'm too tired out from laughing to climb up in my car and go home. Help me, Jack," Aunt Nanny gasped.

"All I need to do is start," said Uncle Percy, holding up his new twelve-link chain he'd whittled. Then in their cloud of ghostly dust they were gone.

"Remember to look on Banner Top when you get to the road!" called Etoyle, running after them, waving. "If you want to see what'll keep you laughing all the way to Peerless!"

**355**

"Granny will be all right in the morning," said Aunt Beck, putting her arms around Miss Beulah. "When she thinks back on today she'll wish she could have it to live all over again." She smiled on Gloria. "And you don't want to be another one any longer, not another schoolteacher, do you, Gloria? And change the world?"

"No ma'am, just my husband. I still believe I can do it, if I live long enough," Gloria said.

Uncle Curtis hugged Granny without words. She kissed him— then saw him leave her anyway.

"I don't know who I've thought about more times today than I have Grandpa. Blessed Grandpa!" said Aunt Beck, softly patting Granny's cheek, then tiptoeing away.

"Don't listen to him," said Granny. "Listen to me."

She watched the old Chevrolet hauler, loaded with so many people that it was almost dragging the ground, go down into the dust, the last one.

"Parcel of thieves! They'd take your last row of pins. They'd steal your life, if they knew how," Granny said.

"Granny, don't you know who dearly loves you?" Miss Beulah asked, clasping her. "Don't you remember the hundred that's been with you all day? Giving you pretties, striving to please you—"

"Thieves all," said Granny.

Uncle Nathan kissed Granny on the forehead, the little vein throbbing there. He was to sleep outdoors under his tent. He declared he preferred it.

"But I don't want to lose ye," said Granny after him into the night.

After Uncle Nathan had gone, only Miss Lexie was left of all the day's company.

"Would you stay with me, please?" Granny asked Miss Lexie. "My children have deserted me."

But Miss Lexie seemed not to hear, staring at the old cactus where another and still another bloom drifted white upon the dark. "Yes, and those'll look like wrung chickens' necks in the morning," she said. "No thank you." She went inside.

"Now, many happy returns of the day, Granny Vaughn," said Mr. Renfro, bending to her cheek, but she only let his kiss touch her little withering ear.

"Suppose something had happened to me while you gapped," she said, and he bowed his way inside.

When nothing of them was left out there but their dust behind them, Granny still summoned them. "Thieves, murderers, come back," she begged. "Don't leave me!" Her voice cracked.

Jack knelt at the foot of the rocker and looked up at her face. Presently her head was brought down. Then she saw he was there. For a little while she gazed at him.

"They told me," she said, her voice barely strong enough to reach him, "you'd gone a long time ago. Clean away. But I didn't believe their words. I sat here like you see me—I waited. A whole day is a long wait. You've found Granny just where you left her. You sneaked back when nobody's looking, forged your way around 'em. That's a good boy."

Jack held still under her eyes. Nobody made a sound except Lady May in her mother's arms, who sent up a short murmur out of her dream.

Granny lifted both her little trembling hands out of her lap and took something out of her bosom. She held it before her, cupped in her hands, then carried it toward him. Her face was filled with intent that puckered it like grief, but her moving hands denied grief. Then, in the act of bending toward him, she forgot it all. Her hands broke apart to struggle toward his face, to take and hold his face there in front of her. It was the little silver snuffbox that Captain Jordan in his lifetime had come by, that had been Granny's to keep for as long as anybody could remember, that rolled across the floor and down into the folds of the cannas.

Jack let her trembling fingers make sure they'd found him, move over his forehead, down his nose, across his lips, up his cheek, along the ridge of his brow, let them trace every hill and valley, let them wander. He still had not blinked once when her fingers seemed to forget the round boundaries belonging to flesh and stretched over empty air.

Jack rose and put his arms around her. Miss Beulah said, "It's her bed she wants!" and swung up the lamp and led the way. Jack lifted the old lady to her feet, she gasped, and then he picked her up in his arms. He carried her, her bare head drooped quiet against his chest, down the passage to where Miss Beulah waited holding the lamp at the open door.

*357*

Later, an arm stretched out of the dark of the passage with some starched gowns and folded mosquito netting laid over a load of quilt.

"Thank you, Mama," said Jack, receiving it.

Gloria sat in Granny's rocker and undressed the sleeping baby. She raised the little arms one at a time and pulled her out of her sleeves. She shucked her out of her petticoat and little drawers and lifted her by her two feet and changed her.

"She's a sweet, trustful little thing. I believe altogether she enjoyed this day more than anybody," Jack said, gazing.

"Do you know what? You fell in love with this baby," Gloria told him. "I watched you do it."

"What a little hugger! And I believe she's going to be smart too."

"She's our future, Jack. I wish you'd look at your baby's bites! Her whole little body's given over," Gloria said. "She looks like she's been embroidered in French knots. Those are what she got going through it all with her daddy." She popped the baby's night-gown over her head. When the little cockscomb came out at the top, Jack laughed.

"I see her new tooth in her little objecting mouth," he said, and then kissed the baby good-night.

Gloria rose and stilled the rocker till it stood like a throne and laid the baby down in it. She opened out the length of mosquito netting and with one fling spread it over Lady May, chair, and all.

Then she took first turn undressing in the dark passage and putting on her gown, and while Jack did the same she ran on quick bare feet to the quilt, flung it wide, and spread it on the floor. Dropping to her knees she patted it perfectly free of wrinkles. It was ready by the time Jack in his gown came running out, catching all the moonlight down his front, and before she could get her hand over his mouth he had given his holler.

The pallet seemed thinner than paper, and was already the warmth of the floor underneath. Long since faded, blanched again tonight by moonlight, it showed a pattern as faint as one laid by wind over a field of broomsedge. It was the quilt that had baked on the line all day, and its old winter cleanness mixed with today's dust penetrated their very skins with a smell strong as medicine. There was no pillow to spare for this bed, no up and down to it.

A female voice, superfine, carrying but thin as a moonbeam, strung itself out into the night: "Ay-ay-ay-cock!"

"I can't help thinking about my luck," said Jack in a hoarse whisper. "I'm a married man and Aycock ain't. And suppose I was in his place!"

"Don't let it go to your head," Gloria said and laid her palm there. His forehead was as burning as Lady May's, and under the bridge of her hand his eyes shone unevenly moonlit.

"Gloria, we won our day," said Jack.

There was a secret sound, something that rasped on the ear over and over like the chirp of a late cricket. In the company room, Judge Moody was winding his watch.

"We've still got in-the-morning, Jack. The Moodys are in our bed," Gloria reminded him in a whisper.

"They've beat us to that," he said. "They got there first."

"Your school diploma is nailed up over their heads. It's all we've got, because our wedding license is burned up along with the rest of the courthouse."

"Our courthouse caught afire?" he exclaimed. "Why wasn't I home! I'd helped 'em put it out."

"My son in the pen," Miss Beulah's voice said, travelling up the passage from the dark bedroom. "My son had to go to the pen."

Jack's head rolled away from Gloria's. "Mama must've been up and at it today for 'most as long as I have," he said presently. "She's bone tired."

"She'll forget what she's saying to your daddy," Gloria promised him. "She's old. She'll soon be asleep, just like he will."

"I wish I could do something for the boy," Mr. Renfro's voice said.

"Not something foolish," said Miss Beulah's.

"I'd do anything in the world to help that boy and his pride," came Mr. Renfro's voice.

"That didn't keep you from putting-out for Judge Moody," said Miss Beulah's.

"I took a shine to the fellow, you're right. I couldn't tell you why," Mr. Renfro's voice agreed. "I just did, that's all. If he'd stay a week, I'd take him turkey-hunting."

"And call it helping Jack?"

"I'd like to help 'em both out, Mother. If I was a little younger, I believe I could help both of 'em at the same time."

"I tried getting home before today," Jack whispered, head still turned to the outdoors. "Don't let on to Mama, to make her feel worse. The day I got there, I started trying finding a way. When I heard about our baby, I went out stooping, went through a watermelon field. Stooping—like I was thumping melons from row to row to find us boys a good one. At the last minute I stooped low out of there, but they knew that trick. Don't tell Mama how easy they caught me—it would break her heart. I put in all my time and every bit of my thinking on the subject. I tried for the reunion last year. They caught me."

"I don't see how they charged all that up to good behavior," Gloria whispered.

"Today was my last chance of making my escape. I took it. One more day, and I'd had to let 'em discharge me."

"Of course the boy didn't do what Nathan did," said Mr. Renfro's voice.

"I've got it to stand and I've got to stand it. And you've got to stand it," said Miss Beulah's voice. "After they've all gone home, Ralph, and the children's in bed, that's what's left. Standing it."

Jack turned to Gloria.

"Say now you'll love 'em a little bit. Say you'll love them too. You can. Try and you can." He stroked her. "Wouldn't you like to keep Mama company in the kitchen while I'm ploughing or fence-mending, give her somebody she can talk to? And encourage Ella Fay to blossom out of being timid, and talk Elvie out of her crying and wanting to grow up and be a teacher? You can give Etoyle lady-like examples of behavior. And on bad winter evenings, there's Vaughn. All you need to do with him is answer his questions. Honey, won't you change your mind about my family?"

"Not for all the tea in China," she declared.

"Once it's winter, Papa just wants to put up his foot and see pictures in the fire. You could crack his pecans for him, perched there on the hearth. And there's precious little Granny—I asked her when I told her good-night if *she* wouldn't love *you* and she said she would, she nodded."

"You're so believing and blind," Gloria said. "About *all* of 'em—they don't even have to be girls."

"The whole reunion couldn't help but love you—the prettiest

one of 'em and still looking just like a bride."

"They didn't hesitate to wash my face in their sticky watermelon juice!"

"Poor face," he said tenderly, drawing his hand down her cheek, turning her face to his.

"What they said was we'd been too loving before we got married!"

"And if we hadn't, I'd like 'em to tell me when we'd had another chance at it!" he burst out.

"They tried making me your cousin, and almost did."

"Be my cousin," he begged. "I want you for my cousin. My wife, and my children's mother, and my cousin and everything."

"Jack, I'll be your wife with all my heart, and that's enough for anybody, even you. I'm here to be nobody but myself, Mrs. Gloria Renfro, and have nothing to do with the old dead past. And don't ever try to change me," she cautioned him.

"I know this much: I don't aim to get lonesome no more. Once you do, it's too easy to stay that way," said Jack.

"I'll keep you from it," she vowed.

"And you'd better."

"Jack, the way I love you, I have to hate everybody else."

"Possum!" he said. "I ain't asking you to deprive others."

"I want to."

"Spare 'em a little bit of something else," he pleaded.

"Maybe I'll learn after a long time to pity 'em instead."

"They'll take it a good deal harder!" he cried.

She drew still closer to him.

"Don't pity anybody you could love," whispered Jack.

"I can think of one I can safely pity."

"Uncle Nathan? Love him."

"Miss Julia."

"I know she hated to breathe her last," he said slowly. "As much as you and me would." He took her hand.

"Are you trying to say you could do better than pity her?" Gloria asked him. "You never laid eyes on her."

"I reckon I even love her," said Jack. "I heard her story."

"She stands for all I gave up to marry you. I'd give her up again tonight. And give up all your family too," she whispered, and felt him quiver.

"Don't give anybody up." He stroked her. "Or leave anybody out. Me and you both left her out today, and I'm ashamed for us."

"There just wasn't room in today for it," she said. "Or for feeling ashamed either."

He said. "There's room for everything, and time for everybody, if you take your day the way it comes along and try not to be much later than you can help. We could go yet, and be back by milking time. There's still the same good reason."

She put her mouth quickly on his, and then she slid in her hand and seized hold of him right at the root. And so she convinced him that there is only one way of depriving the ones you love—taking your living presence away from theirs; that no one alive has ever deserved such punishment, although maybe the dead do; and that no one alive can ever in honor forgive that wrong, which outshines shame, and is not to be forgiven until it has been righted.

◆§

Moonlight the thickness of china was lying over the world now. The Renfro wagon stood all alone where the school bus used to stand, muleless, empty, its spoked iron wheels clear-cut as the empty pods of fallen flowers. The shadows of the trees stretched downhill, lengthened as if for flight.

"You'll never get away from me again," Gloria whispered, "Not in your wildest dreams."

She reached for Jack's hand. It was hot as the day, with calluses like embedded rocks. It was fragrant of sweat, car grease, peach pickle, chicken, yellow soap, and her own hair. But it was dead weight, with fingers hanging limp as the strands of wilted weed that dangled through the crack in Mr. Willy Trimble's wagon. She stroked his lips and they moved at her touch and opened. He let out a snore. Everything love had sworn and done seemed to be already gone from him. Even its memory was a measure away from him and from her too, as apart as the cereus back there in its tub, that was itself almost a stranger now, having lifted those white trumpets.

◆§

Vaughn thought the house was asleep, but for a little distance as he rode away he listened behind him—he might still hear his name called after him. For a year and a half it had been "Vaughn! Vaughn!" every minute, though it would turn before he knew it back into "Jack!" again.

Or would it? Had today been all brave show, and had Jack all in secret fallen down—taking the whole day to fall, but falling, like that star he saw now, going out of sight like the scut of a rabbit? Could Jack take a fall from highest place and nobody be man enough to say so? Was falling a secret, another part of people's getting tangled up with each other, another danger to walk up on without warning—like finding them lying deep in the woods together, like one creature, some kind of cricket hatching out of the ground, big enough to eat him or to rasp at him and drive him away? The world had been dosed with moonlight, it might have been poured from a bottle. Riding through the world, the little boy, moonlit, wondered.

Grandpa Vaughn's hat came down low and made his ears stick out like funnels. Over and under the tired stepping of Bet, he could hear the night throb. He heard every sound going on, repeating itself, increasing, as if it were being recollected by loud night talking to itself. At times it might have been the rush of water—the Bywy on the rise in spring; or it might have been the rains catching up after them, to mire them in. Or it might have been that the whole wheel of the sky made the sound as it kept letting fall the soft fire of its turning. As long as he listened, sound prevailed. No matter how good at hollering back a boy might grow up to be, hollering back would never make the wheel stop. And he could never out-ride it. As he plodded on through the racket, it rang behind him and was ahead of him too. It was all-present enough to spill over into voices, as everything, he was ready to believe now, threatened to do, the closer he might come to where something might happen. The night might turn into more and more voices, all telling it—bragging, lying, singing, pretending, protesting, swearing everything into being, swearing everything away—but telling it. Even after people gave up each other's company, said good-bye and went home, if there was only one left, Vaughn Renfro, the world around him was still one huge, soul-defying reunion.

Bet twitched her ears when he rode her out into Banner Road. In the moonlight the car on Banner Top looked like a big, shadowy box mysteriously deposited there at the foot of the tree, not to be opened till morning. For a moment, he thought he heard somebody up there, moving. He thought he saw men flitting in the moonlight, like bats—he thought he could see the ears of Ears Broadwee.

He could have shouted when he saw the school bus again, peacefully stranded in the ditch.

He trotted downhill to it, reined in. He slid from Bet's back. Then with the chain he'd brought he hitched her to the bus, took her around the neck, and led her; and without the slightest fuss about it, there in the moonlight the bus creaked once, rose out of its berth, and surfaced to the road.

"Without Jack, nothing would be no trouble at all." Vaughn spoke it out. He laid his hand on the radiator, with its armor of moonlit scorch and rust, warm as a stove in which the fire has been banked all day. He carried well water to it in Grandpa's hat. Climbing in through the still-open door, he took the steering wheel. It was warm and sticky as his own hands. He coasted the bus the rest of the way down the first hill, and before it reached the bottom up came a froglike chirping, then a sound like a slide of gravel, then bang, bang, bang—the engine was running for Vaughn just as any engine in the world ought to do.

If it would be morning now! He thought of tomorrow with such sharp pain that he might have just been asked to give it up. He so loved Banner School that he would have beaten sunup and driven there now, if the doors had had any way of opening for him.

Gritting his teeth, he backed the bus up again, far enough to turn in at his own road, accomplishing the drop and hurdle of the ditch.

The row of bois d'arc trees that lined the home road stirred like birds in their feathers in the moonlight. Some of the trunks were four or five trunks sprouted from one old stump, fused now into one, like a rope swollen barrel-thick. Where the big split stump was like two bears dancing, he turned off to the best hiding place he knew. A little way off from the truck, pale oaks hid the moon; heads of stars like elderberry bloom filled the space between the trees. He cut off the engine. Very loud and close he heard:

"Who cooks for you?
Who cooks for me?
AHA HA HA HA HA HA HA!"

He saw the owl sitting in a dead sycamore that had become a wreath of moonlight.

Biting mosquitoes were everywhere; he plucked them from his breast like thorns. But he kept one hand on the steering wheel. The bus, as long as he held the wheel, held him all around, and at the same time he could feel that bus on its own wheels rolling on his tongue, like a word of his own ready to be spoken, then swallowed back into his throat, going down, inside and inside. And at the same time, the sky that he could see went on performing—more stars fell, like a breaking chain.

Before he left the bus here, ready and secret till morning, he made sure of the book he had been sitting on, the new geography that he'd traded out of Curly Stovall. He dragged it to his cheek, where he could smell its print, sharper, blacker, dearer than the smell of new shoes.

Then he got on Bet when she caught up with him and rode her on home. He rode Bet to the barn and attended to her, and rounded the house for the water bucket.

Down past the empty tables, he saw the Wayfarer's Bell against the stars, elevated and gathered into itself. It was just as ever, but nobody was lost any more. Might it give sound of its own accord on some night like this? It was the one voice that hadn't spoken. Vaughn's heart quailed. The Wayfarer's Bell would not speak in silver like the rest of the night. It was iron, with an iron tongue, and it would say "Iron"—and go on saying it, go reaching with it all over the world. Though no one was lost any more, there could be no bell that does not say "I will ring again."

Uncle Nathan's tent was under the pecan tree like a pair of big black-spread wings that had dipped near to the ground to hover there all night. Among all who slept here slept one who had killed a man. But he might not be asleep. Perhaps Uncle Nathan never slept.

Vaughn went to the water bucket, and the dipper rattled in it—it was empty. He climbed the steps, and there lay Jack and Gloria asleep on the porch, in his way. They were lying one behind the other in running positions. Though they lay perfectly still, they looked like race runners all the same. Jack's head was thrown back, but Gloria was in front. He had never before seen her barefooted, much less asleep—now he saw her blistered heels. The moonlight lay on her back-flung hair like ashes over coals. He stepped over Jack and waded through the moonlight around her forward, unshielded arm. Had she still counted as a teacher, had she not married Jack, it would have said in her voice: "I am not asleep." He could smell their sweat—it went against his face as would the moist palm of a hand. Then he saw—the smell must be coming from the flowers. They looked like big clods of the moonlight freshly turned up from this night—almost phosphorescent. All of him shied, as if a harness had bloomed.

Veering, he almost collided with the baby. He had forgotten there was a baby. She was lying up over the sleepers in the hide seat of Granny's rocker, with something gauzy wrapped around her, as though she'd been in that spokey cart clear to the moon and back.

He got by her, and his shirt-tail brushed the spokes of Granny's spinning wheel, which by daylight's gloom stood like a part of the wall but was now lit up. It softly struck like a clock. He tiptoed into the now moonlit passage. A nail nailing its shadow to a high board was where Uncle Noah Webster's banjo always hung before he went to live with Aunt Cleo. There the loom stood, open to the night like the never-closed-in passage itself. The moon picked out its spider web. It looked as tall as Banner bridge, and better made, stretching from the old loom to the ceiling of the passage. His mother's broom tore it down every morning, it was back new every night.

But here, with people on every side and behind every door, no more voices came—only knocks, night-sounds. Even from the heart of the house no sound came now except the beat, beat that was given off by the swifts in the chimney, where they stirred and shifted, a hundred deep or more.

Then all of a sudden there came through the passage a current of air. A door swung open in Vaughn's face and there was Granny, tiny in her bed in full lamplight. For a moment the black bearskin on the floor by the bed shone red-haired, live enough to spring at him. After the moonlight and the outdoors, the room was as yellow and close as if he and Granny were embedded together in a bar of yellow soap.

"Take off your hat," Granny's mouth said. "And climb in wi' me."

He fled out of her dazzled sight. "She didn't know who I was," he told himself, running. And then, "She didn't care!"

He ran on, onto the back porch and past moonlit Elvie reigning on his cot, and forgetting the kitchen where there might be water in the bucket, he stumbled out of the house and ran for the barn. He got himself inside, met the old smells thick as croker sacks hanging from the rafters, so thick he seemed to have to part them with his arms. He heard Bet still feeding, saw the dark shape of the broken buggy, which the muffled clucking of nesting hens seemed to be moving on oars down the night. The stall was full of the electrical memory of Dan the horse, the upper regions full of Grandpa Vaughn's prayers. Granny's side saddle hung on the wall in the dark, invisible but in its place, and he saw it in his mind, the leather crumbling and flaking like sycamore bark. Brother Bethune's mule had found his way to the Renfro barn; Vaughn saw the whites of his eyes, but they were to him only the extra eyes of confusion, and he pulled himself up the ladder into the loft. While saying his prayers, he tumbled over from his knees and was asleep before his forehead rolled on the floor.

<br>

Silent as the pulse itself that went beating on through sleep, there was lightning deep in the south, like the first pink down in the kindling—only a muscle that moved, like a bird in the net. A sky-wide stretch of cottony cloud came up and spread itself, so it appeared, under the moon, pallet-like. A different air streamed slowly toward the house and stirred the moonstruck nightgowns on the porch.

The cloud showed motion within, like an old transport truck piled high with crate on crate of sleepy white chickens. The moon, like an eye turned up in a trance, filmed over and seemed to turn loose from its track and to float sightless. First floating veils, then coarse dark tents were being packed across the sky, then the heavy, chained-together shapes humped after them.

Lightning branched and ran over the world with an insect lightness. Eventually, thunder followed. A ragged cloud ran in front, the moon was round for a minute longer, like a berry in the open beak of a bird, then it was swallowed.

Then thunder moved in and out of the house freely, like the voice of Uncle Noah Webster come back to say once more, "Good-night, blessed sweethearts."

Then the new roof resounded with all the noise of battle. With the noise and the smell as sudden as from water being poured into a smoking skillet, in the black dark it began to rain. Miss Beulah, who sprang up as at the alarm of fire, ran through the house slamming everything tight shut, company room included. Elvie, perhaps in her sleep, rose long enough to set two cedar buckets outside on the back steps.

Jack and Gloria never stirred.

Hearing what sounded like great treads going over her head, the baby opened her eyes. She put her voice into the fray, and spoke to it the first sentence of her life: "What you huntin', man?"

Miss Beulah ran out onto the porch, snatched up the baby, and ran with her back to her own bed, as if a life had been saved.

# Part 6

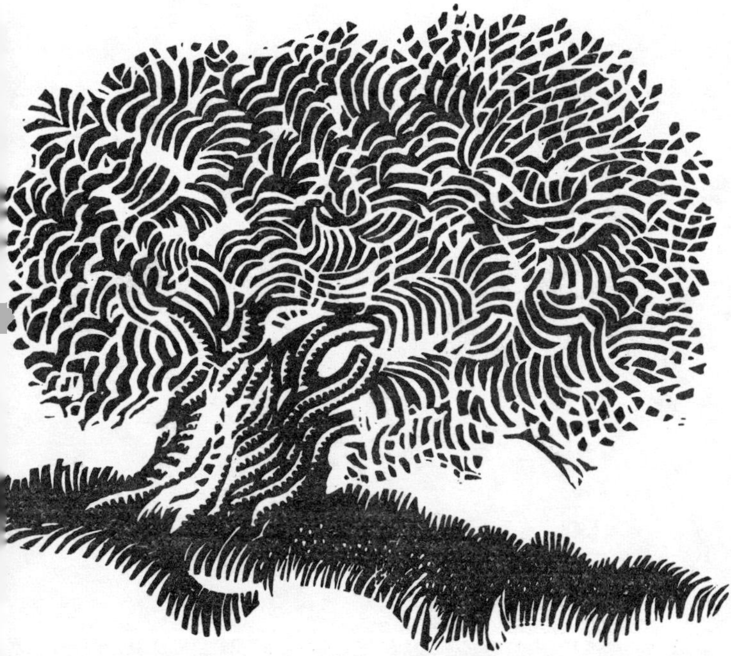

"**G**ranny's sleeping her little head off this morning," said Miss Beulah, running around the kitchen table, where Mr. Renfro, the Renfro girls, Miss Lexie, and Uncle Nathan were eating breakfast by lamplight.

"Paying for yesterday," said Miss Lexie.

"Rewarding herself! Getting a good start on ninety-one!" Miss Beulah corrected her.

"I got my own pants back," said Jack, coming in. Yesterday's shirt was tucked inside, with the starch gone but with most of the dust cracked out of it. He was steering Gloria to the table. A sober-looking Lady May trotted at their heels.

"Jack Renfro, look at you! What's the matter with your blessed eye!" Miss Beulah shrieked.

"Mama, it's just something that happened to it down in the road—away back yesterday, as long ago as before dinner. I can still see out of the other one."

"That's the one to mind out for this morning, when you rush back in," she said, helping his plate from the hot skillet.

Lady May stood up to the table, not tall enough to see, but she could reach plates.

"Where's Judge and Mrs. Judge? Still enjoying the company bed?" asked Jack.

"Why, Vaughn's gone in the wagon to carry 'em to Banner Top," said Miss Beulah. "You never saw two people in so great a hurry. You'd think, after being forgiven in front of a hundred, after eating the most chicken, sleeping all night in the weightiest feather-bed in my house—you'd think they'd feel beholden enough, those blessed Moodys, to eat as hearty a breakfast as they could swallow? Not on your life. I fried up every morsel I had left over to spread company breakfast, and they didn't deign. They left it for you."

Ella Fay laughed. She was all excitement and clattering feet this morning. "You ought to have seen Judge Moody hop right over your nose, Jack!"

"I didn't hear him go hop," said Jack, softly into Gloria's ear. It was brightly exposed. This morning her load of hair, straight as a poker, was carried all on top of her head, close-packed as a fine loaf.

"You was dreaming! Till I took pity on you and shook water on both your faces," said Miss Beulah, nodding to their faces, held cheek-together. "But Vaughn had to hitch the wagon and trot 'em there, they wouldn't wait."

"Why, there's still plenty of time. Both me and Curly got to milk," said Jack. "What drove 'em?"

"It's raining, son," said Mr. Renfro. "Getting pretty slick up there."

"And is that the whole story?" Miss Beulah cried at him.

"Your own daddy's another one that didn't wait on you, Jack," said Miss Lexie.

Miss Beulah put the biscuit pan in Mr. Renfro's face. "All those poor souls down in Banner Cemetery must've thought it was Judgment Day last night. Bang! Right over their heads. I bet you succeeded in waking your own father—for long enough to disappoint him, anyway."

"It would have taken a better job than that to wake Grandpa Vaughn," Miss Lexie retorted. "If he was as wedded as Papa to the Sounding of the Trumpet, he was a lot more of the disposition to sleep through it. Bang, bang, bang, indeed I heard it."

Jack said, with his cheek against Gloria's, "I don't remember the least bang."

"Well, it wasn't the bang I wanted," said Mr. Renfro. "I forgot to cap my fuse. And right to this minute, I can't think of a good reason for it."

"Papa," cried Jack, "what's this story you're telling me, sir?"

"Though for one thing, my fuse was a little dried, a little

caked—at the time I played it out, I was critical of it," Mr. Renfro went on. "Results was a little beneath what I'd term my standard."

"Who told you to try it at all?" Miss Beulah cried.

"I did nick the old cedar to a certain extent, son," said Mr. Renfro. "You ought to find when you get there I made it a little bit easier for you to start out this morning."

"*Sir?*" cried Jack.

"You'd *better* start worrying. Didn't you *hear* your daddy setting off that blast in the night?" cried Miss Beulah. "What's getting wrong with your ears, now?"

"I reckon that's about when I dreamed I was behind the wheel of my truck," Jack said. "Aycock didn't show too strong an objection?"

"He was enough trouble just being there," said Mr. Renfro. "I don't harm a neighbor, you know. I've learned by my time of life you've got to go a little slower than you would be inclined, because wherever you put your foot down there's a fool like Aycock that don't know enough not to keep out of your way."

Vaughn whirled in on them, raindrops flying. "The car's still there and Banner Top's still there, but their looks are ruined. You can't see the worst till it gets good day," he cried. He was back in his knee pants.

"I didn't even rise up when it started to raining," said Jack to Gloria.

"You missed the racket on the new roof?" cried Vaughn. "I give up."

"Well, don't sit down—you haven't got time to eat breakfast, Vaughn Renfro. Scoot! Up, the rest of you children! You've got your chores to finish and then school to track for, and Vaughn's got the teacher to tell he's misput the bus. There's only one new pair of shoes to be ruined, there's a mercy."

"Think how many's waiting on that bus to come along and pick 'em up this first morning. Well, they'll give up, sooner or later, and walk to school like I did," said Miss Lexie. "Do 'em that much more good."

"Vaughn'll catch a whipping at the door. I'll give him one myself when he gets back this evening, with a little extra for the hay he's lost his daddy," said Miss Beulah.

"If everybody hadn't wanted the gathering and all to wait on Jack!" Vaughn cried. "I could have had the hay saved!"

"It was what you felt called on to cut and leave laying in the field, Contrary, that's out yonder to spoil now," said Miss Beulah. "Yes sir, school is right where you're going. Put down that chicken bone."

Ella Fay jumped up clattering, Etoyle and Elvie moved morosely to follow, and they all went around the table telling Uncle Nathan and Miss Lexie good-bye.

"Me and Etoyle wanted to go help Jack," said Elvie.

"A fine way to get to be a teacher!" said Miss Beulah.

"Oh, yes, they'd like all life to be one grand reunion and never stop," said Miss Lexie. "I'm glad it's over. Taking it all in all, Beulah, I consider yesterday came just about up to scratch. It compares with the others. I was only afraid your little old granny might wonder where we got those Moodys. But she didn't."

"She took them in her stride, along with you and the rest of it," said Miss Beulah. "And if you're going to take any of my dewberry jelly, take it! If not, put back the spoon."

"The reunion didn't come up to *my* idea," said Ella Fay. She tarried in the kitchen door in Gloria's old teaching dress—the blue sailor with the flossy white stars on the collar and the skirt with the kick-pleats in it. "Curly Stovall was left out of the invitations, that's why!"

Miss Beulah ran and caught up with her in the passage. "All right, New Shoes! I'm fixing to smack you hard right across those pones of yours, where you need it most," she cried. "And for the rest of your punishment, you're to come straight home from school today and tell me something you've learned."

"Feed the stock. Lead the cows to pasture, Vaughn," said Mr. Renfro. "You heard your mother. The reunion is over with."

"I ain't done anything," said Vaughn.

"Then keep still," said Uncle Nathan. He pointed a loaded fork at Vaughn. He ate something out of his pack for breakfast, with a little home syrup poured over it.

"Everybody is liable to get a surprise yet," said Vaughn, as he struck off for the barn.

"Uncle Nathan, you ain't leaving?" cried Jack, when a moment later Uncle Nathan began handing around tracts out of his pack—the one about the crazy drunkard that he carried the most of. "Are you trying to tell us you won't stay for hog-killing time like you always do?"

374

"I must needs be on my way," said Uncle Nathan. His patched sleeve still smelled of coal-oil and a little scorching from last night.

"Nathan, have you even set long enough under my roof to dry out a little?" cried Miss Beulah. "Let me feel your thatch."

"Sister, I must needs not stop to take comfort."

"You won't even stop in Banner to help bury Miss Julia Mortimer?"

He shook his wet locks. "If the Lord has left me to outlast her, He must want me to go my road further than I ever gone it before," he told her, and hoisted his pack.

"Then put a kiss on Granny's cheek without waking her up," she told him.

"Good-bye, good-bye, Uncle Nathan!" yelled the three girls' voices from the barn lot, when Uncle Nathan's footsteps were heard measuring their way through the mud. "See you next reunion!"

"There's a chink of light out yonder now," said Mr. Renfro.

"They can't start till I get there!" Jack cried, jumping up. He laid a restraining hand on Gloria's shoulder. "Honey, I wouldn't have you get your little feet wet. Don't you come traipsing after me. It won't take long at Banner Top—it can't!" He kissed the baby, who was holding a little ham bone in her lips like a penny whistle, kissed everybody, ran up the passage, shouted, "Milk for me, Vaughn!," gave a warbling whistle, and ran splashing off with the dogs. They heard Bet thudding away with him.

Miss Beulah took off her apron.

"Now, Mother, are you ready to set down for the first time?" asked Mr. Renfro.

She cried loudly, "Set down? I'm going to Banner Top! Why, you couldn't hold me! Stovall and Moody are about to come to grips with their two machines! If my boy's ready to turn in the performance I think he is, it's a mother's place to be there and see it done right!"

"It's raining like it almost means it," said Mr. Renfro.

"I'm neither sugar nor salt, I won't melt. And morning rain's like an old man's dance, not long to last," Miss Beulah recited. "What I'm asking is, is anybody at this table coming with me?"

"Don't believe I'll venture from the house," said Mr. Renfro in mild tones. "If you ladies will excuse me."

"He's got that old dynamite headache," said Miss Beulah. "I'll only say it one more time, Mr. Renfro, and I'm through: from now on, you let other folks go out in the night and blow things to pieces, and you stay home. There's too much of the Old Boy in you yet."

"He'll shortly blow up something else. He won't learn, he's a man," said Miss Lexie.

"Yes sir, your touch is pure destruction!" Miss Beulah told him and ran to her kitchen. "I'll consider you were drunk on lemonade," she said when she marched back, Mr. Renfro's hat on her head.

"I really ought not to keep Mr. Hugg waiting," Miss Lexie said. "Especially when I'm coming to be his surprise. Jack may have to do without me watching him."

"I'm not going to beg you, Lexie Renfro," said Miss Beulah. "You can take your stand at our mailbox and get carried off either of two directions. Elmo Broadwee can carry you on his route and when he gets to Mr. Hugg's he can set you down with his nickel's worth of ice. Or you can change your mind and go the other way with the mail rider. Then you could get put down at that funeral. Couldn't she, Gloria?"

"If she's ready for it. And not scared of Miss Julia any longer," Gloria said, standing up in her church dress of deep blue dotted swiss with white piqué collar and cuffs.

"Still, I missed everything yesterday," argued Miss Lexie, rising too, and shaking crumbs on the floor for someone else to sweep up.

"Nobody's compelled to watch my boy's performance that don't want to," said Miss Beulah.

"Ask 'em who's going to stay home with me," said Mr. Renfro to Lady May, and Gloria handed her over. Lady May went to him as good as gold and gave him her tract, too.

On the ridge of the new roof the mockingbird sat silent, all chest, like a zinc bucket filled to the top, all song contained. What looked at first glance like a herd of strange cows come up into the yard overnight were only the tables of yesterday, stripped and naked, gleaming like hides in their sheen of rain. It was a tobacco tin in the weeds that shone like a ruby; what crouched like a possum under the althea was somebody's lost apron. A peashooter dangled from its sling down the back of the school chair. The night-blooming cereus flowers looked like wrung chickens' necks.

Miss Lexie, coming out onto the porch wearing a pillowcase over her hat, pointed them out.

Miss Beulah came pulling the old wool brim down squarely over her forehead and said, "Gloria Renfro, is all that hair you've got going to be enough to keep you dry?"

Gloria popped a blue straw sailor onto her head and snapped the elastic under her chin. "No ma'am, I've still got the same hat I came here in."

There was a sudden fusillade of sounds at their backs. Vaughn was feeding the pig. They had only to turn their heads to see all the refuse of yesterday—corncobs, eggshells, chicken bones, chicken trimmings, chicken heads, and the fish heads, all jumping together in the blue wash of clabber, all going down. Rusty looked back at them, with tiny eyes. He had the old, mufflered face of winter this morning and fed sobbing with greed, champing against blasts he was never going to feel.

"That reminds me, I've thought of a very good way to fix Mr. Hugg, when I get back to him in a little while," Miss Lexie said, hooking arms with the other two ladies on the slippery yard. "It's to give him every single thing he wants. Everything Mr. Hugg asks for—give it to him." She glared.

"All right, Lexie, go ahead," said Miss Beulah. "Just so it don't mean you cart him here to me."

"He'll get the surprise of his life, won't he?"

"Now Vaughn!" Miss Beulah was calling over her shoulder. "After he's gobbled that, turn the old sinner loose again. There's still plenty he can root out, not very far away. But he did look sassy tied up there for the reunion!"

◆§

"Gloria Renfro, how did you *ever* switch that car away up there? If you told it yesterday, I reckon I was too busy to listen." Miss Beulah stopped still in the middle of Banner Road and stared upward from beneath the row of rain beads on Mr. Renfro's hat.

"I scared it up," said Gloria, giving a skip over the ditch and arriving beside her. "I only wish it was in my power this morning to scare it down again."

No Moodys were in evidence. Jack stood on Banner Top by himself, hands on hips, studying the scene.

The Buick seemed not to have changed its position at all, though there was a lick of scorch up the back of it and its back window had stars. But the tree was out of the ground and hanging top-down over the jumping-off place. All its roots had risen together, bringing along their bed of clay, as if a piece of Boone County had decided to get up on its side. The solid wheel of pocked and bearded clay looked like an old white summer moon, burnt out on the edge of the world.

Miss Beulah was climbing the path up, making haste toward the Buick. "With a living Comfort inside it. I marvel," she said. "Or *is* he inside, I wonder? Comforts generally acts by contraries, but you'd be nothing but a fool to count on it."

"Sure, he's in there, Mama," said Jack, still studying the car. "Asleep on all fours, like a bird dog."

"Right where you left him? Oho!" Miss Beulah scoffed. "If that'd been a Beecham or a Renfro so treated, do you suppose the world had been safe from us last night?"

"Never knew the world *was* safe," hummed Miss Lexie, who had halted right at the mailbox, where she stood a head taller than Uncle Sam. "Well, the sight's not a great deal different from the way I had it pictured."

"Mr. Renfro was being modest for a change when he said he took a little nick out of that tree," said Miss Beulah. "I don't think it's going to be with us very much longer."

"It's clinging," said Jack. "Waiting to see what's the next thing to come along."

Nothing but memory seemed ever to have propped the tree. Nothing any stronger than memory might be holding it where it was now—some last tag end of root, that was all. There was just a round mass of clay, hanging with roots, like a giant lid raised and standing open, letting out an aromatic smell. There in the rain, its underside went on raining, itself, into the hole, the starved clay raining down dryness from the old, marrowless, pink-and-white colored roots.

"What do you think of it now, Jack?" called Judge Moody's voice. He and Mrs. Moody came in sight from the top of the farm track, where they had been sheltering under a tree. They made their slow way down into Banner Road.

"I'll tell you what I think," said Miss Beulah. "It's lacking very little. It's a very nearly perfect example."

"What of?" asked Miss Lexie.

"Man-foolishness," said Miss Beulah. "Ever heard of it?"

"One of these days I'm going to have to agree with your mother about something, Jack," said Gloria into his ear. "I hope she never finds out."

"Papa was trying to help," Jack said. "He's got him a reputation that's going to kill him one day yet."

"I want a good answer," said Judge Moody from the road. "What's the size of the situation now?"

"Well, sir, my way down was already closed off north, south, and east," Jack called. He made a step forward and went down up to his belt buckle. "And now Papa's cut off my west. Well, it's just a hole. Nothing but a hole," he said, climbing out. "And I believe that big pleasure Buick'll clear it! If she's persuaded the right way—and I'm counting on my truck just as strong as I can count!"

"Where is it, then? Is that truck going to fail us too?" asked Mrs. Moody.

They all stared down Banner Road. In the row with them, the cosmos flowers barely stirring on their stems under the fine soft rain were washed bright as the embroidery on the pillowcase Miss Lexie wore over her hat. There came a sound like a swelling, heavier rain.

"Yonder's your answer! Coming right now! Bigger and brighter than ever!" Jack hollered. He seized Gloria and Miss Beulah each by a hand and ran with them down to the road.

"Is that the same truck? It doesn't look the same as yesterday," Mrs. Moody greeted them.

"It's backing," Jack told her. "It's been coming uphill from Banner."

"It even looks to me like it's got a dog driving it," Mrs. Moody argued.

"Suppose you say no more, dear, and just give it a chance to get here," said Judge Moody in heavy tones.

Jack stood in the middle of the road while the truck backed up toward him, holding a muddy chunk raised in his hand ready to brake the wheels on top. This morning, the fishing poles had gone, and draping the rear was a strip torn off a bolt of kitchen oilcloth, on which words written in red paint with a stick were now coming close enough to be read: "Excell (Curly) Stovall for Justice of the Peace. Leave It To Curly."

"Rain curtains!" Jack hollered, as the truck drew closer. "Who parted with those?"

"Brother Dollarhide for a gallon of gas. Where's he hiding—the fellow that belongs to that Buick?" came the muffled voice from within the cab.

"He's standing right here with his wife, waiting on you. Whoa!" The truck drew even with his feet and Jack blocked the wheel. Ten or fifteen of Curly's hounds at once poured out from the bed behind onto the road and surrounded Jack, Judge Moody, and the ladies, their tails like a dozen fairy wands all trembling towards trouble.

"Then tell him it's going to be a dollar to go up and a dollar to come down. The whole business is going to set him back two dollars," called Curly Stovall. "Cash."

"If the fellow doesn't know any better than that, let's just keep him in the dark about what they'd charge in Ludlow," Mrs. Moody murmured to her husband.

"I am not reassured," said Judge Moody.

"It's a bargain, Curly!" Jack sang out. "So stick your head out of them pretty curtains now, it's time to see where you're going."

The curtains on the driver's side parted. A yell came out. "Jack! Hey! Look yonder at Banner Top! Who got here first?"

"Papa," answered Jack. "Don't worry. It's just minus one tree."

"And what am I going to hitch to? Drat your hide!"

"Careful how you talk, Curly. We got a pretty fair crop of ladies scared up for a rainy morning," said Jack. "And lined up here to watch us."

"First and foremost his mother!" cried Miss Beulah, and as she spoke the cab door on the passenger side swung out and down stepped one more lady, with the only umbrella for a mile around already raised.

"Why, Curly, you brought Miss Ora! Who's holding the store down—Captain Billy Bangs?"

Everything waited while the fat lady picked her way through the mud. "Granny Vaughn live through her birthday? Jack get his welcome without it leaving any scars? Get any surprise visitors?"

380

Miss Ora Stovall asked Miss Beulah. "I believe I'm looking at two of those right now." She edged in on the Moodys, so she could stand between them. "How're you feeling?" she began. "I'm Ora Stovall, weigh more than I should, never married, but know how to meet the public, keep up with what's going on. Enjoying your visit? What do you think of Banner? Like to hear about the biggest fish-fry that ever was?"

"All right, Jack Renfro and Curly Stovall!" Miss Beulah called over dogs, engine clatter, Miss Ora and all. "The visitors may have all day to talk, but the Renfros haven't! Now get on up there and perform! And keep in mind a mother's here to watch you."

"I'm the owner of the car, if you please!" Mrs. Moody exclaimed.

Through the rain curtains, canvas that had come to be the texture of old velvet, slit with isinglass lights and a few peepholes, Curly's voice called out, "Lady! This ain't the same job I took on yesterday!"

Jack flung himself onto the running board. "Curly, things change overnight, you got to be ready for that. We got a job this morning as whopping big as both our reputations put together!"

"And how you think we're going to do it!"

"By you sticking to the wheel and me doing the engineering!" He hopped to the road. "All right, Curly! Crawl! Back like you're going, right on up the bank, just back on up to me." He ran up the slippery clay, both arms beckoning.

"Shucks. Hindways?" Miss Beulah objected.

"Mama, in my truck, as long as you want your gas to feed steady, you got to pamper it on the upgrade. Give her the throttle, Curly! Don't be bashful!" Jack called.

From the road they watched it. With a long chain of noises like a string of firecrackers set fire to, the truck began to plough its way upward. The rain had washed it, so now, in part, it was the old International blue. With the spots and circles of oil that had worked their way through the finish, it was iridescent as butterfly wings as it quivered its way up. On the brow of the cab the original wording had emerged, "Delicious and Refreshing."

"What do those blasted horns mean?" Judge Moody asked.

"They mean I made a good trade out of Captain Billy Bangs! Who wants to know?" came Curly's voice back.

Sid, having barked the truck off the road in spite of a dozen hounds, was still after it, and flung himself like a bullet at the windshield, already stuck up with adhesive like a cut face.

"Mind out for your bob-wire fence!" Jack sang, as something flew up from under the back wheels like a whip. "You strung it there—just to trip your own self up with the first time you tried for the top! And the next thing is you got to straddle a hole about the same size you are. Keep your eye cocked on me."

"What caused a tree to just up and get out of the ground?" Curly hollered, over the hole.

"It was old and ready to fall—Lady May Renfro could've pushed it over with her little finger," Jack cried. "All right, whoa!" He skidded to put a chunk in front of the truck's front wheel. "Now! Pitch me your rope!"

The cab door swung open long enough for an arm-throw, and a black coil crossed through the air and slammed Jack wetly in the chest. He spun and crouched with it behind the truck, shoulders pumping as he worked with his knots. In a moment he'd jumped around to the back of the Buick. As he attacked that, a shaking of bells thrilled the air.

"Somebody, somebody for sure, climbed up here in the night and tied cowbells on this Buick!" Jack called. "Only the Broadwees would have had that little to do." Then he rose and yelled into the car, "Wake-up-Jacob! Wake up! Ain't you about ready to quit riding?"

"Is it daylight?" came Aycock's sleepy voice from inside.

"And raining. All right, Aycock, you can get out now—I'll count three. When I count three, Curly, you start pulling!" Jack yelled. "And when you do, remember yours ain't the only engine that's running! Once Aycock jumps and the Buick's out of balance, she'll start pulling against you! All right—ready?"

"Jack Renfro, you can finish this by yourself!" yelled Curly. "I'm going back to Banner right now."

"You're tied!" Jack shouted. "You and the Buick's hitched to one rope and hitched good! *One!*"

"Do you reckon we've got a chance?" Mrs. Moody asked her husband.

"I should say what chance we have depends on Jack," he said, eyes never leaving him.

"I can vouch for that!" Miss Beulah agreed. "Don't count on either one of those two machines. As for the truck Jack's so in love with, it's got parts from everything that's ever passed through Banner and lost a particle. It's an example of a grab-bag to me. And more'n likely it'll fly to pieces the first chance it gets, if you want my unvarnished opinion."

"Two!" yelled Jack.

"I ain't playing!" roared Curly.

"Curly, Aycock, there ain't no time left for anybody to act bashful," Jack said. "If you want any glory, you can't quit now!"

"You want to change places?" cried Curly.

"Two and a half!" yelled Jack.

"I dread this," said Miss Beulah, taking off Mr. Renfro's hat and emptying some rain out of the saucer of the brim, never taking her eyes from on top.

Jack opened his mouth again.

The Buick's rear door shot open then and Aycock came tumbling out into Jack's spreading arms. Both boys fell, Jack rose, picked up Aycock and stood him up stiff with his hair dry and on end. Then Aycock danced sideways into the plum bushes and while they waited on him they could all hear through the sound of the rain what he was doing.

"Three!" Jack was calling urgently. "Three! And watch out down in the road!"

The rope had already stretched out straight—the Buick had already moved forward. A loud report cracked out from underneath it and something went spinning.

"Yonder went Uncle Nathan's sign!" hollered Jack, as the truck backfired, crawled forward, then was jerked to a halt. The Buick, on solid ground, was running the other way. Jack raced to catch it. But even before he got there its wheels rolled to a stop. Then they began to roll the other way. The Buick was moving with the roaring, recovering truck. It was coming on the rope, slowly away from the edge, swaying, like a lady coming out of church— one of its tires was not flat.

"Well," said Jack, watching the car, "she just plain run out of gas. Ain't that your opinion, Aycock?"

"I seen we needed some," Aycock said.

"In a minute she'll be coming down behind you, Curly!" Jack hollered. A whip of barbed wire flew up from under the truck and Curly yelped like a woman scared by a mouse, and braked the truck with a sharp turn of the wheels. The engine choked and died. The Buick, just at the crown of Banner Top, presented with a slack in the rope, rolled back to where it had come from, and on past it. It proceeded on its original forward way over Banner Top, disappearing with the moderate speed of an elevator going down. The truck rose up like a tin monkey on a string, until both its back wheels entered the tree hole and stayed there.

"Well, this isn't what *I* came to see!" said Miss Ora Stovall. "What about you?"

An upward avalanche pounded its way to Banner Top from the road. With Jack holding both arms wide to keep them safe behind him, Gloria, Miss Beulah, the Judge, and Mrs. Moody all crowded together in the clouds of exhaust and cedar fumes, to look down.

The automobile was hanging by the rope and the tree beside it was hanging by its own last roots, like two things waiting for the third.

"Oscar, I feel like I can draw my first breath," said Mrs. Moody. "It's happened."

"Not what you *wanted?*" he broke out.

"No, but now it's not still ahead of us."

"Some of it is," he said.

The Buick had descended as far as the drop of the rope allowed: its nose hung within five or six feet of the ledge below. Its wheels turned innocently in free air. The rope held, held, until holding was hardly believable any longer, until it seemed tenuous as a sound—a long, last, feathered note from Miss Beulah singing "Blessed Assurance," holding even after the rest of the choir and the congregation had given up.

"From here, I would call things a tie," said Miss Lexie. She still stood in position at the mailbox.

"That's right. As long as they're hanging on tight to each other, both of 'em's as safe as you are, Aunt Lexie," Jack said.

The rain curtains were torn aside and a face red as the hidden sun looked out of the truck.

"I see you, you old infidel!" Miss Beulah screamed. "That's all I needed! How do you like what you've done to us now?"

"Tuck back in there, Curly!" cried Jack.

"But the truck's coming out of the hole!" hollered Curly.

"Not this way!" Jack warned him. "Start driving. Drive the other way, Curly, drive as hard as you can!"

The truck engine gave out a piercing, froglike chirping.

"The throttle!" yelled Jack. "The Buick's gaining on you, Curly! The Buick's pulling too much weight!"

"I'm coming out of the hole!" Curly warned. "In spite of all, I'm coming out! Like a old jaw tooth!"

"I just wish you'd gobbled a bigger breakfast before you come!" Jack yelled.

"She's coming!" shouted Curly. "Think I won't jump? You can catch me too!"

Jack whirled, grabbed the rope and pulled leaning back toward the truck, pulled till he sat down pulling, and was hauled to his knees and forward down onto his stomach and dragged, by the inch, till he hung head-first over the drop, yelling, "Gloria! Take ahold of me! Just anywhere you can find!"

Gloria slid behind him into the bucket-like seat that sweethearts had worn over the years into the jumping-off place, and clamped her arms around his bulging legs. His feet locked together behind her. Judge Moody, breathing heavily over her head, wrapped his hands around the rope and pulled with Jack and the truck. Mrs. Moody, planting her feet apart, got his suspenders in her fists and sawed on him, while Miss Beulah dug her hands into Mrs. Moody's girth, rammed herself back against one leg, and hauled on her, setting up a steady rhythm.

"The way to do it is make a human chain," Miss Lexie instructed them from her place at the mailbox.

"I'm driving hard, Jack! But I ain't getting anywhere!" called Curly.

"Just hold things like they are so they don't get any worse!" yelled Jack.

"How far is that thing now from touching the ledge?" asked Judge Moody.

Jack screwed around his head. "In my judgment, about as far as me to you, sir." He slid for an instant. Gloria's arms locked his feet to her breast. "Closer!"

Down there the ledge was spread with rose briars in ten-foot rays and dotted with chewed plum bushes. In the scoop of the gully below it, the little sprung-up cedars pointed up darkly out of the clay, like the hairs in Brother Bethune's ears.

"Are we reaching clear back to my truck, Mama?" Jack called.

"How long do you think I am?" she yelled. "But we got two

**385**

more in the road and one more idler on top! March here behind me, Aycock Comfort. Squat. Sit on my foot. Brace that leg of mine, Foolish!"

"Then if the rope comes in two, all the line'll fall back on top of me," he said, not coming.

"Pore you. And what about Jack, when he flies the other way?" Miss Beulah flung at him scornfully.

"If Miss Ora would volunteer to set her two hundred pounds' worth down on the bumper of my truck, and kind of tread backwards with her feet, that wouldn't hurt anything," gasped Jack. "But even if she could hear me, I can't ask her—it's so little of a compliment."

"Get up here, Ora Stovall!" yelled Miss Beulah.

"I'm going to put you in the paper and that's all! When it rains, I'm a regular little kitty," Miss Ora called at once from the top of the bank opposite, where she had climbed to see better, out from under her big umbrella black as a buzzard's wing.

"Oh, I can't think Providence has delivered us this far in order to desert us now! Surely help will come," Mrs. Moody said faintly over the creaking of her corset as Miss Beulah hauled on her. "But please don't in the meantime cut my wind."

"The ones I'd call for first are already with us, this time," Jack gasped. "There ain't any better than who's right here pulling, Mrs. Judge!"

"I don't trust that infidel Stovall to stick to the wheel a minute, Jack," said Miss Beulah. "You know what he's thinking of? His own hide!"

"I wish everybody would be less loudly critical for a minute and let me think," Judge Moody said.

"Let him think!" hollered Jack.

"Better hurry," said Miss Lexie. "World isn't going to stand still and wait on you."

"Lexie, for the second time, come catch on to my waist!" Miss Beulah said in a loud voice.

"I've got to save my strength for battles later on," said Miss Lexie. "Mr. Hugg is a ton."

"I'm driving but I ain't getting anywhere!" called Curly. "Sinking, that's all."

"That's a fellow!" called Jack.

**386**

"When it falls, will it fall on that little shelf down there?" asked Mrs. Moody fearfully.

"If it don't skip," Jack called. "Uncle Nathan's sign skipped right over it, though. Yonder *it* lays, too far down to even read. I'm glad Uncle Nathan got back on his road before he learned what become of that one."

"But what's at the bottom?" Mrs. Moody cried.

"The Bywy River," said Jack. "Low as it is now, you could walk the sandbar from right under here clear to Banner bridge without getting wet."

She gave a little cry.

"Jack," said Judge Moody, "I think if we could very gently lower the car the rest of the way to that ledge, it would have a better chance. While we still have time. And strength."

"That's giving in, Oscar," protested Mrs. Moody.

"The other thing against it is the rope won't stretch like I will," gasped Jack.

"Jack, what are you going to do?" Gloria pleaded.

"I'm going to hang here pulling as long as you can hold my feet, Possum," he gasped.

A racket was heard in the road.

"Ha, ha, Homer Champion," came Miss Ora Stovall's voice in greeting as the wheels skidded to a stop. "Take a look at Brother!"

"Where?" came Uncle Homer's voice. "Hey, what's going on here?"

"Want to be part of the human chain?" yelled Jack.

"That sounded like Jack Renfro!" exclaimed Uncle Homer. "Where's he? Was he speaking to me?"

"He's hanging over the living edge!" yelled Miss Beulah.

"Sister Beulah!" shouted Uncle Homer. "Here, what's the big idea?"

"Just seeing how long we can keep us all in one piece, I reckon!" Jack said in short breaths. "Glad to have you if you want to add on!"

"Every dog has his day, huh?" laughed Miss Ora Stovall. "Look at Brother right on top."

"On top? Is Stovall in charge of that *truck?*" Uncle Homer hollered.

"Curly!" Jack yelled, but already the truck shuddered as its door opened and Curly hopped out in boots into the naked air, and heavy-shouldered as if doubled over in knots of laughter, he cut a short caper, his face beaming from side to side, and then he was back inside again.

"I saw what you did, you old rangatang!" yelled Miss Beulah. "Not content with all you caused already, you try to make an end of us too!"

"Never mind, Mama. When Curly hit that door open, this one answered," called Jack. "So we're still matched."

The Buick's back seat had been jolted forward and had turned loose all the tools, with a wheel of never-used towline that rolled and wobbled on the ledge, printing its track, then lay down under their eyes.

"Everything in its own good time, Possum," said Jack in short breaths. "There's everything I stood in need of yesterday."

"Look where you've succeeded in raising my rival to!" Uncle Homer cried. "Don't you know what'll happen? Hold him there long enough in the public eye, and they'll vote for him!"

"My boy's keeping one end of this man-foolishness from running off with the other, with his bare hands, and you just think about Tuesday!" said Miss Beulah. "We got no time to waste listening to pretty speeches, get on up here before I throw something at you!"

"Don't fret, Uncle Homer. If Curly had his way this minute, he'd be away from here and down on solid ground where you are," called Jack.

"The heck I would," said Curly. He sounded the truck's horn; it hummed like a distant swarm of bees.

"The heck he would," said Uncle Homer. "Sitting pretty where you got him planted! And if you want the public to decree Stovall is the man better fitted for worthy office than your own in-law, you keep him where he is, from now right on up till when the polls open. The only thing he lacks now is cowbells."

With effort, Jack managed to work the rope a fraction, and faintly the Buick's cowbells rang from below.

"If you want the rest of the story, Uncle Homer, at the other end of this rope we got a Buick out of gas," he called.

"It'll be a landslide!" howled Uncle Homer. "I don't see why you don't charge to see it!"

"Champion, do you really reckon this exhibition is going to

gain Stovall votes?" Miss Lexie demanded to know. "I wonder could you once be right about anything?"

"I know people. I know people," bawled Uncle Homer, as if his heart would break.

"So I suppose you'll stand there wishing the rope would snap!" Miss Beulah yelled. "Till it does! Politics! I wouldn't have son of mine enter politics if it was the last door open to him on earth!"

"Uncle Homer, the ladies are growing a little frail," Jack panted out. "Don't you want to lend your strength to keep Curly where we got him?"

"I'm all that's lacking, am I?" Uncle Homer shouted. "You ought to go back to Parchman, Jack! Next time, stay through the primary and the run-off too!" The van skidded away and down out of hearing, and Curly Stovall let out a rocking laugh from the truck.

"There it came! My guitar," Aycock said, peering over the brink. He took a hop into the air and landed on the ledge with both feet.

"You come off and left it behind when you jumped? I hope you find it still in tune!" Jack called.

The car's headlights just cleared the rusty top of Aycock's head as he loped underneath and picked up the guitar from the mud. "Well, I reckon I better get on home and speak to Mama," he said, as he hauled himself up by protruding tree roots onto the top. Nursing his guitar, he gave a small wave of his free hand as if he were closing a little purse, and started away. "I'll see is she still mad at me."

"Don't you care to see the end?" Jack called.

"I just as soon hear you tell it," said Aycock. "All I'm truly wondering about this minute is how cold will my grits get before I make it home. Cold till the butter won't melt?"

"Trifling! And always will be. Parchman was too good for you, Aycock Comfort! Go home and tell your mother I said so!" cried Miss Beulah.

"All you needed was to get married, Aycock," Jack said. "Ought to brought you a wife home ahead of time, like I did, and had her gripping your feet now."

"Not yet awhile," Aycock said politely. He stopped at Miss Beulah's position and stood with his head on one side and his wetting hair lying on his neck like the feathers of a Rhode Island Red. "Mis' Renfro, I feel like Mr. Renfro kind of aimed to blow me up."

"I've got just enough patience left to ask you one question," she yelled. "How did Mr. Renfro get himself up here last night?"

"He creeped," said Aycock. "Then he creeped down again. If he'd told me ahead what he's going to do, he'd had me out in his lap. Come the bang, I thought I'd wait to see what else was coming, before I set foot outside. His dynamite ain't the freshest in all the world."

"Dynamite?" Curly Stovall's head came out through the rain curtains.

Judge Moody suddenly broke out: "We're all holding on here now by the skin of our teeth! Can't conversation ever cease? Can't anybody offer just a single idea? What're we going to do about this?"

"You could cut that rope," suggested Aycock. "Save time." He tiptoed away across the mud puddles.

"We have now been holding on for eleven and a half minutes," said the Judge.

"Judge Moody, I kind of believe your watch has stopped," Jack gasped. "Can you still hear it running?"

"Please, *you* let me try to think," said Judge Moody.

"What's the matter, Gloria?" called Jack. "When you gave that sigh, it travelled right on through my toes and down me to the top of my head."

"I don't see our future, Jack," she gasped.

"Keep looking, sweetheart."

"If we can't do any better than we're doing now, what will Lady May think of us when we're old and gray?"

"Just hang onto my heels, honey," he cried out.

"We're still where we were yesterday. In the balance," Gloria said.

"Don't give up, baby," said Jack as her chin came to rest between the heels of his muddy shoes, with their wet soles splitting apart, their tops worn down to sandbar pink, their strings sodden and metal-heavy with mud and weed, his wedding shoes. "Just put your mind on what me and you will be doing this same day next year. That's what I told myself last year in the old pen."

"Jack, only you would still think it was all going to be all right!"

"I still believe I can handle trouble just taking it as it comes," he gasped.

"It takes thinking! We've got to think!" Judge Moody broke out.

"Jack, now the blood is all running to your head!" Gloria cried.

**390**

"Just so he don't fall and land on it," Miss Beulah cried from the end of the line. "Precious head!"

Hot tears coursed through the rain on Gloria's face. "Oh, Jack," she whispered to his heels. "I don't see how you've stayed alive for as long as you have."

"He don't know when he's licked. That's how!" said Miss Beulah.

"I ain't never licked!" cried Jack.

The rope went singing in two. As it cracked Jack free he rose, spread his arms, and came down in the fallen tree. The Judge, his wife, and Miss Beulah were flung backwards to the ground, but Gloria dived the other way. Her hat popped off and went sailing down through space.

"And there she goes after him again!" came Miss Beulah's wild cry.

Both Jack and Gloria were in the tree, tumbling toward each other. The cedar trunk rolled once, as if a wave came all the way up from the river and went under it, but it stayed attached, hanging onto its very last roots. Branches sharp-cracked at Jack's and Gloria's knees and shoulders and around their heads, and pitched them against each other, buoyed them up and dropped them. Like runaways caught in a storm and living through it, they drove out with their arms and legs and went down shouting. Still the tree held to its shape—like a summer's-old nest that had itself fallen out of some greater tree or vine, with all its yesterdays tangled up in it now. The two of them fell together through what was once the roof of the tree onto the ledge, landing right side up, looking at each other, weak with accomplishment.

Cowbells were still shaking a little, close to their ears.

"Well, the auto evermore landed where it hurts, didn't it?" Miss Beulah cried.

The Buick stood on its nose on the nose-pink ledge.

Jack was climbing back to his feet. "Curly! If you couldn't bring a better rope than that, I'd just as soon you hadn't brought none!"

"It was a World Wonder Number Two Grade," shouted Curly, still inside the noisy truck.

"I think it was just a plowline with a little pitch on it!" Jack was tenderly lifting Gloria up out of the broken branches. He drew little twigs from her hair.

"What's wrong with the knots you tie!" Curly hollered back.

"They're still tied! They're the same Jack Renfro knots they ever was! Curly, that rope of yours busted in the *middle!*"

"Wasn't ever used but once before. And that was to pull one little calf away from his mother."

"You brought the wrong rope."

"On its very nose. And it wasn't for lack of me trying to see the thing done right," said Miss Beulah. "Well, things could be a lot worse, though. Machines could both be piled up down at the bottom and two or three people with a leg or an arm or two broken."

"I suppose you're happy," Mrs. Moody said to her husband. "There it is. On that ledge."

"It brings some relief," he said. "Of course it's temporary."

"It looks to me just a whole lot like it's permanent," she told him.

"Well, it's temporary, Maud Eva," he said.

At that moment there came something like a thunderclap behind them, and a cloud of larkspur-blue swallowed up all of Mrs. Moody and a part of Miss Beulah. The truck sprang up like some whole flock of chickens alarmed to the pitch of lunacy, fell, bounced, bounced again.

"Curly," Jack was hollering, "I believe you must be driving over one of Brother Bethune's snakes!"

The truck came to rest ten feet away in some plum bushes, the dogs streaking circles around it, barking. Curly Stovall, as soaking-wet as if he'd been outside with other people, leaped the second time from the cab and stamped through mud back to the jumping-off place and yelled at Jack, "All right, what was that?"

"Curly, you know Papa planted a little of his dynamite up here, trying to do me a favor," Jack said. "And he did."

"We already heard from that once!" shouted Curly.

"And now you've heard from it again," said Miss Beulah, looking him in the eye. "Some folks' dynamite blows up once and gets through with it, but you don't reckon on that little from Mr. Renfro."

"He's using dynamite that's mighty old, then!" Curly stormed. "And there ain't no guarantee on what *old* dynamite is *ever* going to do!"

"If it hadn't been good for one extra bang, I can think pretty fast where *you'd* be, Stovall," said Miss Beulah. "Still in that hole! Well on your way to China! Oh, that smell, Mr. Renfro!" She cast up her eyes. "That smell! Worse than a whole roomful of Cape Jessamines at funeral time."

Mrs. Moody let out a cry.

The tree had begun to move. It was leaving them. First it went slowly, and then it was bounding, rolling unevenly down on its wheel of roots and clay, diminishing under their eyes, firing off fainter sounds, until it was quiet and still—only a bundle in the grayness below, of no more size or accountability than a folded umbrella.

"Mrs. Moody scared it down," said Gloria.

"Thank Mr. Renfro instead—it was that last bang shook it," Miss Beulah contradicted her.

"And now the Buick's got a sweet path open in front of her," said Jack. "Back to the road where she started."

"You call that a path?" asked Judge Moody, frowning down.

"It finds its way out here from the road, threading down to the river," said Jack. "Gloria, keep as far back from me as you can." He picked her up and swung her around behind him.

"Hold onto him, girl!" cried Mrs. Moody.

"I'm only fixing to level you, Mrs. Judge," Jack said.

"With what?" Judge Moody demanded.

"Nothing but my own main strength, sir, that's the safest," Jack said.

"Don't move. Wait for me," ordered the Judge.

❧

The car stood with its underside exposed in full to face Judge Moody as he tramped around the fishing path onto the ledge. Away from the road, or even the sight of the road, rising up on a ledge by itself, with a clay wall going up on one side and the rain falling to the houseless distance down the other, it might have been some engine of mysterious invention, its past unknown, its function obscure, possibly even illegal—like some whisky still come upon without warning in a clearing in the woods.

Judge Moody stood there in front of it, Gloria stood behind, Mrs. Moody and Miss Beulah overhead, and Curly Stovall was somewhere back there laughing.

"As Jack's wife, I would rather nobody breathed," said Gloria.

Jack stepped before the car and stood under it with his back turned, flexed his arms, squatted once, then squared his knees. He cleaned off his bloody hands on his pants, then, as slowly as if he were already lifting its weight, he pushed his arms upward and took hold of the car.

"Now watch! Reminds me of Samson exactly!" Miss Beulah cried frantically—she was standing on the jumping-off place. "Only watch my boy show the judgment Samson's lacking, and move out of the way when it starts coming!"

Jack staggered and then jumped as if out from between a set of jaws, and the Buick came down like the clap of thunder after a very near strike of lightning.

"And she's ready to haul!" he yelled, as Judge Moody caught him.

"My cake!" exclaimed Mrs. Moody.

The Buick's other doors one after the other fell open, like pockets being turned out, and up the path from under the ledge ran little spotty wild pigs, like the church carpet come to life, and they gobbled up the cake that had spilled out of the front seat into the rain. Bringing up the wild pigs from behind came Rusty, the pig from home.

"All right, Stovall, now it's your turn," Judge Moody called.

"I quit! I ain't going to drag you no further and you can't make me—I'm the law, mister," said Curly.

"Curly, Judge Moody's the law too," said Jack. "I hope you ain't so ungrateful that you'd forget Judge Moody."

"What Judge Moody? *That* Judge Moody?" Curly cried. "I didn't know I was ever going to see *that* Judge Moody again! Not around here."

"How many do you think there are?" Mrs. Moody exclaimed. "Are you trying to suggest to me there's some other Judge Moody? Don't waste my time."

"Maud Eva," began Judge Moody.

But there was suddenly added to the throbbing of the truck a rattling sound. Curly whirled. Jack rushed the clay wall, grabbing at cedar roots, cedar sprouts, rose briars, his legs wheeling him finally over the top, where Miss Beulah spanked him on.

The empty truck was jolting headlong toward the road, skating in and out of the tracks it had made backing up. It was held back only a little by its laboring engine and by the brief fingering of plum bushes. It banged into Banner Road, a puddle walling up in front of it, then through its shower limped on across the road as if pretending something was broken, and threw itself into the ditch, ushering a part of the syrup stand with it and still dragging a long clay tail behind, which was its end of the rope.

"All right now, that splashed my dress," Miss Lexie greeted it at the mailbox.

"I'm staying right here with mine," Mrs. Moody was calling.

"All right, Jack, *you* done that. You jolted it. You shook Banner Top, letting that Buick down. This truck, the way it's put together, it feels ever' little shake and shiver," Curly accused him.

"Well, one thing leads to another, that's all," said Miss Lexie. "That's why I stay out of it."

Each section of the truck stood just a jot away from its neighbors, like the plated hide of the rhinoceros on its page in the geography book. Everything about it seemed a little out of its place except the license tag, an ancient one turned gold, from Alabama, which still hung upside down. The back wheels were as solid with mud as the balled roots of a tree out of the ground, but the front wheels and both horns were dripping with thinner, fresher mud like gingerbread batter.

"She's a little whopper-jawed now," Jack agreed, while he shouldered the truck back into the road and headed it toward the crowd of cosmos that concealed the fishing path. "But looks ain't everything. I'll do a little more tightening on her, the first chance I get." He climbed into the cab. "Here's hoping I didn't crack the ledge with that Buick like I cracked my truck," he said to Gloria as she reached the road still running.

"Get back to the other one," she said. "The Moodys are having a fit."

On the ledge, Judge Moody stood with his hand on the open car door, one foot on the running board. "I'm on my way out of here now, Maud Eva," he said.

She screamed again. "Jack, don't let my husband set foot in my car! Where's that truck? Drag it away from him!"

"My truck is waiting on a little further encouragement to get her clacking again, Mrs. Moody," Jack said. "I know what it needs, right now."

"Never mind," Judge Moody interrupted. "I'm driving my own car out of this place, young man."

"Don't let him, Jack. Look down under him!" cried Mrs.

Moody. "If he tries, take the wheel out of his hands. Dr. Carruthers would faint!"

"Wait in the road, Maud Eva. Will you young people help my wife to the road? If you don't object, everybody please wait in the road till I come driving out." He added more calmly, "I believe I can do better if you're not standing over me. I may be peculiar that way."

"What you are is out of gas, sir," Jack reminded him. "I'll bring you back some of mine."

"Then I've had my say," said Mrs. Moody. "I'm not going to offer another word, Oscar, until we get home."

Jack hunted up a chewed section of rubber tube in the bed of the truck, unstuck a rusty bucket from the ground under the syrup stand, emptied out the rainy leaves, and then sucked and siphoned into the bucket some gasoline out of the tank. "With the mileage he's been getting, this ought to carry him to Banner," he said, running back with the handleless bucket in his arms.

"He owes me four bits more now," said Curly Stovall.

They heard cowbells before they saw it. Then, streaked with clay, hung with briars, the emblem gone from its radiator top, its bumper swallowed up, both headlights blinded, the Buick bumped its way into view, listing sideways and fanning up mud. Judge Moody was visible at the wheel in spite of the mesmerizing rainbows flashing through the drizzle from cracks in the windshield. It churned hard before climbing its way up into the road, and then coming out between bowed-over heads of cosmos, it bumped around to where Mrs. Moody was waiting.

"You bring it to me covered with mud!" she cried.

"And it's got a few other serious things the matter with it," said Judge Moody.

"Her nose is a little bit out of kilter," Jack said. "And that's reasonable. She's been standing on it."

"The first thing to do is remove those cowbells," directed Mrs. Moody, and already Jack was pulling them off like so many cockleburs.

"Listen to the engine, Maud Eva. The way it's running leaves something to be desired," Judge Moody said.

"She'll make it to Banner," said Jack. "You could call it all downhill. Pull her up where I show you, Judge Moody, sir, in front of my truck—" He was shoving the truck, pointing it down the road.

"Instead of you pulling me, now I'm pulling you?" broke out Judge Moody.

"We'll all go in one," said Jack.

"Rescuing some woebegotten homemade truck that couldn't even get up the steam to rescue me?" exclaimed Mrs. Moody. "I can just see visions of that!"

"We're all going the same place, Mrs. Judge! Curly, I'm going to let you ride in my truck, all the way, sitting high to the wheel if you want to. And Judge Moody's Buick'll bring you in behind him."

"Right under the nose of my trade?" he yelled. "My voters?"

"Curly, make up your mind to be towed," said Jack.

"There's always *something* to come along to shorten the tail of the rabbit. Remember that, Stovall," said Miss Lexie Renfro.

Judge Moody had just backed the Buick into place.

"But I don't hear it choking any longer, Oscar," said Mrs. Moody.

"Neither do I. No, I can't get another spark out of it, I'm afraid," said Judge Moody.

"So you brought it here to me and that's as far as you can go," Mrs. Moody said to the Judge. "That was a short distance.—Stay out! Stay out! I don't want to see you getting in my engine, even with my car on the ground!" she called at Jack's back—he'd rattled up the hood. "Oscar, blow the horn at him!"

Jack put up his head. "Listen!"

It was another horn that blew. The flying school bus came down on them, around the mailbox and past the truck and the Buick, and Jack with a shout ran chasing it.

"Stop! Stop!" he hollered, until the stop-flag dropped down, the bus swerved, and he caught hold of it.

Vaughn put his head out the window.

"Scoot out and give me your bus," said Jack.

"I fixed it easy. I'm on my way to school!" Vaughn cried.

"Just what we need, and just in time, and I hadn't even missed it!" Jack said.

"It's my first day to drive it," Vaughn cried. "I ain't even let my sisters in on it, to cramp my style—they walked the sawmill track." The engine kept on with its excited, sibilant sound like uncontrolled whispering.

"Vaughn, it can be your first day tomorrow." Jack with a still bleeding hand reached in and patted Vaughn's scrubbed one. "Just get it in line at the front of that Buick and hop out. I only wonder if you sparked that battery the way I would."

"It's no blooming fair," said Vaughn, accepting it.

"The rain has washed that thing off some," said Mrs. Moody, looking disapprovingly at where the headlight sockets were still empty and the grille and the front bumper were both still missing. This morning, dimples as big as children's faces were visible, pressed into the yellow fenders. The metal of the body showed itself punctured and in places burned. The words "Banner Bob Cats" had come out across the front under the roof. "It's bound to be the same bus. And we're going behind it, Oscar?"

Judge Moody's cheeks puffed out, holding in his reply.

"All right, Vaughn, you go hunt Judge Moody's towline. Look under the jumping-off place, down on the ledge, if we still got a ledge," said Jack. "I'm going to give his rope a fair try."

"My tools and my towline are back in the car where they belong," said Judge Moody. "Under the back seat." He began to get them out again, while Jack went leaping up the other bank.

In a moment there came a kettle-drumming that went sounding on forever, it seemed, before it was swallowed up. "We got one sturdy fellow!" Jack said, running back to them. Stained red and black, and heavy as a live snake, it hung looped and dripping over his scratched, muddy arms.

"You let that bucket fall back in, Jack, and there went one thing you won't get back just by asking for it," said Miss Beulah. "That well goes to China, and your Great-great-granddaddy Jordan himself was the stubborn old digger. Might even be his bucket."

"And that's what you'll use to pull a truck and a car both from here to Banner?" asked Miss Lexie. "Tied to the Banner School bus? It's a well rope, is all it is."

"If a thing didn't have but one use to it, Lexie, I'd just let you have it," said Miss Beulah. "Mind!" she cautioned Jack. "That soppin' rope's heavier than you are!"

"Mama, I believe this morning it's wetter outside that well than in," he told her, as the two brothers went hurriedly to work knotting, Vaughn doing just as Jack did.

"Still not enough to get us all in one!" said Jack. "Now what?"

"I brought along a rope of my own," said Vaughn, with a glance up Banner Top. "In case what happened to him was to happen to me." From under the driver's chair in the school bus he got out a neatly coiled rope with a big knot in it. Mr. Renfro's axe and a length of chain were stowed there too. Jack had it all out of his hands at once.

Only a few moments later he hopped to his feet and asked Mrs. Moody, "Will you have a seat in the school bus now, Mrs. Judge? It'll give you a front view of the road."

"Not in my seat!" Gloria pleaded.

"Thank you, I'll ride where I can keep the best eye on my car limping along in front of me," she said.

"You choose the truck?" exclaimed Judge Moody.

"Then it's a little bit careful with where you put your feet, Mrs. Judge," Jack said, boosting her into the cab of the truck, "while I work you in from behind."

Mrs. Moody screamed, "Why, there's no floor!"

"Hook one foot onto that good two-by-four across the front end there, Mrs. Judge, and swing the rest of you over," Jack said. "Mind out for biting springs."

"She's got a horse blanket to her," Curly Stovall said, pointing.

"Curly, the only reason I'm letting you back in this truck one more time is my wife wouldn't trust nobody but me to drive the school bus," said Jack. "Judge Moody, I'd be obliged if you'd set between 'em, and while Mrs. Judge keeps her eye on the Buick, you keep your eye on Curly."

"That is what I intend doing. I'll keep my eye on everybody," he said. He climbed in, Curly Stovall pushed in after him and threw his weight on the steering wheel, and Jack's dogs and Curly's dogs leaped into the bed of the truck together. "But I will not travel with those dogs—Bedlam on top of Bedlam," the Judge said. "Dismiss those dogs."

"And they're wet in addition to the rest," said Mrs. Moody.

Jack ushered the dogs out, and they split as if for a race, some of them pounding down the road and the rest trundling one another onto the path that started around Banner Top.

"Now, have you boys got all that hitched perfectly? I'm not sure yet I place what's holding all that array in one piece, exactly," Miss Beulah cried.

"Trace chains, well rope, Moody towline, fence wire, and Elvie's swing, ma'am," called Vaughn.

"Well, I'm not as sure as you are that Elvie was through with that swing. Jack, whatever happens, promise you come back with that swing to give back to Elvie. She'll cry if you don't," said Miss Beulah, all agitation now, her hand already starting up as if to wave good-bye.

Now Jack whistled and was answered by a whinny.

"What do we need with that terrible mule?" Mrs. Moody exclaimed as Bet showed herself at the top of the farm track.

"All going in one," said Jack. "And I believe Bet's recruited me one extra on her own."

The black mule and then a white mule came slipping down the home track, passing and re-passing each other.

"Brother Bethune's mule has just been waiting to be shown the way home," said Vaughn. "He won't need to eat no more for a week."

"By the time we're loaded with children too, we're going to need that extra mule power," said Jack. "Add him on."

"What children?" cried Mrs. Moody.

"The schoolchildren. Vaughn ain't the only one. Mrs. Judge, we got to deliver all the poor little souls that's starting to school this morning," said Jack. "If they're late, the teacher'll give 'em a hiding."

"Now there's Vaughn on Bet, partnered with Brother Bethune's mule, both heading up the school bus with Jack at the wheel, and the truck with Stovall and the Moodys inside, and the Moodys' pleasure car tied on in the middle. Like a June bug about to be hauled home to dinner by a doodlebug and a yellow butterfly and a couple of ants," said Miss Lexie. "There! I've got something to tell Mr. Hugg."

"No, Vaughn! You hitched to the wrong end. You and the mules are going last!" Jack hollered. "You're the brakes!"

"Don't you know how to pull the emergency?" Vaughn said with scorn.

"I know how. But if there's one thing in the world I wouldn't put my faith in, Vaughn, it's the emergency on the Banner School bus," said Jack. "You've got two good mules. Each with their own good record of behavior. I trust one as much as I do the other."

"But they've never worked together," Judge Moody interpreted.

"And they won't gee," said Miss Lexie.

"I'm counting on 'em," said Jack. "I want 'em right behind."

"Here comes somebody else. But I don't reckon he's any help," said Miss Beulah. "He's just the letter carrier."

"You can pass us right here if you whip your pony up fast and follow the tracks through my ditch, Mr. Wingfield!" Jack called.

"No letter for you," said the mailman to Gloria. "You mailing one on the route?"

"I don't ever have to write any more letters," she told him.

"I'm glad *for* you."

"If it isn't the iceman too!" said Miss Beulah. "Look, coming the other way. Watch out, everybody, you'd hate to collide with that ice."

"It's my ride," said Miss Lexie, handing her a wad of damp cloth. "I enjoyed wearing your pillowcase." For the moment, she exposed to the rain Miss Julia Mortimer's birdwing. After the ice wagon had maneuvered its way around, Jack ran back to boost Miss Lexie up.

"Miss Lexie? You still teaching the public?" asked the driver of the ice wagon as Miss Lexie rose foursquare into the air.

"If I said I'd given it up long ago, that make you any happier?"

"I heard they're fixing to bury one now in Banner," he said when she was up on the box beside him.

"Get a wiggle on," said Miss Lexie. "Carry me till you can set me down at old man Hugg's front gate."

"There goes Lexie, back to something she knows," said Miss Beulah, as the ice wagon banged on away.

Then Miss Ora Stovall stepped on the running board of the truck. "Hope you don't mind if I slide in on your lap," she said, and sat down on Mrs. Moody. She was the only clean, dry person left. White powder on her face gave her a complexion that seemed to have a pile, like cat's fur. Her cheeks were burdened down with a pink like that of excitement, which extended all the way to her ears.

Mrs. Moody, with Miss Ora on top of her, put up one hand overhead, exploring. It stayed helplessly raised.

"It's raining." she told Judge Moody piteously. He reached and brought the curtained door shut on roofless, floorless space.

Jack leaned out of the bus. "Now, who're we about to go off and leave if she don't run for it?"

Gloria ran and hopped lightly up the steep iron step, swung

herself inside, and perched on the seat behind the driver's, where she folded her hands over the back of his wobbly chair.

"Don't let that parade get away from you, Vaughn! Vaughn can't rob a hen's nest without Jack to tell him. Vaughn is not Jack, and never will be," Miss Beulah confided at the top of her voice into the truck.

"Oh, Jack," Gloria sighed at the same time into Jack's ear from behind him, "this is the way we started out. Our first day."

They shot forward. Creaks, booms, gunlike reports, the rattling of bolts, splashings underneath, and the objections of mules from behind added themselves to the high-pitched motor of the school bus leading.

"We thought things was bad *last* year," Miss Ora began to Judge Moody. "Thought we was poor *then*. Compared to now we was all millionaires and didn't know it!"

There was not a close fit to the hood covering the truck's engine. A piece of the motor was almost under their noses, glistening like a chocolate cake. Mrs. Moody peeped around Miss Ora and saw it.

"Suppose it starts working!" she exclaimed. "Oh, what'll I do with my feet?"

"Hold 'em!" Jack called back.

The three big hulks ploughed their joined-up way down Banner Road, moving as they'd never been before and never would be again, in one another's custody and in mule custody, above the ragged gullies and under the shaved clay hills that were shining as though great red rivers were pumping through their hearts.

The rain, that was falling on everything more gently than the rays of yesterday's sun, had been just enough to spoil the hay and to part Sid's hair down the middle. He was joining them now, going first, leading them all. As they came along faster he ran faster too, jumping over puddle after puddle, rocking himself like a little chair to jump over the big ones.

"I'm taking the liberty of unsnapping these rain curtains," said Mrs. Moody. "If they were doing any good for the roof of my head, I wouldn't object, but they are decidedly mildewed."

"Don't ask me to hold 'em! I've got all I can hold. All," said Miss Ora. In her lap, besides the umbrella, was a big purse of black leather that was turning gray along the seams and around the corners, the same gray that hair turns in old age.

Mrs. Moody gave the curtains to Judge Moody to hold. She peeped again, ran her eyes up and down the claybanks and frowned at the sky on top. The procession dipped across a creek bridge, limber as a leather strap.

"It's just some more of what was served to us yesterday," she said.

"No, the world doesn't do much changing overnight," said Judge Moody.

"And this is the edge of nowhere, no two ways about it. Don't try telling me there's people living along here," Mrs. Moody said, when big shepherd-type dogs ran out from where they guarded the entry to some little track, barking to greet Sid, trying to bite at the tires of the school bus, barking everything on past.

"Follow them buggy tracks back far enough and you'll see houses for 'em. Oh, there's plenty customers still hanging on." Miss Ora laughed there on Mrs. Moody's knees.

"Brakes, Vaughn!" Jack sang out, and the line of them jerked, tugged almost to a stop. A handful of children with schoolbooks held over their heads waited by the side of an Uncle Sam mailbox.

"To the back!" Gloria commanded as the children scrambled shrieking inside with her, while their dogs, the shepherd-type, like members of the neighborhood family, then tried to get on the bus.

"Get back in that road, Murph!" said Jack. "Get that tail out of here. Sid's the only dog that knows how to ride with me." He whistled and Sid entered and sat up by the gear box, panting. He sat as close to Jack's foot as Gloria sat close to his head.

Judge Moody pointed suddenly across the two ladies. "I believe there's my ditch. There it is, Maud Eva! Take a look."

"Horrors, you made me see a snake in it about nine feet long," said Mrs. Moody. "Dead, I devoutly trust."

"Yes sir, along here gets to be a fairly good-size dreen," said Miss Ora. "Don't it, Brother? Panther Creek gets in a hurry sometimes to get to the old Bywy."

"Brakes!" called Jack.

"My opinion is we're going to bang together so hard next time we stop that I'm going to spill somebody," Mrs. Moody warned.

"But Mrs. Judge, we got to gather up all these children regardless!" Jack called. "They've got one in every cranny, waiting in the rain, with nothing to their poor shaved little heads but a schoolbook or two. You wouldn't want 'em left behind and missing a day of school."

A sled, with a front guard like the foot of a little bed, stood hitched to a gray mule, waiting where there was no mailbox but only a clearing in the cut-over woods to let a track through. A little boy jumped off the sled from behind his father who stood to drive.

"Patient as Job," said Jack, throwing open the door to let the little boy in.

"Now let that be enough," Mrs. Moody prayed to the dripping sky.

Judge Moody pointed again. "No, *that's* my ditch! There it is, Maud Eva. This is the right one."

"You've already forgotten," she said. "Well, that one's got some kind of a warning planted down in there, plain to see. Take a look yourself."

It was a new sign, its paint shining wet in long black fishtails.

" 'Where Will YOU Spend Eternity?' " Miss Ora read off for them. "I can tell you without a bit of trouble who to thank for that."

"I'm not going in again," said Judge Moody.

"Old Nathan Beecham. He's a crank. He comes this way once a year and you never see the last of it," Miss Ora told him. "I'll tell you who else lives on that road, Mr. Willy Trimble. He's a bachelor. Down yonder's his chimney." It was of mud, lumpy as an old stocking on an old leg. "He's a pretty old fixture of this community."

"Well, just keep on twisting and winding," said Mrs. Moody to her own car going in front of them. "I suppose we've got to get past everything there is before we're there."

On top of the bank could be seen a roof and, higher than that, gourds hanging in rows, strung on lines between thin poles, like notes on a staff of music, each painted skull-white with a black opening.

"All right, that's Brother Bethune's house," said Miss Ora. "He's a Baptist preacher and a moonshiner, and that's his bluebird houses."

Now, election posters for races past and still to come embraced the bigger tree trunks. There were the faces of losers and winners, the forgotten and the remembered, still there together and looking like members of the same family. Every time there was Curly Stovall on a tree there was Uncle Homer on the next one, but only Uncle

Homer's qualifications were listed in indentation like a poem on a tombstone:

> EXPERIENCED
> COURTEOUS
> LIFELONG BAPTIST
> MARRIED
> RELIABLE
> JUST LEAVE IT TO HOMER.

"It ain't far now! We're coming to Aycock's house," said Jack.

Against the sides of the road bank, like the two halves of a puzzle, lay a parted bedstead, every iron curlycue of it a flower of rust.

"Look what little Mis' Comfort is trying to wish off on the public now," said Jack. "I believe that's Aycock's own bed."

"No," said Gloria. "That's been rusting even longer than you and Aycock have been gone. It's Mr. Comfort's."

"If he ever is planning on coming home, he's got one of the poorest welcomes I ever saw waiting on man. I almost hope he's dead," said Jack. "Brakes!"

"What are we stopping for now?" protested Mrs. Moody, as they slowed down under a big blackjack oak that a little path climbed up under.

"Aycock!" Jack hollered. "Where's the teacher?"

Over their heads was a house perched even with the edge of the bank, on struts. Aycock was visible sitting on the porch floor with his knees crossed and legs hanging over; he was crouched over his guitar. Without interrupting the rise and fall of his hand, he called, "She hoofed it. I told her the school bus wasn't anything to count on."

"He's happy right where he is. He'll sit there serenading himself till he's seen the train go by," said Jack as the procession leaped forward.

"The train?" repeated Mrs. Moody.

"You know, Maud Eva, it's due in Ludlow at ten fifteen," said Judge Moody, looking at his watch.

"Banner's on the crossing," said Miss Ora. "They call it a blind crossing."

"The train better stop for it," said Mrs. Moody.

"*We'd* better stop. The Nashville Rocket doesn't know Ban-

405

ner's on the map," said Judge Moody. "Any more than you did yesterday."

"They know now!" Jack sang out. "Ever since he got stopped by my truck, Mr. Dampeer always blows for Banner about forty times! Don't worry, Mrs. Judge, he won't hit my truck a second time!"

"On the last dip, I bet you a nickel we're going to give 'em a free show, Brother," said Miss Ora.

"I swear you Bob we've risked life and limb every inch of the way since we left home, Oscar," Mrs. Moody said. "And going on a mercy errand!"

"Listen, now somebody's coming up behind us," Curly Stovall said.

"Who?" objected Miss Ora.

"I can hear 'em. It's another horse or mule back yonder, crowding the two we got," said Curly.

Miss Ora stuck her head out. "I'll tell you who it is, it's old Mr. Willy Trimble," she said, and yelled, *"Willy Trimble?—Hope not!* What're you coming after us for?—He's pulling a load of flowers in his old wagon," she told Judge Moody. "He's funeral-crazy. I can tell you where he's going."

"I know already," he told her.

"Well, excuse *me*," Miss Ora exclaimed. "Excuse me for living."

For a straight strip downhill the road ran between equally high carved banks shining wet on either side and too close for comfort, like the Red Sea in the act of parting as pictured in the Bible. Two wooden churches hung over them from opposite sides of the road, as if each stood there to outwait the other and see which would fall first.

"Methodist—Baptist," said Miss Ora Stovall with a wag of her head. She asked Mrs. Moody, "I'm Methodist, which are you?"

"I'm neither one, and gladder of it every minute."

Jack was waving his hand out of the school bus. Brother Bethune stood on the Baptist porch watching them go by, in a coat from which the pocket flaps stood out like stove lids, a sheltering dog under each drumming palm.

"Looks like I've been stood up!" he called back. "Where's my crowd?"

Mrs. Moody gave a little shriek and, even under the weight of Miss Ora on her lap, she drew up her legs and held her feet. They were looking down a gap between banks red as live coals onto a streak of river with a bridge across it.

"Brakes!" Judge Moody said loudly.

"School bus goes down this hill every morning and crawls back up every evening!" Jack called as down they plunged. "If anything ever happens to put a stop to that, it's going to be about twice as hard to get an education!"

"It's running away with us," whispered Mrs. Moody. "With all of us!"

"Now I can see it! Almost under my nose!" Jack called. "The blessed water tank that spells out Banner." He let out a shout. "Brakes, Vaughn! Whip 'em just as hard as you can labor—in the direction of home!"

"Oh, Jack!" said Gloria.

"Blow my horn, Curly, if you're coming that close behind!" yelled Jack.

"Pray!" cried Mrs. Moody.

And the children all with one accord began to sing,

> "O hail to thee, Banner School so fair,
> The fairest school in the land!"

"I'm going to put it all in the *Vindicator*. Watch out, Freewill! Banner's going to beat you this week! You won't have as much as we have to toot your horn about," bragged Miss Ora Stovall.

"Be ready for the shock if that engine catches, Curly!" hollered Jack. "We're gonna level out in a minute!"

The claybanks flew up behind them, the smell of the river came forward in their place. Honeysuckle and trumpet vines whipped out at the school bus, at the Buick, the truck. A little crossroad peeped up for a minute. "The blind crossing!" Judge Moody cried, warning, while the children all sang the louder, *"Beyond compare! Beyond compare!"* and they rushed upon the railroad track and were bounced in quick turn over it, while old circus posters on the side of a store went by like a flurry of snow in their faces, and they rushed on to where the road widened at a water tank and just as quickly narrowed again to meet the bridge, and just before the bridge they swung off to the right into the open level of a school yard and around it in a pounding circle, taking the shocks of humping tree roots, and seemed to be running straight into the schoolhouse—it pressed close like a face against a windowpane—while the children yelled to finish the song,

> *"We rally to thee!*
> *To the purple and gold!"*

and the truck engine suddenly caught and fired off and braked them from behind as the bus came up against the basketball goal post and stopped to its tired crack.

"Oh, Jack. It was like it used to be," Gloria sighed. She had been sprung over his chair from behind him, into his lap.

"I ain't lost my touch?" he asked tenderly.

"Hardly any."

"You can sit up and look, Mrs. Moody!" Jack called. "You're in Banner!"

"Praise Allah," she said.

Only Mr. Willy Trimble, with hat lifted, had kept going straight ahead, taking mules and wagon on the jump onto the old cable bridge that ran unsupported as an old black tongue put out by Banner at the other side. The noise was like forty anvils making a chorus.

"Run for it!" Jack cried, throwing open the bus door. The laughing children poured out, jumped the puddles to the school-house step, and shoved their way inside.

"All right, Vaughn! Cut a-loose!" said Jack. "We don't need you any longer!"

Immediately the mules, unshackled, ran past the school and then, one with neck laid over the other's neck, turned back the way they'd come.

Vaughn stood on the bus step. "Sister Gloria, would you please to find me my books? They're where I was going to sit on 'em to reach up to my steering wheel."

"Rise up, Jack. They're still as good as new," Gloria lied, placing the warm books in Vaughn's arms.

"You can drive it home," said Jack. "Don't forget all you learned on the way down, and remember it's the opposite."

"He's drenched," Gloria said to Jack. "That green teacher ought to excuse him from sitting three in a seat until he dries out in the cloakroom."

"No'm, it just feels good to my skin," said Vaughn. "You can't be the teacher any longer."

Painted in another year, the schoolhouse had the ghostly white-

**408**

ness of a bottle from which all the milk had just been poured. A line of crayoned and scissored bonnety daffodils, pasted on the window-pane before the break-up of school for spring planting, was still there. Now the window filled from behind with laughing faces. The teacher Vaughn was so ready to worship appeared in the doorway. The jonquil smell of new pencils ground to a point for the first day, smells of rainy hair and flattened crumbs, flowed out of the school-house around her as she held out her hand.

Holding his books circled close to his ribs, Vaughn cleared the mud puddle and the mountain stone both in one leap and landed almost in the teacher's arms.

"Vaughn's big brother he's been to the pen," some children's voices began to chant as he got inside.

Jack plunged out of the bus and jumped Gloria to the ground. He raced to the truck, pulled Curly bodily out of it, then leaped into the driver's seat himself.

He ran both arms under the steering wheel and embraced it. Butting the Buick ahead, he drove the truck at thirty miles an hour, while it roared back at him, swinging it under the sycamore boughs to bring off a wide left turn out of the school yard, straddling the mud puddle as he crossed the road, roaring past the giant sunflowers lined up all the way to the store like a row of targets, with Miss Ora sliding from Mrs. Moody's lap onto Judge Moody's and back again, and stopped with the Buick's nose an inch short of the tele-phone pole. He unhitched the two machines and drove the truck to the other side of the yard and evened it with the Buick so that they stood matched.

An old man sat on the bench on the store porch above them, feet planted and wide apart, hands gripping the seat.

"Well, if it's not Captain Billy Bangs, gathering up strength to vote tomorrow!" cried Jack.

"Today is election day," said the old man. "Ain't it?"

"No sir, you're going to have to wait for tomorrow to get here," said Jack, and he leaped onto the porch to shake the old man's hand. "Captain Billy, I want you to know Judge Moody and Mrs. Judge Moody from Ludlow—they spent last night in my bed and they just had a ride from Banner Top in my truck."

"Train's late," Captain Billy told them. "Life ain't what it used to be." There was still some red in his beard.

"Well, all I hope is when they read about it in the *Vindicator* they'll appreciate what I went through," said Miss Ora Stovall. "Give me a strong pull out of here, Brother."

When she was out of the truck, Judge Moody helped his wife slide off the horse blanket to get her feet on the ground, where rivulets the orange of inner tubes played over the clay-packed gravel in front of the store.

Banner School and Stovall's store sat facing each other out of worn old squares of land from which the fences had long ago been pulled down, as if in the course of continuing battle. The water tank was shimmering there above the railroad track like a bathing pigeon in the fine rain. Around its side, under the word BANNER, letters that stretched so wide as to appear holding hands spelled "Jack + Imogene." Beyond that, there were two ancient, discolored sawdust piles standing in a field of broomsedge like the *Monitor* and the *Merrimac* in the history book, ready to fight again. A beckoning fringe of old willows grew all around their bases.

Once through Banner, the road climbed steep as a stepladder onto the bridge that was suspended narrow and dark as an interior hallway between the banks of the Bywy, somewhere down there out of sight.

"Why, we're right back in mortal sight of *that!*" Mrs. Moody's face, looking at the way they'd come, became mapped in pink. "For all we've travelled!"

"It's never been any secret that on Banner Top they've almost got Banner in their laps," said Gloria. "I'm glad it's further than it looks, or nobody'd ever be out of everybody else's call."

"And is that the road we just came down?" Mrs. Moody demanded.

"The thing that looks like a sliding board is. That's the straight part," said Jack.

"Those same two churches!" protested Mrs. Moody.

"And here is Curly's store, where you can ask for anything you want," said Jack.

As he spoke, a busy-walking little person switched out of the store and down the steps. She popped her eyes and put out her tongue at Gloria.

"Hi, Imogene," said Jack.

"Jack Renfro, listen-a-here, the first thing you do, I want you to climb up and scrub your name off that water tank where you wrote

**410**

it up there with mine," she said. "You can leave my name up there *all by itself*. I evermore mean it."

"Just as cute and bowlegged as ever," Jack said to Gloria as Imogene Broadwee wagged herself away. "And the very one for Curly here to marry. I'm going to tell him a good way to go about it."

"I'm going to use the telephone," Judge Moody interrupted. "Better late than never." He climbed the steps of the store. Nailed one to a post across the front were posters, each with its picture of Curly wearing a hat, and coming out from the crown on rays were the different words "Courteous," "Banner-Born," "Methodist," "Deserving," and "Easy to Find." A hide was stretched and nailed on the wall over the doorway, where it appeared to hover, like a partly opened black umbrella not too unlike Miss Ora's. Judge Moody stumbled over the scales as he found his way in.

The smells of coal oil, harness, cracker dust, cloth dye, and pickles clung about the doorway. Judge Moody could be only dimly seen where he stood at the telephone; among the boots and halters hanging from the beam above his head, shirt-tails of every description, old and new, were visible like so many fading banners of welcome.

"Hey, Curly, today is here at last!" Ella Fay Renfro cried.

There where the sawmill spur came out of the bushes into the railroad track, she and Etoyle and Elvie stepped off into Banner. Ella Fay piled her books on the little sisters and sent them dragging themselves inside the school. With a skip she came running across the road.

A fatuous look spread over Curly's face and he said, "Well, look who they're sending to pay the store!"

Jack punched him in the nose.

"And there go Brother and Jack again, not looking a bit different or a day older since the last time they was at it. But you do, and I do," Miss Ora Stovall remarked to Gloria. "Just don't bring it in the store!" she yelled at them, as Captain Billy Bangs drummed his heels on the porch floor and gave a clap once or twice with his hands.

Jack drove his fist again and Curly, losing his baseball cap, staggered backward until he fell against the open door of the truck and slid to the ground. Some whimpers began coming out of his mouth like small, squeezed tears.

"Jack, that hurt!" Gloria cried. "I hope landing that blow was an accident, not something you learned at Parchman."

Ella Fay squatted down, put both her little white hands around the ham of Curly's arm, and said, "I was only coming to ask him for a dime's worth of candy corn."

"Haul up, little sister!" Jack told her. "Didn't you learn you a lesson when he took Granny's gold ring?"

"I should worry, I should care!" said Ella Fay. "I made *him* give *me* something!" With all the haste her wet fingers could manage, she unlaced the throat of Gloria's sailor dress, turned back the collar, and displayed what she wore on a calendar cord tied around her neck: a pearl-handled pocketknife an inch long. Both little fingers extended, she rapidly undid the knot behind, and with a brief scream of pleasure showed it to them in turn, laid on her sweet, horny, greedy little palm. "So we're evens. We exchanged," she said, blushing at last.

"Why, you little sneak!" cried Gloria.

"But that's all we did," said Ella Fay back. "So what if the old ring did go down the mouse-hole? I know who'd get me a new one. Hear, Curly?"

Curly Stovall laughed and sat up. Re-tying her calendar cord, dropping the knife expertly down her front while she gave a brimming glance around her, Ella Fay told Gloria, "Watch and see! I can be a bride too. You can't always be the one and only!" She turned and pounded splashing into the schoolhouse.

"Curly! You threatening to marry Ella Fay? Curly! That's coming into my family!" Jack said.

"Jack, you're turning red all over," said Gloria. "You're going to pop."

"Curly! Our battles'll be called off before they start! We'll all be one happy family!" Jack cried. "I'll have to bow you a welcome into my house where I can't lather you!" He pulled Curly to his feet and yelled in his face, "With Uncle Homer out of the running, we'll even have to vote for you from now on!"

"And you all vote as a family. That's a hundred votes right there," said Curly. He put his baseball cap on again, visor to the back.

"Curly, I'd give you something. I'd almost give you the truck, like it stands, not to marry into us. Want it for a present?"

Curly stopped laughing and put out his jaw. "I ain't going to take no present off of you."

"I'd just as soon give it to you as look at it," said Jack hotly.

"Jack!" screamed Gloria, running to stand beside it.

"It's yours! It's yours, Curly, take it! I dare you!" said Jack.

"I ain't gonna!" shouted Curly.

"It's yours on a silver platter. Take it right now! And get out of my family before you get in it."

Curly's fist landed under his jaw. Jack rose on his toes as if about to fly, then toppled, and the foot of the telephone post cracked him on the forehead. He rolled over and spread out on his back. His good, wide, blue eye was still fixed where he had just turned it—the blue was nearly out of sight in the corner, as if something might still be coming around the edge of his cheek.

"Jack! Jack!" said Gloria. "Can you see day?"

"Now gimme that shirt-tail, boy!" Curly shouted. He whipped out his big hunting knife, and rolled Jack over and cut his shirt-tail off.

"Oscar, aren't you going to referee?" cried Mrs. Moody, as the Judge reappeared on the porch.

"Maud Eva, I am not a referee," said Judge Moody.

"Well, *I* am! Listen here, Buster, Jack was down there on the ground lying helpless as a babe!" Mrs. Moody cried to Curly. He ran with the shirt-tail past her into his store. "And you big bully you, you cut his shirt-tail off!" she called after him. "That's no fair!"

"I knew it would happen some day," said Gloria. She had Jack's head in her lap, and sank back against the telephone post that rose like the gnawed pith of a giant stalk of sugarcane behind her.

"It'll learn him! Trying to give me his truck! What's he trying to call himself? Rich?" cried Curly, hammering the shirt-tail to the cross-beam with all the other shirt-tails.

"I can't even get hold of the operator," said Judge Moody through the blows.

"If anybody's dead, she's at the funeral," said Miss Ora Stovall. "Gets her a crowd and *goes*. Try her about dinner time."

"Just lie there," said Gloria, stroking Jack's brow. "You don't know a thing that's going on."

"We're stranded. Worse than yesterday. Stranded," said Judge Moody to his wife. He pointed. "And what's the boy doing down on the ground?"

**413**

"Didn't you hear the crack to his head?" Mrs. Moody asked. "I don't see why his wife doesn't simply shake him."

"Completely stranded," Judge Moody said, and over the river a church bell rang. In the rainy air it was no more resonant than a bird call. Now, on this side of the river, from up the road, a car descended into Banner and ran through it onto the bridge.

The air rang as though anvils were being struck for a mile around. Before the bridge had stopped swaying, another car followed the first one down Banner Road, and two more, travelling close together as if keeping each other company, ploughed splashing up out of the crossroad coming from Foxtown, streaked and red-wheeled with mud, all of them. They all went the same way, onto the bridge, under the old tin sign saying CROSS AT OWN RISK. Miss Ora Stovall had already put her finger out and started counting them.

"These people don't know it, but they're lucky not to be meeting that funeral," shouted Mrs. Moody over the racket. "It's nothing but a one-way bridge."

"They're going to the funeral, I should say," said Judge Moody, looking at his watch again.

"Oh, Jack," Gloria said under the clanging, "you don't even hear our bridge. When we were young we used to chase each other on it, back and forth, like running through a cat's-cradle."

Another car bounded past. "Not one soul looks this way. You'd think they'd inquire if there'd been an accident," shouted Mrs. Moody.

"They're from Ludlow," said the Judge.

"Then I should be thankful they're *not* looking."

"They're driving like they're mad," said Miss Ora Stovall, looking satisfied.

"I expect they've already tried every other road they can find," said Mrs. Moody.

Finally there was only the barking of the dogs and the chirping of the truck in their ears. The truck motor, all by itself, still ran, having never been cut off. Mud still poured from it as it shook, thick drops like persimmons being steadily rolled out of buckets.

"Well, you only had to wait," said Mrs. Moody, still speaking loudly. "It comes without being called, Judge. Here's your wrecker."

"Now *that's* something *new*," said Miss Ora.

A wrecker clattered up out of the crossroad and over the railroad track into Banner. It had had a coat of red paint, but the black hieroglyphics of a more recent soldering job overlaid the paint on most of the body parts. Rocking and splashing through the puddles, it made its way past the Buick and went straight for the truck. It backed up in front of it. On the driver's door was lettered in black, as if by a burning poker, "Red's Got It."

The driver got out, hopped a puddle, landed in front of Curly Stovall, and said, "How much did you bet you'd never see me again?"

"Mr. Comfort!" said Curly.

"And look there. Who give him that souvenir?"

"He bumped his own head to make that rising. And his eye just got a kick from a dear little baby," Gloria retorted. She held Jack's head in her lap. His good eye was still rolled as if to see around the corner of her knee.

"You give us a shock, Mr. Comfort!" cried Curly. "Who's letting you run around loose in that wrecker?"

"Started working for old Red this morning. First job he give me was come over to Banner and haul him in this truck."

"Come back and see me day after tomorrow, Mr. Comfort. Better make it Saturday," said Curly urgently.

"I may not have to work on Saturday," said Mr. Comfort. "Hope not."

"Oscar, aren't you going to speak to him?" cried Mrs. Moody. "He'll go off without my car if you don't speak to him. He's shifty-eyed."

"Just a minute, there. Mister, do you see this Buick?" asked Judge Moody.

"Yes sir, looks like a booger's had a fit in it," said Mr. Comfort. "But I didn't have no orders about a Buick. My orders was Stovall's truck."

"Well, it just don't do any good to say good-bye to anybody," said Miss Ora Stovall.

"But you can't carry it off now!" Curly cried, blocking the older man's way.

"Old Red got wind a while ago he better git it while the gitting is good," said Mr. Comfort. "Make way, Curly."

"What's he want with your truck, Brother?" asked Miss Ora Stovall. "Is it a prime secret?"

"Wants the parts," said Mr. Comfort. He ducked around Curly, hopped puddles to the truck. He started thumping its sides as if it were a watermelon and he were a judge of ripeness. "Is it at all in good shape?" he asked with pursed lips. "Seems like I already smell a little smoke somewhere."

"It's most likely coming out from a thin place in your own hide," Captain Billy Bangs said from the bench.

Curly was splashing around Mr. Comfort, who was trying to hitch a chain, while his dogs came and tried unsuccessfully to bite through Mr. Comfort's boots.

"Hey, Jack!" Curly hollered. "Jack, are you dead, possuming, or what?"

"Wake him up, girl! Give him a slap!" Mrs. Moody called. "We need him quick."

"He's sleeping so trustfully," said Gloria. She laid her ear to his chest. "His heart is beating right along with mine."

"Do you want him to be *sorry?*" cried Mrs. Moody. "Listen, that rascal's running off with his truck when he doesn't know it—and won't take the Buick to the shop like Judge told him. Swat him!" she cried to Curly, as Mr. Comfort put out a hand and cut off the truck's motor.

"He's an old man!" bawled Curly. "He's Aycock's long-lost daddy!"

Mr. Comfort wiped off his hands and vaulted the step into the wrecker's cab.

"Mr. Comfort, ain't you staying here even long enough to vote?" cried Curly.

"I'm voting in Foxtown now."

"Mr. Comfort, I could tell you some news you might be interested in hearing," called Miss Ora Stovall. "This very morning they're burying another lady in your grave. Don't you want to stay for that?"

"No, I'll just be running on. I just come to git this truck while the gitting's good. Tell my little family hello and to keep praying for me," called Mr. Comfort.

The wrecker engine started with a sound as mild as a sneeze, then delivered a volley of backfiring. The two vehicles began moving together. The wrecker shook harder than the truck; it looked as if the pieces of the bed they had passed on Banner Road might have gone into making it.

The melodious hoot of the diesel streamliner made itself heard in the distance. It warned Banner softly over the river hills, coming closer, sounding louder and sweeter, its pitch rising.

"Pour a bucket of water over his head right quick, girl!" said Mrs. Moody.

"This is *my* husband," said Gloria.

A roar began to dip and wave on the air, and Gloria with her hand warded them off as the wrecker drew the truck around them and out of the store yard, on toward the railroad track.

A deep organlike note vibrated throughout Banner. Jack reached out a hand, feeling about in space, and as the train sprang as if out of the store onto the blind crossing, he got to his feet, staggering. Eyes focused ahead, he moved his lips. "Where went my truck?"

Gloria pointed for him, and by the time he turned right-about there was only the train to see. It was going at eighty miles an hour, all heat, with the sunflowers and the elderberry bushes bowing, sucked in as if by a storm running on its belly. For a moment or two the heads of strangers rode by at lighted windows, and when the road could be seen again on the other side, it was already empty, only a few live sparks dancing on it. The dogs that had raced the train to the other end of the school yard stood convulsed with barking until their voices became audible once more. Then the last, soft, lapping sounds of the train were gone too. Like the truck and the wrecker, it had vanished.

"The junk man got it!" Gloria cried.

"You're dreaming!" cried Jack.

"Took it away while you didn't know the difference."

"But I hadn't been at my wheel but a minute! Didn't drive it a whole lot over thirty yards!" Jack cried.

"Now it's going to Old Red in Foxtown. And Old Red is going to take it back to pieces," said Gloria. "That's what he wants with it."

"He's the renderer!" said Jack. "He's who got my horse! My horse first and now my truck!"

"That's how the world treats you, Jack, when you don't know any better. Now do you see?"

"Curly!" Jack spun around. "What new bargain have you been striking behind my back?"

"Jack, what that truck was was my vote getter!" hollered Curly. "Old Red owns Foxtown! Like I own Banner. And he swore—"

"You traded this truck for the Foxtown votes. *I* see," remarked Mrs. Moody. "There's no abiding mystery to me about politics."

"I thought I could trust him till tomorrow. But he's pulled a triple double-cross," cried Curly. "I sure wasn't looking for nobody to come for the truck till after the votes was in and counted!"

"But it's gone!" Jack cried again. "And in the twinkling of an eye!"

"Homer Champion is an everlasting unmitigated blooming skunk," said Curly, grabbing him. "He's the lowest thing that crawls."

"And he must have a mind like chain-lightning to go with it," said Jack. "To come back with an answer that quick after you were crowing over him on Banner Top."

"He's thick with Old Red, as thick as he can be!" cried Curly.

"Uncle Homer may be doddering before long, but this time he wasn't asleep at the switch. He won't lose by much," said Jack. "Thanks to you for selling away my truck!"

"Old Red knew it wasn't in the bargain for him to come for that truck till after Tuesday's celebration. And you didn't reckon I was going to let him *have* it, did you?"

"You just did!" cried Jack.

"I couldn't hit Mr. Comfort! He sent Mr. Comfort!"

"Yes, Jack, to add insult to injury, Mr. Comfort came back to be the one to haul it," said Gloria. "And nobody stopped him."

"To think that's the way Mr. Comfort elected to put in his appearance. After all this time, being given up maybe for dead!" said Jack.

"It's these daddies that need the whippings," said Miss Ora.

"At least he gets a better mark than Ears Broadwee for beating the train to the crossing," said Jack.

"He didn't have a minute to spare," said Gloria. "Suppose the train had been on time?"

"You're a fine one to criticize!" Mrs. Moody exclaimed. "Who wouldn't throw a bucket of water on her husband? Just let him lie there while that old monkey got away with it."

"I wanted you to wake up right on time to see what they all would do without you, Jack," said Gloria. "Judge Moody showed his colors too—all he did to help was stand there and say 'Stranded. Stranded!' "

"*Stranded?*" Jack cried. "Who's stranded?"

Over the water, the bell rang again, faint as an echo. "I missed the funeral service in Alliance," said Judge Moody.

"You ain't going to miss the burying in Banner!" cried Jack. "No sir. I made you a promise to get you back on your road, and I'm going to keep it yet. They ain't in sight yet. I'm going to patch you up in time to join in with the parade to the cemetery. And that's your road home, Judge Moody—after we bury her, you just keep on going. With good luck getting through Foxtown, you'll be back at the courthouse by dinner time." He spun around. "All right, Curly, where's your newest tires?"

On a pipe coming out of the wall three used tires hung like ringers in a game of quoits. "You're going to need ever' one I got," said Curly, rolling them out. "I'll put 'em on for three dollars and your old tires, mister."

"Three won't take me anywhere," said Judge Moody, coming down the steps into the yard.

"The best-looking one in sight is Judge Moody's spare," said Jack. "All it ever had was one blowout. Patch it and it can go on a front." He dived down in the bob-tailed shirt and crawled under the Buick with the jack.

When the Buick stood up on four slick, gray, pumped-out tires, Judge Moody climbed into the driver's seat.

"I'm still unable to get a spark," he said. "I didn't expect to."

"Keep your head out of my engine, Jack Renfro!" Mrs. Moody cried.

Jack's hands and face were hidden from them. "One wire is pulled just a little bit loose from your coil," he said. "There, it's hanging in two."

"Leave it. Leave it in two. Leave it that way, Jack," Judge Moody said.

Jack shuttered down the hood, clambered inside the Buick as Judge Moody squeezed out of the driver's seat, and seized the wheel as if it were a pair of vibrating handlebars on a motorcycle. With the noise of a motorcycle, the engine leaped to life.

"How do you account for that? How do you suppose you fixed that wire?" Judge Moody asked over the motor's singing.

"I used some of my spit. I believe it might even hold you as far as the courthouse," Jack said as he jumped out.

Judge Moody heaved a long sigh.

"Was it all that hard, Oscar?" asked his wife, getting in beside him.

"Everything's hard," he said. "Or it's getting that way."

"Do you want me to tell you what your next birthday will be?" she asked.

"No," he said, and she told him.

"Pump me in a dollar's worth of gas, then," he called to Curly Stovall.

"That makes two. And it's a dollar for the trip to Banner Top and a dollar for the trip down," Curly reminded Judge Moody as he paid him. "And three tires."

"Seven whole dollars! And I want to add to that that you've been thoroughly objectionable and I won't soon forget you," said Mrs. Moody.

"And sixty cents more for the rope," said Curly. "I ain't going to be able to use it again or sell it either."

"Sixty *cents!*" Mrs. Moody screamed. "Is that the rope we were all hanging onto? Is that what he supposed our life was worth?"

"Keep it. I'll charge the rope to Jack," Curly said, as Miss Ora Stovall came and took the bills out of his hand, folded them, and snapped them inside her purse.

Curly Stovall went into the store and came back with his candidate's hat on, placed down low over his brow.

"Now, hurry up, funeral!" Miss Ora called. "It's just quit raining for you."

"Funeral coming?" asked the wavery voice of Captain Billy Bangs. He put his old hands tight on his knees. "Is it Elvira Vaughn?"

"No sir, she started on ninety-one this morning," said Jack.

"Just wanted to see if I could catch you," said the old man. "She still putting up with Billy Vaughn?"

"We buried Grandpa, Captain Billy," said Jack in a low voice.

"Well, I like to see who I can catch," said Captain Billy. "Who are they fixing to bury now?"

"Miss Julia Mortimer, sir."

"Oh, is that the case with her," he said and fell silent.

"I want to get home," said Mrs. Moody from the Buick. "Bury the woman and get home."

**420**

"There's been some starch taken out of you too, dear," Judge Moody said then, and he put his hand down on her knee.

"White piqué wasn't intended to be worn a second day. Much less to graveside services in falling rain," she said. "But can we *not* go, Oscar? And then be able to forgive ourselves?"

"Oh, we're going," he said. "We always were."

"If you so decree. But I wish you could see yourself!" she cried. She aimed a finger at his seersucker trousers where he had gone down in the mud. "People from Ludlow, and Presbyterians from everywhere, will wonder what you've been doing down on your knees."

"Let them wonder," he said.

She gave him a short laugh. "And when they see this car, and look for the winged Mercury I had especially put on the radiator! They'll say it's lucky you had me along to vouch for who you are." Judge Moody glanced at her and she said, "And I'll tell you something. One thing along with us is still snowy—Maud Eva Moody's gloves! They've never come out of my purse until this minute." She drew them forth.

"Put them on," he said. He turned and leaned out of the Buick. "We'll say good-bye. You kept hold of us all for a pretty good little while there this morning, Jack."

"I was proud to do it." He blushed. "The one thing I wasn't ready for was a poor excuse for a rope!"

"Well, I hope—I hope you save the hay," said Judge Moody.

"Thank you, sir."

Judge Moody put out his rope-burned hand, Jack put up his bloody one, and they shook.

"The one you'd been happy to see in the ditch, you saved and shook hands with," said Gloria in a low voice.

"I know it," said Jack.

"I didn't want you risking your neck either time."

"I'm proud you helped me in spite of yourself," said Jack, bending to kiss her cheek. "Like a little wife."

"It's hard to help somebody and keep them out of trouble at the same time," she said. "But through it all I tried to keep my mind on the future."

"Leaving what was going on to me. That was a good wifely way," he said.

"But you'll do it again," she cried. "Put me in the same fix!

**421**

You risked your life for them! And now look at you."

"Look at his eye," Mrs. Moody called over to her. "That's from his own family. His own child gave him that."

"It was a love-tap," said Jack and grinned as he went to shake Mrs. Moody's gloved hand.

"And look at your hands, Jack! They're rags!" said Gloria.

"You can put a little goose grease on 'em for me when it's all over and we get home," he said tenderly. He washed them under the pump, then said, "Come stand close." He kissed a finger and rubbed her cheek with it. "I think I must have given you a little smear on your cheek."

"Blood?" she asked.

"Only about fifty percent. The rest is pure Banner clay. Now I reckon we're as ready as we'll ever be for that funeral."

"Come on, funeral!" called Miss Ora Stovall.

"You and the girl haven't got a way to ride," said Judge Moody. "You can ride in the back seat of our car to the cemetery."

"I'd hate us to sit on that velvet," said Jack. "The Buick on the inside is as good as it ever was—when you get it home, you can find something and pound the dust out of it."

"They're young, Oscar," said Mrs. Moody. "They can walk."

"We're not tired," agreed Jack. "There's a pretty good short-cut. Aren't you ready for a march, Gloria?"

"You still don't know the worst," Gloria said. "Prentiss Stovall finally got your shirt-tail, Jack. And nailed it to his beam."

Jack went scarlet. He brought up a clenched fist, but Gloria laid her hand on his arm, over the muscle. "Too late now," she said. "You can't get another minute of it in. I see what's coming."

Slowly their arms went around each other's waists. Moving together, they walked the last few steps down the road to the old plank platform of the bridge.

The opposite bank of the river was high, and not red clay but limestone. It rose shell-white out of the water, washed and worn into the shapes of tall, waisted spools, of forts with slits, old towers cut off at the top. The high-water mark was a golden band of rust nearly as high as the bridge floor. Where the bridge reached it, the stone was wrinkled in rings like a pair of elephant legs braced to hold it up.

As the slow-moving procession followed the line of the bank and then turned to pour down its road toward the bridge, down-floating wands of light and rain tapped it here and there. As it reached the bridge, loose planks began to play like a school piano. The stringy old cables squealed, the floor swayed. Behind the hearse the line seemed to narrow itself, grow thinner and longer, as if now it had to pass through the eye of a needle. And the eye of the needle was the loudest place on earth.

Yet a moment came when the procession stretched and covered the full length of the bridge. The clatter of the cables stopped, the floor drummed in a different key. As it ran full from one end to the other, the bridge become nearly as quiet as the river.

"Hope they don't fall through with her at our end," said Miss Ora Stovall. "That wouldn't do our reputation very much good."

"Miss Julia came over that bridge every Monday morning for a good many years," said Judge Moody. "It would do well to bear her weight one more time."

Arms entwined, Jack and Gloria stepped down out of the way, their feet on a path that led down under the bridge. Below, the river bed reached out from the bank a bare, pocked, uneven white floor, over which ran strands and knotted ropes of red water. Beyond the farthest shelf of rock, nearly all the river there was was flowing by in one narrow channel. A child might have jumped it. And between here and there, the whole limestone floor was ignited with butterflies, lit there and remaining as if fastened on. Without rising, some of them opened and closed their yellow wings, like mutes speaking with their hands.

As Jack and Gloria waited, the hearse trundled down off the bridge almost over their heads. Its most recent coat of paint, wrinkled like oilcloth, shone in the lightless air because it was wet.

Curly Stovall, standing at attention beside his gas pump, removed his hat and held it over his heart. Miss Ora stood beside him, counting those going by with a gesture from her folded umbrella. Cars with headlights burning on dim followed close one behind the other, and now and then would come a wagon, all alike filled with hatted passengers. At every departure off the bridge, the noise of those still coming was increased a little more.

The church bus came off the bridge washed to a blue as acid and strong as a stand of hydrangeas nobody could ever make bloom pink. It crawled past Jack and Gloria, windows packed with returning faces. "You haven't got very far since yesterday!" the driver called as she went by.

Behind that came school buses, one after the other. Two looked worse than the Banner School bus, two looked better, and one was like the Banner bus all over again. Their special racket brought the children inside Banner School to the window. Through the paper flowers they watched the buses ride past full of schoolteachers.

"It's a holiday!" cried Miss Pet Hanks, leaning out of one of them. "News went out far and wide! Spread like wildfire! Everybody knows it but Banner! I couldn't get anybody to answer the phone. Children running wild all over Boone County so the teachers could come to her funeral."

Judge Moody at the wheel of his car softly groaned.

"That's your fault, Oscar, for not being on the job," said Mrs. Moody. "You were supposed to prevent anything of the kind."

Rocking over the railroad track, the procession was turning down into the Foxtown road that ran almost hidden between high banks of elderberry, following the track and the river.

"Count the license tags from away!" Miss Ora Stovall's head turned from one side to the other for every vehicle that passed. "She taught all those folks. They're all sprung from around here, no doubt about that. Those're the ones got up and left home. I never supposed they'd show up here again till it's time for us to bury *them*."

On the bench by himself up on the porch, Captain Billy Bangs didn't rise—he was too old to rise. "She taught me. She taught her elders. Because after the Surrender, they didn't leave us no school to go to. She taught me the world's round," he said. " 'We ain't standing still, Captain Billy,' she says. 'No sir, the world's round and goes spinning.' 'And if that's what it's doing, daughter,' I says back to her, 'I'd hate to think there's a can of kerosene setting anywheres on it.' " Captain Billy, who had slowly been raising one hand, finally touched one trembling finger to the brim of his hat.

The hearse had reappeared heading the long line climbing now up the cemetery hill. And at the same time, with a masterpiece of racket, Mr. Willy Trimble came last off the bridge and brought silence. His wagon was loaded with what looked like a bale of honeysuckle. The little boy who lived down the road from Miss Julia's house in Alliance rode among the vines to keep them from flying loose. As they passed Banner School, he faced the window-packed schoolhouse, laid his thumb to his nose, and played on all his fingers at the imprisoned children.

"Now or never!" cried Mrs. Moody, grabbing the wheel along with her husband and helping him make the turn. The Buick moved slowly out of the store yard and edged into place behind Mr. Willy at the end of the line.

"His steering's going to veer him a little from now on," murmured Jack. "But I believe Judge Moody would rather I left him to find that out for himself."

"Well, they every one of 'em made the bridge. It'd been something extra if they hadn't," said Miss Ora Stovall. "But there's hardly an inch I've got left to fill up my Banner Notes anyway. With the crowd for the fish-fry and the crowd for that reunion and the crowd for this funeral, that's a big set of names. Willy Trimble is getting his in three times. Wait for me!" She was stopping to put Orange Crushes and Grapettes and Cokes into the barrel with the fresh ice. "They won't be very cold, but they'll sell. After you been to a funeral, you're glad to drink 'em warm or any other way you can get 'em," she said.

Then she and Curly, Jack and Gloria set off to follow on foot. Jack's little dog Sid was at Jack's heels, jumping the puddles.

"I'm staying right here," said Captain Billy.

᭥

"Honey, I'm sorry I can't put you in my truck," Jack said as they trudged up the short-cut. "So I could carry you like Judge Moody's carrying Mrs. Judge."

"Jack, do you know what that truck turned out to be? It was just a play-pretty," said Gloria. "A man's something-to-play-with."

"It was my sweat."

"It finished up being nothing but a bone of contention."

"But I wasn't through with it!" he cried. "And neither was old Curly!"

"I'd already learned enough about it to satisfy me. It was never going to carry *us* anywhere. We'd always have to be carrying *it*," said Gloria. "I didn't feel all that sorry to see it go."

"Honey, you're a soldier," he said.

The path was one that led to the dinner grounds lying back of Damascus Church. Here it was empty like an empty room, exhausted of sound like a schoolroom in summer. There was a smell that had steeped for years, of horses and leather and waiting and dust, and the ghost-smell of mulberry leaves and wet mustard belonging to the tables that had gone to yesterday's reunion and were waiting now on Jack to bring back. Where each table had stood was a trough in the ground like that under a children's swing or an old person's chair by a roadside.

When they came to the old iron fence in its honeysuckle, Jack helped Gloria over it where two waist-high homemade ladders clasped in each other's arms made a stile. Across an acre of billowing ground, the funeral procession was now inching to its destination.

Grandpa Vaughn's grave was the brightest thing in sight. It was still an elevation, red as new brick, with only a few strands of grass hanging out of the clay, each a foot long, bleached but alive. The fruit jar of Granny's seed dahlias stood on it; having lived through yesterday's sun they had bowed to the rain this morning.

Jack dropped down and with his planting hand he straightened and firmed the small wooden cross, frail as kite-sticks.

"And I'm going to afford him a tombstone some day if it's the last thing I ever do," he said, jumping up.

The billowy Vaughn graves seemed to be shoving against one another for first place, tilting with their markers—some of iron, crested like giant doorkeys that might unlock at any moment.

"Where we're walking now is where Granny'll go," Jack said. "The last Vaughn in the world! And not weighing much more for all her years than our baby weighs now. When I lifted her up for her birthday hug, she near-about shot out of my hands!"

The whole expanse they were crossing had the look of having been scythed yesterday. It smelled of hay that had been rained on. Even though it was wet, their own footsteps sounded on the bristles as though they were walking over some old giant's stubbled chin. They walked faster.

"There's Mama and all of 'em's mother and dad going by," Jack said, his hand going out to the double-tablet over the single grave, with only one grave close to keep it company. "Yet when you think back on the reunion and count how many him and her managed to leave behind! Like something had whispered to 'em 'Quick!' and they were smart enough to take heed." An old crape myrtle stood with branches weighted down by rain and casting the preponderance of its bloom over Sam Dale Beecham. It grew with half a dozen trunks, not round but like girls' arms, flat-sided; with the drops of rain to honeycomb them the panicles of bloom looked heavy as flesh and twice as pink. Sam Dale Beecham's marker had darkened, its surface like the smooth, loving slatings of a pencil on tablet paper laid over a buffalo nickel, but the rubbed name and the rubbed chain hanging in two, its broken link, shone out in the wet. A grasshopper of shadowless green and of a mouse's size sat hunched there. It flew up before their hurrying steps and vanished in the stubble.

"Let him hop!" said Jack. "Sam Dale Beecham wasn't hardly older than I am now when they put him in that grave of his."

"He'd be old like the rest of 'em now. Even if he was just the baby brother," Gloria reminded him, "if he hadn't died, he'd be old, and expecting to be asked to tell everything he knew."

Her feet almost stumbled—there were also three small stones, three in a row, like loaves baked by different hands but all bearing the same one word, "Infant." Two were Aunt Nanny's and Uncle Percy's, all they'd had, and the other was Miss Beulah's last.

"Honey, no time to stand still! They can bury people before you know it," said Jack, swinging Gloria over a mud puddle.

"You didn't hear Brother Bethune bury Grandpa. It was like the reunion, never-ending."

"I hope nobody got forgiven before he was through!"

An army of tablets, some black as slates, marked half a hill-load of husbands and wives buried close together—all the Renfros. This time, Aunt Lexie and Auntie Fay, Uncle Homer Champion, Mr. Renfro and Miss Beulah, their children—Jack and Gloria themselves, and Lady May Renfro—were the skips. The original grasshopper was repeated here too, repeated everywhere and a hundred times over, grave-sitting or grave-hopping in the stubble, rising up in front of their hurrying feet and dropping behind them after they passed, grasshoppers by the hundreds.

They had made the short-cut to the little road, and along its side, in among the honeysuckle-shrouded trees and the Spanish daggers in their lowlit bloom, the cars and wagons, horses and buses had been already left behind. There was the Buick, its engine softly running at low throttle. Next to it was the postman's pony and cart, mail left in a cigar box, gathered in by a rubber band. There was Uncle Homer's van with a fresh sign decorating it, "It's Homer's Turn." The school buses had put new scrapes on one another's sides trying to line up where they wouldn't get stuck. The church bus had been left with its door open; every seat was laid with a hat, for a little rain still dripped from the branches of cemetery trees. Mr. Willy Trimble's mules stood docile, cement-gray, like monuments themselves, quietly eating honeysuckle off the fence.

"We made it," Jack whispered, lips warm at Gloria's ear. "We're just in time."

The hearse was already backed in among the graves. It was standing still, and Gloria and Jack flew past it and joined the crowd.

They rounded a great clump of ribbon-grass as high as a hay-stack, out of which Rachel Sojourner's grave seemed to slide, ready to go over the edge of the bank, like a disobedient child. The small lamb on its headstone had turned dark as a blackened lamp chimney.

The crowd was forming around three sides of the new grave hole. Where Mr. Comfort had been supposed to go was the last grave at the river end of the cemetery. At its back stood only an old cedar trunk, white against gray space. Its bark was sharp-folded as linen, it was white as a tablecloth. Wreaths and sprays of spikey florist flowers from Ludlow—gladioli and carnations and ferns—were being stood on their wire frames around the grave, and the homemade offerings—the flower-heads sewn onto box-lids and shirt cardboards, and the fruit jars and one milk can packed with yard lilies and purple phlox and snow-on-the-mountain—were given room to the side.

Jack held Gloria's hand and led her out in front of the known and the unknown faces around them, making for right in front. As though magnetized to the tallest monument in the cemetery, both Curly Stovall and Uncle Homer Champion stood at Dearman's grave, both glaring straight in front of them, both with their candidate's hats laid over their hearts. A little taller than they were, Dearman's shaft rose behind them, on its top the moss-ringed finger that pointed straight up from its hand in a chiseled cuff above the words "At Rest."

"That boy walking in front of you has brought himself to a funeral without a shirt-tail behind," said a voice at their backs.

"It's Jack Renfro. I feel like telling his mother," said somebody else.

"*She's* not much better. Look at *her* collar and cuffs. Look at her skirt."

"They're married. And I heard that before you could shake a stick at him, he'd gone to the pen for a hold-up."

"She'll have to stick to him now. They've got a baby not even weaned. I've laid eyes on it."

"He's probably the best she could do. Little old orphan! If she didn't want to teach school the rest of her days."

"Look at his eye when he turns around to look back at us. You know what? I saw his baby kick him in that eye. Right out in the public yesterday. I saw his baby jump and saw him catch her and she delivered him something special."

"He could still wear a shirt-tail to a funeral."

"Just keep your mind on what's coming, honey," Jack whispered to Gloria. "You've done grand so far, been a soldier as good as Mama."

"I don't think they've got any business at a funeral," said the voice of a very old man or a very old woman.

The grave hole, up close, smelled like the iron shovel that had dug it and the wet ropes that would harness the coffin down into it. As though thirsty and greedy enough to take anything, it had swallowed all the rain it had received and waited slick and bright. The raw clods grubbed out of the ground outshone those on Grandpa Vaughn's now older grave; they had been piled un-gravelike as a heap of dug sweet potatoes on the far side of Mr. Earl Comfort standing there on a trampled clump of cemetery iris.

"I never saw so many grayheads in one place at one time," said Miss Ora Stovall's voice. "There wouldn't even be time now to count 'em. And look at that one! What does *he* call *him*self?"

It was the priest in his vestments. His skirts dragged rhythmically over the objecting stubble. Behind him marched the pallbearers; Judge Moody with his own bared head was first on the right.

"That pallbearer came in such a hurry he hasn't even shaved," came a voice.

The coffin had been draped with the Mississippi flag.

"If I know that flag, it's one that's been wrapped up all summer, lying on top of a school piano with the march music. Let's just hope it didn't sour," came a carrying voice from where the school-teachers stood, all sticking together.

As the pallbearers reached where they were going, owls in a stream, one after the other, came up out of the old cedar tree. Owls lifted like a puff of smoke over the priest and the pallbearers and the coffin as it rocked once, suspended over the grave, lifted over the morning's crowd, over monuments and trees, and away. Even the last old cedar was inhabited.

The priest stood imperturbable, waiting on the pallbearers' final success, on the silence of those present. A little blackface robin sat reared back near the opened ground, watching all their moves, as if to see what was in it for him. Then the priest opened his mouth and words came out—unfamiliar in Banner Cemetery, not a one of them understood. His syllables following one another fell like multiple leaves in the rain. Then he made a movement with his hands, and his head turned an inch or two. He seemed to be yielding gracefully to some offer of assistance.

"Where's Brother Bethune? It's his turn," whispered Jack.

The priest gave him only a moment, wherever he was, and went on without him. He lifted both hands and spoke in a low voice and rapidly, keeping to the same tongue. When he came to a stop, Mr. Willy Trimble came scrambling toward him with the agility of a roof-climber over the graves between, both his arms loaded with honey-suckle, and said for Brother Bethune, "Amen." Mr. Earl Comfort took a step forward in a patched red rubber boot, and then the first clods fell.

At once the crowd broke, moved, and started streaming away. The priest had got away first, before they knew it.

"And I reckon all that was just to say 'Ashes to ashes and dust to dust,' " said a voice. "Worshipped himself, didn't he? Just loved hearing the sound of his own voice."

"Where was good old Brother Bethune? He's going to be disappointed when he gets here."

"Neglect!" said a heavy, red-flushed pallbearer in a limp Palm Beach suit, striding there between the Moodys towards the cars. "Neglect, neglect! *Of course* you can die of it! Cheeks were a skeleton's! I call it starvation, pure and simple."

"She's past minding now, Dr. Carruthers," said Mrs. Moody.

"And now I mind!" he said.

"And she'd already completed her task here on earth. But I do think she could have given in enough to allow down-to-earth Presbyterians to take charge of her funeral. All that jabber we got here in order to be served with! Just because she once taught that fellow algebra!"

The three of them picked their way out among the graves and

disappeared through the trees. "You pick a funny time to laugh, Oscar," Mrs. Moody's voice said, fading.

Then there was only the racket of departure, and Mr. Earl Comfort, with a groan as though he needed help, was filling the grave.

"Look! We're to ourselves, Jack," said Gloria.

He drew her close and led her a little distance away, toward the edge of the bank. Rachel Sojourner's ribbon grass had a rainy sheen—it was like last night's moonlight hanging in threads. Down below their feet was the river.

The Bywy, running close to the Banner side here, where it was called Deepening Bend, was the color of steeping tea, clearer at the top. Stranded motionless just under the surface, a long and colorless tree lay crosswise to the current they couldn't see, and heaped in its arms, submerged, were white and green leaves and the debris it had caught. Lying under the water with the drifts of fine rain on it, it was like a fern being pressed in a book.

"Oh, this is the way it could always be. It's what I've dreamed of," Gloria said, reaching both arms around Jack's neck. "I've got you all by myself, Jack Renfro. Nobody talking, nobody listening, nobody coming—nobody about to call you or walk in on us—there's nobody left but you and me, and nothing to be in our way."

He stood in her arms without answering, and she dropped her own voice to a whisper. "If we could stay this way always—build us a little two-room house, where nobody in the world could find us—"

He drew her close, as if out of sudden danger.

The first sun had started to come out. Light touched the other side of the river, the other bank went salt-white. A shadow plunged down a fold of rock where the cave was, a black opening like a mouth with song interrupted. The banks of the other side shelved forward with the sun, close enough to show the porous face of the stone. It was like a loaf sliced through with a dull knife. The high-water mark was yellow and coarse as corn meal, and travelling along its band some wavery letters spelled out "Live For Him."

"I'm glad Uncle Nathan didn't ever have to go to the pen. They would never have let him put up his tent and bring his own syrup. Or be an artist," said Jack presently. "As long as I went and took my turn, maybe it's evened up, and now the poor old man can rest."

**431**

"He'd have to be talked into it," said Gloria.

"At the next reunion I might get a chance to speak to him."

"He only washes in the Bywy River. I hope he won't come."

"He loves his grandma," said Jack. "And I rather hear his cornet blow for a poor soul than a hundred funeral orations, long or short." He took her hand to lead her out the way they had come. "I'm sorry you had to lose your teacher," he said. "But I'm glad I could get you here on time and you got your respects paid."

Gloria didn't speak until they got to the fence. Then she said, "Miss Julia Mortimer didn't want anybody left in the dark, not about anything. She wanted everything brought out in the wide open, to see and be known. She wanted people to spread out their minds and their hearts to other people, so they could be read like books."

"She sounds like Solomon," said Jack. "Like she ought to have been Solomon."

"No, people don't want to be read like books."

"I expect she might be the only one could have understood a word out of that man burying her. If he was a man," said Jack. "She was away up over our heads, you and me."

"Once. But she changed. I'll never change!" she cried out to him, and he clasped her.

While he helped her back over the stile, the sun came following fast behind them. The cemetery everywhere began to steam. The gravestones looked small and white and alike, all like one gathering of eggs let carelessly roll from an apron.

They came out through the dinner grounds and on around the church. Damascus was a firm-cornered, narrow church resting on four snowy limestone rocks. It stood even with the bank to face Better Friendship Methodist Church across Banner Road. This morning the rained-on wooden face of Damascus had a darkness soft as a pansy's. The narrow stoop was sheltered by two new-looking boards at a right-angle; under this, like an eye beneath an eyebrow, a single electric light bulb was screwed into the wall. Its filaments showed a little color, like weak veins—somebody had turned on the current and it was working. Two wires bored into the wall, and a meter box hung by the closed door, bright as a watch. Up above, the steeple was wrapped around and around up to its point in tin, like an iris bud in its gray spring sheath.

**432**

"Jack, the last time we stood together on the steps of Damascus, we were just starting out! Getting up the courage to walk inside and down the aisle where Grandpa Vaughn was waiting at the foot, ready to marry us," said Gloria.

"Too late!" said Brother Bethune, coming out. "I waited and nobody came. 'Where's my bride and groom?' I kept asking. 'Where's my crowd?' It's a shame the way you all treat me. I wasn't even sure your floor was going to hold me. And I drawed my finger 'cross the lid of your Bible, and if I could've thought of my name right quick, I had enough dust right there to write it in. And look at me teeter! Porch like this could pitch a hungry preacher right out on his head. Pitch him clean to the road! You're letting 'em undermine your church, clawing up here with that road, and what's fixing to cave in the hind end—your river? Front and back, you're being eat out of here." Brother Bethune inched down the steps, leaving the door wide open behind him. He pointed back up with his gun. "Why don't you paint it?" he asked. "It's going to rot! There's only one thing I feel like is going to save this church at all—I just know it's Baptist. The same as I know I am. And why don't you try getting married on a Sunday? That's what Sunday's for."

"If Grandpa was back on earth to hear him, he'd bore a hole right through him now with his eyes," whispered Jack, as Brother Bethune tramped over the irises down to the road. "Grandpa Vaughn *built* Damascus."

"One ordinary look should have told even Brother Bethune we were married," said Gloria.

His mule walked out of the hitching grounds and trotted down to the road after him, while Bet stood waiting her turn in the shade.

"He's climbing on," said Jack. "As long as his mule knows him, he's safe. He'll get carried to the right place."

The sun came out as if for good. All at once they were standing again in a red world. Their skin took the sharp sting of heat. At the foot of the road, on which Brother Bethune was trotting down to Banner, the shadow of the bridge on the river floor looked more solid than the bridge, every plank of its uneven floor laid down black, like an old men's game of dominoes left lying on a sunny table in a courthouse yard at dinner time. Along the bank of the river, the sycamore trees in the school yard were tinged on top with yellow, as though acid had been spilled on them from some travelling spoon.

**433**

The gas pump in front of Curly's store stood fading there like a little old lady in a blue sunbonnet who had nowhere to go.

"Between 'em all, they've taken away everything you've got, Jack," said Gloria.

"There's been just about a clean sweep," he agreed.

"Everybody's done their worst now—everybody and then some," she said. "They can't do any more now."

He set his lips on hers. "They can't take away what no human can take away. My family," he said. "My wife and girl baby and all of 'em at home. And I've got my strength. I may not have all the time I used to have—but I can provide. Don't you ever fear."

"I'll just keep right on thinking about the future, Jack."

He interrupted her with a shout. Down on the dim, steamy pasture between Curly Stovall's back shed and the river, something white was moving, erratic as a kite in a windy sky.

"Dan!" he shouted. "I'm looking straight at Dan!"

The horse ran lightly as a blown thistledown out of the open pasture gate, around Curly's house and store, over the road, across the school yard and once around the school, down the railroad track to the water tank and around it and back, running on his shadow. He ran all over Banner in those few bright minutes. He ended up in the school yard, and paced deliberately up to the basketball goal post, his old hitching post, which leaned over him with its battered ring of sunlit rust. He stood as if listening for his name.

"Dan!"

The horse lifted on his hind legs and turned around on his shadow. He came down in a red splash that shot up man-high and fell behind him. He came a graceful step or two up Banner Road, and there was nobody out to see him, tossing his mane and tail, while Jack laughed until tears popped out on both cheeks.

"Dan, you're alive. You lived through it!" He stood in the road and threw open his arms.

The horse came a little way farther, close enough to show he was still white, though his coat was rough. His mane and tail had been combed only by the rain. Jack gave his sweet, warbling whistle. But the horse with a wayward toss of his head turned around in the road and trotted back down again, his tail streaming bright as frost behind.

"He's fickle," Gloria told Jack. "Dan is fickle. And now he's

Curly's horse and he's let you know it. Oh, Jack, I know you'd rather he was rendered!"

"No, I rather he's alive and fickle than all mine and sold for his hide and tallow," said Jack. He still stood in the road with his arms out. "Why hasn't Curly already pranced out on his back in front of me then? What's he saving the last for?—There's just one answer. He's waiting till he can catch him." Gloria slowly nodded. He went on, "And I expect this morning Captain Billy Bangs let him out of the pasture. We all went off and left Captain Billy with nothing else to do—he can't vote till tomorrow." He cupped his hands to his mouth and yelled, "All right, Curly! I saw him! I'll be down to get him when the time's good and ripe!"

"That's what Prentiss Stovall wants you to do," said Gloria. "He'll be justice of the peace by day after tomorrow. Oh, Jack, does this mean it'll all happen over again?"

"It's a start," said Jack. Then he swung around. "But for right now, Gloria, there's a lot of doing I got to catch up with at home. We got to eat! That's the surest thing I know. But I still got my strength."

Bet came down into the road.

"The surest thing I know is I'll never let you out of my sight again. Never," Gloria swore. "I never will let you escape from me, Jack Renfro. Remember it."

"It's the first I knew I was trying," he said, with his big smile.

He lifted her and set her up on Bet's waiting back, and took Bet by the bridle and led her. They started for home.

"And some day," Gloria said, "some day yet, we'll move to ourselves. And there'll be just you and me and Lady May."

"And a string of other little chaps to come along behind her," said Jack. "You just can't have too many, is the way I look at it."

Sid twinkled out of the church. He had gone straight through Damascus Church, in at the back and out at the front, as though it were a tree across a ditch. He came in springs down the bank and ran up the red road, tail jumping like a ringing bell as he sped for home, and growing smaller and smaller up ahead.

Jack and Gloria went along behind him, and the sun gave Banner Road no more shade now—it was noon. One of his eyes still imperfectly opened, and the new lump blossoming on his forehead

**435**

for his mother's kiss, Jack raised his voice and sang. All Banner could hear him and know who he was.

> *"Bringing in the sheaves,*
> *Bringing in the sheaves!*
> *We shall come rejoicing,*
> *Bringing in the sheaves!"*

# VIRAGO MODERN CLASSICS

The first Virago Modern Classic, *Frost in May* by Antonia White, was published in 1978. It launched a list dedicated to the celebration of women writers and to the rediscovery and reprinting of their works. Its aim was, and is, to demonstrate the existence of a female tradition in fiction which is both enriching and enjoyable. The Leavisite notion of the 'Great Tradition', and the narrow, academic definition of a 'classic', has meant the neglect of a large number of interesting secondary works of fiction. In calling the series 'Modern Classics' we do not necessarily mean 'great' — although this is often the case. Published with new critical and biographical introductions, books are chosen for many reasons: sometimes for their importance in literary history; sometimes because they illuminate particular aspects of womens' lives, both personal and public. They may be classics of comedy or storytelling; their interest can be historical, feminist, political or literary.

Initially the Virago Modern Classics concentrated on English novels and short stories published in the early decades of this century. As the series has grown it has broadened to include works of fiction from different centuries, different countries, cultures and literary traditions. In 1984 the Victorian Classics were launched; there are separate lists of Irish, Scottish, European, American, Australian and other English speaking countries; there are books written by Black women, by Catholic and Jewish women, and a few relevant novels by men. There is, too, a companion series of Non-Fiction Classics constituting biography, autobiography, travel, journalism, essays, poetry, letters and diaries.

By the end of 1986 over 250 titles will have been published in these two series, many of which have been suggested by our readers.

*Other books by Eudora Welty published by Virago*